Glimpse, Memoir of a Serial Killer

by

Stephen B King

Deadly Glimpses, Book 1

Glimpse, Memoir of a Serial Killer

Cover Art by *Kim Mendoza*

The Wild Rose Press, Inc.
PO Box 708
Adams Basin, NY 14410-0708
Visit us at www.thewildrosepress.com

Publishing History
First Thriller Rose Edition, 2018
Print ISBN 978-1-5092-2268-1
Digital ISBN 978-1-5092-2269-8

Deadly Glimpses, Book 1
Published in the United States of America

Dedication

I will be forever grateful to Mica S Cole for help and guidance. She took my book and told me all the things I'd done wrong in telling it, and that was a lot.

Special thanks to my editor Melanie Billings who loved the story, as did everyone at TWRP and wanted Rick and Patricia's tale to see the light of day—Thanks, Melanie.

My wife and family put up with a lot, having an author in the house, who only wants to spend time writing instead of quality time with them.

Lastly, my daughter Tania has been my constant rock, and biggest supporter. None of this would have happened without her behind me, pushing and giving her constant praise. Love ya, babe.

Chapter 1:
1999–The Beginning

Melanie Cartwright disappeared on a Sunday evening. Storm clouds gathered in the West as her husband's car pulled into a spot of the busy parking area of the suburban shopping center.

She turned to her husband with one hand on the inside door handle of the car. "Are you sure you won't come with me? You never know, I might meet another man." She smiled, and he knew that was a joke.

"You've had me working my bum off all day; the football's on and I think I can trust you to buy a couple of steaks to throw on the barbeque without being tempted away by some passing gigolo." He winked at her.

She grinned as she flicked her head to clear her blonde hair from her face in the warm breeze. They had been stripping the bathroom for new tiles to update the three-bedroom house they had bought the year before, and it had been backbreaking work. Once they cleaned up, it was past closing time for the big supermarket she usually shopped at, so Allan agreed to drive her to the smaller grocery store in an adjoining suburb. During the drive, he insisted he would stay in the car, to listen to the radio, while she ran in to get things for dinner.

His team, the West Coast Eagles, was playing Hawthorn and it was the third quarter in what was a very tight game. "Don't be long, or I'll come looking for ya," he joked, watching her light cotton dress ride up her thighs as she climbed out of his battered old SUV.

She waggled a finger at him before spinning around with a little skip, which lifted the back of her dress almost to her panties. "Back soon, lover boy." She closed the door quietly, then with a spring in her step, headed off toward the supermarket.

Allan settled back into the seat and turned the volume a little higher as Hawthorn scored a goal. He watched people come and go in front of his car, backlit by the setting sun, their gray plastic bags overflowing with vegetables, cans, and freshly baked bread. His stomach rumbled with hunger.

The fourth quarter had only just started when Allan wondered what was taking Melanie so long. *That woman is such a tease; I bet she's doing it just so I go looking for her.* He smiled, but the Eagles goaled again, and ten more minutes went by as the two teams fought in a tug-of-war for supremacy.

Allan glanced at his watch and scowled. *If this is her idea of a joke, it's not mine.* He yanked the keys out of the ignition, wound the window up, and got out of the car slamming the door so hard it rattled.

He entered the building through the automatic glass doors and scanned the checkouts. He moved through the turnstile then walked up and down each aisle.

He searched the supermarket three times before his anger turned cold. *Maybe I missed her, and she's back at the car?* He ran back outside, but she wasn't there, or anywhere else that he could find.

Melanie Cartwright had vanished.

****

The police arrived in a light utility truck with a fiberglass canopy with two fresh-faced officers who were approaching the end of their shift. One was male, and the other female. They took down his statement and description of Melanie in a little notepad. Allan could tell what they thought; he could read them like a book. In their minds, they thought the couple had argued, and she had run off in tears, despite his assurance that they most certainly had not.

The officers asked a few cursory questions of the supermarket checkout staff to see if they remembered serving her, which they did not.

"Look, Mr. Cartwright, I can see you're upset," Constable Wilkins said in a placating, patronizing voice, once Allan had finished his statement, "but I'm sure there is a perfectly reasonable explanation. She'll probably turn up later at home."

"Why are you not getting this? She wouldn't do this; she had no reason to run off. She just went in there to buy a couple of steaks for dinner, for God's sake."

"Well, let me ask you: what do *you* think happened to your wife?" He stuck the end of his biro in his mouth and waited with a stupid know-it-all look on his face.

"I don't know. If I did, I wouldn't have called you, would I? You should be helping me find her. She may have been kidnapped."

"Why would someone want to kidnap your wife from a tiny suburban shopping center on a Sunday evening? Is there something you're not telling us, hmm?"

Allan shook his head. There was nothing, no reason he could think of. "I don't know, I just don't know. Look, it's been well over an hour, something bad has happened to her, I'm telling you." He looked down, he was wringing his hands and hadn't even realized.

"All right, Mr. Cartwright, best you go home and wait there, she may turn up, or you may get a phone call from her. We will have a drive around the area see if we can spot her wandering around. We've put a bulletin out for other cars to be on the lookout and notified the hospitals to keep a watch too. If she hasn't turned up by the morning, come into the station and we will get CID, and Missing Persons, to have a chat with you. I'm sure you have nothing to worry about."

****

It was fifty-eight-year-old Harvey Broughton, who made the find which would feature in local newspapers and TV bulletins, for months to come. Fit and healthy for his age, with hair that was snow white, he finished emptying his six-by-four trailer full of branches pruned from the Bougainvillea plants, which populated his front garden, and grew like wildfire. He was at the Midland City garbage dump, four weeks after Melanie's disappearance.

He wiped his sweat-covered brow and glanced around as he wrinkled his nose. The place stank to high heaven and he knew he would need a shower when he got home. He realized he was alone at the tip face and spotted the new looking saddle-brown suitcase halfway down the slope. Always on the lookout for a bargain, or better yet something for free, he thought the case looked to be in fine condition, far too good to have been left there. At that distance, he thought it looked brand new, and that was odd.

After a furtive glance, to make sure he wasn't

being watched, because there were signs everywhere warning patrons: *NO SCAVENGING*. He clamored down the short incline and squatted down on his haunches. It had twist locks, which he turned counter-clockwise and to his surprise, they popped open. He lifted the lid and peered inside.

It took several seconds to understand what he was looking at. The opaque plastic was wrapped around what appeared to be butcher's joints of meat, yet in the back of his mind, somehow, he knew they couldn't be that.

With a dawning horror, he realized what he had found. He screamed, and in a blind panic, ran back up the slope, bent at the waist, and vomited into the dust.

Melanie Cartwright's body, which would later be identified from dental records, had been discovered, packed inside a large suitcase at the Midland City Rubbish Dump. She had been neatly dissected, her pieces individually wrapped in plastic sheeting, and carefully stacked inside the sturdy case.

****

Detective Sergeant Richard 'Rick' McCoy had drunk three cans of beer, and just opened his fourth, when his mobile phone rang. It was his boss, Detective Chief Inspector Colin Harris.

"Rick, sorry to call on a Sunday, but we've got a dissected dead body found in a suitcase at the Midland Refuse Dump. Meet up with Forensics and the M.E., will you? The local cops have secured the scene," he said in his usual no-nonsense, gruff, tone.

If the mental image of a body in a suitcase hadn't sounded so interesting, Rick would have told him that he had been drinking and to take the next officer on the roster. Instead, he shrugged and said, "I'm on my way."

Just for a moment, right after he hung up the phone, he thought about calling back and declining. It was Sunday, he had been drinking while watching a boxing match on TV, and he had hoped to drive back to his old neighborhood a little later. He didn't have visitation rights for that weekend, but he still hoped to watch Amy, his daughter, from afar.

Rick was forty years old. He had salt-and-pepper graying short spikey hair, that never seemed to sit right, but because he wore a six-day growth beard, somehow it looked good on him. He wasn't overweight, but not a picture of fitness either, and he always looked like his shirt had missed the iron before he had put it on. In short, he looked like the married, but recently separated man that he was.

He lived in a tiny one-bedroom apartment and was forced to play what he thought of as mind games with his ex-wife, Juliet, over visiting rights for their daughter. Unfortunately, it seemed that whenever they reached an agreement, his job would take a bow, and he would be forced to work all or part of the agreed day. The separation hadn't been formalized, with a judge setting custody rights. The bitterness Juliet displayed when they spoke on the phone, when he tried to arrange an alternate visit, shone like a beacon as it seemed she tried to make life as difficult as she could.

Rick didn't have to think too long and hard about where things had gone wrong in the marriage: he resolutely blamed himself. Though at the time, he blamed his work, Juliet, and anything *but* himself. It was a common story among a lot of senior homicide detectives: long hours working, booze to help them forget the hideous things they saw, and the people they had to deal with. Worst of all, detectives often had a reluctance to talk about it with their wives, so they felt excluded. That had been true for him.

In Rick's case, the final nail in the coffin that was his marriage was Angie.

Angie had been a victim in a mugging gone wrong. One interview with her, and the spark of instant attraction had struck, ending in a short but torrid affair. When Rick came to his senses and tried to end it, Angie took great delight in giving his wife graphic descriptions of the sex they had shared.

When he got home from work that night, the locks had been changed, his clothes haphazardly crammed into two suitcases, and a scrawled note pinned to the front door to tell him why. No amount of pleading for the chance to explain made a difference. Two hours later, he grabbed his cases and went to a motel, where he drank a bottle of scotch.

Rick was sometimes thought of as morose by colleagues, although he was the life and soul of any party after hours. When his marriage ended, he became moody, but threw himself harder into his job. His arrest rate increased as his alcohol intake decreased; the hope of winning back Juliet never far from his mind. He knew that to have any chance of reconciliation, he had to sort himself out, grow up, and become again the man Juliet had fallen for years before.

At three fifteen that Sunday afternoon, going back to work was the last thing he wanted to do, but a dismembered body in a suitcase was far too interesting to let go of. Using his mobile phone, he called his partner, Tyler Dundas, and left a message with his answering service, telling him of the job that he was attending.

He changed from his grubby T-shirt and shorts into the least crumpled shirt in his wardrobe, adding slacks, a dark woolen tie, and a jacket to conceal the gun at his hip. He was out the door in ten minutes, popping mints to cover his beer breath.

It was almost four in the evening by the time he got to the dump, which had been locked to restrict access. A uniformed cop nodded, recognizing Rick without the need for him to show his I.D. and got into the passenger side of Rick's standard police issue dark blue sedan; and they drove over the rutted gravel road to the tip face.

Rubbish dumps all over the world have the same horrible odor, and Rick wrinkled his nose as he climbed out of the car and concentrated on not retching. He walked over the uneven ground to the staked, taped off area, which designated the crime scene. Off to one side, a policewoman comforted a small, nervous man, the one who'd likely found the body, Rick thought. He gave a small wave of acknowledgement to the woman and kept walking toward a group of men who wore white coveralls. They were combing the area.

Thank God I don't have their job. Some were on hands and knees, raking through garbage with their gloved fingers, searching for clues.

Rick sighed inwardly. *How would anyone recognize what was evidence and what wasn't in a rubbish tip, for Christ's sake?*

Clearly whoever dumped the body had driven in, picked a quiet spot, threw out the suitcase, and left. There would be no usable tire tracks among the hundreds they'd find. *So, what if they find used cigarette ends, or gum wrappers?* He knew it had to be done procedurally, but what a complete and utter waste of manpower it would undoubtedly turn out to be.

He ducked under the tape and walked between the string lines which showed where had been swept, to the edge of the slope, within meters of the case. He nodded to the officers and forensic investigators and stood waiting with hands in pockets for the medical examiner to acknowledge him. The man squatted next to an open suitcase while a photographer worked alongside him. It didn't take long; the ME stood, shook his head, and picked up his bag. He methodically climbed up the slope toward Rick.

"Mike, how're you doing?" Rick asked.

Mike Roundtree wheezed and shook his head, motioning for Rick to follow him out of the taped area. Thirty meters away, he sat on an old oil drum, dropped his bag, and took out a packet of cigarettes. With trembling hands, he struck a match and cupped his hands around it as he lit up. He took a deep inward breath and then slowly puffed out a huge cloud of smoke.

"I fucking needed that." He shook his head. "I'm just getting too old for this shit."

"It's a dog eat dog world, Mike. What can you tell me?"

"Not fucking much at all. I daren't open any more packages here and risk contamination. There may be fingerprints we can use on the plastic, so I only opened one to confirm it's human. And it is. The rest you're going to have to wait for until we get back to the lab. I want to help you get this fucker, so I will work on it

9

overnight, and have a report for you in the morning." He took another deep pull on his cigarette.

"Male, female, old, young?"

"Female, I could see the head through the plastic. That's all for now, but by the looks of things, she has been dead only a matter of a day or two. Now, don't quote me, but I'd say this woman was malnourished."

Rick raised an eyebrow. "You mean like a homeless person?"

"Possibly, or someone who had been starved. The skin had contracted on the portion of the arm I uncovered. Also, there were minor cuts and stab wounds; I'd say it's a fair bet she was tortured before death."

"Oh, I see. Give me one of your smokes, Mike."

"I thought you quit?"

"I did. And I will again, this is just a momentary relapse."

****

Rick watched as the suitcase was lifted out of the pit and set gently inside the coroner's vehicle. He turned and walked gingerly to the witness, who looked like he could cry at any moment. "Mr. Broughton, is it? I'm Detective Sergeant Richard McCoy, sorry to keep you waiting. How are you feeling?"

Harvey shook his head and blinked back tears. "I never seen nothing like it. Jesus, I'm gonna have nightmares about this."

"Is there anyone at home, Mr. Broughton? I don't think you should be on your own, this kind of thing can be quite a nasty shock." He gripped the man's arm to show empathy.

"The wife is there, waiting for me. This lass

phoned her so she wouldn't worry." He pointed at Helen, whose name Rick recalled from a party some weeks before.

"Good, good. Now Mr. Broughton, I hope you understand I need to ask a few questions. Did you see who left the suitcase, or notice anyone suspicious hanging around who might have dumped it?"

"I wish I did. It gave me a nasty turn opening it up and seeing that mess. When I was backing up my trailer, there was a white van leaving, but I'm not saying that was who did it. It's just that that was the only other vehicle here."

Rick nodded thoughtfully. "Okay, so just to clarify, can you think back for me? You were backing up your trailer when you noticed the van, are you saying that it left from the area where the suitcase was located, or somewhere else?"

"Well, I'm parked over that side." He pointed to where his beige colored Chrysler was parked, "and the van was over that way. It could have been. But I couldn't say exactly, because he was driving away as I was driving in."

"So, it was a man driving?"

"Oh no, sorry, I just assumed it was a man, you know, driving a van and going to the dump. Well, it's hardly something a woman would do, is it? The sun was reflecting off the glass so I couldn't see who was inside, not that I really looked, if you know what I mean."

"No, I suppose that's a fair assumption, Mr. Broughton. So, just to confirm, you didn't see anyone else around, and you didn't see the driver of the van, but it was a white color? Do you recall what make or model it was?"

He looked blankly back at the detective. "It was just one of those Japanese ones that look like an oblong box on wheels, I'm sorry."

"So no stickers, or signwriting on it, you wouldn't have noticed part or all of the license plate?"

"Not that I can remember, no." He shook his head, emphatically, but still looked close to tears.

"All right, Mr. Broughton, that will be all for now. You go home and have a nice cup of tea. This is my card—" he took one from his inside jacket pocket and handed it over. "—If you think of anything else, especially about this white van, please, give me a call. I will visit you tomorrow to see if you've recalled any other details and take a written statement from you. I will also bring a book full of images of vans to see if can recognize a make or model."

They shook hands and Rick walked him to his car. "Are you sure you're okay to drive home, Mr. Broughton?" He opened the driver's door, and watched as the man gingerly climbed in.

He nodded, and grimaced climbing into the seat. "As you say, a nice cup of tea will help."

Rick thanked Helen for spending time with the witness, then watched as he drove away, with her alongside him, acting as his chaperone to see him out of the gates. *Poor old bugger, not the best Sunday he's ever had.*

He spoke with the senior Crime Scene Investigator and confirmed his earlier thought that no significant evidence had been found so far. *Nor are they likely to find anything no matter how long they search.*

Rick's next stop was to the transportable building

which served as an office and lunchroom for the staff. He knocked on the door and entered without waiting for a reply. Inside a man sat with his feet up on a desk, reading a dog-eared adult magazine. The office had a dusty and damp smell to it, and clearly hadn't seen a cleaner for weeks.

"You're the police I take it?" he said in a disgusted tone, tossing the magazine back onto the cluttered desk. "Harry Melton, site supervisor. I was told to wait around till you showed up." Harry was a big man. Rick was shocked that he could be so overweight and still hold onto his job, as he seemed incapable of being able to walk too far without being out of breath.

"Detective Sergeant Richard McCoy, thanks for waiting. What can you tell me about the operation here? I'm trying to narrow down a time frame of when the suitcase might have been left."

Melton sat up, waddling his body from side to sit to gain leverage. He shook his head and took the card Rick offered to him. "Since the council cut back on staff we don't have the manpower here like we used to. So, what we do is this: We run two tip faces, one for the weekend warriors, where you've come from now, and the other, on the Western side, for during the week, mainly for commercial and councils. At the end of each shift, and twice during the day, we come along with our D9 Dozer, the one parked out back, and crush everything in, cart away what we need to, and tidy up the area by burying everything under sand. That's how the tip face moves every day."

"So, as the case wasn't buried, the only thing I can tell you is that it was dumped there sometime this afternoon, but as to what time?" He shrugged. "I'd say it was quite recent, as I'm sure one of us would have seen it sitting there on our walkthroughs, but I couldn't swear on a Bible exactly when. Occasionally, we wander through to make sure everything is okay, and see if we need to run the D9 over the area specially. People are often messy with how they leave their stuff. But, we didn't today because it was quiet. We probably got only three to four hundred vehicles through."

"Three to four hundred?" Rick couldn't keep the disbelief and frustration from his voice.

"Yeah, some Sundays it's much higher than that. Well, we don't count them as they drive in. Being rate payers we don't charge patrons to dump, so anyone can enter during the hours of seven and four. I'd say three to four hundred conservatively, but it might be five hundred for all I know."

"And, stupid question I'm guessing, but no CCTV?"

"What, at a dump? What are they going to steal, rubbish?" He laughed.

Rick could see this was another dead end. *Fuck it. I hope there is some forensic help from the body or suitcase.*

He looked at his watch and realized with a sinking heart that it was too late to go past his old house. On weekends, when he wasn't working, or had rights to see Amy, he liked to go and sit in his car on the far side of the playground and see if she was there, with her mother. Sometimes, if the weather was nice, Juliet would take Amy to the park, across the road from their house, and Rick could watch and remember when his life was good. He knew that by the time he got there, it would be too late, and yet another week had gone by without him seeing his beautiful daughter.

"Thanks for your help, and hanging around to talk to me, I appreciate it. I'll be back around tomorrow to interview everyone who worked here today, so if you think of anything that could be useful, please let me know."

Rick left the transportable building and made the decision there was little point in staying any longer. As he walked back to the car, bitter and twisted at the situation that had seen him estranged from Juliet, his mobile phone rang. He took it from his jacket pocket and pulled the aerial out if its socket so hard it almost came off in his hand.

He barked into it, "McCoy."

"Boss, its Tyler, sorry I missed your call, I was at the movies with Bette and the kids. What's up, do you need me there?"

"Nah, it's Ok. Enjoy your family time, mate. Not much else to do here. It's a dead end until we get forensics and an ID. I'm about to leave."

"Have you eaten boss? Drop in, Bette would love to see you, come and have dinner with us."

Rick was tempted, very tempted. "Give Bette my apologies, tell her I have a date, otherwise I would."

"You've got a date? That's fantastic."

Yeah, a date with a bottle of scotch.

"See you in the morning." Before his partner could answer, he hit the end button, and shoved the aerial closed.

Chapter 2: My Memoir Entry
The First Glimpse

I was five years old, when I first saw someone bleed out. *Bleed out* was one of my father's expressions. I remember it as if it was yesterday. But, what I remember most, wasn't the sight of the blood, and boy, there was lots of that, but how it affected me; how it made me *feel*. If I had to use one word to describe it, it would be euphoric. I hasten to add, that at that age I didn't know what the word euphoric meant; that was an adjective I came to learn much later when I analyzed my feelings after my first kill.

I had been out at the country fair with my dad; he was a big man. When we walked, he would always hold my hand, and when I looked up at him to answer a question, or ask him one, his face would often be haloed by the sun. It would make me blink and I always thought of him as a saint. During Sunday school, at Father Charles's Church of The Immaculate Conception, we used to color in pictures of the Disciples, with worn down stubby pencils that had been sharpened repeatedly over the years. Those holy people always had a halo, just like my dad did in the noon-day sun when I looked up at him.

He was a butcher by trade, tall, with huge sideburns and a haircut that has been described since as a 'mullet.' He had his own shop in Mundaring, which is in the Eastern hills of Perth, in Western Australia, and all the locals loved him. This was back when it wasn't part of the metropolitan area as it is now with urban sprawl. It was treated as a day trip to visit the National Park, which people did then for a picnic and a bush walk.

Sometimes, when he worked, he would let me watch him cut up the big carcasses of pigs and cows as they hung upside down on a long chain that ran along the roof in the cool room. I used to sit on the cold floor, with my favorite collection of Matchbox cars, and make roads in the sawdust, while he cut joints of meat from his *babies*, as he called them.

Looking back now, that was where it all started. The first spark, if you will, that eventually became a conflagration—an obsession that went on to rule my life. It began with dreams of using a knife to hurt and dismember my victims, and later, became a reality.

I sat surrounded by my toy cars, in the sawdust which was there to absorb any spilt animal blood, as my father lovingly, seductively even, used a cleaver to cut through bone and muscle. I loved watching him. The harsh overhead lighting used to glint and flash off the polished steel as he sculptured his carcasses into jointed slabs of meat.

I often wondered why the carcasses didn't scream when he cut them into big chunks, so I asked Dad that very question. He had his arm up to his elbow in a sheep, as it hung upside down from the chain at the time. Just for a moment he looked at me, then burst into a hearty laugh. He must have seen I was serious, and he told me that the animal most certainly would have screamed, if it wasn't already dead.

Naturally, that evoked a long conversation about death, and how the animals he cut up every day had been killed. He explained that that was why there was minimal blood dripping on the concrete floor beneath the swinging sheep: it had been humanely dispatched in an *abattoir*. That, he explained, was a place where death was the only outcome for those beasts that went in. Once dead, it had been bled out, that was how he described it, *bled out,* and then had been eviscerated. He went on to say that his *babies* were no longer animals, they were *meat* for the dinner table.

I suppose he meant well. I was an inquisitive child, always bombarding him and Mother with questions. That was before she left us, which she did suddenly one stinking hot March weekend, when the temperature had climbed to forty degrees Celsius for the third day in a row. He was trying to show me, at the tender age of somewhere between four and five years old, that all things die, and, sometimes there is a purpose in death. I don't think he meant to indicate we should find pleasure in killing and carving up animals, but forever after that conversation, I had dreams.

I didn't dream every night, and if I did, not all dreams luridly involved flashing knives, scarlet rain drops, and screaming animals. But some did. And the older I got, the more colorful and detailed they became. Is it any surprise that as time went on, in some dreams, the incidence grew to where *I was the one wielding the blade? And, when people made me angry, I imagined it was them hung upside down on the chain, as I hurt, and cut them up.*

I suppose it is no shock to you reading this missive, with all that has since transpired that when I first saw *the blood drenching,* as I always referred to it, rather than bleeding out, as my Father called it, that it resonated. And I think it was *because* of that conversation that the pleasurable link between bleeding and dissecting was formed within my imagination.

Of course, being a boy child, I had my fair share of bumps and grazes growing up. Although, unlike Johnny Mortimer down the street, I had never broken a bone. Johnny fell off his dad's motor cycle while pretending he was riding it and broke his left leg. We all wrote things and our names on the plaster cast he wore for weeks afterward. I couldn't write my name at the time, so I drew, in purple crayon, a pirate with a curved sword. Johnny said he liked my picture and named me Pirate Prince Paul. I loved that name; it made me feel special.

So, I don't mean to infer I had never seen blood; I had. There was always some at dad's shop from the *babies.* Once I saw dad cut himself shaving, which I always thought as ironic, him being a butcher, when I was old enough to know what the word meant. And, I had my own injuries in minor doses throughout my early childhood too. But, during the drenching…well, that was something else.

It happened on the weekend of the Mundaring and Districts Country Fair. Mum had been gone several months by then and I still missed her. Dad got fed up with me asking when she would come home, and he lost his temper one night and hit me, I lost count of how many punches. When he was done, he slammed the bedroom door on his way out, and forgot to leave my night light on. I cried myself to sleep, in a fetal ball, and that night the dreams were in Technicolor. I never asked about her again, and years later, when I found her body, it no longer mattered.

On the day of the drenching, Dad had shut up shop at three o'clock and told me to put away my cars, and that he was taking me to the fair. Usually he closed at five on a Saturday, but that day he promised me fairy floss, a hot dog, and, if I was very good, a ride on the carousel.

It had rained the night before and right up to about ten o'clock that morning, but then the sun had come out and it was quite warm when dad paid our fee at the main gate and we walked into the show grounds. The grass had turned muddy in some areas, and once I almost slipped over and would have if dad hadn't yanked my arm half out of its socket to stop my fall.

He led me first to the judging section, and we looked at lots of animals that had won various color ribbons, for breeding and appearance. The area stank to high heaven, and I could barely breathe. Dad's animals never smelled of excrement, and I could hardly wait to get away from the fetid stench.

Then, we traipsed into a huge tent where we saw cake decorating, pies with intricate pastry designs, and even sausages, which hung by their strings. They smelt wonderful after the stink of the animals. But it was crowded in the marquees and I kept getting jostled, and dad got angry as the human snake of viewers slowly weaved its way in and around the display tables in the hot and humid tent. His grip on my hand got tighter and tighter until finally we got outside in the last of the evening sunshine. My hand hurt quite a lot by then.

I suppose I got used to Dad hurting me. Now, I'm not saying he deliberately did that, it was more like I was…a distraction. Most of the time he was a loving, caring dad, but other times it was like he was someone else. And when he was like that, he lived in some sort of fugue. I didn't exist as *his son*, but as an annoyance. And then he would hurt me.

For me, that was normal. I didn't know any better; that was just the way it was, especially living with my father after my mother had run off. I suppose the thing that hurt me the most about her, was that she never even said goodbye.

So, once we got outside the big tent with all the pies, we followed the throng to side show alley. Oh, it was fantastic. The noise, the neon lights, rides that whizzed around and up and down while loud music tried to overpower the screams of teenagers, thrilled me to my soul. Everywhere was the smell of fresh popped corn, and cooked doughnuts dipped in cinnamon sugar.

All I had had for lunch was a wafer-thin slice of polony and tomato sauce sandwich. I knew better than to ask for more, no matter how hungry I was, since asking once before made Dad's eyes glaze over. Then he hit me. He yelled about how *lucky* I was to have what I'd been given.

"When I was a prisoner of the Viet Cong army, I would have done anything, *anything* to have that to eat," he screamed at me, as I cowered and cried.

He spoke at great length, at odd times over the years, of the months he spent in a bamboo cage half suspended in muddy river water, with rats as friends, while his tormentors poked him with sticks and threw rotten scraps down for him to eat.

I'm sorry; sometimes I digress.

Dad and I walked down the center of sideshow

alley, I had his oversized hand wrapped around my right, and something rather wonderful, called a dippy dog, in my left. For the uninitiated, a dippy dog is a hot dog sausage on a wooden skewer, dipped in batter, deep fried until golden and crispy, and then smothered in tomato sauce. It was, without doubt, the best thing I had ever eaten in my life.

I had just watched him in the shooting gallery while he shot down small dented cans from a shelf with a cork-firing rifle. Perhaps it was his army training that came to the fore, but he won me a brown and white stuffed dog and said I should name him. For some reason, I called him Bobby, but I have no recollection why. I think it was supposed to resemble a Basset hound, but it was so poorly made it only lasted about three weeks of cuddling and the stuffing began to seep out from between the stitching. Of course, Dad blamed me for being too rough with Bobby, but I promise I never was: it was just cheap tawdry rubbish. For those three weeks, I loved that dog.

Dad stopped quite suddenly, so I did too, to watch a group of four teenagers laughing and giggling around the strength test game. The two men went first but failed to send the ball all the way up the pole to ring the bell, and they were teased mercilessly by their girlfriends. The challenge was laid down, and one I heard named Louise agreed to have a go.

She took the oversized hammer, stood wide legged, and appeared to struggle to lift it from the grass. She intended to bring it down onto the pad. I suppose it was her boyfriend who stepped in to help her, putting his hand under the shaft and helped yank it up. Looking back now, I think she had given up and wanted to drop it, but the man was already jerking it upward.

The end of the hammer traveled through its arc and hit her in the face.

She screamed as blood squirted out from her smashed nose. She lifted her hands, but there was so much it spilled through her fingers, gushing like a waterfall. She was wearing a tight, white V-necked jumper, but that soon turned deep red.

I've tried to work out why, many times over the years since, and can't come up with a valid, conclusive reason. Possibly it was because she was female, and the only woman I had known up till then was my mother who had abandoned me when she went shopping and never returned. Maybe it was because of the increasingly vivid dreams that assailed me almost nightly, ever since the conversation about death while my father cut up that sheep. I don't know why, but that was when I first fell in love with the sight of blood.

I knew, as an undeniable fact in my soul, I wanted to see more; lots more.

Chapter 3:
The Y2K Bug

The body in the suitcase was sensationalized by the media, but in many ways, it was overshadowed as the year 1999 drew to its inexorable close. There was real fear that the world might come to an end when the clocks reached midnight on the thirty first of December.

The eighties and nineties had seen the explosion in computer technology with the invention of the microchip. This wondrous piece of technology had seemed to find its way into the heart and soul of every electrical and electronic device imaginable. For years, things got smaller, faster, and more efficient as machines were being used to design faster, smaller, and more efficient computers.

Ticking away inside the brain of all these pieces of brave new world equipment was a simple clock. For a clock to be useful it needs to have a reference point in time, and no one thought when designing these clocks, what would happen when the two-digit measurement for the year reached 00. Surely, people argued, something like a machine couldn't understand that 00 was a year, when mathematically it meant it wasn't that, it was nothing.

Some said things would simply shut down, computers, trains, planes, cars, traffic control lights, bank alarms; it seemed the list of things people had to worry about ceasing to work was endless. It was such a concern it was given an acronym Y2K. Businesses cropped up, with software solutions, which promised, for a fee they could ensure your home or business computer wouldn't shut down, never to be able to be turned on again.

The West Australian Police force, like all government departments, also had its concerns. IT technicians were working frantically in December to ensure that at midnight on New Year's Eve, the entire police communications and computer network didn't shut down, unable to be re-booted.

For McCoy, it was just another problem in a life of continual annoyances. It seemed that every time he wanted to use his computer, the system was down for Y2K proofing. In his opinion, anyone who gave credence to such ludicrous scare-mongering conspiracy theories needed their heads read.

The suitcase murder case had dragged on, seemingly going nowhere. He and Juliet had been separated for three months. She appeared to be in no hurry to forgive him, but more recently, he had noticed a change in her. He could sense it in the tone of voice she used on him, as if she considered him to be a human being again, rather than a rat.

The change in her started with a relenting of her refusal for visits to see Amy at times other than every other Sunday. Rick believed that it had been her way of hitting back at him where it hurt the most in the early part of their separation.

On a Sunday afternoon, in early December, Rick was sitting in his car, secretly watching Amy play in the park. Suddenly, his mobile phone rang, he thought it would be work, and he almost didn't take it from his pocket, but old habits die hard. He had been under considerable pressure because his investigation had stalled.

He answered in his usual way: "McCoy."

"You know, Rick, you are absolutely crap at hiding. Whatever you do, don't go into undercover work, will you?" Juliet said.

Oh, fuck. He sat up straight in the seat and mumbled an apology. "I'm sorry, Juliet, I didn't think I was doing any harm, I will leave."

"Don't do that. Come on over, Amy would love to see you."

He almost ran across the park, and when Amy saw him, she screamed "Daddy!" and clapped her hands with obvious glee.

He squatted down and hugged her, mouthing: *thank you* at Juliet over her shoulder. "Hi baby," he whispered. "I missed you, so I thought I'd come and say hello."

"I missed you too, daddy. Can you read me a story in bed tonight? You haven't done that for such a long time."

He stared at Juliet, questioning her with his eyes, but she stayed motionless. "Well, baby, we'll have to see about that. I may have to go back to work." He tried not to let any disappointment show in his voice.

As was her way, she changed tack. "Daddy—" She leaned her head back so she could look at his eyes. "— I've been talking to Mummy about having my own puppy, and she says I have to wait. What do you think?"

He glanced up at Juliet, and she shook her head,

mouthing the word *Christmas* so he knew it was to be an upcoming gift for her. "Well, sweetheart. I think maybe you need to be just a little bit older so you can take care of him."

She frowned. "But I am older now. All my friends have pets you know!"

His heart melted, as it always did with her, "I promise you, baby, one day soon, you will have a puppy, when the time is right."

She nodded, her big brown eyes opened even wider as she smiled. "I love you, Daddy. Can you push me on the swings, really, really high?"

While Rick could see, that Amy loved seeing her mother and father together again, he could still feel the thick atmosphere. But, he was happy for the chance, no matter how small, to try to build a bridge with her. As he pushed Amy on the swing, Juliet stunned him by asking about the investigation.

"I saw you on TV, doing the re-enactment. That poor woman in the suitcase. You looked tired, Rick. How is the case going?"

At first, he didn't want to talk about it to her, especially as the results from the press conferences had been so meagre. But in a blinding revelation he realized one of her many complaints about him from the past: He never spoke to her about his job, and that she felt excluded from his world.

"Jules, I know I never talked about the job to you much when we were together, and I'm sorry for that. I suppose I was trying to protect you from all the crap I deal with day after day. Plus, to be honest, when I got home I wanted to get away from all of that, not relive it. I was wrong to exclude you. If you want to know about this case, then I'd like to talk to you about it, but not while Amy is around us. How about we go to Pizza House for dinner like we used to, then after we put Amy to bed you and I can sit on the back patio with a glass of wine, and I will tell you all about it?"

She stared back at him, open mouthed, and nodded.

"Pizza House for tea, *yippeeee,*" Amy yelled, as she swung through the air.

A little later, she surprised him again while they watched Amy playing with another little girl's puppy. "Are you seeing anyone, Rick?"

He shot her a look. "Jules, I swear to you, since you kicked me out, I haven't seen anyone."

"Not even your slut, little Miss Angie-fancy-pants?"

"*Especially* Angie. My God, Jules, that whole thing was the biggest, most stupid mistake of my life. There isn't a single day goes by that I don't hate myself for it."

She nodded again and turned away to swipe at her face with a hand before stroking the puppy alongside her daughter.

That evening, the Pizza House was packed with families. On Sundays, it was all the pizza, salad, and dessert you could eat, and Rick felt as if he was living as a family again, though he kept reminding himself, he wasn't.

He limited himself to a single beer and bought a Wine Cooler for Juliet. They talked of normal things, like cartoon shows Amy was watching on TV, her friends at play school, and the possibility of her getting her very own puppy just like the one at the park.

Back at home, they both bathed Amy. "So, Daddy,

wasn't that puppy, Maxi, in the park so cute? That's the sort of doggy I would like." Rick had to bite his lip to keep from laughing at her persistence, as he shampooed her hair. He glanced up and Juliet was trying to hold in a laugh too.

When Rick brushed her long brown hair as she stood in front of him, while he sat on the couch, Amy again talked about how lovely her life would be if they could just have a little puppy. When he put her to bed he read her a bedtime story while she cuddled her favorite teddy bear, named Pinkie. He kissed her goodnight and she hugged him and whispered that she loved him, and he replied that he loved her too. He hadn't felt so complete in a long time.

When he got to the kitchen, Juliet handed him a can of beer as she held a glass of white wine in the other. She tilted her head toward the rear glass sliding door, and he smiled nervously. He didn't know or understand why Juliet wanted to spend time with him, but he was overjoyed that she did. *Don't fuck this up.*

When they were sitting down, opposite each other across the glass-topped patio table, he began. "You might call it karma, that during the worst three months of my life, I've also been working on the worst case of my life."

"How so?"

He took a long slow drink of his Lager before putting the can down. "Well, the Forensic inspection of the suitcase showed it was a cheap brand, available through lots of shops and had been on sale for three years. We tried tracking it through the stores that sold them, but it was a dead end, far too many people bought them that couldn't be identified.

"The body parts fitted almost exactly inside it, except for the one piece that was missing, the right upper thigh, and we assume it was left out because it wouldn't fit. No sense risking the case popping open, I suppose. God knows where that is, buried in his back yard, I guess."

Juliet shuddered and Rick noticed she picked up her wine glass to try to hide it. Yet her face glowed in a way he hadn't seen before, which looked like barely suppressed excitement.

He pressed on, not wanting to break the spell of closeness he felt. "The plastic he used for wrapping each body part was the type sold in hardware stores. It's the kind used as drop sheets for painting and decorating. We did recover good, usable fingerprints, but they led nowhere as he has never been arrested before. When we catch him, we will have more than enough physical evidence to put him away. We have DNA from his semen; he had sex with her some time before death, but even his blood type is the most common, so no help there."

"He left his blood on the body?" she asked, incredulously

He looked into Juliet's eyes, wondering if he was giving her too much detail, but she looked fascinated, and she almost imperceptibly nodded her head to urge him to continue.

"No, Jules. They got the blood type from his semen. Through dental records we identified the body, Melanie Cartwright, twenty-six years old. She disappeared while shopping in a supermarket. Her husband waited for her in the car, while she went inside, and she vanished without a trace. Apparently, he was listening to the football on the radio, a decision he will regret for the rest of his life. We know that she was somehow abducted, but no one saw how or who took her. If someone did see anything unusual in the car park, they didn't volunteer any information when we had the televised re-enactment."

Juliet finished the last of her wine with one large gulp and put the glass down on the table. "Go on, please," she said almost breathlessly.

"Staff working there did not recall seeing her, so she probably didn't make it inside, which means she was grabbed in the car park, or the mall. It had to be random, as she didn't usually shop there, unless they had been followed, but that didn't make much sense."

He again paused and took a long sip of beer, surprised at how easy it was to talk about it to Juliet. *Why did I never do this before?*

"She appeared to have been tortured, starved, and raped. The ME tells us this because the skin was drawn and shrunk, and she had lost a considerable amount of weight when they weighed everything that was left and allowed for what wasn't. Then bizarrely, she had been hung upside down, we think, while she was bled, by having her throat cut after death. The exact cause is impossible to determine; heart failure seems the most likely. It's not conclusive though, because there were numerous wounds to her body, mainly knife wounds. She was dismembered by someone who seemed to know what they were doing, possibly with medical training. The cuts were neat, joints separated not hacked through, the murderer took his time, this was no rushed job. For a while we looked at some sort or religious or cult related killing. Being hung upside down suggested some type of ritualism, but like everything else it didn't lead anywhere.

"We found no witnesses to the dumping, though, and we spoke to hundreds of people who admitted to being there on the day, along with all the staff. But whoever had been driving the white van hasn't come forward, so maybe that's something. But we have no idea how many other vehicle drivers didn't come forward either because people just don't seem to notice others at the dump. There was so much garbage, as you can imagine, left around the suitcase it's impossible to know what's relevant and what's not. It's also hard to know when the case was left, some said they thought they noticed it there, but others said they hadn't seen it. About the only thing of note was a heap of pruning's from a lemon tree. But whether that's anything to do with our killer or not, who can say? A lot of people took tree trimmings that day.

"We don't know why Melanie was abducted and killed. We have turned her and her husband's life upside down trying to find why she was targeted. The best we can come up with is plain bad luck; a random killer who just was in the right place at the wrong time for her. Perhaps she reminded him of someone else, perhaps in some sick twisted way he was offended by her, but if he never kills again, I don't think we will ever catch him."

"Do you think he will kill again, Rick?"

He nodded slowly and picked up his can. "He likes it, Jules. At least that's what I think. My boss wants to play that down, doesn't want a panic, and rightly so. It's a particularly brutal, horrific murder, and the victim went through seven kinds of hell before she died. You would think a woman should be safe going to the supermarket."

She shook her head and looked every bit as angry as Rick felt. "How could someone do that to another human being?"

"That's the scary part, Jules. We just don't know. Outwardly he could seem quite normal. He is clearly intelligent and methodical. I doubt there'll be a neon sign saying 'killer.' He obviously got some sort of perverted pleasure out of torturing and killing Melanie; her death didn't appear to be frenzied. He is a cold hearted, calculating, merciless murderer. I so badly want to catch him before he does it again, but deep down, I know I won't." He took another long drink of beer.

"I wish you had opened up like this to me when we were together. I always wanted to feel like I was a part of your life, and call me morbid, but I find this sort of thing frightening, but interesting. Does that make sense?"

He nodded sadly. "I didn't want to burden you. I deal with scum, and normal people who do hideous things to other human beings, often people they love, day after day. It gets you down, honestly it does. I wanted you to be my escape valve from all of that. I'm sorry I didn't share with you, if I had my time over again, I would."

"And Angie? Was she a relief valve too?"

He stared at her and saw the sadness in her eyes. This was the first time she wanted to talk about it, to understand how he could do what he had done. He had to handle this right.

He shook his head, slowly. "There is no excuse that

holds up to scrutiny, Jules. There is nothing I can tell you that says x plus y equals z. But it's taken all of this for me to know that while at the time I blamed you, it was never you, it was me. When it started with Angie, you and I seemed to be arguing a lot, and we hardly ever found time to be intimate. I thought you were nagging me: I was drinking and smoking too much, going to the pub with the guys, and working too many hours. It was crap for you, and you tried to make me see that, but all I did was expect you to take the shit I dealt out. I see now that you were trying to save our marriage, not end it. But at the time…it felt different.

"Anyway, when I interviewed Angie, she had seen a mugging go wrong, and the guy attacked her, and she stood up to him and fought back. God alone knows what she saw in me, but suddenly a young attractive woman wanted me at a time when you didn't. Pretty much as soon as it started I came to my senses and tried to stop it, and you know the rest."

The silence dragged on between them. Rick had no idea what Juliet was thinking, but he knew he felt better for having tried to explain. At least they weren't arguing.

"You know Jules, the stupid thing is that I deal with people who don't think of the consequences at the time; they just react, and someone dies. And here I did the same bloody thing. I could never say sorry enough to you, and I will never stop regretting what I did."

She blinked away tears that had appeared, making her eyes twinkle. "What ever happened to us, Rick? Life used to be fun. we went out, we shared things, we laughed, and then it all stopped."

He leaned forward, in his chair, trying to convince

her of his sincerity. "I think like a lot of other things in life, it was a combination. You might think it was Angie, but it wasn't. She ended the marriage, but if I had been more mature, more understanding, then she never could have tempted me away. It was, and always will be you I love, I lost you through my own stupidity."

"God knows things were not great before Angie. Jesus, I can't believe I can even say her name. But since we broke up, I'm scared all the time. I don't sleep well, and you'll think me stupid, but under my pillow is one of your T-shirts. It's there so I can smell you in bed with me. Sometimes when I wake up because I heard a noise in the house, the only way I can get back to sleep is to hold it over my face. Amy asks about you all the time, and that hurts. And then, on top of all that, there is this thing about the Y2K bug."

Rick had to bite his lip. In the old days, he would have ridiculed her for being silly, he was fed up with the whole doom and gloom thing that bordered on mass hysteria. "What about it?"

"Well, what if everything does shut down, like some are saying? They are warning that all planes will be grounded, and trains won't be running. Power could go off, gas supplies could end, the list is endless what if all the computers that look after the American and Russian nuclear missiles go haywire and we have World War Three?"

He stared at her, dumfounded. *Is she for real?*

Rick watched as she held back real tears, and he was reminded what a gentle soul she was. He stood and walked around the table and her eyes never left his. He squatted beside her and wrapped his arms around her and she cradled her head in the crook of his neck. He felt her tremble as she cried, she was obviously scared and lonely.

More than ever Rick realized how wrong and bad he had been, to have mistreated her, and not just over the affair, it had been lots of other things too. He could smell her shampoo, and body spray, and the essence that was her. She shuddered slightly, and he could feel it throughout her body.

"Baby, you don't need to be scared, everything will be all right. We've got government IT guys working on our computers at work, and I was talking to one the other day. He said it's all a load of rubbish, and that it's all scare tactics by businesses selling solutions. With all the brains that they have with the US and Russian governments, do you honestly think we would go to war because the clocks stop working inside missile launch controllers? Honestly, love, you don't have to worry."

She lifted her head off his shoulder and blinked back tears. She looked at him before answering. "Rick, I gave up my life and career to be with you. We had our daughter, and yes it wasn't perfect. But, at least you were here at night, and I felt safe. Then my secure little piece of the world was destroyed, by you, and I hated you for what you did to me. But the worst thing was that after you left I felt scared all the time, especially at night. Every little creak and groan the house made. Every time Amy fell over and hurt herself, every time I see you on the TV with the re-enactments, looking for this killer. At night, I would lock the house, then I'd have to get up out of bed and check to make sure I had done it properly. This used to be my haven, Rick, and now it's my worst nightmare."

"Let me come back, Jules. I've learned my lesson, believe me I have, I will never let you down again."

"But, how will I ever be able to trust you? If you call me to say you are working late, how will I know you are? I will think of you off with another Angie, giving you whatever it is that I can't."

He shook his head. "I know trust will be an issue, and probably there isn't anything I can say that will make that better overnight. Trust is earned, never given, but I swear to you, I will never allow another Angie to happen."

Another tear rolled down her cheek. "I know you missed the sex, I suppose I'm wired differently. I miss the closeness, the intimacy, and the talking to each other. My days are boring being just a mother and housewife, but yours...you chase criminals, and are trying to make the world a safer place, and I love that about you. I don't want to be shut out of that."

"I understand that now. Take me back Jules, please? I've missed you and Amy so much."

She nodded, and he cuddled her again, not daring to speak, not trusting his voice wouldn't break, and worried that he would say something to ruin his chance to find his balance in the world again.

Chapter 4: My Memoir Entry
I Spy, With My Little Eye

So, there it was, me: a super star, featured in all the papers and on TV. I can't describe, dear reader, how it all made me feel, but I shall try.

They said she was my first; the body in a suitcase. What a laugh I had at that. There had been others. Because I know you are paying such close attention, dear reader, I shall tell you about all of them.

****

My father's moods got worse as I got older. Previously, Dad got into his more distant and violent phases once every two or three months or so. Well, slowly, they became more frequent, and unpredictable.

During the days, when he worked in the shop dealing with customers, he was often friendly, even flirtatious with the housewife customers, sometimes. I thought people came in for a chat with him, rather than because his meat was cheaper, or even particularly good; after all, within reason, meat is meat, right? But when he was alone with me, he would often get a faraway look in his eyes and tell me how *lucky* I was. That was always a precursor for a beating.

There was no rhyme or reason to it. It wasn't as if I did one thing that set him off. If it had been, believe me, I would have been very careful not to do it. No, it could be all manner of trivial things that set him off, from asking him a question about the weather, to getting a word wrong in a book.

I think I was probably about six or so when I did that. I had brought home from school that day's reading book, which was to be done with a parent. The story was about a caterpillar who ate cake, lots of different types, and I think it was a lemon one I called orange. I admit I didn't read the word, I wasn't that dumb, I guessed it from the picture, and, I guessed wrong.

It was summer, and I had my summer pajamas on, as I was ready for bed. That meant it was shorts and a T-shirt. That's why the first slap on my bare thigh hurt so much; I didn't have any covering over the skin. It took me by surprise. There was no faraway look or any warning. I was reading, and suddenly SLAP. It took my breath away, the pain was so sudden and intense, I wet myself right there on his lap.

That made him worse. The slaps became punches, before he carried me to my room and threw me on the bed before storming out. But the next morning it was as if nothing had happened. At breakfast, he told me to cheer up: it was a beautiful day, or some such thing. That, was even scarier than the beatings. One time he took me to the hospital with a suspected broken arm, but all the way there he chatted like it was a sporting injury. But, I never had any interest in playing sport; I was studying when he grabbed my arm and dragged me into the living room because I had left a cup on the coffee table which had made a wet ring. Thankfully it wasn't broken, just bruised and sprained, but I remember thinking, he didn't know he had hurt me so badly.

I never knew what that day's father would be like:

loving and friendly, or distant and violent, with him telling me I was lucky. It got to the point, where I began to think that I *was* lucky. There, now you'll agree with the newspapers when they tell you I'm insane. But, I stress that growing up, I didn't know any different, for me it was my life, and, so far as I knew all kids were brought up that way. No one ever asked me if my father was abusing me, in fact, it's true to say that even the word abuse, was not one which was used at school back then. No one cared, really, and so it continued with me thinking I was the one at fault, not my dad.

It's not something that was discussed at school, and generally I could keep the bruises hidden from view. On occasions when I couldn't for some reason I always lied: I had fallen over, been play fighting in the park, a ball hit me in the face, and so on.

It was just before my twelfth birthday when life as I knew it came to an end. On that Sunday morning, I got out of bed, and couldn't find my father anywhere. I thought he must have been in the shop working, though that would be unusual for a Sunday. But, I soon discovered there wasn't anywhere else he could be, so I went to look.

The family home adjoined the butcher shop through a long passage, which ran along the side of the cool room through a solid timber door with opaque glass panels. I entered the shop but he wasn't there, so I turned to look at the massive door to the chiller, which was about ten centimeters thick. It was secured by a large chrome handle that took all my strength as a child to unlatch. Once I navigated the handle, it was quite an effort to open the door, because of its weight. The handle and latch had a hole which lined up, and dad kept his big sharpening steel hanging through. I don't know why he did that, because it wasn't as if he needed to keep the door locked; the carcasses couldn't escape after all could they?

I think he kept the steel there just because it was a convenient place for it to hang, being within reach of the wooden carving block. But, in doing that, it effectively locked the door, and that was one of the combination of things that stuck in my memory. The image of the permanently locked door, led me to think that the cool room would make an excellent prison. The walls, being so heavily insulated, meant it was soundproofed; all the better to hide the screams. My dreams had a home, and they came thick and fast, with people I disliked I imagined hanging from the chain, as I cut them up with my knife.

Dad and I had been watching horror films together on Friday nights since I was nine, and they helped fuel my imagination. They had always been his favorite, and he let me stay up till very late at night, I think to keep him company, it was as if we were best mates, and I enjoyed those nights.

He had never just not been there when I woke up before, and I was scared. I searched the house twice before wondering if he was working in the shop, though why he would do that was beyond my comprehension; he'd never done it before on a Sunday. When I ventured to have a look, I noticed the steel wasn't hanging through the handle, it was on the butcher's block, and that was strange.

Is he in the cool room? If he is, should I go in?

I agonized over that question quivering with fear. You see, I knew that if I upset him he would hurt me again, and I certainly didn't want that. I stood there, in my pajamas, with slippers on my feet, pondering for what seemed like ages. Eventually, I sighed. I needed to know, so I yanked on the door handle and flung it wide.

Oh, my God! There in the middle of the cool room hung a pig carcass. It had been stabbed, hacked, and chopped until it was just a bloody obliterated ghost of its former self. Bits and pieces of meat had been left hanging from what once was a carcass, and a long-bladed carving knife stuck out of its flank. It looked for all the world as if dad had tried to murder the pig.

You, dear reader, are probably thinking I was horrified? Shocked and surprised, yes, but horrified I wasn't. It was, somewhat inspirational, and more than anything else I wanted to go and pull the blade out of the side of the pig and plunge it back in a few more times. So, I could be more like my father.

I did go and remove the knife, out of respect for dad. He would *never* intentionally leave one of his favorites like that, if he had been thinking straight. I closed the cool room door as I left, knife in hand, and slipped the steel sharpener back through the handle out of habit. Holding that piece of Sheffield Steel's finest was a comfort, as I was alone, and frightened by what had happened to him.

Quite likely, though I can't remember exactly now, I thought the knife would help me to be able to protect myself in a house where Dad had vanished. The monsters that had abducted my father could return for me at any moment and I could ward them off with it. Was I being melodramatic? Possibly. Having been drip fed a continual dose of horror films it was easy to think the worst.

So, there I was, in the house, with a mutilated pig carcass in the fridge, and a knife in my hand, alone for the first time in my life. My mother had run away while shopping, and my father had vanished.

I went back through to the house, sat on the couch where dad and I watched *Zombie Terror* and *Dracula's Minions*, two nights before. The former was such a good movie; we had watched it a second time the night before. I thought about my options. Firstly, I could make my own breakfast, and wait it out. But if I did that, and dad came home with Croissants, it would lead to a beating for not waiting, so that was out. I looked up at the clock, and it said nine twenty-three, so I knew he wasn't at church. At that thought, I broke out in a fit of the giggles. My dad in church? Now *that* was funny.

Then, out of the blue, I thought about the shed in the garden.

The back shed was a place that I was not permitted to go. Dad had threatened me with a fate worse than death if I did. *A fate WORSE than death.* How bad could that be? Did that mean that my eyes would be poked out, or my legs put through the mincing machine, or that I'd be hung upside down on dad's cool room chain, and hacked to pieces like the poor pig? Was that realistic or even feasible? Of course, it wasn't. But remember: I was a child who had a violent upbringing in conjunction with a vivid imagination fed by regular doses of horror films.

Still holding the knife in my hand, I went to the kitchen, put my hands on the sink, and hoisted myself up to look through the window out into the garden. I use the word *garden* with a certain amount of poetic license. Outside, a concrete path dissected two beds which had become long-since overgrown with weeds. The only other thing of note was a very old and overgrown lemon tree.

In the back corner stood an access gate which led out to the lane, which was shared with the neighbors. Fifty meters along that exited into the street. The gate hadn't been opened in years. Over on the right-hand side sat the back shed I had been forbidden to enter. Constructed of corrugated iron, long since showing rust, with a window that had been boarded up and painted over with white enamel paint by dad a few years before. It always looked mysterious, especially in the dark. It was secured by an old oak door which had always been permanently padlocked with a big brass Yale. I knew inside resided dad's big freezer, in which, he kept cuts of meat he had frozen *before* they had reached their use by date. This we sometimes ate, when dad felt like cooking a dinner, such as steak, lambs fry, or pork chops; the list went on. Dad never liked to throw anything away, as was evidenced by telling me how *lucky* I was to have toast and jam to eat for tea. If I was lucky to get toast, how fortunate was I to eat rump steak which had been frozen the day before its best by date?

I noticed, perched as I was high on the sink, that the shed door was open, wide open. And then my heart just about stopped. No one was supposed to leave dad's shed door open, not even dad. All sorts of ridiculous fears raced through my head. What if criminals had come to break into the shed, and he had gone out to investigate, and been hurt? Maybe he was bleeding, close to death, laying just inside the shed door from a violent beating. How would I know if I didn't investigate? But then, if I did, and dad was inside, working away, it would be another beating, or worse, for me. *A fate worse than death,* came back to me.

Unsure what to do, I went and sat back on the couch; my tummy rumbling with hunger. I agonized over going to investigate or making some toast. What seemed like an hour later, I realized that my father couldn't be working out there. Firstly, he only worked in the shed while I was at school, and secondly, he would have been out long before, if he was just moving meat in or out of the freezer. There was nothing for it. I had to go and look.

Carrying my knife, just in case, I opened the back door, realizing as I did it had been *unlocked.* Therefore, my dad had to have come out that way. I was so scared though, that didn't sink in through my subconscious until much later. I crept across the weeds in the beds, rather than the path, not daring for my foot steps to be heard. Lifting my feet high before bringing them down softly, I slowly made my way across to the shed. Even then the weeds made a scrunching noise.

Dad and I had watched a film a couple of weeks prior, I think it was called *Killer Marines,* and that morning, I felt and acted like a US Marine. When I reached the outhouse, I stood flat-backed against the wall, alongside the door, which was swinging in the breeze, twisting the knife in my hand. If someone other than my father had have come out, I swear I would have stabbed them, without blinking an eye.

It may have been seconds or minutes, but eventually the pounding in my ears slowed, and I inched along the wall and peered around the doorframe. It took a while for my eyes to adjust to the dim light inside, but slowly the shadows cleared, and I noticed shapes. On the back wall, I could see the long white outline of the commercial grade chest freezer, and there kneeling in front of it was my father.

Now, when I say kneeling in front of it, it was more like he was on his knees, but with his arms and head over the edge, like he was peering into a wishing well.

"Dad," I whispered urgently, "are you okay?"

There was no reply.

"Dad!"

Silence was the only answer. Slowly, I crept inside. At all times, I was fearful, that he would suddenly sit up, yell at me for being in the shed, and give me a beating for disobeying his most basic rule. But, something didn't look right, and I had called out before I entered, so surely he would forgive me, right? Wrong. I knew that he wouldn't.

I'm not sure what I noticed first because looking back it's hazy. Was it the blood from my father's slashed wrists and throat, or the frozen body lying in the freezer looking up at me. Face forever locked in an icy scream, squashed into the confined space, lay a woman. As I stood there, trying to make sense of what I was seeing, one thought worked its way through my foggy brain. The dead body wore the red shirt I had last seen my mother wearing, when she had gone shopping, and vanished. Right then, that was when I saw it all.

My father had murdered my mother and kept her in the freezer, while slowly, every day, he went more, and more, insane. I realized something else too. I would have been a constant reminder to him of her, and what he had done. I understood then, that was why he beat me so often and hard. It was my fault she had run away. If I hadn't been such a bad child, she would have stayed, and Dad would have loved me. I'd not only made her run away, but eventually, caused my father to kill himself. The guilt descended around me like a cloak.

Chapter 5:
Into the Noughties

While January the first, 2000, and the supposed end of the civilized world, loomed ever closer. The media in all forms seemed to take great delight of telling lurid stories of doom and gloom, and a large percentage of the populace, like Juliet McCoy, believed them. For those who thought it nonsense, life went on as normal. They wore an incredulous grin at the gullibility of people who worried that a state of anarchy would follow the destruction of the technology we had come to rely on.

Rick and partner Tyler had been working long fruitless hours, trying to find a breakthrough in the *body in the suitcase* murder, without success. Hundreds of witness statements had been taken, every possibility had been looked at under a microscope, and they had nothing to show for it.

Meanwhile, Rick and Juliet had spent some, at first, uneasy weeks living together again, trying to find their way back as a being a loving couple. Rick spent his time teaching himself to be a better husband, and Juliet, tried to learn to trust him, not to stray again.

At 5.37 on Christmas morning, they were woken by a very excited Amy, jumping onto their bed. *"Merry Christmas,"* she screamed. Her face was a picture of wonder, and boundless enthusiasm.

Rick reached for her and dragged her, kicking and giggling into bed to lay between them. "Merry Christmas to you too, Pumpkin. What do you think, do you think Santa has brought you something?"

She nodded in somber response. "I've been jolly good, you know, so I deserve lots of presents."

He looked up at Juliet. She was smiling, and he thought she too remembered the night before, when they shared a bottle of wine while wrapping Amy's gifts. They ended it making love in front of the brightly decorated tree adorned with flashing colored lights.

"Well, Munchkin, maybe it's still too early for getting up, maybe Santa hasn't been yet. How about we go back to sleep for a while, just in case?" He snuggled her against him, and just for a moment, she seemed to consider his suggestion.

"Daddy!" she whispered. "How about I creep like a little mouse and go and see if he's been. I left him cookies and a glass of milk cos I knew he would be hungry, so he won't be mad at me if I meet him."

"Good idea, Baby, you do that, but be very careful he doesn't hear you if he is still unloading the sled," Juliet suggested, as she stroked her daughter's long hair, which had been mussed up through sleeping. She had drunk the milk, and they had a cookie each after their lovemaking, just before midnight.

Rick sat up, picked her up under her arms, and twirled her through the air to put her softly on the floor by his side of the bed. He put a finger over his lips and whispered: "Shush."

She nodded earnestly, her big brown eyes wide as she turned and crept to the open door. Juliet sat up and cuddled into Rick's back wrapping her arms around him to watch her. "I love you," she said softly. He slid his hand behind, to find her thigh and squeezed it through her night dress in response.

Amy rested one hand on the wall, then leaned around the edge to see if the coast was clear down the passage. Rick's heart swelled with love for his daughter, and her gentle soul, as she turned back to her parents and nodded it was safe. In an instant, she had disappeared on her way to the lounge room on her voyage of discovery.

Rick only ever slept in shorts so he grabbed his T-shirt and hurriedly put it on, knowing they had only seconds remaining. Juliet swept the bed covers aside and swung her legs over the edge to slip her feet into her slippers. As if choreographed they got out of bed at the same time, just as Amy's excited squeal echoed to them: "Mummy, Daddy, come quick and see what Santa has brung me."

At seven a.m. Rick stepped over the mountain of discarded wrapping paper, announcing he was just going to pop next door and wish their elderly neighbors Will and Edna, a Merry Christmas. They were holding something rather special for Amy, and he had arranged he wouldn't pick it up before seven, so as not to wake them too early.

"Say hi to them from me," Juliet said with a wink.

"Don't be long, Daddy, I'd like you to help me pick out clothes for Molly to wear for Christmas lunch at Nanny's," Amy added.

She put down a large jigsaw puzzle she had been studying to pick up the teddy bear which had slipped off her lap. Molly was the name she had given to the blonde haired, blue eyed, near life size doll she had received as a Christmas present.

"I won't be, baby," he replied, with a grin to Juliet.

Five minutes later, he returned carrying a box with an oversized red ribbon on the lid. "Look what I found on the doorstep, Amy. Santa must have left it there by accident, but I know it's yours because it has your name on the tag."

She looked up sharply and did a double take when she saw the size of the box. With an incredulous look on her beautiful face, she whispered: "Is that for me?"

Rick nodded, and squatted down, gently putting the box on the floor. He looked up to see Juliet wiping a tear from her eye as she watched Amy leap to her feet and run to the doorway. "Let me take the lid off for you baby, this is a special present, from Mummy and Daddy, are you ready?"

She nodded, and clasped her hands together, as if in prayer.

"One, two, three." He took off the lid, and Amy screamed with joy at the sight of the fluffy brown and white, crossed Pomeranian, puppy that jumped up, wagging his tail. He put his front paws on the rim of the box yapping at his first sight of Amy.

Bedlam ensued. It was love at first sight between Amy, and as he was set to be called, Minty. Though Rick never discovered why or how she came up with that name for him, they were inseparable. He laughed when the puppy peed on the carpet half an hour later, and Amy, ensuring Minty didn't get a telling off, said quite calmly: "It's because he's just a puppy, you know."

Later, Juliet and Rick sat on the garden steps just before they were due to go to her parents for lunch, her arm through his, watching Amy giggling while laying on her back while Minty licked her face. "You know something, big guy?" she asked, squeezing his arm.

"What's that, Jules?"

"I never thought I would say something like this, but I think Angie was the best thing that ever happened to us. You've been amazing since you moved back in, and I've never felt happier."

He turned to look at the sincerity she displayed on her smiling face. He had stopped smoking, cut his drinking habits dramatically, never went to the pub after work anymore, and talked with her about his day over dinner each night. He too had to admit, life was far better than he could ever remember it being before the break up. He also felt better about himself. He had taken up rising early and going for a jog around the park where he used to sit in his car, and watch Amy play from afar. He had dropped a few pounds, increased his fitness, and felt his life was complete, again. "I love you too, Jules. That man is gone now, the old me, and he's never coming back. I guess it's true what they say: *'you never know what you have, till it's gone.'* Thank you for taking me back and giving me another chance."

They kissed, long and lovingly, while their giggling girl and her new puppy played on the grass. Life was good.

****

Rick had taken the week between Christmas and New Year off work, to spend with Juliet and Amy. He had done it not only because of wanting to be as a family at such a time, but also because, despite her brave face, he knew Juliet still worried about the Y2K bug. The closer it came, the more she seemed panic struck. She inexplicably feared the life of happiness she had found with Rick again, could all come crashing down if all the computers in the world stopped working. Worse, for her, was her irrational fear for Amy, that if disaster struck, her daughter would suffer.

Often, she admitted to Rick it was madness, and she knew she was being silly, but she worried none the less and was powerless to stop it. Then her nightmares started. She dreamt of lawless streets, of gang of hoodlums raping and taking whatever, they wanted, the police and armies long since disbanded. The dreams broke her sleep and left her crying and sweating, while Rick did his best to comfort her. It was irrational, she told Rick often she knew that, but would then add, "But what if it does happen?"

He had offered for the three of them to go away for a few days and get out of the city. But, such was her fear, she worried if they did go, would their car work after midnight on the 31st, and not let them get home again. Surely, she argued, there were micro-chip computers in motor cars these days?

The old Rick would have lost his temper, but the new and improved version was kind and considerate. He understood her fear was almost phobia like in proportion, and while she refused to seek counselling, she appreciated the time he took from work to be with her. But, the time ticked away like a deadly countdown, and the closer New Year's Eve got, the worse it was for her.

Rick never lost sight of the fact that were it not for Y2K bug, she may never have let him back into her world, so ironically was grateful. With his new-found lease on life, and love for Juliet, he was determined to be her rock in her time of need.

Minty bonded completely with Amy, and they were inseparable. He slept by the side of her bed, content to sleep only when she did. She fed him, gave him treats when he deserved them, which for her was continuously, and insisted on walking him with her parents in the park. She did draw the line at cleaning up after him when he had his inevitable accidents, but she was quick to remind Juliet or Rick whenever he left a little present for them: "He's still just a puppy, you know." Each time she said it, they couldn't help but smile at the obvious love she had for her dog.

Rick was very worried when on the night of the 30th, Juliet was incapable of sleeping. She tried, but her tossing and turning kept Rick awake, until he got up and made them both a cup of tea. That was around two a.m., and he could see she was bordering on a state of hysteria; her fear threatening to take over completely. During the day, with things to do and occupy her mind, she had been good, with only long periods of silence when she would stare into space. That night, her imagination was running riot, and for her sanity, he knew he had to do something.

They sat, with the backs against the bed head, sipping tea, with a plate of biscuits between them that he had found in the pantry. They listened to the silence of the house, while Rick decided what he could do to help.

"What about Amy, how will she cope if everything turns bad tomorrow? It's so unfair," she said, shaking her head.

"Jules, did I ever tell you about Peter McGrigor?" Rick asked quietly, as he took a bite from a jam coated shortbread.

Since moving back home, each night he had taken great pains to share with Juliet what had transpired at work during the day. Unfortunately, with the body in the suitcase investigation, there wasn't a lot to tell, but she listened with rapt attention anyway.

"No, who is he?" Her voice brittle. *She is barely holding on*, Rick realized.

"Well, he murdered his wife, but he did it in a very clever way. He almost got away with it, and two million dollars in insurance money."

She looked up, their gaze locked, and Rick knew this was the best way to help get her mind off the end of the world which she imagined was coming. "How did he *almost* get away with it?"

"Well, he killed two other women first. He found two who resembled her, to make it look like she was a victim of a serial killer. This was back in ninety-four, one of my cases when you were pregnant with Amy. It was an investigation I didn't want to talk about back then because I didn't want to upset you. But, it's one of the most fascinating investigations I've ever been involved with."

The next three and a half hours sped by, as Rick recounted the intricate details of how he and his partner at the time, Detective Ramos, had eventually unmasked the true murderer, and brought him to trial.

When he finished his tale, Juliet looked at the clock, and smiled at Rick. She got out of bed and softly closed their bedroom door. Coming back to his side of the bed, she stood, with one hand on her hip, and head tiled to one side. "I know what you did, Rick. You told me that story to help get me through the night. Thank you. I love you so much."

She straightened up and pulled her nightdress over her head. shaking her long hair free of it and threw it on the bed. Her white lace panties followed to land on top. "We've got about thirty or forty minutes before Amy wakes up. Can you make love to me in that time?"

Rick nodded, licking his lips, instantly hard at the vision of beauty standing before him. As the dawn broke, and early sunlight filtered through the blinds, they reached a shattering climax together.

****

"McCoy," Rick answered his mobile phone later that afternoon, as he and Juliet watched Amy tossing a small ball for Minty to chase in the park. Juliet was still worrying, with occasional outburst of venom at the 'stupid fuckers' who had brought this technological terror upon her world.

"Rick, it's Rita, can you talk without Juliet listening?"

"Sure, just hold on a second will you, boss?" He stood mouthing the words, *'work'* to his wife, and walked away a few paces out of earshot. Rita was Juliet's mother, who had never quite forgiven him for the affair and hurting her daughter. Really, Rick couldn't blame her for that, and they had abided each other since, but any closeness they had once felt was gone.

"What's up, Rita, is everything okay?" he asked quietly when it was safe.

"How's Juliet? Herb and I are so worried about her, with this Y2K thing, she seems so upset about it all. Tonight, it's all going to come to a head one way or another, and we are frantic here about her state of mind.

We'd like you all to come over and spend the night with us, so we can make sure she is going to make it with her sanity intact."

"I'm worried myself, Rita. Last night was bad, she didn't sleep at all. I helped her, by telling her stories until morning. Today she's been better, but now she is so dog tired that's getting her down too. She can't bring herself to leave the house because she is scared she won't be able to come back if everything else stops working, or the bombs start to fall. There's no way I could get her to go over to your place. I'll tell you what though, why don't you and Herb come over here for a barbeque, and you guys spend the night in our spare room. I think she'd love the company."

There was a silence for a while, and Rick wondered if the line had dropped out, which was not an uncommon occurrence with mobile phone technology. 'Rick, I'm going to say something to you now, I hope you don't mind. When you hurt our daughter, I could have scratched your eyes out, you were an asshole and there is no other word for it. But, since you made up, we've seen the change, not just in you, but how Juliet has come to life again. You inviting us over is a nice thing to do, we will take you up on it, and I thank you. Maybe you're not such an asshole after all."

When he got back to Juliet, she wore a scowl. "Why is your boss phoning you when you are on holidays, and its New Year's Eve?"

With all that had happened, he was not going to start lying. "It wasn't work, love, it was your mother, and she asked if she could talk to me out of your earshot. She's worried about you and wanted to make sure you are going to be all right tonight."

She hung her head and cried. "What's happening to me, why am I so scared? Everyone must think I'm stupid."

"No, they don't babe." He put his arm around her shoulders. "They say everyone has one fear. Tyler is shit scared of rats, a guy I know at work turns to jelly if he comes across a spider. Some fear small spaces, others open ones. I knew a girl at school who was incapable of walking under power lines, she was petrified of the electricity, and it she could hear one humming she was a basket case. This is your phobia, and it's not something to be taken lightly. The good news for you, is that at one minute past midnight, you will be relieved of yours, never to recur. I love you, even with your phobia."

She snuggled in to his shoulder. "Thank God you're here, I could never have gotten through this without you. But, what if it's not a phobia, what if at midnight, everything does stop working, and the missiles are launched?"

"Then we will be together, to face whatever comes. But, honey? I've spoken to so many I.T. guys at work, the WA Police has had the best of the best check out our computers, and every one of them says we have nothing to worry about. Now try and cheer up. I've invited your mum and dad for a barbeque, and they are going to stay the night. We all love you, and we will all help you through this." He squeezed her to him, trying to share his inner strength with her.

"It's Amy I worry about most, not me. She's five years old."

"And she's going to have a whole lifetime ahead of her, try to stop worrying, love. We need to go and buy some things to do for dinner, now your parents are coming. What do you think we should do? I think steaks would be nice."

She wiped her eyes and sat up. "You know Dad doesn't enjoy steak since he got his new teeth. He can't seem to chew things with them. The butcher does those nice rissoles, and maybe chicken sausages. I can do salads, maybe a cauliflower cheese." She stopped in mid-sentence. "you've done it again, haven't you? Distracted me from worrying. Thanks, Rick. Okay, I feel better again. Let's get Amy and Minty, and go to the shops, I will be all right now."

But the gain was short lived. After dinner, during which she could hardly eat a thing, Amy had been bathed, story read, and put to bed with Minty, her fears returned, crashing like waves. She couldn't sit for too long and her pacing while looking so distraught, worried Rick.

Rita went into the kitchen and came back with a glass of water. She stood in front of Juliet who was forced to stop pacing and held out the glass and a tablet. "Take this, I insist. It's just a tranquilizer and will help calm you down, help you get through the next four hours." Silently, Juliet took the offering and swallowed it, before resuming walking up and down.

They attempted several games of cards once the pill had worked its magic, but Juliet couldn't concentrate and seemed drowsy. At 10, Rick put the TV on to watch the celebrations and slowly the new millennium crept ever closer.

Suddenly Rick had a revelation and cursed himself for not thinking of it sooner. He turned to his wife who looked more upset than at any time he had known her.

He grasped her hand in his and shook it to get her attention. "Jules, it's over, don't you see? Why didn't I think of it before? Melbourne, Sydney, New Zealand, they are all ahead of us, their clocks have already clicked over into the new year there. We are not seeing news bulletins of mayhem happening, nothing went wrong, you can stop worrying."

She looked up questioning in her gaze, the tablet was slowing her down and she seemed incapable of understanding him.

He stood and grabbed his phone, and with shaking fingers dialed the number for his elder brother who lived in Sydney. He was a senior Sergeant at a regional police station. Herb clapped his hands "He's right, love, you can stop worrying, there's lots of places ahead of us in time, it would be all over the news if they were having problems when they reached midnight."

"Bob? It's Rick, sorry to call you so late. Happy New Year, Bro. Are you celebrating or did I wake you up?"

He listened for a while, nodding. "Good to hear, Man, so hey, listen, answer a question for me, will you? It's what…around 1am there, what happened with this Y2K bug thing, did anything go wrong at midnight?"

Juliet stood on shaky legs, and gripped his upper arms, her face showing a mixture of hope and worry. Silently, she pleaded with him for good news.

"Okay bro, that's good to hear, I will let you get back to it, give our love to Kate and the kids, bye for now." He pressed the disconnect button and tossed the phone aside on the couch and wrapped his arms around the quivering body of Juliet. "He's on duty Jules so couldn't chat, busy night for the uniform boys, New

Year's Eve. But he says it was just a hoax. Nothing at all has stopped working, everything is fine, you can relax now."

****

Ironically, other than Juliet who had panicked, the people who had worried the most almost felt as if they had been cheated when electrical grids didn't fail or computers turn on their Masters when January first arrived. The Y2K bug had been nothing more than a conspiracy theory, and the new year entered with a whimper, rather than a bang. In the lead-up to the big night, many had held Y2K parties, almost daring things to go wrong at midnight. Planes did not, as had been predicted, drop from the sky, busses and trains didn't crash, and war didn't break out between superpowers. TVs still worked and life went on pretty much as normal.

****

All leads in the case had dried up, and eventually Rick and Tyler had been assigned new jobs to focus on. As was usual with unsolved crimes, it would come up for review once a month during a round-table conference with all detectives in the squad, headed up by the Chief Inspector himself. No one liked cold cases. Everyone knew that the more time passed, the more difficult it would be to catch the killer.

Rick's confidence had taken a battering over Melanie Cartwright's murder, and he felt he needed an 'easy' investigation to get him back on an even keel. He was glad he had been handed one, but not the circumstances. A domestic violence attack had got out of control. Martina Roberts stabbed her husband in the chest when he approached her with a clothes iron, intending to 'burn her face off.' A victim of years of abuse, as proved by hospital records, Rick thought that she might escape an overly long custodial sentence, and could get off altogether with a good lawyer. He gained no pleasure from her arrest.

The day-to-day business of homicide continued normally, right up until April the fourth. It was just as he had got inside his kitchen after a long day, and hugged Amy, when his mobile phone rang. He popped a piece of the roast chicken Juliet had been carving into his mouth and pressed the talk button on his phone.

"McCoy."

"Rick, its Colin, sorry to ring you after hours."

He stood up straight. "No worries, sir, what's up?"

"I think it would be best if you came back in, this is not something to go into over the phone, and it will take a while to discuss this. I will wait till you get here, Tyler is coming back in too. Apologize to your wife for me, this is important, I wouldn't drag you here at this hour if it wasn't. I can tell you this much, your least favorite killer is back."

The phone went dead and Rick was left wondering what it was all about. It had been weeks since Rick had given up on Melanie Cartwright's case, but it had never been far from his mind. They say that every cop has one unsolved case that haunts them, and that was his. Was there another victim, or could it be fresh information for Melanie's case?

"Jules, I'm sorry, but I have to go back to work. I think our man may have left another suitcase."

"Oh, God, no. Call me later, will you please? Let me know what's happening and when you will be home. Please don't work all night."

He hugged her, relishing the way her body molded to his, but this time his mind was elsewhere, worrying what had happened to cause his recall. He kissed her, then crossed the kitchen to the dining table, where Amy was drawing with her crayons, her puppy asleep under her chair.

He squatted by her side, his gun digging into his hip making him grimace. "Daddy has to go back to work, sweetheart. Mummy will read you the story tonight, but I promise to read you two tomorrow. Is that okay?"

She nodded, looking up at him with her big brown eyes through her fringe, and his heart melted, as it always did. "You promise, daddy? Two stories? Can I pick which ones, and can Minty lay in bed with me when you read them? He likes stories too."

He grinned; she was becoming quite the negotiator. "You know we don't like Minty on the bed, even though I know you sneak him up there sometimes, don't you?" He grabbed her sides and tickled, making her giggle. "Two stories, you can pick them, and Minty stays on his blanket to listen. Deal?"

"Okay, daddy. I love you."

"I love you too pumpkin. Night, night, sleep tight."

At headquarters, he used the back entrance into the CID offices, which, without a major crime case going on, was deserted. In recent times police budgeting, had become more critical, so without a pressing need, overtime was kept to a minimum. Most dedicated detectives would still do it to chase a lead that couldn't be done during the day, but often these were unpaid hours, or time given off in lieu. In Rick's case, he sometimes worked longer hours because that was how he was; an old-school cop who pursued criminals outside the nine to five working day.

Tyler looked up from his desk where he sat, completing a crossword from that day's newspaper, as Rick entered the squad room. Nothing was said, but when Rick raised his eyebrows, Tyler shook his head and tilted it toward the closed door of the Senior Detective's office. He stood as Rick approached, and together they knocked.

"Come in, guys."

Rick entered with Tyler behind, but he stopped suddenly and his partner walked into his back. There sitting to the side of the DCI's desk was Assistant Police Commissioner Darryl Monkton. His office was situated on the top floor, and he was renowned for working only nine to five hours. To see him on the Major Case Squad floor, and at night, was highly unusual. That, inferred the case Rick and Tyler had been called in for, was extremely important.

"Sergeant, Detective, thank you for coming in at such short notice and giving up your evening. Take a seat. I'm not sure if you've met, Mr. Monkton," Colin Harris began.

They moved to two chairs on the opposite side to Monkton, but the four large men filled the small office. Rick, as protocol decreed, spoke for both officers. "Good evening, Commissioner, and sir. What's up?"

Rick noted the commissioner was not in full uniform, but suit and tie. He nodded at the two officers. *Maybe he's on his way to the ballet?*

"For the time being, guys—" Colin Harris shifted in his chair to sit more upright. "—you are sworn to secrecy about what we are about to show you. I want you to work exclusively on this job. You will have any help you need including manpower, but anyone you bring in will also be told in no uncertain terms that this is top secret. You will answer directly to me, and only me. If this story gets out, there will be a witch-hunt."

He opened a red manila folder on his desk and took out a clear plastic sleeve. Silently he slid it across to the two men. One look revealed a scene from a horror movie.

It was a black and white Polaroid photograph. The shades of gray made the picture itself look even grimmer than it would have been in full color. Center stage was a naked woman, wrists encased in handcuffs, secured to a gray concrete wall above her head. Her long blonde wavy hair obscured her face, which was tilted toward the floor. Whether she was unconscious or forced to keep her head down couldn't be gauged, but it made any identification of her impossible.

"Is this all we have?" Rick asked, after scrutinizing the harrowing picture.

"Oh, no, we have more. We have a note." He slid across another sleeve which encased a piece of lined notepaper; the type that could have been torn from a child's cheap school notebook.

To Sergeant Richard McCoy
Homicide Department.
She is still alive, but every two days that pass, I will cut something off her and send it to you. Stop me if you can.
Are we having fun yet?
P.P.P.

Rick felt his blood turn to ice water as he heard Tyler gasp. "How did we get this?"

Colin slid a third plastic cover across the desk. It contained a cheap letter-sized envelope. "Anonymous call from a public call box telling us there was an envelope for the Homicide Department between page ninety-nine and one hundred of the phone book. The caller said it was about the Body in the Suitcase investigation. Uniform thought it was a hoax but were smart enough to preserve the scene, as best as they could, when they found the envelope. Fortunately, they got it to forensics to open.

Rick shook his head, dumfounded. "Why address it to me?"

"Probably because you were lead investigator on the case, and you ran the TV re-enactment for Melanie Cartwright's disappearance at the shopping center. Our man must have seen you, there was no way he couldn't with all the publicity," the commissioner answered.

"But surely we don't know that this is the same killer?"

"We do. Bottom right hand corner of the photograph is a perfect thumb and forefinger print. It matches the ones on the plastic sheets; he's back."

****

There wasn't too much more they could do that night. Forensics had checked out the phone booth and envelope already. Rick and Tyler had earlier been interviewing witnesses to a shooting, on a case, at the Yanchep National Park, and it wasn't until the fingerprint results came in to the Inspector, that he decided to bring them back in after hours.

The discussion between the officers went on for an

hour, when behind them, the night cleaning crew arrived. A plan of attack was drawn up. They agreed that this story must not, under any circumstances, be leaked to the press. The first murder had been horrific enough, but that this man would hack pieces of the poor women slowly over time to taunt the police beggared belief. There would be mass panic and total loss of confidence in police officers, if the vitriolic media got hold of the story.

"Sergeant, I am relying on you to make sure the media do not link these two cases if the news breaks of the abduction, is that understood?" Commissioner Monkton insisted.

Rick nodded, seeing the logic in the argument. He glanced at Tyler and knew him well enough to know his nod affirmed his agreement too.

The DCI leaned forward in his chair, "any interviews, must be conducted in a way that does not give away the truth, Rick. Are we clear on this?" He did not wait for a response. "Any assistance you need, anyone else who is brought into the investigation, must be told of the secrecy. One whiff of this gets out and we are all toast. I will suspend anyone caught leaking this story to the press; we cannot afford a mass panic."

Inwardly, Rick groaned at that decision, although he agreed in principle. He was going to have to break the rule almost immediately because he had promised Juliet he would keep her informed. If he now kept secrets, and she found out later, it would destroy what trust they had re-built.

"Tomorrow you will both begin the investigation at the phone box, to find anyone who witnessed a man acting suspiciously. We will source phone records of all calls, and back-track it to the people who made those calls in hopes they saw the killer hanging around. There is also a slim chance he used the phone to call someone other than us to divert suspicion."

Rick had a feeling the killer would be far too smart for that, though he would not voice his opinion; the mood of his superiors was far too serious for him to show any negativity.

They knew from previous cases, there wasn't too much that could be done to enhance the quality of an instant picture, however he suggested they seek out an expert who may be able to find something to help them identify the location where she was being held. They would also take the note to a handwriting expert.

The assistant commissioner had remained relatively quiet to that point, and Rick thought that he preferred to leave the operational side to the Detective Chief Inspector. He cleared his throat. "Sergeant, I will make a phone call in the morning and introduce you to Patricia Holmes; a senior lecturer at UWA in criminal psychology. She may be able to give some insights into the kind of person we are hunting. The FBI have a Behavioral Unit, specializing in serial killers, which Patricia has spent some time with. They are making great strides in understanding what makes these kinds of people tick.

"Thank you, sir; that may indeed be helpful, because, let's face it, so far we don't have much else to go on." *What a colossal waste of time that will be*, was what he thought, though he dared not voice it.

Colin cleared his throat to gain control again. "While you are doing that, Tyler can trawl through the missing person's reports. We know she's blonde, we know her build, and we can guess her height. Once you've found her we can consider where and how he took her. Anything we've missed?"

"I have a suggestion, sir, but it's pretty far out of left field," Rick said.

"Go on."

"Well, for some reason, he has focused on me. Why don't I try to lure him out?"

"How do you propose to do that?"

"Well, I could announce publically that we are re-opening the Melanie Cartwright murder due to new evidence. We could say we have a witness that has come forward from the rubbish tip and are now pursuing a new line of inquiry as to the vehicle that was used to dump the suitcase."

"I don't think I like this idea, but go on," he said, shaking his head.

"Well, I'm thinking on my feet here, but the witness who found the body said he saw a white Japanese van which we deliberately withheld. Suppose I ask for public assistance in finding the man who drove that van, because he never came forward. I could even give a vague one size fits all description of him. If he wants to play games, let's play back, and try to catch him off-guard."

"But you don't know that he was the murderer," Commissioner Monkton interjected.

"No, that's correct, sir, but that's the whole point. If it's not him, the killer may contact us to gloat about how stupid we are, and if he did that, he may make a mistake. But, if it was the murderer who was driving the white van, he may worry, and try to throw us off the scent in some other way. He may want to be interviewed to clear his name, and again, he might make a mistake that allows us to catch him. My gut feeling is that unless he mucks up, we won't find him, and this woman will die. Remember his quote: 'Are we having fun, *yet?* '"

There was silence while everyone thought that through. Eventually the DCI leaned forward and said: "The worry here is that he may panic and kill her, then go to ground."

Rick shrugged, he could not deny the obvious. "That's true, he may, sir, but I don't think he will. My gut feeling is that he loves this. He *wants* to engage me in conversation, and if I do nothing, that may make him angry, and he kills her anyway. Not giving this to the press, may also piss him off if he is seeking recognition. He strikes me as being like a petulant child saying: *look at me.* If we don't find him quickly this woman is dead regardless."

"Sergeant, we cannot afford that kind of defeatist attitude. I tell you what, why not ask Patricia Holmes what she thinks he might do if you take that course," the commissioner offered.

"With respect, sir, should we let this woman dictate police procedure, no matter how talented she is?"

"No, Sergeant, *we* will dictate that. But she may well agree with you, and if she did, and it all blows up in our faces, we can say we did get psychological advice."

Rick nodded. He could see the wisdom in the words. "And if she advises against that tack, sir?"

"Then your Detective Chief Inspector will give you guidance," he said, with a brittle tone of voice. Rick knew not to argue further. He nodded again.

****

Rick got home after nine, and Juliet was waiting for him. The smell of his dinner gently keeping warm in the oven made him realize how hungry he was, and he hoped it wasn't too dried out. "Hi, Babe; that smells sensational."

She opened the fridge door and took out a can of beer for him and nodded for him to sit at the kitchen table. She opened the can with a pop and fizz but held onto it for a moment. "Call me stupid, and I'm sorry to ask, but I have to: you have been at work, haven't you? Don't get mad at me."

He smiled, understanding her doubt. This was the first time he had worked this late since moving back home; it was to be expected. He stood up and hugged her to him.

"Jules I'm not mad. I've been at work, with no less than the assistant commissioner, Darryl Monkton himself, along with Tyler and the DCI."

She dipped her head and smiled "Okay. Sit down have your beer. I haven't had dinner either so you can tell me all about it while we eat."

He took the offered drink. "I will, but you must promise to not breathe a word of this case to anyone else. There is a total blackout of information to stop the press getting hold of it. This is without doubt going to be the worst case I've ever dealt with."

"I won't, I promise, Scout's honor."

Two minutes later she was peeling the aluminum foil from the two plates and using her oven-mitts to shield her hands from the heat placed them on the table. She picked up her glass of Moselle and sat down next to him. "Okay, I'm all ears, why so hush-hush?"

He explained in detail what had happened at headquarters, holding nothing back, while they ate. She listened in rapt attention.

"Oh, my God, the poor woman. Why has he sent you a picture?"

"Who can say? I think that it's all a big game to him, and he feels uncatchable. He is no doubt intelligent, but he thinks he is so much smarter than us mere mortal cops. For some reason, he has latched onto me, the note was addressed to me by name, and I think he wants to play some sort of cat and mouse game, with this victim as the prize."

They ate in silence for a while, lost in thought. Juliet stopped with a fork on its way to her mouth. "Rick, you don't think he knows you, do you, personally I mean? If he does, he may know Amy and I."

That was a something he hadn't thought of. "Err, I can't imagine that he does, how could he? He would have seen me on TV doing the press conferences, so he knew who to address the letter to, but he couldn't know any more than that, even our phone number is unlisted. I'm sure there is nothing to worry about."

Chapter 6: My Memoir Entry
Life in Foster Care

I stood in a daze for an hour or more. Well, it seemed that long but probably it wasn't. When I came to my senses I knew I was starving hungry, and second, I realized I had to tell someone about Dad. I went back into the kitchen, found some bread in the pantry, and popped two slices in the toaster. While waiting for it to pop up I got the margarine out of the fridge and the strawberry jam and put them on the table along with a side plate. I also lit the gas under the kettle for tea. Then I went into the hall where on a sideboard cupboard was the phone. I dialed the emergency triple zero number for the police.

"What is the nature of your emergency?" a snotty sounding female voice asked.

"I want to report that my father has killed himself. He has slashed his wrists in the garden shed."

There was silence for a few seconds, during which I heard the toaster pop. "Can you repeat that please?"

"My name is Paul and I live at 1606 Phillips Road in Mundaring, it's the house behind the butcher shop. My father has killed himself by cutting his wrists in the back shed. My mother is in there too."

"She is in the shed with your father? Is she trying to stop the bleeding?"

"No, she is in the freezer."

It was at this point, I began to see how funny this conversation was, and it reminded me of a kind of sketch you would see on a comedy TV show. It was all I could do not to burst out laughing. "What is she doing in the freezer if you father has cut his wrists?"

"She is dead as well."

"*Dead*? Did she kill herself too?"

"No, my father killed her about eight years ago, he's been keeping her in the freezer."

"Sir, you do realize there are serious consequences for hoax calls?"

"I'm eleven years old."

"What?"

"I'm eleven years old, there is no need to call me sir."

"I'm dispatching a police patrol car to your location, please stay where you are, do not go back into the shed."

"Oh, don't worry, I'm not going back in there, I'm going into the kitchen to finish my breakfast." I hung up the phone.

I admit that my thoughts were torn between sadness at the loss of my father, shock at finding my mother had not run away, and bewilderment of what it all meant for me. What was going to happen next? Was it selfish to be thinking of what effect events were going to have on my life? Probably, but what can I say? That was what I was feeling at the time.

I was licking the remnants of jam off my thumb when the doorbell rang. *That was quick,* I stood up to let them in.

I guess old habits die hard; Dad always told me if I was ever home alone to *never* just open the front door without knowing who it was, in case they wanted to rob the shop of the takings.

"Who is it?" I called out through the door.

"Is that Paul? This is the police, you called for us?"

I twisted the key, undid the floor bolt, dropped the privacy chain, turned the old brass handle, and swung the door wide. Two uniformed policemen, with guns on their belts, stood on the concrete step. One was old and tired looking, a bit plump with graying tufty hair, but the other one was young; almost too young looking to be a cop.

The young one spoke first, while the older one looked bored: "Hi Paul, I'm Richard, this is Ben. You called for us?"

'Yeah, come in." I stood aside as they passed by and entered the hall. I closed the door and led them to the kitchen. "Jeez that woman on the phone sounded real dumb."

"Did she now?" Ben said, and I knew he was being sarcastic.

I thought I had some tea left in the cup and wanted to finish it. I sat down at my chair and picked up my cup. As I thought, there was some in the bottom, so I finished before it went too cold.

Richard, who seemed much nicer than the old bloke, pulled out a chair and sat opposite me, while Ben took up station by the door; in case I decided to make a run for it, I suppose. "So, Paul please tell us everything, why did you call for us?"

"Dad was a good man; I want you to know that. Yes, he has been getting crueler to me over the years, but he was a good man. He was in the war and got caught behind enemy lines. The Viet Cong had him as a prisoner for months until their camp was overrun and he escaped. I think that was what caused his…problems. Anyway, I was about four when mum just vanished. He said she had run away, but after a while I was forbidden to talk about her. My dad always called her: *Persona-non-grata,* and he used to beat me if I asked when she was coming back. Now I know why; she was never going to be able to do that."

"Do you find this upsetting to talk about?" Richard asked, and I liked him for caring enough to ask that.

"No, not really. I should, shouldn't I? But for some reason I just feel, well, alone. I suppose, what I'm trying to say is, he wasn't always like that, he had his good moments too, and he was my dad."

"So, it's been just the two of you ever since? No other family?"

"I've got an uncle, but he and Dad didn't get on, so I haven't seen him for years."

I saw them exchange glances and it dawned on me, they didn't believe me! I nearly laughed at that, *well they will soon*, I thought. "So, Paul, where is your father now?" the older one asked.

I sighed, loudly. *Are all police this stupid?* I wondered. "Sorry, but what part of this don't you get?" That made the old guy cringe, and suddenly stand up straight, but the young one could barely conceal his grin. I liked him even more.

"Okay. Look, my dad has been slowly going around the bend over the years and I think it started when he murdered my mother when I was four. He kept her body in the freezer in the back shed and told everyone she had left him. I could show you the old bruises from the beatings he gave me, but like I said a lot of the time he was good. Last night we watched a movie together, the video tape is in the player. It was about dead people coming back from the grave to haunt the living, and I think it must have played on his mind. When I got up this morning I couldn't find him anywhere until I checked the back shed. He went out there to be with mum one last time and cut his wrists." I shrugged. "I guess because he wanted to join her."

The old guy leaning against the doorframe suddenly stood up. "Stay here, with him. I'll go and check."

"What school do you go to?" Richard asked, when we were alone.

"Mundaring, I hate it."

"Why? I thought that was a pretty good school."

"They keep putting me in the wrong classes. They should put me up a year or two, I'm so much smarter than the kids in mine."

"Ah, I see. Yeah don't you just hate it when that happens?"

I felt a kindred spirit in him, though I did wonder if he was being patronizing, but he seemed to be genuine. "How long you been a cop? Can I hold your gun?"

"Well, Paul, I wouldn't be a cop any longer if I let you hold my gun, would I? I graduated from the academy seven months ago, I'm what's called *probationary*."

Just then we heard the older cop yell out from the back garden: "Radio in, get the detectives sent out, there are two dead bodies out here."

"See? I told you so," I said. Then I got up to put the kettle on again, I thought there would be lots of tea drinking going on.

****

Richard stayed with me pretty much the rest of the day, and it was he who walked me to the car when I left to go to the foster home. I was to be a 'Ward of the State' doesn't that sound awful? Well, it was awful, in fact it was a horrible place, but more of that soon.

I was interviewed by detectives, but they kept Richard close. I was, after all, only eleven, nearly twelve. I believe they realized I needed a friendly face. When asked questions, I didn't feel like answering, he would get involved and I found I didn't mind responding to him. He was kind, and the others weren't, at least that's how it seemed to me.

So, firstly, I told the whole sad and sorry tale again to Detective Wilson, then some woman turned up who said her name was Cynthia. Really? I mean who would name their kid that? She said she was head of children's services and wanted to make sure I was safe. What a joke that turned out to be. Talk about the lion tamer delivering food to the lion.

I had to tell Cynthia my story all over again, and by that time I was pretty fed up with it all, I mean seriously, how many times did they expect me to tell it?

Richard was good to me, though; he made me a sandwich, and it was a good one too, with double polony and heaps of sauce. He could have taught my dad a thing or two about making a sandwich, that's for sure. I asked for a second one, and he smiled and made me another. I could have hugged him.

I watched through the window as they carried Dad's body out on a stretcher to the coroner's hearse-like vehicle, and it was shortly after that that I got a fit of the giggles that just went on and on *and on.*

It's funny how the mind can play tricks, isn't it? Sometimes you see something, and you imagine things to fill in what you don't see. I heard some muffled comments about how they couldn't get Mum's body out of *"the fucking freezer."* That's their words, not mine; I never use profanity. But, in my mind's eye I could see them huffing and puffing and struggling as they tried to get a frozen corpse that had been in situ for seven years out of the chest freezer. In the end, they carried the whole damn thing out between four of them, power chord dragging in the dust, and put it on the back of a police Ute. And that's how they transported my mother's body to the morgue.

Shortly after that Cynthia said it was time to leave, that she was taking me *into care*. Richard walked with us to her car, a yellow station wagon, and held the front passenger door open for me. Once in, he squatted down by my side and gave me a piece of folded paper.

"Hey, buddy. That's my home phone number. If you ever find yourself in danger or trouble, I want you to give me a call, will you do that?"

I nodded; I thought it was nice that he would care enough to give me his phone number. "Thanks, Richard. Will you ever let me hold your gun?"

"I tell you what, if you can stay out of trouble, when you're eighteen, I will take you to the gun club, and teach you how to shoot, how's that?"

"Deal." I held out my hand, and he shook it. Then he stood up, adjusting his gun belt as he shut the door, and I tucked the piece of paper in my jeans pocket. He stood and watched as we drove away with me waving through the window.

It is distressing to recall what happened between

the age of twelve and eighteen. My dad had been a brute to me, but he was also loving when he wasn't in a mood. No one was loving to me after he died.

****

Cynthia took me to Harkerville Children and Youth Services Center. The people who ran the place were a mixture of nuns, and government staff, most of whom seemed to me to care about us. Some of the kids there had been abused, abandoned, or had serious mental health issues. Some were short term stays; others were long termers. A few, having escaped an awful past, were delighted to live there, while most hated the place with a passion bordering on insanity. One lad hated it so much he ran away on a regular basis. The police would eventually bring him back, then within a week or two he would disappear again. I asked him once how he survived on the streets, and he told me, quite graphically how he gave old men head jobs for money so he could buy hamburgers to eat. That turned my stomach, but he just shrugged and said it was better than being in Harkerville.

After Cynthia introduced me to Sister Kate, I was handed over to one Jeremy Stubs, a fourteen-year-old 'inmate.' He was to show me around, where I was to sleep, where I would eat, crap and shower and say prayers. It felt like I was in jail.

It all started well enough when we were in front of The Sister and Cynthia. They had explained until a family member came forward, or they could place me in a private foster home, this would be where I was to live. The complex was hidden behind a fourteen-foot-tall brick wall with iron gates.

Jeremy, or Stubsy, as all the other kids called him,

I was to find out, knocked and entered the room. "Paul, this is Jeremy. Jeremy this is Paul, he's a new boy. Will you show him around please? He will be in the Wattle dormitory with you, so you can keep an eye on him, and make sure he settles in.

He smiled broadly and shook my hand, like an adult. "Hey, man, welcome."

"Jeremy, why don't you show Paul where he will sleep, then take him to the dining area, he might like a sandwich or something?" Sister Kate said.

"Sure, no worries, Sister, come on man, I think you're going to love this place."

So off we went, and he smiled and joked, and stupid me, fell for his crap. We wandered around and turned a corner into a corridor flanked by brick walls on both sides, and a strong breeze blew down it. Jeremy suddenly stopped.

"Oh, hey man, just one thing you should know."

That's when he punched me in the stomach. Now, I had been punched by my father when he was in a *dark place*, but then I was expecting it so I could clench my muscles. There is *nothing* as bad as a full-blown punch in the solar plexus when you don't know it's coming.

The pain was excruciating. I couldn't breathe, I couldn't see for tears that sprung to my eyes, and I fell to my knees vomiting bile and the remnants of my polony sandwiches. I felt him rummaging through my pockets while I tried to catch a breath again. The one and only thing I had was the scrap of paper with Rick's number on it, and I saw it disappear after he looked at it and threw it away. The strong breeze picked it up and it flew out of sight.

Next, he grabbed a handful of my hair and jerked

my head up to punching height. "Now listen here, fart-face. I run this place, not them. Any money you get, you give to me, any smokes you get, ditto, and if there is even a hint of a foster family showing interest, you make sure they don't pick you. Get me, dick features?"

A random thought filtered through my foggy brain: *fart-face, dick features? This guy was an idiot if that was the extent of the insults he could come up with.* I grinned, unintentionally, and he punched me in the face, hard. I was vaguely aware of my nose crunching, sickeningly, and gushing blood.

I think even he realized he had gone too far. My hands were cupped over my face, and I watched the blood cascade through my fingers down over my T-shirt. In one of those flashes of memory that seem to come out of nowhere, I recalled the girl at the fairground, all those years ago, when I was five years old, and I guessed I looked the same.

The feeling of nausea, and that I would faint passed, as the blood flow slowed, and I was aware of him sitting cross-legged in front of me. "Listen up, dog breath." I was careful not to grin again. "I'm going to take you to the nurse. Now, you can do one of two things. You can rat me out, or say you fell over. I'd recommend the second option, if I were you."

I suppose, reading this, you, dear reader, might had ratted him out, and called his bluff. But, I was like a fish out of water; life had been bad with my dad, but he was gone. For all I knew I could be in this place for years. So, I reasoned maybe Jeremy would be better if he wasn't my enemy.

"You see, cocksucker, if you tell the nurse on me, yeah they will punish me, but really, what can they do, send me home? So, no matter what they do, I will still be here, and I will get you back sooner or later. And, if you think this is bad, well, just wait till me and my mates get you for ratting. What's it going to be, shit for brains?"

He half-carried me, half-dragged me to the infirmary, where Nurse Jackie looked after me. All the way there, Stubsy repeated what he would do if I told what had happened. He assured me they would never believe me, and even if they did, he would get me back the very next chance he got.

"Oh my goodness, what's happened here?" the nurse said as I stumbled into the room.

"New boy, Miss. This is Paul Rankin, he stumbled and fell and banged his nose on the corner of a brick wall. I was worried he might have done some real damage, so I thought I'd bring him here."

"Jeremy, tell the truth, have you been fighting again?"

"No miss, ask Paul. We were walking along and he tripped and fell onto the wall."

She stood with hands on hips, clearly not believing him, and that was without me saying a word. I realized then he had a reputation, which only gave his threats more validity. I was the new boy, and he ruled the roost. If I was going to survive in this hellhole, I needed him off my back. I mumbled a few unintelligible words, and she looked at me.

"I fell, he's telling the truth," I said slowly.

She shook her head, I don't think she believed me, but what could she do? "All right, Jeremy, you did the right thing. Now, Paul, let's have a look at this nose."

And that was my initiation to Harkerville.

****

If you ask me what I learned while at Harkerville, I would say survival. At least twice a week, Stubsy, or one of his cohorts; there were three of them, would punch me, often more than once. Sometimes he would kick me instead if his hands had hurt too much from punching others before me. Either way it hurt like a bastard, as my dad used to say. What it meant was that no sooner had the bruises faded, then I was given more.

It wasn't just the beatings; it was the constant living in *fear of* receiving a beating. Did it change me? Mold me into something else? That's not for me to say, but I'm sure the psychologists will say it did.

Stubsy had a habit of creeping up behind his younger, more vulnerable victims like me, and letting fly with a kick like a mule. By that, I mean he did not hold back for fear of braking bones. We never knew when we were safe from his bullying, and if some of us stood around talking we would do it with our backs to a wall. At least then we would see him coming and would have some time to prepare for the pain.

He was punished regularly, but as he had once told me, what could they do? He was also a very adept liar, and for some reason I could never explain, I think the adults liked him. In a way, I suppose you could say he kept a lot of other kids in line who might otherwise be troublesome.

One boy, Michael O'Connor, tried to rally several boys to take on Stubsy, and stop the bullying once and for all. It was a plan doomed to failure. I was almost the only one who could see the futility and abstained. The other renegade, Clarence Spinney, naturally, told Stubsie. Maybe he gained a reward, or maybe he was promised some sort of relief from the beatings, I will never know, but it was a rout.

Michael was found in the vegetable garden, beaten to a bloody pulp, some said a steel star picket was used. An ambulance took him away, and I never saw him again.

The technicolor dreams from my childhood were constant friends. I had them frequently at Harkerville. In the best ones, I tortured Stubsy and his friends with all manner of household items I had fashioned into weapons. It helped sustain me, knowing I could always fall back on my imagination for making them bleed. How I loved to make them squirt copious amounts. Every night I enjoyed doing just that. I stabbed, cut, slashed, poked, and stomped them over, and over again.

What else can I say about Harkerville? Well, the food was good, the bedding warm, and the *adults* cared, at least.

While there, a representative from the Office of the Public Trustee visited. Sister Kate was there too, obviously to ensure that I had a 'guardian' with me. It seemed that my father had left a will, where everything had been left to me, in trust, until I reached the age of eighteen. The property was freehold, and there was around twenty-six thousand dollars in the bank, which they would manage for me, less their percentage, obviously.

What I didn't know then, was that if I had foster parents, especially a family member, they could claim a wage from the estate, in addition to a government allowance, to look after me. While at first, I thought of him as my savior from the relentless beatings from Stubsy, my Uncle Phil was not to be so. Never was there a truer saying than: *out of the frying pan, into the fire.*

Three months later, it was like I was being paroled, and I left with him. Cynthia and Sister Kate waved from the veranda, and in the distance, I saw Stubsy, and he looked pissed.

I thought I had been rescued, but I hadn't. I learned why Dad didn't particularly like his own brother; because he was a homosexual pervert. It was a week before I found that out, when he whipped me with his belt, tied my wrists to the iron bed frame, and raped me. When he untied me, I was bruised, crying, and bleeding from my anus.

Uncle Phil was huge, like his brother, and any resistance from me was futile, and painful; I had always been slight, you could even say under developed. Once or twice my father, when he had been hurting me, said I wasn't even his child. He accused mum of screwing the milkman, newspaper man, or anyone other than him. Remember, he was a very big man, and I was tiny in comparison, and he often reminded me of that discrepancy, which, he said, proved he was not my father.

I want to stress here that my uncle didn't turn me into a homosexual. I hated every single moment. But, I knew there was nothing I could do about it, so I just went along. There was no alternative, and to avoid being hurt more, as well as raped, I suffered in silence. So, for the next five years, I was Uncle Phil's sexual plaything, and slave.

In the beginning, I would have loved to have had Richard's phone number and would have called him and begged for help. For a long time, I even believed he would come to my rescue. I thought about trying to locate him, but I was sure the police department wouldn't give out the phone number of a fellow officer. Worse; I could not remember his last name. For all I knew there could be five hundred Richards in the West Australian Police Force.

But after a while, I realized he had been just doing his job, and what I thought had been kindness was just an act. I reasoned that if he had cared, even just the tiniest bit, wouldn't he have come to check up on me at Harkerville? He knew where I was and I didn't know where he was, or how to contact him. I realized he didn't know his phone number had been taken from me, but I was eleven years old and thrust into a home with other troubled children, yet he never once thought to see how I was coping?

I still had a sort of childish hope that he would turn up one day, so I could tell him what Phil was doing to me. But he never did. I could have called the police myself, but my uncle had convinced me that no one would believe me. That happened during a conversation early in my stay with him. He had just used me, on a miserable night in June. My wrists were tied to the bed head, his favored position for me, he held a knife to my throat, and I was crying.

"Paulie, my boy. Don't you be thinking of telling anyone about what we do. You know they won't believe you, don't you? And, if you do tell, I will kill you. I know you like the sex; your crocodile tears don't fool me, so just keep your mouth shut, and all will be fine."

Cynthia visited, but was in the same room at the same time as was Uncle Phil. I wanted to scream out what he did to me almost nightly, but his eyes bored into mine, and I was just too scared. He allowed no time for me to be alone with her, obviously so I couldn't inform on him. I suppose, if she cared enough to insist she could have interviewed me on my own, but like my father, Uncle Phil was such a charmer she thought the sun shone from his smile. I remember clearly how they laughed and joked with each other; I was an afterthought, so the rapes continued.

Uncle Phil was always on at me to give him the house when I inherited it, as repayment for him taking me out of Parkerville. I knew that was never going to happen, I would never agree to his terms because at night, after he had used me to satisfy his lust, I often cried myself to sleep, and enjoyed a series of recurring dreams.

They began with sadistic images of what I wanted to do to Stubsy, and after a few weeks, when I tired of torturing him in beautiful, bloody ways, my fantasies turned to what I wanted to do to Uncle Phil. One kept me sane during those years. I had Uncle Phil tied upside down suspended from the chain that ran across the ceiling of the cool room in the shop at home. I recall watching his terror-stricken eyes as I stood before him, sharpening the knife on the steel that hung in the handle of the door. He was gagged with thick sticking tape across his mouth, but his eyes begged me to set him free. I skinned him alive, but slowly in inch wide strips designed to increase his pain, and my pleasure. I would ask him, repeatedly: "Are we having fun yet?"

Once that seed was sown, there was no way I would ever have given the place up for sale, it was fueling my fantasies. I yearned for the day when I could use it for what I saw as its true potential: a torture chamber for those I wanted revenge on.

****

Karma has a funny way of popping its head up like a Meerkat.

Three months before my eighteenth birthday, I was working as an apprentice butcher. There was never any other career I wanted to pursue; for me it was natural to follow in my father's footsteps. My teachers at school thought I was capable of so much more; university, a doctorate, law, there was no doubt in anyone's mind that I had the intelligence. If I had done anything else, it would have been psychology. The thought of playing around in people's minds was almost as attractive as cutting up carcasses. The appeal was so great, at night I studied psychology text books, but it never seemed to beckon me toward a career, it was more of a deep-seated interest.

While Uncle Phil enjoyed using my body whenever he wanted, he would always go back to his own bed to sleep, and in the mornings, one of my 'chores' was to take the filthy, pig, his toast and coffee so he could have breakfast in bed.

Why did the abuse continue for so long? Why did I not fight back? Well I am only small; weak if you will, not at all built like Dad, or uncle Phil. Resistance would have been futile, and while I dreamt of murdering him in the goriest ways, the harsh reality was that had I done that, the police would have found out. I would have gone to jail, or back to Harkerville. The more time slipped past, the harder it was to do something about it, does that make sense? I had my dreams, and they had to be enough; I suffered in silence; it was always less painful if I did.

On my unluckiest mornings, I would have to perform oral sex on him when I delivered his breakfast, which would make me want to vomit afterward. However, if the Gods were with me, either he wouldn't be in the mood, or I was running late for work. Uncle was a believer in my being on time for my job. After all, he took every cent of my wages, so it was important that my pay wasn't docked for being late.

On the best day of my life to that point, I entered his room, tray in hand, and discovered Uncle Phil had suffered a stroke. I never felt so happier at any time in my life as when I discovered him awake and dribbling out of the side of his mouth. Oh, my God, how good was it to walk into his room that day and see him like that? One look at his face told me all I needed to know. There he lay among his scrunched-up pillows, with the left half of his face having slid lower than the other half. One eye was open, the other closed, spittle pouring from the side of his crooked lips making a puddle on his shoulder. I could have broken out in song.

He waved his good hand at me feebly, while he muttered incoherently, and I knew he was begging for help; like that was ever going to happen.

"Well, Uncle Phil, I don't think you'll need your breakfast today, will you?" I teased, as if nothing was wrong.

I sat on the end of his bed, made myself comfortable, and sipped from his cup of coffee, having first perched the tray on my lap. I chatted away to him, telling what my plans for the day would be at trade school, and that for him not to worry, but I might be a bit late home that night. He moaned, and pointed to the door, as if asking me to call him an ambulance.

I ate his toast and marmalade. "Well, they say what goes around, comes around, and I guess your time has come. Isn't payback wonderful?" I could hear the glee in my voice.

I looked at him and could tell he knew I wasn't going to help him; that I was going to let him suffer, as I had suffered. The really, *really,* great news was that I would be blameless. I stood up, brushing the crumbs from my top. "Well, Uncle, I have to get off to work now. Sorry you didn't feel like breakfast today. Oh, one last question: Are we having fun yet? Wasn't that what you used to ask me?"

I picked up the tray, and whistling, I closed the bedroom door behind me, and went to the kitchen to wash up the dishes. When I got home from work I would have to call an ambulance. They in turn might call the police, and if they were called, I wanted no indication that I knew he had been ill earlier that morning. My story would be that I had gotten up and had gone to work as per normal. How was I to know he had had a stroke? That would be how I would act. The paramedic could call the police, protocol might demand that, because one way or another, Uncle Phil would be dead. If he was still alive when I got home, I would turn him in bed, so he was face down, and smother him with his pillow.

I cautioned myself to make sure I appeared completely normal to everyone I encountered during the day. Perhaps that was all elaborate and over the top in planning that far ahead. But I wanted to leave nothing to chance. I was going to be free for the first time in my life since I was four years old; nothing was going to spoil that.

I'm not sure what time during the day he died. But, when I got home about seven thirty that night he was lying on the floor, halfway to his bedroom door, and I reveled in the knowledge that he had tried to save himself and get to the phone, and failed. I stared down at his body and it took all my will power not to start kicking him. Thankfully, common sense prevailed.

With phone in hand, I practiced what I would say in my most serious voice, but no matter how hard I tried I kept giggling with sheer unadulterated joy.

Then, a sudden idea hit me: *what if Richard is the officer to turn up for the call out? Nah, couldn't be, over six years has passed. It was a Mundaring patrol before, and this is East Perth, won't that be a different patrol?*

The thought was enough to sober me up, so to speak, and I could make the call for an ambulance, without bursting into hysterical laughter. While I waited for them to arrive, my thoughts of hatred for Richard returned with a vengeance.

Now, I feel I should explain something here. I wasn't angry at that other cop, whose name I couldn't remember without a struggle, who attended my father's death. He didn't give a shit in the first place, and so I couldn't hold that against him. But Richard? Who would give a scared kid some sort of hope that there was another human being out there that gave a damn, only to not follow it through? In my opinion, only the worst sort of person in the world would do that.

Sitting at the kitchen table, sipping from my cup of tea, waiting for the ambulance to arrive, I made a vow to myself. A sacred promise that no matter how long it took, no matter what I had to go through, I would find him, and make Richard's life hell. I smiled at the thought and felt more content than I had in a long time.

Chapter 7:
June

Her name was June Daniels, thirty-two years old, slim and very attractive, and she was due to fly out to Melbourne on the Qantas four a.m. plane. Because it was such an early flight, she had her bag packed and ready, so if she was running late, it was one less thing to worry about. It was a very important business meeting she had to attend, and if she was successful, it would mean a very large promotion, and a bonus.

Her husband worked away on an oil rig and was home only one month out of every two, so it meant calling on her mother for babysitting duties. June was on her way home after dropping her son off, as her mum had gladly volunteered to look after Joshua for three days.

Her favorite song, Mascara, by Killing Heidi, came on the radio as she drove along, which was enough for her to crank up the volume and sing the lyrics.

Up ahead the flashing lights for her local supermarket beckoned, and she smiled as she decided she deserved some ice cream. Milk was also getting low and as her return flight was a late one, it made sense to buy supplies now. There was a vacant car parking spot alongside a Nissan, which she gratefully accepted. Her only regret was that she turned off Heidi, halfway through the song.

"Oh well." June Daniels jumped out of the car and almost ran across the car park, deep in thought which flavor to buy, the choc mint or indulgent strawberry. On her way back to her car, having decided on choc mint, she saw someone struggling on crutches while carrying an over-full shopping bag. She debated going to help, when the person fell, making the decision for her, and she dashed between two parked vehicles to assist.

June put her bag down on the ground, "Hey, how are you doing, can I help you?" she asked, as the person turned around.

That was when she felt the razor-sharp point of the knife being held to her throat, and she realized she had been fooled. The person didn't need crutches at all.

****

The list of dialed numbers made from the phone box totaled eighteen in the three hours preceding the call, and two within ten minutes afterward. A team of six detectives were sent to interview the recipients, and from there to question the people who had made the calls. There had been a serious assault on the street, was the cover story, and they were looking for witnesses.

When those interviewed stated they had not seen anything even remotely resembling an attack, they were asked to describe everyone that they could remember they had seen, along with any vehicles parked on the street. The detectives were hoping for a description of someone who looked out of place, nervous, or just hanging around. However, being forbidden to tell the truth of why they were asking such questions, only made the job more difficult. Most people are not very observant of the mundane, especially in busy city streets, and asking for witnesses to an assault that didn't happen, only made the job more difficult.

Other than the phone users themselves, they had only a few scant and vague descriptions. When checked against the list of people seen at the shopping center and the garbage dump, it did not show anyone that warranted a closer inspection. Comparing vehicles was equally unhelpful. Even if a description was of the killer, they had no evidence; therefore everything was background information only. The best hope was that someone would show up more than once during the investigation that married up with a previous interview, or witness.

Rick and Tyler questioned the local business owners situated near the phone box. They said they were looking for someone who had used the phone to make a bomb threat hoax call to a school. That garnered more interest than an assault, but again, was not very successful.

The killer had used the call box the day previously at one-fourteen in the afternoon, a time when lunch breaks were taken. Rick and Tyler were at the phone box, at the same time, stopping people as they walked by to ask if they had been there the day prior and had seen anyone using the phone. That was when they had their first break through.

"Excuse me, Ma'am. Sergeant McCoy, West Australian police. May I ask you a couple of quick questions please?"

The woman was in her late forties, dressed in a business suit with white satin shirt under her blue pinstriped jacket, and was clearly in a hurry. "I'm in a rush, officer, what's this all about?"

"I won't keep you, I promise, I just need to know if

you were here, about the same time yesterday?"

"Yes, I was, why?"

"That's great, we are looking for a man who used that phone box about this time yesterday, he made a bomb threat, and we want to catch him before he does it again."

She looked blankly for a few seconds before a light dawned in her eyes. "You know what? I did notice someone coming out. He seemed to time his exit with the lights going red, so the traffic had stopped. He opened the door and walked straight across the road, weaving between the cars toward Hay Street. That's the only reason I noticed, I thought he had perfect timing."

"And this man left the call box right about this time?"

She nodded and looked at her watch. "I have to be back at work at one thirty, so yes it would have been right around now; I'm never late. I work at the Commonwealth Bank building and have my lunch a Cissy's Café back up the street there."

Rick was taking notes in his book, trying not to get too excited. "May I get your name, please?"

"Yes, it's Bridget, Bridget Schaeffer."

"Thank you, Mrs. Schaeffer, can you describe the man you saw, please?"

"It's Ms., not Mrs., however, I forgive you. I'm in a rush; I work in overseas transfers and can't be late."

Rick stood with pen poised, looking at her expectantly. "I understand, Ms. Schaeffer, but please, tell me as much as you can, it is important."

She nodded. "Well, I didn't see his face, he was turned just slightly to the side, and then he had his back to me as he crossed the road, but he had longish straggly blonde hair, and he wore sunglasses with thick black plastic rims. More like a women's if I'm honest."

"This is very helpful, Ms. Schaeffer—build, and height?"

"Hmm, well, he wasn't anywhere near as tall as you, and he was much slimmer, not that I'm saying you are overweight, he was just more, I suppose what you would call delicate. Quite thin and maybe about this tall." She held her hand up above her shoulder to show his approximate height."

"If you had to hazard a guess as to how old he was, what would you think?"

"Gawd, no idea, maybe thirty-ish? But honestly he could be older or younger."

"Did you notice what he was wearing, and how long was his hair?"

"Just slacks and shirt, could have been jeans, I suppose. Well, as I recall his hair was quite long, and thick; dirty looking, like he was at least three months overdue for a trim. That's about all I can tell you, and now, I must get back to work."

"Can I have your address and phone number please?"

She gave him her apartment address in South Perth.

"Ma'am I need a statement from you, would it be all right if either myself or that detective over there call on you this evening to get it, and if you could have a really good think during the afternoon, just in case you can remember anything else. I promise you anything at all would be very helpful."

"Detective, okay, I'm intrigued, yes you can call on me after six, and I will give you a statement."

She walked away abruptly, her stiletto heels

resounding noisily on the pavement, and Rick watched her go, knowing it wouldn't just be a detective that called that night. It would be a police artist as well. This was their first breakthrough, they now knew the height, build, hair color of their target, and that he wore glasses. They could now go back and re-interview previous witnesses to show that description, and picture when they had it. Perhaps they might get lucky, at last.

****

Within thirty minutes the two detectives realized the window of opportunity had gone for people who were passing by at the same time as the day before. They re-visited the shopkeepers they had spoken to earlier with the new description. They also crossed the road in the direction of Hay Street, the direction Bridget mentioned, to ask if anyone had seen the man. They knew the chances were somewhere between slim and none.

Rick had also passed the news on to the officers tracking down phone users, to be wary if one of them had overly long untidy blonde hair, because he could well be the suspect. Also, had the users seen anyone hanging around who matched that description?

Once Rick had called the news into the DCI another team was sent out from headquarters to the people who had admitted to being at the Midland dump, and the shopping center where Melanie had been abducted from.

An hour later, the detectives were dejected. It was as if the Gods had given them a glimpse of the killer, and then drawn the curtains back down. For the first time since the first day of the suitcase murder, Rick wanted a cigarette.

His mobile phone rang.

"McCoy."

"Sergeant, it's Assistant Commissioner Monkton."

"Yes, sir?"

"I've arranged for you to meet Patricia Holmes at five thirty at her home in Applecross, it's 223 Mountsview Crescent. I've authorized as much overtime as any of you need, we must try to save the victim. We have a probable MISPER report; we think her name is June Daniels. Four nights ago, she stopped to shop at her local supermarket, and never came home."

"You realize she is probably dead by now, don't you, sir?"

"Not necessarily. His last victim he kept alive for around three weeks before he killed her, we have to hope, he will use the same method again."

"God knows what state she will be in, even if we do find her alive."

"Well, Sergeant, that's your job. Make sure you get to her in time. One last thing. When you meet Patricia tonight, try to keep an open mind. I got the distinct impression you were against her involvement."

"Yes sir, I will."

But what he thought, when he hung up the phone was: *bollocks.*

Rick, like most detectives of his age, had little time for psychologists, or lawyers whose job it was to keep killers out of jail. When a defense lawyer used a psychologist to testify that a murderer should be freed because of his or her state of mind, it made him feel like punching them. But, that night he had to consult with one, to him it was akin to consorting with the enemy.

****

At five-thirty he rang the ornate doorbell and heard the chimes from deep within the home. The house was grand, with a large sweeping driveway and steps leading up to the front door, underneath a huge veranda supported by carved stone columns. *Typical, my whole house could fit in her front garden; I'm in the wrong job.*

Mentally he cursed the intrusion into his personal hours for what he was sure would be a complete and utter waste of time. He had called Juliet to explain why he would be late and exactly whom he was seeing; of course, she had been fascinated despite his annoyance.

The door opened, and the woman who greeted him was nothing like Rick had imagined she would be. She was slim, yet full bodied, with very neat short black hair, and he had to look very closely to gauge her age which he put at late thirties. She was well dressed, in an opaque cream shirt with lace slip underneath, a mid-thigh black skirt, but had bare stockinged feet. The air she gave was that of a sophisticated, intelligent woman, not at all the mousey, bespectacled professor he had imagined.

"You must be Rick. Come in, I'm having a red wine, care to join me?"

"Umm, well, thanks, but I'd prefer a beer if you have any."

"Oh, I think I can manage that."

She led him through the cavernous entrance hall, with intricate parquetry flooring and a curved staircase off to the left leading to the upstairs area. "Pop yourself in there in my study, while I go and find you a beer."

Rick walked into a huge room that reminded him of a library. Every wall housed book shelves, even the wall with an open fireplace had crowded shelves on both sides and above. On the mantel above the fireplace were family pictures: mother and two daughters, who looked like twins, wearing graduation robes. Another when the girls had been younger, and one with whom he assumed was her husband wearing a tuxedo, and she in a glamorous ball gown.

Classical music played softly in the background, but not enough to be intrusive. Rick was more of a rock, or blues man, but the sound of a full orchestra was relaxing, he had to admit.

The desk was neat and tidy, though clearly used, two chairs in front of it, and an old red leather chesterfield couch which looked inviting, facing the fire place. Being that it was the tail end of summer, the fire wasn't lit, but it would be a lovely place to be in winter.

"Rick, if you don't mind I'd like you sitting at the desk. I'm happy to give you some preliminary thoughts tonight, but I want to record everything you tell me, then give it a lot of serious consideration over the next day or two in hopes I can be more specific. Will that be all right do you think? Here's your beer, I hope this brand is okay?"

Rick smiled. It was a secret favorite that he rarely indulged in.

He took the offered glass and sat on an antique chair, also with red leather and curved, carved arms. She sat opposite him and put her glass down, so she could open her drawer and take out a portable cassette recorder. She ferreted around and came out with a green covered tape cartridge, wrapped in plastic film. With practiced ease, she peeled it off, opened the cover, and slid the tape into the deck. She pressed the button for record, then picked up her glass of wine. She curled her legs underneath her, which gave just a hint of her thighs, and sat back in her chair cat-like. She sipped from her glass and licked her lips. "God, I needed that, it's been a tough day."

Rick almost burst out laughing. In this luxury house, which he would never be able to afford, she seemed so damned *normal*.

"What?" she asked, taking another sip of wine. "You don't think we psychologists can have tough days? I have a psychiatric degree as well and have two long-term patients in the high security wing of Graylands Mental Hospital. One cooked his wife and child before eating their organs, and the other murdered three random strangers because, he says, God told him to do it. Trust me; digging around in their minds constitutes a tough day." She shuddered.

"I'm sorry Pat, I meant no disrespect."

"No, I don't suppose you did. But, I'm guessing you feel like you've been press-ganged into coming here, haven't you? You believe using psychology to try to understand why someone would do horrible things to another human being is a waste of your evening. You've a wife, and probably a couple of children at home you'd rather be with, don't you?"

He blushed, knowing she would tell if he tried to lie, and he found himself, against his earlier intuition, liking her. "Just one child, Amy, she's five years old. Pat if you could just jot down this killer's address for me, I would think you were amazing. But it's going to be long hours of painstaking, often boring police work that tracks this guy down. When we've caught him, you can analyze him to death, I just want him off the streets."

"Fair enough, we know where we stand. But, did you know that a high percentage, and I do mean a *very* high percentage, of serial murderers had been previously interviewed by police, sometimes more than once, during an investigation? They are often let go, unsuspected, to kill again before they are eventually apprehended. Now I'm not saying great police work didn't catch them eventually, but, had the cops had access to a good, insightful criminal psychologist, maybe, just maybe, they'd have him locked up earlier, and innocent lives saved."

Rick nodded, thoughtfully, then raised his glass in a silent toast to her and took a sip.

"So, let me guess, you think you better be nice to me, because Darryl and I went to university together? You think if you speak your mind, I will dob you in to him?"

He blushed again, *just maybe this woman is indeed insightful*.

"Pat, I know you went to uni with the boss, because he told me. I am an old-fashioned cop who believes in what I do. This is a hideous case, with clearly a deranged murderer who takes delight in abducting, raping and torturing women. If we don't stop him, he will keep going because he likes it. Believe me, I'm willing to take any help from you that will get me closer to this guy."

"He's not deranged. He just sees things differently than you or I do. To him his behavior is normal, and you cops are the abnormal ones. That's probably because of his upbringing. Tell me everything you know, let me try to get a feel for this guy, Daryl has already told me quite a lot, but I want your take on the facts. I will tell you one thing I think already, he lost his mother at a very early age. I think she went out to the shops and never came back. She abandoned him, that's why he selects his victims from shopping areas."

"Oh, come on, how can you know that?"

She uncurled her legs and leaned forward on her desk. "My role, if I am to be any help at all, is to theorize. To observe the facts and make deductions from them. It would be fair and reasonable if I were wrong twenty percent of the time. I could live with that; eighty percent is good for this kind of work. Our man abducts women, from supermarkets, therefore he does it for a reason and not by random chance. By him replicating that, it would make sense if he is hurting his mother for leaving him. Rick, people who commit these sorts of crimes don't do it just for fun, although often they enjoy the act. They can feel driven to do it; it satisfies an urge or need that they have. Psychopaths hear voices, which tell them what to do and how to do it. But Sociopaths have no conscience, they don't feel guilt, and you can't argue with them logically. They often will feel incredibly superior, and they will lord that over you; tease and taunt, just to show how clever they are. They will shift the blame so if you don't stop them it's your fault, not theirs. Rick, this is my field, I'm not going to be able to tell you where he lives, because I don't use a crystal ball. But, I might be able to tell you the kind of place he might live in, the sort of up upbringing he may have had, and most importantly, the kind of things to look out for if you interview him.

I'm only offering to help you, so, please, tell me everything, don't hold back; what do you have to lose?"

He nodded slowly and took a long draft of his beer. *She's right, what do I have to lose?*

After a few seconds, Rick gathered his thoughts and began, and didn't stop until forty-five minutes later when he was about to divulge the description they had received that day.

"Stop," Pat said suddenly, and held a hand up.

"Why?"

"Let me tell you. He is small, almost, some would say, diminutive, possibly effeminate, but not necessarily gay. He's been bullied in some way or another most of his life, well, ever since his mother abandoned him. Your witness, didn't see him full frontal, I'm guessing side on or from behind. Because he let her see him, and that was all he allowed. He was probably wearing glasses and his hair, straggly or over long, probably an unusual color or style. That would be a wig. If it's not that, then he wore something distinctive, like a bright yellow jacket."

Rick closed his mouth, which had been open in shock. "Did Monkton give you the description?"

"No, he didn't, Rick." She shook her head emphatically. "Look, if this were a 'normal' murderer, I'm sure you would have caught him before now. But let's be honest, you have nothing. I believe he wanted you to get this description, because it's false. There are two possibilities I can see. One: he paid someone to make the call and leave in such a way that you had a convenient witness, or two, and this is more likely, he wore some sort of disguise so he would stand out. A wig and glasses, or sunglasses, more likely. Was the wig blonde, or red, something distinctive?"

"How could you know that?"

She stood up and walked around the desk, and perched herself on the edge, her leg almost touching his thigh, and Rick found himself wishing that it did touch. She took a long sip of her wine and savored it in her mouth before swallowing. "You must understand all this is conjecture, only what I think, not what I know. It's not mumbo jumbo or black magic, its deductive reasoning, and an understanding of this kind of psyche."

"Go on."

"What bothers me more than anything, is why you? Yes, it could just be that you were lead cop on the high-profile suitcase murder, but, I don't think that's the reason. If I'm right about some other things, then this guy is a planner, and he doesn't do things for no reason. I think it's more likely he has selected you and I don't know why, but I can tell you it's *not* because he saw you on TV. No let me re-phrase that, he probably did see you on TV, and because of some past association, he has targeted you. He isn't just in this for the thrill of his kill this time, he wants to engage you in his glory to make you suffer. You probably won't remember him, but for some reason he blames you for something, and now he wants to make you pay. And, I'm sorry to say, he will not stop until you have. So, he is smart, intelligent, and capable of very clear and strategic thinking and planning. He will be at least two, possibly three moves ahead of you, if you think of this as a chess game."

"But why the elaborate disguise to stand out and be noticed? I don't get it. Wouldn't he do that to avoid being remembered?"

She shook her head. "Yes, well, to answer that question we should think about the kind of person he is, and what is motivating him; what drives him to do things. I don't think he will mind getting caught, when he is ready. I think he looks forward to the day when he can tell the world how clever he's been and just how stupid you police were. In fact, he will possibly give himself up, eventually, or kill himself, but there will be a lot of dead bodies before he does. No, he has given you this gift of a witness so you go public with it. He will be laughing his head off with you on TV adamant you are hunting a blonde-haired man, when all the time he is bald, or has black hair. And even when he is caught, you will be the one who went public with the wrong description. I believe he is diminutive, because he is so ordinary and follows the pattern of being victimized. He has been abused, I would say on a regular basis for a long time. He hates the world and everyone in it who allowed that to happen to him. Why female victims? Because he's small, so he is more able to abduct a woman than a man, and as I mentioned, this revolves around a hatred of his mother abandoning him. That said, he won't care if he kills men, women or children, everyone is just cannon fodder. He is getting back at the people that have hurt and mistreated him all his life."

She finished the wine in her glass and turned to go back behind her desk for a refill, her skirt brushing his leg as she twirled.

"What about the sunglasses?"

"You mean how did I know he wore them, or how did I know he had something about him that was outlandish, like oversized glasses?"

"Both, the woman thought the glasses were more like the type a woman would wear."

"There you go, that's how I knew. Rick, once you accept that he wanted to be seen, but seen in such a way as it would never be a description you could fit to the real him, it becomes obvious. He did it *so he would be noticed.* By wearing oversized glasses, of course she noticed him on a busy street at lunchtime. It was discordant and made him stand out from the crowd. While she focused on the glasses, she didn't take note of his face. Am I, right?"

Rick nodded, slowly, understanding dawning on him.

"So," she continued, "let's look at this another way: the witness. He knew she walked past every day, therefore he timed leaving the box when he knew she would pass by. He was watching her, for days probably to learn her habits, and he selected her to be your witness. Remember I suggested that this man plans everything to the last degree. I think he wanted someone who was a creature of habit, smart, intelligent, and believable. So, once he picked her; the perfect witness, he watched, her, followed her; he knows more about her than you do. Then on the day he wore things that he knew she would notice, he spent a lot of time planning this. I'm afraid she is a possible future victim, now that her job is done. He has used her, she followed the script he wrote, and to give her fake description more validity, I think he might kill her. By doing so, it is another thing that you can take the blame for, and he will revel in your failure."

****

Tyler and police sketch artist Hugo Mann arrived at Bridget Schaeffer's apartment and found the front door ajar. Tyler drew his revolver and pushed the door open with the barrel.

There, on the floor in the entrance hallway laid a mutilated woman. The remnants of her blue pin stripe jacket had been slashed and hacked, and the body was surrounded by a puddle of her own blood.

Tyler's mobile phone rang; it was Rick calling to advise him to put Bridget into protective custody.

****

Just before ten o'clock that night, June Daniels cowered up against the cold wall of her prison. The maniac had returned carrying a tray with a tea-towel covering most of the things on it. One thing that wasn't covered was what looking like some sort of old fashioned tool, and it looked like it was red hot. He put the tray down on the concrete floor, to her side so as he lifted the cover, she couldn't see what was underneath it.

Her arms had long since lost any feeling in them, chained as they were above her head. She was bitterly cold and shivering, naked as she was. Every part of her body hurt, and he hadn't even bothered to clean the blood from her where he had used his knife to cut into her skin. "Please, please let me go, I won't tell anyone what you've done."

He smiled, except it wasn't a smile, it was like he was trying to make her think he was smiling, when really, he wasn't; he was grinning. He spoke in the squeaky, high-pitched monotone he possessed: "I've told you before, I will let you go, but you and I have to send some messages to the cops first, so they have a

110

chance to rescue you. Now, be a good girl, and keep still, this won't hurt too much."

He held up a knife, and the fluorescent light glinted off the blade. "Oh God, no, please no, don't hurt me anymore."

She screamed, begged, and pleaded until she passed into unconsciousness. Once her finger had been removed, Paul Rankin seared the joint closed to stop the bleeding with the old-fashioned soldering iron. It had been sitting on a roaring gas flame on the stove until it was glowing red, though it had lost its glow by the time he used it. It took longer to stop the bleeding because of it.

He covered her removed digit in tissue paper and packed it in a small cardboard box along with a note. He then wrapped it in brown postal paper, with stamps applied that he had purchased some weeks prior and addressed the outside to Detective Sergeant Richard McCoy. Rankin left his home, wearing a long coat and baseball cap pulled low over his face.

He drove into the city, parked in a quiet spot, and walked to where he knew a post box was. Without breaking stride, as he passed, he dropped his parcel in through the slot.

It was a pleasant evening, and he was in no rush. He took a long circuit back to his van. With hands thrust deep in his pockets, he whistled a tune to himself.

Chapter 8: My Memoir Entry
Enjoying the Fear

People think it's about the killing, that it is the act of committing murder that is the attraction; it's not.

For me, it's about the control. You could say that I had a miserable life, and I want others to share in my misery; and that would be true. But, I enjoy controlling their *fear*. I can give them hope, then snatch it away. I can watch their eyes and see that moment, when finally, they give up, and retreat inside themselves, and just want it all to end. And then, right there, that is the moment I live for.

You could say I am a product of my upbringing, and I would have to agree that I am. Is evil inherently evil of its own accord, or do circumstances cause people to become that way? Is anyone ever truly bad, or does what happen to them as they grow up, make them become something other than they would have without those influences? I often wonder if you took two different people and subjected them to the same upbringing, would they turn out the same. I have read that studies have been conducted along these lines, but there is nothing conclusive. I am writing this scrapbook so you, dear reader, can be my judge.

My Father wasn't naturally evil, I'm convinced of that, and I loved him. He went away to war, so far as I know a perfectly normal young man and came back deeply troubled. My mother had waited for him and tried to help him as best as she could. I believe, now, that she took to seeing other men when she went out at night, and it was that infidelity that sent my father over the precipice, to a point where he could take no more. While I believe, he loved her, he killed her, and kept his memory of her alive in the freezer.

For the longest time, I thought she had run off. Even when I discovered that she hadn't, I still hated her as if she had. In my mind, she was unfaithful – which is a hideous thing. Because she was unfaithful, she also abandoned me. Logic does not, after all, overcome emotion. And though I know she didn't run off, I'm sure she was unfaithful, so in the final analysis, she deserved what Dad gave her. Am I, right?

I remember the evening it happened like it was last week. Mum was dressed up to go out; it was a Thursday evening, she wore a new red shirt, she had make up on and her best perfume. As she and Dad put me to bed I asked where she was going, and she said she was off to the shops. Once they had left my room, they stopped outside my door, and I heard dad say, "Please don't go out again, stay home with me."

I never heard mum's reply, but a little later I heard the door slam and then silence. I thought I heard him crying, but it could have been the TV, the mind sometimes plays tricks on us, doesn't it? But he did plead with her to stay home, and she refused.

****

When Uncle Phil died, I expected them to put me back in Harkerville. I dreaded the thought of Stubsy, and his cronies, beating me up on a regular basis all over again. If I'd been thinking clearly, I would have realized that couldn't have happened, because he would have been too old by then to still be a resident. By the time I realized that, it was no longer an issue. Maybe it seems incongruous with what the last few years had been like for me, and the only way I can try to explain it is that with my uncle, things were predictable. As unpleasant as it was, I knew what to expect. With Stubsie, I never did. The violence, was ultra-violence; if that makes sense

Either way, for some reason, they didn't. A social worker named Norma came around and spent a few days helping me sort out his affairs. She made sure I was coping by visiting from time to time, and I suppose she could see I was perfectly capable of looking after myself.

He had not left a will, but I inherited the house, as he had no other living relatives. The same Trustee helped with that paperwork. I suppose, as I only had three months to go before I became an adult legally, they decided to leave me there under Norma's supervision. She had given me her phone number with the instruction I was to call her any time; day or night, if I thought I wasn't coping. Little did she know; I was overjoyed with my new life, and not troubled one little bit.

I had had the presence of mind to destroy his pornography collection. He had an old fashioned concrete cinder block incinerator in the back garden and I took great delight in destroying the magazines in it. I even found it, therapeutic to burn everything. Even now, dear reader, I shudder at the thought of those obscene homosexual images.

The other thing I destroyed were all the Polaroid

photos he had taken of me, and things he had made me do. They had been taken with a camera which I put to good use later in life to record my own triumphs. Uncle Phil was a disgusting perverted man who had deserved to die, and the only regret I had over the whole affair, was that it hadn't been me that killed him. I even had a fantasy of digging up his coffin and taking his body home so I could mutilate him, hung from the chain in the cool room, though of course that was unreasonable.

The day following my eighteenth birthday I had an appointment with Mr. Bridges at the Public Trustees office. He was a very nice man, or so I thought at the time. Stupid me; what I thought of as kindness he showed me, was, once again, something else.

My dad's small estate had grown under his management. The shop and house had been leased out, which, while being pragmatic, because it had made money, was now an issue because I had to wait for the lease to expire before I could move back in. Luckily, I had uncle's house to use until that time. Once I had got rid of all the reminders of his sexual deviations, I didn't mind being in the house at all, whereas before Id expunged it all I felt nervous and skittish all the time.

I suppose, looking back now, it was all rather inevitable. Mr. Bridges offered to bring all the paperwork to the house for me to sign after our initial meeting. That was because by the time I finished work at the Carousel Meat Market, I couldn't get into town during his office hours, having used up my quota of leave with the funeral. Once there he took off his jacket and said: "It's quite warm today, isn't it?"

I expected him to sit at the dining table, but instead he made himself comfortable on the couch. He patted alongside him for me to sit there. I've wondered since if Uncle Phil had let on what he did to me to Mr. Bridges. I will never know. Probably not, I suppose, it's more likely that me being the small stature, and slim build that I was, he mistook me for being gay.

He went on about how he had helped me and worked long and hard to grow the twenty-six-thousand-dollar nest egg into sixty-two thousand, and how I should be grateful to him. He also said he was going to continue to help me with selling my uncles house when the time was right, and that he would take me under his wing. Silly me, I believed he was genuine. That was when he undid his trousers, pulled them and his underpants down, and said it was now my turn to do something for him.

I wanted to kill him there and then, and could have, quite easily. I had made a conscious decision after Uncle Phil died not to be anyone else's victim any more. But there was a dilemma. My rapid-fire brain worked out the consequences within seconds. If I murdered him there would be a body to dispose of, and no doubt people knew he had come to see me. I would be jailed, and life would end. Killing the pig, Mr. Bridges, didn't bother me, but I had to be smart about it if I wanted to live my life on my terms. I had only had the freedom I was feeling for such a short time; I was unwilling to throw it all away.

I could have said, no. Accused him of misconduct, called his employer, the police, done one of a dozen things. Why didn't I? The explanation is quite simple. I knew I wanted to kill him, yet if I did it out of anger, I would be the prime suspect. What he wanted me to do, was disgusting, but no worse than I had been performing with my uncle. The turn-around for me, was to let him think he was using me, but I was leading him along, all the way to his death.

****

It took five months, but I got even with him. The final icing on the cake, and the last nail in his coffin, was that good old Mr. Bridges was married, and had children. He justified it by saying he had always been bi-sexual. His wife was aware of his predilection, apparently, and they had an 'open' marriage. I didn't believe a word of it. My thoughts were that he shouldn't have married and brought two kids into the world if he wanted to have his cake and eat it too.

I had to wait until the tenants had vacated the shop where I grew up, my uncle's house had been sold, and all the money had left the Trustee's bank account and taken up residence in mine. During this time, I had to show my gratitude to him at odd times when he demanded it. As the day drew near for my revenge, I told Mr. Bridges I wanted to take him out for dinner to say thank you, but he told me not to be silly; that he couldn't afford to be seen with me in public.

What an insult that was! That inspired me even more. I told him that I still wanted to show him how truly grateful I was for all he had done for me, and that I had a 'friend' who wanted to join us in a threesome, at his house. I was a very good actor, and he had no idea how much I hated what we did. He thought I was enjoying it. You should have seen his face when I described this imaginary person whom I based on my recollections of Stubsy. I described him as being well endowed, and that he was very keen to meet Mr. Bridges; and that his name was Jeremy.

I set him up beautifully. I told him that on the arranged Tuesday night, Jeremy's parents were going out to a movie so we could have the promised threesome as soon as they left. I said he lived close to a small park, and we should meet there in the car park at seven pm.

He asked me all sorts of questions about what we would be doing, and he was like a panting dog as I laid on the depictions of the vilest acts I could imagine. I asked, discreetly, what he would tell his wife he would be doing.

"Like I always tell her, work, work and more work." He grinned, reminiscent of the famed 'Cheshire Cat.' I grinned back, knowing his wife wouldn't know he was meeting me.

I got there early, my adrenalin high, wearing dark clothing and a beanie woolen cap, and gloves. I had planned meticulously. The cap was to ensure I didn't leave any stray hairs for DNA testing, and of course the gloves were so I didn't leave fingerprints. The long-bladed boning knife I had concealed up the sleeve of my jacket was razor sharp, honed to within an inch of its life, earlier that afternoon.

I grinned to myself as I watched his silver station wagon glide into the car park and park under a light, four minutes before the appointed time. *Like a lamb to the slaughter.*

After one meticulous last look, around, to make sure we weren't being watched, I left the shadow of the tree, walked over to the car, and tapped on the passenger side window. He opened the door and I got inside. No sooner had the interior light gone off, he kissed me; he was like an octopus with eight hands all over me.

By the time he finished, I had the knife removed from my sleeve and positioned under his rib cage on his right-hand side. "Are we having fun yet, Mr. Bridges?" I asked, as I pushed it inside him.

I watched his eyes closely, and noticed he looked down and saw the handle of the knife in my hand sticking out of him. All nine inches of high quality stainless steel were reaching up toward his heart.

He tried to pull away, but I put my hand around the back of his head so he couldn't. When he tried to scream, I said, "Shush, Mr. Bridges," and covered his mouth with mine to give him what I've since named *the kiss of death.* I pulled the knife out, and stuck it back into him over, and over, again.

It was a lot messier than I would have liked, and all the blood made the handle of the knife slippery. It reminded me again of being five years old as I watched him bleed out.

****

I avidly read the newspapers afterward, as they described what they thought, not too incorrectly, as a homosexual park encounter gone wrong. I had stabbed Mr. Bridges more than forty times, apparently. I wouldn't have thought it was anywhere near that number, but there is no point denying it, I was having fun so I could have lost count. I controlled his death, and that was awesome.

After that first kill, I didn't have any compunction to do it again, for a long time. I had never seen myself as a serial killer. That first one was retribution, and it was justified. He took advantage of an eighteen-year-old, even though he was married with children.

Seriously, isn't the world a better place for him not breathing our oxygen? If he had stayed faithful, he would be alive today.

For a while I did worry that the police might knock on my door. I had worked out in my head all the answers I would give to any question they would fire at me. Yes, I knew Mr. Bridges, he was very good to me, and he was a nice man blah, blah, blah. But, they never did come calling, and as time went by, I worried less. I realized they thought they were looking for a gay hater, which took the pressure off considering Mr. Bridges' clients. I supposed getting details of people like me, many of whom could have been underage, would be a complex business, and once they decided it was a gay bashing murderer, it probably wasn't worth the hassle of gaining a court order. For all I knew, maybe they tried to get a warrant, and had been declined. Whatever the reason, I was never questioned.

I finished my apprenticeship at age nineteen and was a fully qualified butcher. The shop had been closed for quite a while, when I quit my job at Carousel, and opened it back up again. I'd like to say it was a raging success, but it wasn't, it was more a dismal failure. It had been closed for too long, and the clientele had gone elsewhere. Besides, I was the son of a murderer, so as you might imagine: people stayed away in droves. I suppose, though they would never admit it, the locals thought the fruit never fell far from the tree, and I could be tarred with the same brush as Dad. Whatever the reason, the shop never made money.

I wasn't as good a businessman as my father was either. I didn't have his flirtatious and self-confident air, so the customers didn't like me anywhere near as much.

I struggled on for nine months, trying to make a go of it, and one morning in late May I woke up thinking to myself, *I'm not going to bother anymore.* And I didn't. That afternoon I went and bought some whitewash and painted out the front window and glass door. I put a sign up CLOSED UNTIL FURTHER NOTICE and that was the last time I opened the shop.

I still had close to two hundred thousand dollars in the bank, as Uncle Phil's house had sold nicely, and there was no pressing need to work. But, I was bored, so eventually I did get a job, as a butcher, in the Meat section at Dalton's Homestyle Supermarket in Midland. And that was where I met Carly.

I fell madly in love with Carly Biddle, very soon after meeting her. She was older than me, but not by enough to matter. She worked in the office doing ordering, accounts receivable, and payroll. Her hair was like the finest silk, long and flowing, and even though she wore reading glasses and was a little bit chubby, she was incredibly pretty with the biggest blue eyes. I was always nervous and mumbled like an idiot whenever she came near me, and soon enough I was the brunt of jokes about her with the other butchers. I didn't like that they belittled her, she didn't deserve that.

Andrew called out one time: "Aye-up Carly, lover boy's been pining over you. He's gonna pluck up the courage and ask you for a kiss any day now."

"He better bloody not," she replied, but she was smiling when she said it. I just knew she was kidding. I still blushed and pretended it didn't bother me, but I'm sure she would have seen how red my face was. I knew in my heart she wanted to kiss me too, but the protocol of being work colleagues stopped her from following her heart.

Another time I remember walking out of the gent's toilet, head bowed low as I made sure my hands were clean. Carly happened to be walking out of the ladies and we collided. She jumped back like a startled rabbit, but before she could I had felt her large breasts squashed against my chest. I put out my hands in part to steady myself but also to stop her falling over, and they closed over her hips. It was like a bolt of lightning traveled through my body, and I'm sure she felt the same.

I wanted her to notice me, but she never did, and I lacked the courage to ask her out on a date. I thought that in time, she would just know how I felt. Sooner or later, she would fall in love with me. I just *knew* it would happen.

I began to worry about her all the time, and wanted to make sure she was safe, so I started walking her home after work. She lived quite close to the shopping center and insisted on walking every night, but there were some bad elements living in Midland at the time.

I had been fretting that I might not be able to protect her for quite a while when I came up with the idea of carrying my boning knife; the one I had killed Mr. Bridges with. But how to do it unobtrusively, I wondered? It came to me one weekend at home, and I made a leather scabbard for it, and two elastic straps to hold it tight and secure against the inside of my left leg, under my trousers. Suddenly I was transformed. I felt confident, and strong, and knew that when we were walking to her home every night, if anyone attacked, I would be able to take care of Carly. I only wanted to keep her from harm.

It was horrible when she discovered I was following her. I had no idea that she knew.

It was just like every other night, with me thirty to forty yards behind, using the shadows of the tree lined streets to hide behind if she looked like turning around.

On the fateful night, she turned the corner into Riddell Street as per usual, which had this huge weeping willow tree on its verge. I hurried to the corner and turned, but she was gone, vanished. I was frantic, looking up and down the road. Suddenly, she stepped out from behind the willow, hands on her beautiful hips, head tilted to one side.

"What the fuck are you doing following me, Paul?" She sounded so angry, and the use of a swear word shook me from my head to my toes.

I mumbled: "I wasn't, I umm was just going this way." I didn't know where to look so my head was bent low, as I kicked the dirt, and felt like the sky had caved in on me.

"You're fucking sick in the head; you're a fucking stalker, Paul. I'm going to tell the boss tomorrow at work, and the cops too. I'm going to get you the sack and then they will put in a mental home, you fucking degenerate."

Now, dear reader, you must try to understand this was my angel, who had suddenly turned on me, shouting filthy words. It rocked me to my very core. I wanted to shut up her potty-mouth.

I don't remember bending and lifting the knife out of its sheath, but the next thing I knew was she was staring down and I had stabbed her in her chest. By the look on her face she was as shocked as I was, and while I hadn't consciously aimed for her heart, I think I hit it through a gap in her ribs, because she didn't make a sound other than a kind of 'ouff.'

She fell into the gravel and dust on her back, eyes staring blankly upward.

Just for a moment, and I know you will find this hard to believe, I thought someone else had done it. It was only when I noticed her blood on my hand, that I realized it had been me; I had killed her, my angel was dead. My next thought was that the foul-mouthed tramp deserved it. Imagine, her abusing me and swearing at me, when all I was trying to do was make sure she was safe. *Stupid cow!*

I put my foot on her tummy, so I could get leverage to pull the knife out. Just for a moment, it wouldn't come. I worried that if I couldn't get it, the police would know it had been me, because my name was engraved on the blade to stop other butchers stealing it. Luckily it did come out, when I yanked it, and I nearly fell on my backside. That almost made me giggle, I mean, really; it was funny.

I was about to run off, back into the shadows, when I had a sudden thought: I had been wondering for ages what she looked like without her clothes, and now I could find out. I wasn't in the mood to manhandle her; that would have been sick, but surely, I thought, a look couldn't hurt. So, I took the knife, slipped it under her uniform, and slit it all the way up her front. Her titties were big and floppy, even though she wore a bra, which was a cheap and nasty type, hardly sexy. Her under pants too were an ugly shade of purple and looked like something a grandma would wear. *Whatever did I see in her?*

She most definitely had not lived up to my

fantasies. I wiped the knife on her clothes, put it back in its scabbard, turned, and walked away quickly, without running. I had a handkerchief in my pocket, and I used it to clean the blood off my hand.

I walked back to my car, feeling liberated. I had bought myself a car by then: a pale-cream sedan. I reveled in knowing that I had found my true vocation in life. I had killed two people and not batted an eyelid or worked up a sweat doing it. Maybe I could do that for a living, as a contract killer. Then I did have a laugh to myself.

Over the next few months, I began making serious plans for using the cool room as a torture chamber. It was time for me to have some fun. That night, when I arrived home with a bag of goodies from the hamburger place, I had quite a few ideas of how I would go about it.

Now, it didn't happen overnight. I had to first make sure I was going to get away with Carly's killing, accidental as it was; I knew the police wouldn't see it that way. I set myself a three-month time limit. I mean, if the idiots hadn't arrested me by then, clearly they were never going to.

The following day I turned up at work, smiling as if nothing had happened and by mid-morning the police detectives were there in the manager's office. Only I knew why. Word hadn't filtered through, so I had to be careful I didn't give myself away.

I waited for the page over the speaker system for me to attend, or cops to come to my work area, knowing that someone would be only too quick to say the weirdo in the meat packing department had the hots for her. Yes, dear reader, I knew what other people thought of me, morons that they were. But, I had had all night to plan how I would handle being questioned, and I wasn't concerned. I had studied numerous books on psychology, and police procedure, and had a good understanding of what they would ask me.

First, the department managers were called one at a time to the lunch room and two hours later, I heard my name come through the speakers. Mick, the senior butcher said as I left: "Been nice knowing you, Paul." Then he snorted as if he had made the joke of the century.

I stopped in my tracks. "What do you mean by that?"

"Cops have come to arrest you, man. They know all about what a freak you are." He laughed again, and the others in the area joined in. I kept my dignity, shook my head to show them I thought they were being stupid, and walked out. After all, officially I still didn't know what the cops were doing there, though the rumor mill was saying they had been brought in because of stolen cigarettes.

I didn't knock, I just walked straight in, wiping the drying pigs blood off my hands with a cheesecloth cleaning rag as I went. The store manager stood to one side and made the introduction: "Paul this is Detectives Barlow and Millicent, they want a few words with you."

"Sure, what's up?"

Two big guys, I mean one was *really big*, stared up at me from behind the Formica table they were sitting behind. I don't think they liked what they saw. One screwed up his face and shook his head while the other nodded in my general direction.

"Sit down, Mr. Rankin, and tell us what you know about Carly Biddle."

I theatrically stopped halfway between standing and sitting for a moment and stared between one and the other. "What do you mean, tell you what I know about Carly?"

"It's a simple request."

"Is she sick or something? I haven't seen her around today. She works in the office, I see her around the place, and she is nice. I don't understand what you mean. I know about as much about her as I do Mr. Potts, the manager."

"That's not what we've been told."

He didn't say another word, just stared at me, obviously thinking I would get nervous and open my mouth and make their job easy for them, so I just stared back. I was determined that he would be the one to speak next, not me. Eventually, he weakened, as I knew he would.

"You seem like a smart-arse to me, Mr. Rankin."

I shook my head and allowed a certain amount of indignation to enter my voice. "I haven't got a clue what you're talking about, but you say you've been told something else about me and Carly. But I still have no idea what you are on about. So, I was waiting for you to elaborate. I work in the meat area; she works in the office. What do you want me to say?"

"She was murdered last night walking home from work, you both signed out about the same time and we know you were fixated on her."

I put my hand over my mouth, hoping I looked suitably shocked. "She's dead? Oh, my God that's terrible. Hang on, what do you mean I was fixated on her? I thought she was married or had a boyfriend. I finish work at six o'clock every night, so did she. Why do you think I killed her? Why would I do that?"

"Maybe you followed her home, told her of your undying love, and she laughed at you, how about that?"

That was scarily true, but he couldn't possibly know that for a fact. He was trying to bluff me. If he had any sort of idea what had happened, he would have arrested me. "Are you mad? Seriously, do I look like a murderer? You think I killed her because I liked her and she didn't like me? That's insane."

"Maybe you are insane."

As I theatrically shook my head, I found that I was enjoying myself. This dunderhead wasn't worthy to clean my shoes, let alone trip me up intellectually. "Detective, I think we have thirty male staff here, including night fill, and every one of them fancied Carly. If that's your motive, I hope you brought lots of handcuffs."

"You think this is funny?"

"In a way, yeah. But it's more worrying if you think I'm your best suspect. I didn't even know she was dead till you told me."

"So you say."

"I liked her, she is, sorry was, a nice girl, but only from afar. I finished work at six, went to my car, and went home. I don't know what more you want from me. This is all very upsetting If you think I'm so unhinged I would murder a work colleague just because I liked her, I suppose you had better arrest me."

"We will, of that you can be sure. We need a DNA sample from you, the killer left a trace behind, once we match it to you, I will personally make the arrest; I don't like smart-arses."

He was lying, obviously. "Happy to help, honestly, I didn't kill her, and I hope you catch who did."

The cop that had remained silent stood up and took from his case a glass type tube which housed a long stick with a cotton swab inside it. "Open your mouth wide, please," he said. I did and he ran it around the inside of my lips before screwing it back inside the tube and then labelled it with a felt tip pen.

****

I watched the TV news and read the papers for a few weeks. I was never questioned again by the police other than once, very briefly when I stopped and asked him how the investigation was going during my lunchbreak when I saw them in the center. He stared at me for a few seconds, trying to remember me, I thought. "Mr. Rankin, isn't it?"

I nodded and took a bite from the sausage roll I was eating.

His gaze seemed to bore right through me. "We're getting very close to arresting our suspect."

"Good. A person like that doesn't deserve to be walking the streets."

I turned and walked away; feeling him staring at my back.

The media consensus seemed to be that it was a sex attack gone wrong, because her uniform was slashed open. Had I been the investigator I would have known that couldn't be true. She had been stabbed through the dress, and then it was cut open afterward. But, who was I to correct them?

Slowly, the Midland Murder, as the papers had dubbed it, became yesterday's news until I realized, the three months had passed that I had set myself as a period of watching and waiting. I began thinking about the next stage of my life.

I had made a conscious effort to be 'normal' at work, and not show that I was grieving for Carly. But then I realized I wasn't feeling much anyway. Did that mean I hadn't felt anything real in the first place, or was it the result of her disgraceful behavior which tarnished my ideals for her? I no longer gave a damn about her either way. In trying to protect her she had ridiculed me. Not just called me names but said she would try to get me the sack and in trouble with police. Surely, you can see how I could feel nothing toward her after that debacle?

For a few days, I acted a bit sad, that would be expected of me. After her death, some of the women did look at me sideways, like they were being wary, but again, it was nothing I couldn't handle. As per normal, I just kept myself to myself, turned up on time, did my job, and spoke pleasantly to others when I needed to. I have always been so much smarter than everyone else, but I practiced hard to hide my disdain for the people I worked with.

So, time passed, the cops turned up at work less and less, and life returned to the same level of normality as before. Slowly my thoughts turned to my cool room, and what I could be using it for. Then one day, out of the blue, I had the most amazing epiphany.

Who knows, dear reader, where random flashes of inspirational thoughts come from? I think artists and great writers are sometimes hit like that. They go from normalcy to being inspired in a flash, and when that does hit them like a lightning bolt, they must act on it.

So, it was for me.

In our branch of Dalton's, we made our own sausages, not just for our retail sales, but other stores as well. We had a huge mincing machine into which we put the meat offcuts, spices, and flavorings into the big hopper, and out of the other end came a never-ending supply of meat which was squirted into the skins. In Dad's day, he used to use intestines to retain the meat, but at Dalton's we used synthetic ones, because they were cheaper.

Clearly, the problem I faced with killing people was what to do with the bodies afterward? I'm not a big man, neither am I terribly strong, so corpse disposal was an issue that was never far from my mind. I had already concluded that if I killed someone in the cool room, getting them out of there would be in pieces. But then what? A body in pieces still takes up a lot of room and weighs the same.

I was standing at the machine, holding a casing over the spout, as it filled with sausage meat after filling the hopper up with an assortment of beef offcuts, when it suddenly hit me. I could take the meat from the bones, bring it in to work in plastic bags hidden in my rucksack, and drop them into the meat tubs to be turned into sausages. Customers would unknowingly be buying human meat mixed in with the pork, or beef, for dinner. *How funny would that be?*

Once I had the idea, I knew, I just knew that I had to follow it through. It would mean from a practical point of view, all I would then have to dispose of would be the bones, but that would be a lot simpler than the whole body. The thought of my customers eating my victims, was an added attraction, and something, I felt I was *compelled to do*.

Chapter 9:
Mind Games

Rick had left Patricia Holmes' Applecross home in a hurry, with the promise to report back to her in the morning at her University Campus office. She had given him her word she too would listen to the recording she had made, to see if she could glean any further insights for him. She also asked him, if he was permitted, to take some crime scene photos for her. Possibly, she volunteered, she might notice something.

All the way to the South Perth Apartment he asked himself: *How could she have known that?* And then a second question: *How come I didn't think of it first?* He shook his head, and muttered under his breath, cursing himself for being so blind to what then seemed obvious.

Two patrol cars, with lights flashing, had cordoned off the street either side of the small apartment block and uniformed officers kept onlookers at bay. Rick's car screeched to a standstill at just the same time as the DI approached from the other end of the road. No sooner had Rick's foot hit the asphalt road surface a thought crashed around inside his head like a pin-ball. With blinding clarity, he knew something, something important; and he had Patricia Holmes to thank for it.

Jesus, the killer had been watching us interview people at the phone box! He stood and closed his door, then leaned on the roof, completely still; he had to think this through. *Hold the fucking phone, hold everything. If the killer had set up Bridget Schaeffer, how could he know they had interviewed her before he killed her? Answer: he was watching the phone box himself and saw them question her. Then he must have followed her home, let her get inside and killed her before she could be re-interviewed.*

Everything clicked into place, and for the second time that evening, he cursed himself for not being more observant. He could have been standing right next to the killer, damn it.

If this were a chess game, he would be two to three moves ahead of you. That was what she said.

Very slowly, Rick turned a full three hundred and sixty degrees and looked at every shadow, then studied the faces of the people watching, in case he was there. But, that would be too easy, and nothing about this case was easy.

"What's wrong, Rick?" the DCI asked as he approached.

"Hi, Boss." He quickly explained the result of his meeting with Patricia Holmes, and her thoughts on the false description that led to Ms. Schaeffer's murder. He explained he had been scanning the area in case the killer was watching them, as he must have been earlier when he interviewed her.

"Rick, you aren't making a lot of sense."

Rick shrugged. "The thing is, I believe her, and let me tell you there was no bigger sceptic than me before this. She told me this witness was in danger and that she would be a future victim. She has a knack of looking at facts in a different way, from the killer's point of view if you like. If I'd thought of this before, Bridget

Schaeffer would still be alive."

"Stop that right now. There was no way to have predicted this."

"Patricia Holmes did. What if we could bring her in as some sort of advisor, get her to think like him and help us?"

"What would she charge do you think, to be a consultant? I'm not sure I could get approval for such a thing. I don't think any force in Australia has a psyche on the payroll."

"I've no idea. I don't even know if she wants to be involved, she doesn't need the money but the looks of her house. Maybe a word from the assistant commissioner could go a long way. But, I think, whatever she charged, she would be worth it, if it helps get this guy locked up."

He nodded thoughtfully. "I will talk to Mr. Monkton in the morning, get his thoughts."

"No need to wait till morning."

He nodded to where a black Holden Caprice smoothly parked, and the commissioner got out of the rear door. With a determined stride, he walked over to them, looking irritated. "What have we got here gentlemen?"

"We've not long arrived, sir, Sergeant McCoy has been updating me on his meeting with Patricia Holmes.

"So, do we know this is the work of our man?"

"Has to be, sir, it's the only thing that makes any sense." Rick explained again his interview with the witness, and the meeting with Pat that told him of the danger Bridget Schaeffer was in.

"And why does she think that?"

"Well, to be honest, I didn't get time to finish our

chat. I'm going to see her again tomorrow morning. But, she does have amazing instincts and insights, and I'm very glad I met her. She likened the investigation to playing chess with him, but he will always be two steps ahead."

"Why you, McCoy? What's his beef with you, did she have any thoughts there?"

"I have no idea, but she thinks it's possible that somewhere in the past our paths have crossed, but I can't see it. Over the twenty years I've been a cop, I can't tell you how many people I've come across. I've no idea if he was a victim, or offender, someone I've arrested or tried to help. Without more information, there is no way to know. That's why I think I need to try talking to him through the media."

"McCoy thinks we should ask her to be a part of the task force," Colin Harris interjected. "Can we get funding to pay for her services?"

"You won't need funding; she would love to be involved with a murder investigation, she has been on at me for years; this is her dream. She will want to write a paper on the guy when we catch him, but for someone with her credentials, that's a small price to pay."

****

For the first time in many years, Rick felt like vomiting when he saw the crime scene.

The woman whom he had interviewed only hours before; a vibrant, healthy person with a strong personality had been slaughtered, for the sole purpose of making him look bad. *This is total madness.*

The irony of the situation wasn't lost on him. There was to be no statement to the media about June Daniels being held by a madman with blonde hair or otherwise.

They had invented a story to hide the real reason why they were looking for witnesses at the phone box, and that told Rick that the killer had not been close enough to know that, just enough to know they had spoken to her.

Rick thought he saw a chink in the murderer's armor. While he was capable of planning far into the future to show off his supposed superior intellect, the fact was that that also made him fallible if they could act in a way that hadn't been predicted. PPP was not going to get the publicity he wanted, so possibly things would escalate, that could cause him to make a mistake.

Forensics was all over the apartment, checking for DNA and fingerprints. But to Rick, the scene told its own story. She had come home from work, entered, but the doorbell had rung. She had not had time to change, or even take her jacket off. She had opened the front door to greet her killer, possibly assuming it was the police. Rick shook his head when he saw the chrome security chain hanging loose, unused, which possibly could have saved her life, if only it had been latched.

They canvassed the neighbors, to ask if they had heard or seen anything unusual. No one had. It appeared Bridget had not had time to scream.

There were two entries into the building, one at the front and the other from the car park at the rear. There were only enough car bays for residents. Visitors would need to find street parking so it was possible, but unlikely, the killer had parked there. The street itself was jammed with cars as the area was full of apartments. He would have been covered in blood spatter, so he wouldn't have walked far without being seen. There were no CCTV cameras to aid them, how the murderer had got away was a mystery.

By ten that night, the interviews were finished, and Rick and Tyler compared notes. The only thing they had that seemed out of place was one witness who said they saw an old man who looked like he was homeless, shuffling down the street away from the building. Only seen from the rear the witness, Michael Highgate, said that the only reason he noticed him at all was the gray shabby long raincoat he was wearing when it wasn't raining or even cold. When pressed for a description, he said the man had unruly gray hair, he was quite a small man who walked with a stooped gait and seemed to be wearing very dirty running type shoes that once in their life had been black.

At first, Tyler had discounted him and only mentioned it to Rick in frustration that he was the only person seen in the area. But, the description rang a warning bell with Rick. Patricia had said that the man wore stupid looking sunglasses so that if he was seen by a witness they would remember the glasses rather than the face. Was the description of this homeless person not similar? If he was the murderer, he had given the impression he was an old man whose appearance made him look like a tramp, and therefore people would be more inclined to remember the overall picture, rather than anything specific. In fact, could it not be ultimately very clever because mostly, when people saw homeless tramps, they didn't *want to look them in the eye.*

Again, Rick had told himself, and Tyler, that their suspect was capable of extreme cunning. He had not come here to kill Bridget Schaeffer in a blind rage or panic, even though that was how the murder scene looked. He had planned this down to the last degree and must therefore have thought about how he would stop a witness giving a good description of him. Rick shook his head, he found himself both sickened at the brutality of the murder, but admiring the killer's ingenuity, and that thought didn't sit right with him.

****

He got home close to eleven that night, feeling weary and depressed. Before he could turn the key in the lock Juliet opened the door for him. She smiled crookedly and hugged him.

"Hey, babe, you are a sight for sore eyes," he said.

"You look worn out, dinner is still warm. Do you want a beer?"

"No, I don't think so, Jules, thank you."

"Come and talk to me while I get things ready."

He leaned against the sink, and changed his mind, he needed a beer to help him get through talking about the case. He took out a can and popped it open.

"So how did you go with the psychologist?" she asked over her shoulder.

"Funny thing, Jules, but I thought it would be a complete waste of time, but I really like her, and she is smart as a whip. I had to cut it short as we now have another body, but I have permission to ask her to join the task force as a consultant."

"*Another body?*"

He told her about it all from start to finish, and she listened with rapt attention. She held up a hand to stop him at one point.

"So, wait a minute, he picked a phone box, then watched it for God knows how long, picked someone who walked by at the same time every day, then donned a disguise, made the call to you and left the box so she

139

could see him? That is unbelievable enough, but then he watched to make sure you interviewed her, and then killed her? Oh, my God Rick, that's incredible."

"I know, but then he wore another disguise so that when he left her apartment we would think he was a homeless bum."

"But why, Rick? Why go to so much trouble? And why not wear the blonde wig again?"

"That's the question I want to ask Pat tomorrow. I guess the change is because after the murder he wanted to get away unnoticed, whereas he wanted to be seen before. Patricia thinks it's because he wants to make me look like an idiot. That sometime in the past we met, and I let him down. But it just doesn't seem real enough to me, yet I can't think of another explanation that makes sense, other than some warped need for playing around in our collective heads for fun."

She stared at him across the dining table. "You knew him?"

"Well, yes, apparently. But, she says that to me it may have been inconsequential, but to him, it meant the world. I have put plenty of people in jail, but she thinks it's not that, it's more of disappointing this person. I'm buggered if I can think of anyone I've done that too, but then I've not had a lot of time to think."

"Oh, Rick, this must be terrible for you."

He smiled at her, loving her understanding, because he did feel terrible. "Not as terrible as it is for June Daniels, and it seems like it could be my fault."

She stood and walked around the table, sat straddling him on his lap, and put her hands on his shoulders. "How can it be your fault? Ever since I've known you you've tried to help people and find closure for the families of victims of murder. The first person he killed, he wasn't taunting you then, he didn't even know you would be on the case, surely?"

"How Patricia explains it is that he saw me on TV during that investigation and it awoke memories for him, *that's* when his focus shifted to me."

"So, that's why you mustn't blame yourself. He was already a killer; there was nothing you could have done about that. He is a madman, doing things for his reasons. I know you will catch him. Come to bed; let me help you feel better."

She kissed him softly at first, while his hands slipped up inside the back of her shirt. For a while, Rick did forget about the case. The silky-smooth feel of her skin, the soft little moans she always made when she was aroused and the way she responded to his touch drove the thoughts of a demented killer, from his mind.

He carried her to bed, and undressed her slowly, kissing her skin as he uncovered it. Her nipples were hard, and her fingernails sharp, as she dug them into his back when he entered her. Within minutes she climaxed, biting his shoulder, which took him over the precipice to join her.

****

In the morning, Detective Chief Inspector Colin Harris reviewed what little they had so far while standing and making notes on the huge evidence white board in the Major Incident Room. He read from his notes as he went, to the now twelve officers.

"Listen up please; let's recap where we are at. I want to remind you all that if anyone leaks the details of this investigation to the media, I will have their badge."

"Our killer is named PPP, but we have no idea what those letters stand for. We now know that he abducted Melanie Cartwright, kept her for almost a month torturing her before he cut up her body and packed the pieces in a suitcase and left it at the Midland Dump. That investigation yielded no witnesses for either the kidnapping or at the dumping site of the body. He now has June Daniels and given us limited time before he starts sending us pieces of her body. Questions?"

"How was she cut up, do we know what weapon was used?" Detective Riggs asked.

Colin nodded and pointed to the blown-up picture of the suitcase. "Good question. The Medical Examiner believes it was done neatly, with a very sharp knife or possibly a scalpel. Perhaps by someone with medical training, or at least with knowledge of anatomy. The joints had been de-boned, rather than hacksawed through. This was no frenzied murder; it was carefully thought out, planned and executed."

"Six months almost to the day later we received a call that a note had been left for us in a call box in the city about the body in the suitcase murder." He pointed to an enlarged picture of the letter. "It was addressed to Sergeant Rick McCoy who had headed up the original investigation. The note included this picture." Again, he pointed to the board.

"We canvassed people at the phone box at the same time on the following day in hopes we could find a witness to who had left the note. Rick found Bridget Schaeffer. She gave a reasonable description of the person at the right time who she only saw in profile. An arrangement was made to speak with her at home that night after work, and for a police artist to work with her. Unfortunately, someone murdered her before that could happen.

"Now, it's possible that the description could have been false, that PPP wore a form of disguise, namely a blonde wig and oversized sunglasses. He then killed her to perpetuate that incorrect description. If that theory held up it would mean he is toying with us, as a police force, and Sergeant McCoy, in particular. He then, we believe, wore a different disguise, to escape detection. This time a witness described an old man, with shuffling gate, dressed like a hobo in a long raincoat. We believe the raincoat was reversible, so he could turn it inside out and hide the blood stains."

"We are consulting with a very well-credentialed criminal psychologist, Patricia Holmes. She will be working directly with Sergeant McCoy who has operational control, reporting directly to me. Questions?"

"Why a psychologist, sir?"

"To help give us an insight into the mind of this killer. He has shown very clear planning ability, but why? Clearly, he is insane, and not like any murderer I have come across. We need to have some idea of what he might do next, because otherwise we are just playing catch-up, responding to what he does, when what we need is to try to get one step ahead of him. I ask you to give Ms. Holmes every assistance, and make her feel welcome, and a valued part of the team. Do not, and I repeat: do not hold anything back from her. If she asks anything, and the questions may seem odd, answer as well as you can. She is going to try to get inside the mind of this killer for us. She has extensive experience, having spent six months as an intern with the FBI's profiling team."

There were several mumblings. "Right, areas to focus on: we are continuing with the interviews of the people we know used the phone box. We also need to go back and re-interview people there because we now believe the killer had that call box under his own observation trying to find who he thought would make the right witness for his next victim. Someone must have seen this man, find him."

"One team is to question again people we know used the dump, another at the shopping center where the first victim was taken from, as well as the supermarket that the current victim was taken. Despite the disguises we know some things about this man we didn't know before. Have a good look at the incident board, get out and find me a witness, there's a bottle of whiskey for the best lead today. Get to it."

****

Rick and Tyler were escorted to Patricia Holmes' office at the University of Western Australia by a young student working at the administration reception. She tapped on the door and opened it wide for them to enter the rather small office, adorned with books on every ledge and shelf.

Pat stood and welcomed them, with a broad smile. She wore a red woolen V- necked jumper and black slacks, and Rick's first thought was she had the art of making ordinary cloths look exceptionally good. She held her hand out to Rick first who shook it warmly.

"Pat, this is my partner, Tyler Dundass."

"Hello, Tyler, that's a good strong name, sit down both of you."

"Good to meet you Ms. Holmes."

"Call me Pat, everyone does. So, Rick, what happened last night?"

He placed a beige manila folder on her desk between them. "As you predicted, Pat, Bridget Schaeffer was murdered before we could get her in front of an artist. Those are the crime scene photos you asked for, but I should warn you they are very graphic, and not for the faint hearted. It may be better if I give you a description."

"Thanks for the warning, but I pretty much know what I will find. A frenzied attack, I'm guessing just inside the front door. She probably died quite early, but he kept on attacking her, am I, right?"

Rick nodded. "How can you possibly know that?"

"Good question. I think I'm getting a feel for our killer, but again I must remind you I would expect to be up to twenty percent wrong while I know so little about him. If what I've thought so far is correct, then our man is a deep planner, to the point of obsession. So, he would want this killing not to resemble either Melanie or June's cases. In his mind, he would want to be diametrically opposite to those murder profiles. Also, he would want to avoid being caught while he is playing this game with you. So, it makes sense to attack her the moment she opened the door, else why would she let him inside, or why not scream blue murder, if she had a chance."

Pat reached for the folder and opened it. She visibly blanched as she looked through the photographs, but took time to study each one, before putting it down in front of her.

"You know, we psychologists love to categorize

our patients into neat little descriptive boxes like: Sociopaths, Multiple Personality Disorders, Psychopaths, Bi-Polar etcetera, but this man is not so easy to do that to. I want you to think of him as a puppeteer, with several different puppets for different situations. He only shows you the one he wants you to see, but the one you are seeing isn't the one who is behind it all. Does that make sense?"

"Not really, Ma'am, no," Tyler answered, but Rick looked at Patricia and nodded.

"Let me ask you this, Tyler. If you didn't know it was the same man who killed Melanie Cartwright, and Bridget Schaeffer would you ever consider it was one and the same, bearing in mind that both murders were planned down to the last degree?"

"No, I would think they were two different offenders."

"Right. So, he plans everything, and I mean everything, but it's all show. He killed Melanie for his own pleasure, but he wanted you to find the body, why? I think he wants fame. If he didn't want you to know about it, he would have buried her in the bush somewhere, or his back garden. So, he is a showman. Sure, there was a risk the suitcase might have gone unopened, but that would be unlikely. *Look at me, aren't I clever? Look at what I can do, and how stupid do you look when you can't stop me.* When you interview him, and possibly you already have, he will be completely believable as a witness who saw nothing. You will have no idea you just spoke to the killer, and he will be laughing his head off. I think, during this investigation you will interview him several times, and you won't know. Because the puppet he puts in front of you will be exactly what you expect to see in that circumstance."

"But why? Why go to all that trouble?"

"Why do I like skiing at Falls Creek every winter, reading Jane Austen, and eating chocolate cake? Because that is who I am. I, like him, am a product of my upbringing, and circumstances. You must understand that. I don't know what led him to get to where he is specifically, but it's the sorts of things that would send most people into depression, heavy drug use or suicide. In his case, he created this persona to protect himself from all the suffering in his formative years. You know they say that by the time a child is seven years old they are programmed for life?"

"I read that somewhere, I think," Rick answered.

"I know you would like me to give you some information to help catch him, and I've given a lot of thought to that. I've been up half the night, listening to our recording and thinking, Rick. So here is what I think is the most likely scenario, and the best advice I can give you right now: Melanie was not his first victim. What she was though, was the first time he *wanted* you to know about him. He has done many things leading up to this, and if you can find some of them, then he would have made mistakes while he was perfecting his craft. Some of the things I am talking about would have been done through anger, or because he reacted to a situation, ergo he killed. And as he did, he learned. Firstly, he learned that he liked it, and was good at it, and so after the first two or three killings, then, and only then did he start planning them. Don't misunderstand me, the earlier ones he thought out carefully and plotted, but they were for a purpose or because he reacted to a situation. The later ones were for pleasure. But, as he developed into a full-blown murdering machine, it wasn't enough. He wasn't getting the credit for them, so he evolved into what you see now, this puppeteer showing you what he wants you to see, and playing the real game of Life, and Death. He's even come up with a name for the game which he put in the note: *Catch Me if you Can.*"

Rick was fascinated, and could listen to her for hours, and never get bored, and he could tell by the thoughtful silence from Tyler, he felt the same way.

"Pat, with his early victims, how will we catch him, even if we could identify them as his work?" Rick asked.

"Because he knew them, Unlike Melanie, June and Bridget. So, if you find a couple, or more, of his early unsolved murders, and look at the acquaintances of those victims, you will find our man. And, when I say he knew them, he knew them well. I suspect he was questioned at the time and dismissed. That, and the fact that he knows you, Rick, have constructed him into who and what he is now. He wants all police to acknowledge his *greatness*, and you Rick, I believe he wants to make you look like a failure, because I get the feeling, you once failed him. It's possible, but not likely, but a slim possibility, he applied to join the police force, and was declined, or if he didn't apply, he wanted to, but knew that he would be refused. Probably by his build, being so small and slight in stature. He would be far too smart to fail any IQ, or intelligence testing.

"What you and I find horrifying, he thinks is fun. He has no conscience, feels no guilt or shame, and this is all a thrill to him. But like any addiction, he must up the dosage to feel the same thrill as he did before. So, he killed once or twice, maybe even more, because he was used, abused, threatened, or ridiculed. To those situations he reacted, as only he could, and he learned. Possibly he worried about being caught at the time, but he wasn't, and that sowed the early seeds for this game he is now playing. From here on in, for each killing he will up the ante. He wants recognition, he wants the whole world to see how clever he is, and I am sorry to say, that you, Rick, I fear will be star of his show."

Rick shuffled forward on his chair, feeling uncomfortable. "Pat, I've wracked my brain, and I can't think of any situation I've come across where I've let someone down or treated someone so badly they would want to get back at me like this. Other than locking up criminals, of course. Should we be looking at my previous arrests?"

"Look, I might be wrong about this, it may just be because you were heading up the first investigation. But that just doesn't feel right to me. If I'm on the right track with his psyche." She tapped the top of her desk with her fingernail. "If I'm right, you're thinking about this from the wrong angle. This isn't about what you did, it's about what he thinks you did, or possibly didn't do. Maybe he wanted you to do something for him, and you failed, and he never forgave you for it. You need to cast your mind back, you would have been doing your job, but think about the kind of person you may have come across. He might have been vulnerable to whatever situation he was facing. Possibly a victim of crime, rather than someone who committed one."

"So, could he have been a child when I met him? If

so, how many years are we going back if he is an adult now?"

She shrugged, "yes, it's possible he was, and he harbored that hatred for years. But it's also possible he was an adult. Either way, this has been brewing for a long while. Sometimes 'Revenge is a dish best served cold.'

"Will he attack me personally, try to kill me?"

"It's hard to know, I need more to go on. But you should take all precautions. Remember, he must up the dosage each time to get the same thrill. I think he had lost track of you, then he started killing, and found you again. He saw you on TV, and, miracle upon miracle, you were investigating him. Imagine that, from his perspective. He kills, and you are now hunting him. So, what does he do? He decides to make it personal and taunt you. It's personal, and yes, Rick, you should be very careful. You may well be his endgame, the point where it all finishes, because, once he gets even with you, what else is there to get him the same thrill from?"

"I hope he does come after me, then I can put a stop to him, permanently."

She shook her head. "Rick, you still don't get it. If, and when, he decided to make it more personal, you won't see him coming, because you will be expecting a frontal attack. That's not his style, and if you don't get that now, you may never catch him until he wants you to. He won't act, or react, as you think he will. Probably, whatever you do, he's already envisioned it and planned accordingly. When he does something, he has already allowed for your reaction, and has a contingency for it. Your best chance of stopping him is through his footprints. Whatever led him to this state, he left his mark. You need to find those footprints in the sand, and look at all of the suspects again, he is there, trust me."

"I had an idea, before this latest victim, and the DI and the commissioner thought I needed to run it by you and get your thoughts."

"Oh, I do hope you are not going to say what I think you are."

"What do you think I will say?"

"You're going to use the media to try to talk to him, taunt him back." She looked at him with one eyebrow raised, a particularly sexy look, he thought.

He shook his head, knowing that his idea was not going to go down well. "Yes, well, kind of. I thought I would go to the media and plea for help. Say that there was new evidence in the body in the suitcase murder, that a witness had come forward. Then I was going to give a description of him with what we now have, and a vehicle. How did you know that was my idea?"

"Oh, let's just call it a hunch." She smiled. "It's what I would expect someone of your experience and dedication to do. Do you know his vehicle?"

"No, I was going to pick one that we know was there that day but the owner of it did not come forward. You see, we narrowed the time frame down by talking to people who didn't see the case at the dump, and those who did. The van is a possibility, but we have no idea of the make, model, or license plate. My thinking was that if it was him, he might worry, and respond, and my doing so could make a mistake. And it if wasn't his car, then he would want to gloat about us being wrong, and so still might make a mistake."

She sat back in her chair and tented her finger tips.

She stayed silent for a minute and Rick could almost hear the cogs of her mind turning as she examined the idea from every angle.

"Rick, I think it's a very good idea, and credit to you for thinking abstractly. But, I feel like I must caution you. There is no way to tell what effect it may have on him, and therefore, what he may do in retaliation. One things for sure, it will make him sit up and take notice. Here is my suggestion, don't announce it; he may see through that. Have it leaked, and don't be specific about the vehicle, just say you now know what vehicle he used. Say you have a good description of it and the driver. Let a friendly reporter think you are closing in, and don't talk about this case. Make him worry, make him wonder why you've not gone public to find the missing woman, or track him down. Please though, just remember that once you start the snowball down this mountain, there is no telling where it will stop, or how big it will be when it does."

Tyler leaned forward in his seat, "could it make him kill June Daniels and head for the hills?" he asked.

She turned her gaze to Tyler and shrugged once more. "Tyler, that is an awfully good question, and one I am not one hundred percent sure of the answer to. My instincts tell me she will be dead before you get to him anyway, because it's going to take time to track him through past case files. If so, what will he do then? I don't think he will run away; that would not be true to the profile I have of him. This type of murderer, generally, will do one of three things, in a situation where he knows you are closing in."

She held up her fingers and touched them as she counted down. "One: commit suicide once he has taken as many with him as he can. Two: permit you to capture him, or even hand himself in for the infamy it will attract. Three, attempt to kill Rick and go out in a blaze of glory."

"Pat, would you like to join the task force that been set up, have a look at the evidence as it comes to hand, actually be involved in tracking him down." Rick asked, hoping she would agree.

"What, you mean like a deputy; me?"

"Well, we were thinking more as a consultant, or advisor."

"Personally, I'd like nothing more, but there are some complications; I don't think it would be such a good idea to be on the front line."

"We need you, Pat. Why do you think it's not a good idea?"

"You can come and see me any time, for a chat, I'd love to help. But, sooner or later the press would get wind of my involvement if I worked with you at the station. Then you'd be ridiculed, sadly we do not live in an enlightened age in Australia where psychologists are valued in an investigative role. That would play right into our man's hands. Plus, I'm not sure he would take kindly to a psychologist working on the case, he would see that as an insult to his intellect, and that could be very disadvantageous to his prisoner. Whatever you do, don't let him think that you think he is insane; to him he is the sane one. Let's just leave things as they are, with me in the background for now."

****

Later that night, after Amy was in bed, and they had eaten dinner, Rick knew he had to talk to Juliet about the case, and one aspect more than anything else.

"Jules, I need to talk to you about something that has been bothering me." He patted the seat alongside him on the couch for her to sit.

Juliet had finished tidying the kitchen after dinner and was rubbing moisturizer into her hands. "This sounds ominous, what's it all about coach?" she asked, with a wary note in her voice.

"It's been in the back of my mind ever since Pat told me that at some time PPP's and my path crossed. She has reiterated today that's her belief. As you know, she thinks I've done wrong by him, possibly a long time ago. But, for the life of me I can't think of a situation I've been responsible for harming anyone, physically or mentally."

She sat down next to him, smoothing her pink skirt underneath her thighs as she did. "Go on, this is sounding more and more like bad news."

He shook his head, emphatically, "no, not bad news, more being prudent. I guess there are two issues that bother me. First and foremost is your and Amy's safety. You asked me the other day if I thought PPP knew where I lived, at the time I said no, I couldn't see how he could. But one thing has become clear since Pat became involved; she believes this man is seriously into long-term planning. So, I'm wondering if somehow he *does* know where I live. If he does, then he knows you and Amy are here. For your safety, I think you should move in with your mum and dad for a bit."

She stared back, and he couldn't hold her gaze. "Go on, what's the second thing?"

"You'll think me stupid, but, if that was the case, I should stay here alone, in hopes he comes for me, so I can put a stop to him abducting any more women."

"Why you, Rick, exactly why do you have to be the bait?"

"Sweetheart, I didn't choose this role, and I certainly wouldn't volunteer for it. It's him that's picked me for some obscure misdemeanor I've been guilty of. But it does make sense to move you and Amy to safety, and then for me to lure him into the open because he thinks I'm alone."

"He's made no direct threats though, has he?"

"Nope, nothing. But, he didn't threaten the women he abducted either. He is a sociopath, and if he makes the decision to come after me, and you are here, he won't hesitate to hurt you." He raised his hand and put it on her shoulder. You and Amy are everything to me. I love you, I would feel a lot happier if you stayed with your parents, if only for a week or two, just till we catch him."

She turned in her seat, dislodging his hand so he dropped it to her hip. "But, what if you don't catch him for months? I can't stay away forever. And it would be a dreadful imposition on Mum and Dad, especially now Amy has a puppy. I wouldn't want to be in your shoes if you told Amy the dog stays here, and she moves out; they are inseparable."

He grinned and nodded. He hadn't thought that far ahead, Minty would be an added problem, and it would be a long drawn out screaming match if he tried to separate them. "You're right Jules, I hadn't thought of that. But, I am worried for your safety. Could you at least run it past your parents, and see what they think?"

"No, I won't. You know as well as I do, Mum would say yes in a heartbeat, and then all the comments would start all over again about you and Angie, and how I shouldn't have taken you back. I know things have been brilliant with us, and I've told her that repeatedly. But this would open all those old wounds all over again. No, wait, don't interrupt, please, let me finish." She paused, just for a moment to gather her thoughts. "I love you for thinking of us and worrying. I love that you want to keep us safe, and if there was a threat made, fine, I would move out. But there has been no hint of that. A little while ago, I was a basket case of fear over the Y2K bug thing. For the life of me I don't understand that; as you said it was like a phobia. But this is different, and I am not scared. This is my home, and I will be buggered if I'm going to give it up over this maniac when he hasn't made any threats."

Rick knew her well enough to know her mind was made up, and there was little point in pursuing it further. "You're one tough lady, aren't you? Just promise me you will take all precautions when I'm not here, keep doors locked, don't let anyone in the house, for any reason. Oh, and watch yourself when you go to the shops, he seems to be grabbing his targets there."

"Aye, aye, sir." She gave a mock salute. "Did you want to take me to bed now and make love to me, or watch a movie first?"

Chapter 10: My Memoir Entry
Step into My Parlor

I didn't rush the next killing. I wanted to savor every morsel, like eating the finest steak. At the back of my mind constantly was how disappointed I was when I finally saw Carly's body, so I counselled myself against having higher expectations than could be delivered.

It had to be *right* this time. No hurried stabbing under a willow tree, no, I wanted it drawn out. I began to realize, that was going to be the best part—enjoying their suffering and fear, *before* their death.

I enjoyed thinking about it; planning how it would happen, and so on. It was at first as good as I imagined how the real thing would be. So, for a long time, knowing I was going to embark on the journey was enough. We are all creatures of fantasy, I think.

First job had to be setting up the right environment. I had decided to use the rear garden entry to bring victims in through the house to the cool room. It was at the end of a long laneway with high-galvanized iron sheets down both sides for fencing, so it would give me the privacy I needed. No nosy neighbors to spoil the party. To that end I spent a Sunday afternoon oiling and cleaning off the rust from the hinges, making sure that the gate opened quietly. I created a parking space alongside the back shed where I had found the two bodies. In my mind's eye, I could see myself driving in through the gate, parking by the shed, then calmly locking the gate. Inside the car she would be cowering, handcuffed, and gagged.

Those thoughts led me to consider my car. Was it suitable for transporting a prisoner? I realized it was not. Even crammed into the boot area she could kick and make noises, which, if stopped at a traffic light, or something, could be embarrassing. It had to go, but what *would* be suitable? It came to me late one night, while going through a McDonalds drive through when I saw in front of me a courier's van. Instantly I had a mental image of four sets of handcuffs positioned against the pillars of the cargo area so that a person would be spread-eagled. Then with a ball gag in place and perhaps an old rug thrown over her, she would be virtually invisible, and best of all, silent. Yes, I had decided my victim would be female. I had never had sex with one, but I knew I hadn't enjoyed it with men. It was a no-brainer.

Once I had made up my mind, I saw those types of vehicles everywhere, and that added to the appeal; anonymity. I would look like any other delivery driver. Where to buy one from that would ensure I couldn't later be identified was the next question to be considered. It was then that I made my plans when the idea hit me, late one night watching a horror film. I would buy the van in a private sale, wait three or four weeks, and then kill the previous owner. No sense leaving a witness who could identify me. I would make it look like an unrelated attack like a burglary gone wrong.

It took two weeks, but I found the perfect buy. The owner, Mr. Joel Ringwood, had resigned as a sub contract courier when his wife got cancer and died. He seemed a broken man when I visited him one Sunday morning to inspect the van he had advertised in the paper. He was in his mid to late fifties by the look of him, and not too much bigger than myself. I thought, as we were chatting away, that I would be doing him a favor.

We agreed on six and a half thousand dollars, and I paid him in cash, that way the money couldn't be traced. I had been hiding in an old shoe box a good part of my weekly wage, in notes for quite a while. Well, you must understand my needs were minimal. The house was paid for, so there were few bills to meet, just a few horror movies I hired each week, and my meals.

The van showed signs of wear and tear but there was nothing ugly to make it memorable. It was the obligatory white color, and as I drove it away I thanked my lucky stars that it had recently been re-registered for twelve months, meaning I could put off transferring it into my name for as long as possible. He wrote me out a receipt in his extremely neat handwriting, and we shook hands before I drove off.

Patience is a virtue they say, and I watched my target on and off over the next several days and learned his habits. I had made the decision to make his death look like a robbery gone wrong, but I wanted to make sure no family members came to stay with him. Seventeen nights later, I broke in through a downstairs window using washing off the line to muffle the sound of breaking glass. Once inside I deliberately made a noise he would hear and waited in the shadows of the staircase for him to come down to investigate.

It was so ridiculously simple. It was as if I had

written the script and he followed his part exactly. He walked past me on the way to the lounge room and I stepped up from behind, clamped a hand over his mouth and yanked my freshly sharpened boning knife across his throat.

There was a lot of blood, and it was fantastic to watch it squirt out. He didn't struggle. The genius of killing him that way, was that all his blood flow was directed away from me. I had worn gloves, as I knew a good burglar would, and once I was sure he was dead, I ransacked the house at my leisure; in no rush, whatsoever.

I came across the money I had given him, still in an envelope, tucked into his bedside drawer. I had to stifle my own nervous laughter for fear of becoming hysterical as I tucked it into my pocket. There was also bits and pieces of old jewelry, a mobile phone, and some other junk I had no interest in, but took to complete the picture. I crept away into the night, knowing that even if the van became suspect in the future, it would now be a dead end back to me. But, as I was driving home I realized that would be a mistake.

We had signed a transfer of ownership form and he may have lodged his part. I hadn't found it when I had searched, so once the cops knew his vehicle was missing they would track me down through that form and wonder why I hadn't completed my part and paid the stupid government fees. As I now had my money back, I decided I would transfer it the next morning. I would probably be interviewed as part of the investigation, but that would add to the fun. I might need a reason for buying it, and if so I would say I was considering opening the butcher shop again and needed a van to carry home deliveries. Yes, I thought, that would work nicely.

It made the papers, naturally. There was a sympathetic outcry: how could some callous thief murder a man who had just lost his wife to cancer? It took two weeks to find the body, and only then by a neighbor. No family had come to visit the poor old bugger. I had a good chuckle at the media's indignation. I couldn't help myself, I wrote a three-paragraph letter to the editor joining in with the general flow of comments saying that jail was too good for such a scumbag. I signed it 'An Outraged Citizen' and I laughed until I had tears rolling down my face. The idiots published it.

Three days later, around seven in the evening, I had just finished my dinner of fish and chips when there was a knocking on the door. Call it a premonition if you will, but I was completely unused to visitors, so I knew who it was. I smiled to myself as I went to the door.

"Mr. Rankin? I'm Detective Constable Whitaker, could I have a word please?"

I looked at his ID and shrugged. "Sure, how can I help?"

"It might be better inside, Sir."

"Oh, of course, sorry, I'm not used to the police knocking on my door at night. Come through this way."

I led him to the lounge and sat on an armchair, while he sat on the couch. Knowing I would be visited, I had tidied up, even vacuumed and dusted the week before. I sat quietly, waiting for him to tell me why he was there, though of course I knew. Dear reader, I cannot describe how much fun I was having.

"I believe you are the owner of a Mazda van,

registration number 1AET 165, may I ask how you came by it?"

"Why, what's wrong with it? Don't tell me its stolen?"

"Please answer the question, Mr. Rankin."

"I bought it as a private sale about a month ago, from an old bloke who had retired from courier work as his wife had just died."

"What was his name, and how did you pay for the vehicle?"

"Joel something or other, Ringbark? Something like that. He asked me for cash, and I obliged him. Six and a half thousand."

"Mr. Rankin, Joel Ringwood has been murdered, his van is missing, and he never banked that money. I'm sorry to say it's missing, which doesn't look too good for you."

"What? He was such a nice man. What do you mean it doesn't look good for me? You think I killed him to steal his van, and was dumb enough to transfer it into my name?" I stood up, went to my chest of drawers, and ferreted around inside, all for show of course. I walked back to him and held out the handwritten receipt. "Ask his family if that's his handwriting. I value human life at a bit higher than a second-hand vehicle." I had to hold back a chuckle at that last bit.

He stared at it for a moment and made notes in his book. "Why did it take so long for you to transfer ownership?"

"Because I work for a living and had to wait until my next rostered day off. Do you know how long it takes to go and stand in the queue at the Department of

Transport? He was a nice old man, I felt very sorry for him, that's why I didn't haggle too much on the price."

Of course, he swallowed it, hook, line, and sinker. I wondered if all police were that dumb, *probably*.

****

The ringbolts had been secured to the wall in the cool room, the rear gates opened quietly, and handcuffs and mattress had been installed in the van. All I needed, was a victim to play with. I was ready, and experienced a nervous excitement continually in the pit of my stomach. It was edging ever closer; I could almost taste it.

Like most things in life, when it happened, it was quite unexpected. I was at home after work, I had had my dinner which that night had been in memory of my father: polony and tomato sauce sandwiches, but, the polony was *really* thick; almost like slabs, and I permitted myself a second one. My favorite TV show had just finished, *NYPD Blue*, and I fancied a cup of tea. I learned a lot from watching crime shows on TV. Anyway, I went to make my cuppa, and found the milk had gone off. *Damn and bugger It,* I remember thinking, which was as close to swearing as I ever came. I looked up at the clock; it was eight twenty, and the local supermarket shut at nine. There was nothing for it, I had to go and get some milk.

The Ford had long since gone, I had sold it a few weeks prior, and so, I took the van. I was even whistling the theme music from NYPD and every now and again would say 'let's be careful out there' in the voice of the station Sergeant. I pulled up in the car park alongside a station wagon which had just parked too. I looked in the back, not being nosy, I promise, I just happened to look, as you do, and there was a suitcase. Next thing a woman got out of the driver's side and hurried off toward the glass doors of the shops.

My blood chilled in my veins. The bloody woman was running away, probably leaving a four-year-old in her haste to escape, just like I had always thought my mother had. Right then I knew she was the one.

I had planned for this time in my mind a hundred times, maybe even a thousand. Everything was in place, and I felt remarkably calm. I got into the back of the van, clutching the tire iron in my hand, and waited for her to return. The minutes dragged by, until eventually I heard her high heels click clacking toward us. When I heard, her trying to open her door, I flung mine open wide.

Time appeared to slow down for me, and I saw everything crystal clear. She jumped in shock at the noise of the sliding door crashing open and dropped her bag of shopping. I heard glass break as it hit the ground. I hit her over the head with the wheel spanner and distinctly heard the 'thunk' sound as it connected through her thick hair. She fell, right into my arms, and, like a ballet dancer pirouetting, and I used her momentum to half drag, half carry her inside the cargo area of my vehicle. Once I dropped her top half inside I then lifted her legs, climbed in behind her and closed the sliding door again.

Went like clockwork I recall saying to myself. I handcuffed her feet and hands with the cuffs I had purchased some time before from the Army, Navy, and Police Surplus store on William street in the city. Next, I slid the elastic over her head and positioned the red ball of the gag in her mouth. I had purchased that from a disgusting sex shop with a lurid display in the window and I had hated every moment I spent in the awful place. I needed a gag, though, and I couldn't think where else I could buy one from.

I gazed down at my handiwork. She wasn't an unattractive woman. I would guess her age was in her early thirties, probably about the same age as my mother had been when she took off. She had long black hair and a trickle of blood ran down her forehead. I couldn't help myself and I know I shouldn't have, but I felt her breasts, which was a first for me, and I quite enjoyed the experience.

I was giving them a good squeeze when she stirred. I leaned over her and licked the trickle of blood away. I had often wondered what someone else's blood tasted like and of recent times it had featured in some of the dreams I still enjoyed. That was when she freaked out for the first time, but I knew it wasn't going to be the last.

I had spent many long hours working out how and when things would progress, and I am pleased to report it all went as well as I had imagined. At home, I parked inside the back garden. Then, with the gate shut, I hopped into the back of the van with her, and with glee saw her trembling trussed up like a hog, looking for any chance to escape.

I took out my boning knife and pressed the tip to her lily-white throat. "Shush, shush, Angel. Now listen carefully. Like everyone does in life you have two choices, are you listening?"

The poor thing blinked her eyes rapidly and nodded. "Okay, first choice you come meekly inside and have some fun with me, then I blindfold you so you don't know where you are and take you back to your car. Second choice, I kill you and bury your body in my garden. What's it going to be? Oh, blink once for the first option, and twice for the second."

I thought, this was what I was born for. I had given her some hope, and she had jumped at it. Of course, she blinked once, but I knew she would look for any chance to run.

I undid one handcuff from the side of the van, reached over her and joined it to the one on her other wrist. I giggled, just a little; she did not look comfy at all in that position, but I could hardly let her hands free while I undid her feet so she could hit me over the back of the head. Next, I unclasped her feet, then, holding the knife to her throat again I freed her last captive hand leaving them manacled together in front of her.

"Now, we are going inside, remember be good, and play nice and I will take you back to your car. Try to run and you die."

Ok, I was lying, so shoot me. I held onto the connecting chain on the cuffs and helped guide her out of the van, knife at the ready. "Oh, by the way, if you scream you die too, did I forget to mention that?"

The garden was pitch black as we walked to the kitchen door, but I knew the way. My heart was crashing in my chest. It did take a little dexterity to unlock the door, hold the knife and handcuff chain and I did sense her stiffen as she intended to make a run for it. Once I showed her how sharp my knife was by touching her arm with the blade though, she stopped.

She began to realize, I think, things were not going to end well for her when we walked through the old butcher shop and into the cool room, but by then it was too late, and she knew it.

"Please don't hurt me, I will do what you want," was the first thing she said when I took off her gag.

Looking back now, at that time of night without the main lights on, it did look eerie, almost reminiscent of the horror movies I watched. She began to moan and sob as I undid the cuffs and re-chained her to the eye bolts in the wall, then stepped back to look at my captive.

Quite calmly I went and closed the huge thick vault-like door, and switched the overhead lights on, *all the better to see you with, my dear* I thought. Then, very slowly, enjoying every moment, I undressed. This was going to be my first time with a woman, and I wanted to make it special for both of us. Plus, I didn't want to get her blood on my clothes.

"So," I said when I was ready, "you are running away, abandoning your children? Tsk, Tsk, Tsk."

She denied it, as I knew she would. But I realized that that was all just part of the game. I used the knife to cut all her clothes off, then stepped back again for a good look. *Oh, yes, much nicer than Carly.*

I've been told by people who have gone away for a long holiday, that when they return, no matter how good a trip they have had, they feel wonderful when they get home. That was how I felt that night, making her suffer: as if I had come home, at long last.

Chapter 11:
Cut and Thrust

Excerpt from the front page of The West Australian Newspaper May 16th 2000

BREAKTHROUGH IN BODY IN SUITCASE MURDER?

By Crime Reporter Simon Rollins.

Police are tight lipped and angry about the leak from police headquarters regarding the grisly 'Body in the Suitcase' murder breakthrough. A senior well informed source has told this reporter they have had a surprise witness come forward and describe in detail both the driver and vehicle used that left the suitcase at the Midland Refuse Center. The secret witness has been away overseas and only recently returned and is believed to be credible.

When pressed for a response, Sergeant Richard McCoy, who has been with the case from the beginning became angry and would only repeat "no comment," before walking away. Sergeant McCoy has been criticized for the lack of an arrest in the brutal murder of Melanie Cartwright. Insiders say he could have been demoted because of his handling of the case but with the latest development and a possible imminent arrest he could be looking at a promotion.

****

"McCoy." Rick distractedly said his name into his desk phone while sitting reading a report.

"Oh, Rick, I've just read the paper and its brilliant. I especially like the part saying you could be up for a promotion; that is going to drive him bananas," Patricia Holmes said, breathlessly.

"It already has, he's sent a parcel with a finger in it, and another note to me."

"How did he send it this time?"

"Oh, just through the mail, post marked in the city."

"That's a relief, and it's good news, in a way."

"Not for the victim it's not Pat."

"Well, no, sorry. I didn't mean to sound flippant, but she is most likely dead already, you know that, don't you? And if she is alive, you are not likely to get to her in time. No, I meant it's good news because he must have sent it *before* the news story hit the streets. It's unrelated, he was sending it to you anyway."

"The M.E. is sure it was removed while she was alive."

The silence hung in the air between them as each imagined the horror of having a finger removed while awake. "Rick, as hard as I know this must be, especially for you, you must try to take the emotion out of this, it's playing right into his hands.

"Yeah, I guess."

"He is a narcissist. It's all about him, and him being on top of the heap looking down on you. To fight him you must be up there on his level, not down in the dumps about the victim. I think he is going to contact you, directly, possibly quite soon. I don't know how or when, but if he buys the story in the paper he could worry that things will come to an end before he wanted them to. Do you have a witness who saw him at the dump, do you know the car he used, are you about to knock on his door with a search warrant? Oh, and he will also be annoyed you've not gone to the press to announce his latest victim."

"Yep, he is annoyed about that all right." Ricks fingers drummed on the desk in anger and frustration. "The note I mentioned? If we don't go to the press about him, he will send us her leg, up to the knee, then her arm up to the elbow. He has upped the ante; he was threatening one piece of her every few days, now it's one a day until we acknowledge he has her."

"I was afraid of that. I understand why you wanted it secret, but he was never going to stand for that, I'm afraid. He wants his time in the sun. But, by doing it now, all it's going to do is buy time. He is still going to send you her leg next regardless."

"I know, that's what is really getting to me, no matter what we do, she is doomed." He looked down at his hand; his knuckles were still bruised from where he had punched the desk in anger and frustration when the finger had been unwrapped.

"Unless you catch him first. How are you going looking at old cases?"

"We are looking at narrowing the list down, the parameters were very wide. We started with all unsolved assaults, violent home invasions, sexual attacks and of course murders going back five years. There are a lot of them to wade through."

"Not to burden you further, I'd also look at cruelty

to animals. Often it is where this type of personality disorder starts. Knowing what you now know though, those will be easy to spot, I think. They will be cut up, not beaten or kicked; it will be more like a dissection. And if you find any of those, they will be near where he lives, works, or went to school. They will be opportunistic, rather than planned."

"Okay, Pat I will get those looked at too. Can I see you this evening, and bring you any files that look promising?"

"Yes, but we are going out for dinner, so bring them between say, five and five-thirty. It takes an old broad like me a long time to get ready these days."

"You're kidding, right? I think you look good wearing anything."

"Why Rick, are you flirting with me?"

"No Ma'am, I'm just stating the facts. I will see you later, I must go and meet with your old buddy Monkton, and brief him, he is holding a press conference later. They have decided to not let me be in front of the cameras, in case it antagonizes our man further."

"Oh, no, don't let him do that, he has to see you there, Rick. I'm sorry but he wants to see you suffer, and if you don't let him see that, then I shudder to think what he will do next to make sure you're there. Let Darryl hold center stage, but you must be there, looking suitably chastised, and defeated."

"But won't that conflict with the leak about the suitcase and the possibility of an arrest?"

"Yes, it will, and that's what's so beautiful about this, it will contradict, and he cannot possibly have foreseen this development. You not talking about the lead will intrigue him, especially looking so crestfallen at the press conference. Do you see what I mean?"

"I suppose."

"Think of it this way, he is the ultimate planner. He thinks about things and imagines scenarios and comes up with contingencies. Suddenly in the space of one day, he will worry he has lost control. It could mean the end for his captive, but it could make him rise to the challenge, make him do something he hasn't spent weeks planning, and then, if he does, you might catch him out. How are your acting skills?"

'I once played a tree in a primary school Christmas play. Mum said I was very convincing, why?"

Because you are bound to be questioned about the leak, and he will be watching you very closely. What I think you should say is that you cannot and will not talk about operational matters, but make it sound like you are about to knock on his door any time soon. Make him think you are genuine, make him come to you."

****

The press conference was scheduled for three o'clock, so there would be enough time to make the six pm news broadcasts. At one-thirty the team, now totaling twenty officers of both plain clothes and uniform, gathered in the incident room for a briefing. Assistant Commissioner Monkton was there waiting as they all took their seats.

As usual Colin Harris held center stage. His tie was loosened, collar undone, and sweat stained. His hair looked clumped and he needed a shave. Detectives who had worked with him before saw all the signs, simmering below the surface, of a man who was about to lose his temper. No one wanted to be the one he would turn his erupting Mt Vesuvius-like rage on.

"Listen up everyone. There have been some developments in the case and we need to ensure we are all up to speed on what's going on. Thank you all for your individual reports to me. What I want to do is share those reports with the rest of the team, so we are all going in the same direction. You all know of the assistant commissioner who is giving us the benefit of his experience and overseeing the case because of its complexity, and seriousness."

Monkton nodded to the group and sat on the edge of a desk. Thin and gaunt, he looked seriously aloof, if not disdainful.

"Okay, make sure you note any new developments on the incident board and check it often to see if someone else has made a comment which you may have some impact on. I'm pissed off majorly at the lack of headway we are making. Things have taken a turn for the worse. We have had another note from our killer, again addressed to Detective Sergeant McCoy. For those who don't know it, it is thought possible sometime in the past, the two have met, and the killer holds Rick responsible for some real or imagined harm. I want to stress there is no implication of any wrongdoing, we have the utmost confidence in Rick's integrity and professionalism over the twenty years he has been on the force."

Everyone nodded their agreement, signifying that those that had had previous dealings with Rick attested to his high standards as a police officer.

"The note, which accompanied a human finger, which the ME informs us was removed while the person was alive, tells us he is angry that he has not been given credit in the media for the abduction of June Daniels. He wants the world to know of his threats to dismember her slowly over time if we don't catch him first. He has threatened to speed up the process from a dispatch of a body part every couple of days, to a daily one, all the time we do not notify the public. If he is going to use the mail system, then she is due to lose a part of her body today." He paused for effect.

One of the detectives held up his arm to ask a question: "Why would he want that? Most people try to get away with crime, not be in the spotlight."

"Graham that's a good question, and one not easily answered. As you all know we have asked a very well credentialed Criminal Psychologist, named Patricia Holmes, to consult with us. Clearly this offender has some serious mental health issues. She has agreed to provide some limited help though she thinks it best to be in the background giving advice rather than on the frontline with us. Suffice to say she has given us some very helpful insights and a possible line of inquiry, which I will come to. It's important though, she insists, that her involvement in this case remains secret so as not to enrage the killer, does everyone understand?"

Everyone nodded so he continued: "I'm not familiar with all the technical mumbo jumbo, but I do know that she knows her stuff. She says the man we are dealing with is a narcissistic, sociopathic killer capable of complex thought processes allowing him to strategically plan his moves. He has some sort of God complex. At the same time, she believes, he wants to drag Rick McCoy through the gutter. Mr. Monkton and I have decided for the victim's sake; we must agree with his wishes to buy as much time as possible to save her. We have a press conference at three pm."

"Other areas of investigation are not going as well as we had hoped. Re-interviews are progressing with as much as we know about the killer, being small and diminutive. So far we are drawing blanks everywhere. This man is like a chameleon, he blends in with his surroundings and no one remembers him, unless he wants them to."

Graham held up his arm again and the DI nodded for him to speak up. "What's the story behind this leak that we have and the new witness?"

"There is no witness. And the leak was created by myself. Rick came up with the idea to his credit, and Patricia Holmes was in full accord that it may put our killer off his stride. For this reason, you must all, and I repeat YOU MUST ALL be on your guard. Now we have put this story out into the media, we must make it believable. No one can let it slip that it was a hoax. When asked, your response will be that you cannot comment on operational matters, this is a serious murder investigation and we are closing in on a suspect. That is all you are permitted to comment do I make myself clear?"

Everyone agreed. Another detective, Clive Peppercorn held up his arm and got the nod to speak up. "Sir, you mentioned earlier that our shrink has given a line of inquiry?"

"The use of the word shrink I find disrespectful, detective," Assistant Commissioner Monkton interrupted.

"Sorry sir, I didn't mean it to sound that way."

"Rick, why don't you take the floor and explain about this," the DCI said, taking control back. It showed to everyone in the room, the eruption was creeping ever closer.

Rick stood and walked to the incident board. He clasped his hands together in front of him and cleared his throat. "Firstly, if I can, guys, I want to agree with Mr. Monkton. Before I met with Patricia Holmes, I thought they were all shrinks, and bleeding heart liberals, who wanted to get violent offenders out of jail and into hospitals. But, can I tell you I find Mrs. Holmes to be extremely helpful and insightful? Let's not forget, that just by listening to me about him, she predicted the witness, Bridget Schaeffer, would be murdered, and that the description we had of him was fake. Her understanding of the type of person we are hunting I find not much short of incredible, so please, do not call her a shrink, or anything demeaning in front of me. I don't want to get bogged down in this, just don't do it, okay?"

The murmurs of assent traveled around the group, and Rick thought he had made his point. "Right, what Pat says, is that this man did not suddenly come to who and what he is now, he evolved." He spent the next few minutes explaining the profile, scant though it was, she had provided him, watching the faces of the officers. He wanted to try to pick the ones who would be supportive of the radical step of bringing in a psychologist, and those who would be against it.

"We thought that Melanie Cartwright, was his first murder. Patricia says it most definitely was not, it was just the first one that he wanted us to know about. She says that that is how we will catch him. That he killed others where he did not use the same level of planning. Not only that, but those victims he would have known.

If we can find, as she calls it, his foot prints in the sand, we will catch him by looking at the victim's acquaintances. We are currently pulling files and looking again at unsolved violent crimes, and murders. We are also looking at extreme cruelty to animal cases, because she says this type of personality often starts on domestic cats and dogs. She adds that if we do find any that he did, they will be close to where he lived, worked, or went to school."

"So far I have pulled about thirty files, where the victim has been attacked with a knife. Clearly he isn't responsible for all of them, but each need to be re-examined and hopefully find something that may point to our man. In the months that I've been working this case, I feel that this is the closest we've come, the next couple of days could be critical if we are going to save June Daniel's life, it must be now. Another avenue to investigate are the wigs. We are putting a team of detectives onto every wig reseller in Perth. We know he has used at least two, one blonde, one gray, possibly it's a way we can track him down."

****

The press conference started on time. In front of over a dozen reporters, TV cameramen and radio journalists was a desk where the three police officers, led by the assistant commissioner, sat. Above them was the Western Australian Police logo and a phone number.

"Thank you all for coming, I am Detective Chief Inspector Colin Harris. This is a very serious situation we find ourselves in, and we are pleading for the public's help to find a very dangerous offender. We have prepared a handout folder with maps and locations, to which I will be alluding where offences occurred. We can now confirm that all of the events we will be describing today have been committed by the same man, who would like us to call him PPP."

"Everyone is aware of the abduction and one month later the murder of Melanie Cartwright, and the subsequent dumping of her body inside a suitcase left at the Midland Refuse Tip last year. Naturally we investigated thoroughly the possibility it was someone in her acquaintance, but we now believe her attacker was not known to her."

"Is this because of the mystery witness that has come forward?"

"The commissioner shook his head. Please keep your questions until the end, but even then, we will not answer on matters of procedure, obviously. We must be mindful of the safety of any witness who comes forward, and secondly we don't want to give too much information to the murderer, do we?"

There were some mumblings, not all of which sounded supportive but before any further questions could be raised, the commissioner interjected. "Eight days ago, Mrs. June Daniels was abducted from outside the supermarket shown on map two in your handout; we can now announce this abduction was carried out by the same man. He is currently holding her captive." He paused.

"Four days ago, we received an anonymous phone call from a call box at the location marked on map number three in the pack. We have also marked all relevant times on that handout so we don't get bogged down here. A note was left for us at that call box addressed to the head of the Melanie Cartwright investigation, Sergeant Richard McCoy. The note says that PPP has Mrs. Cartwright as his prisoner and he challenged the police to capture him before he murders her. He has threatened to send us a piece of her body every few days that he remains free."

Every reporter exploded at once shouting questions. Predominantly they wanting to know why it had taken four days to make the announcement. Monkton nodded to the DCI to take over. He raised his arms up and held his hands out to plead for silence and waited impatiently for it.

"If you people cannot calm down, we can call a halt to this now. This is not a circus, it's a murder investigation." He couldn't conceal the quivering of his voice, and the barely controlled temper that he was struggling to contain.

"I can tell you we get crack pots confessing to crimes, and crank calls every single day, and if we came to you with all of them, you would soon get fed up. So far as we knew, it was just an anonymous call and note with no supporting evidence. We investigated it and came up with a list of missing persons that *could* be relevant. The man had sent us a picture, which could have been fake, of a woman, but her face was obscured making identification impossible. We must be mindful of families of missing persons and we do not want to spread panic. Until we had solid evidence and an identity, it would have been foolhardy to have gone to the press."

The general mumblings of the crowd appeared to Rick to be understanding, where before they had been outraged. But, he wondered how understanding they would be soon, with the news to come.

"During the investigation we found a witness, Bridget Schaeffer, who gave a description of a man leaving the phone box at approximately the right time. The man was of slight build, wearing thick rimmed glasses, and thick blonde hair. Unfortunately, she was killed in an apparent home invasion that night, before we could get an identikit picture of the suspect. Investigations are continuing into her death. Today we had a new development, a parcel arrived, with a note, and a human finger inside it. We do not have DNA results yet, but we have matched the blood type and believe it to have belonged to June Daniels. The note is signed PPP, and he has threatened to send a piece of her body each day unless we acknowledge him in the media as being her abductor, and the murderer of Melanie Cartwright."

There was suddenly a cacophony of noise, and there was little point in answering questions until it died down. Eventually, like a bush fire, it burnt itself out. Colin Harris shook his head and visibly took a long slow deep breath. Then he began again.

"Ladies and gentlemen, this man, is playing the game of his life. He is a very clever, intelligent man, who has no morals, scruples, or conscience. He wants the adoration of an audience to show us all just how clever he is. We need witnesses, and we need them fast if we are to have any hope of saving June Daniels. We have several good lines of investigation which we are following, and naturally I cannot go into them. But we need more. We need anyone who saw anything, no matter how small, or that they think is inconsequential, to come forward, which is why we need your help here today."

"Our thoughts and prayers are with June Daniels, and her family. We hope for the public's help to save her, before it's too late. We will take questions, but I warn you there are elements we will not discuss." He sat down, abruptly, and taking a handkerchief from his jacket pocket wiped the sweat which had beaded on his forehead.

An overweight man, wearing an orange open necked shirt, stood up to the rear of the group, with his arm held high to gain extra attention. "Sergeant McCoy, Jim Nichols for Channel Nine News, you've been strangely silent, what's your take on all this?"

Rick stiffened, he had been dreading being singled out, but at the same time, he had wanted the chance to speak directly to the killer. He slowly stood to his imposing full height. "What's my take? What's my take on a man who is so low as to prey on defenseless women because he is such a weakling he can't take on a man? He thinks he is clever, plotting and planning, but it's not intelligent to terrorize a woman and cut her into pieces, it's juvenile. Clearly he has never grown up. He is still the scared little boy who has been through a tragic life, and I feel sorry for him. But he lost any sympathy I could have had when he started murdering defenseless women."

"Why do you think he is doing it?"

"Why? Because he likes it. It makes him feel important, to be in control. I think in his normal life; he is scared and far from that; a weak insignificant little man. He's a bit like a wannabe super hero, he puts on a cape, and it makes himself feel special. But a murdering sadistic control freak isn't a super hero, he's a demi-God, a monster. Do I feel sorry for him? I feel sorrier for his victims. You know what I'd like? I'd like to sit down with him, and just talk, see if I could help him, maybe over a beer or two, see where he went wrong in his life. Then I'd arrest him and lock him away for fifty years so he would be too old to do this again when he gets out of prison."

There was a stunned silence among the most hardened of journalists. Then everyone had a question at once. But, Rick had turned on his heel and walked out, shaking his head, both enraged with the murderer, and self-recrimination, for possibly making a terrible situation, worse.

****

At five-fifteen Rick rang Patricia Holmes' doorbell, with a pile of files under his arm. She opened the door with a half empty glass of red wine in her hand. She was wearing a white long flowing bath robe, tightened at the waist with a belt and tied in a large bow. Just for a moment, Rick found himself wanting to reach out and yank the end of it, to see what she wore underneath, and was shocked at the thought.

As if she could read his mind, she smiled, and bit her lower lip; her eyes twinkling, and she tilted her head to one side. "Hi, Rick," she said. "How did the press conference go?"

He shook his head and shrugged, "Oh, I opened my big mouth, and put my foot straight in. I tried to talk to him, reach out, tell him I wanted to talk to him about his problems over a beer, and help him. I also insulted him a bit."

"Oh, I see. Well I set up the video recorder so I can watch it later. Do you want to come in?"

"I'd love to, but I can see you're busy getting ready

to go out. I just thought I would drop these off for you to have a look through. I've brought sixteen unsolved case files; I've discounted a heap of others. I'm not sure if he did any of these, but I thought you might be able to see something I missed. These are just the summaries, the witness statements, crime scene photos etc. can't leave the office. But if you see anything and want to dig deeper you'll have to come in to go through it all. As you can imagine, in an unsolved murder, there is a lot of paperwork. The top one, I thought was a likely candidate, missing person's report basically, but the woman was last seen at a supermarket, and her car was left there in the car park, with shopping left lying on the ground by the driver's door."

She nodded, thoughtfully. "I wish you hadn't told me, now I'm going to be thinking about it at dinner. And, to be honest, the two couples we are going out with are quite a stuffy lot. I'd much rather be here, working through this with you. It would be a much more interesting night."

He smiled, and for a moment, wondered if she was now flirting with him. He discounted the idea almost immediately. *A beautiful, sophisticated, university lecturer and a cop like me? Nah, I don't think so.* His very next thought was of Juliet waiting at home.

"Well, you enjoy your dinner and I will chat with you tomorrow. Give me a call when you've found some time to have a look through. Oh, and you can also tell me off for trying to engage our PPP in conversation. I know you told me not to."

She nodded, taking the files from him, being careful not to drop them, or her wine. "Goodnight, Rick, I will talk to you tomorrow." She looked deep in thought, troubled even, But Rick thought better than to ask why.

He turned, giving her a little wave, then turned back. "Pat, something has been bugging me, why PPP? You'd think a serial murderer would come up with something more imposing than that, wouldn't you? It's hardly going to strike fear into the public, is it? I mean why not fluffy duck, or wilting sunflower?"

She burst into laughter, and he joined her; a release from the stress of the day. As they slowed down, they looked at each other, and started all over again. "Oh, sweet Jesus, I haven't laughed like that in ages, she said a few minutes later, using one finger from around the wine glass to wipe her eyes." Then she snorted, in a very cute way, Rick thought, then started laughing all over again. "Fluffy Duck the killer?" She choked.

"Well, PPP, what a wuss name," he said, bringing himself under control.

"Honestly, I have no idea why he chose that. It's an interesting question though. My best guess is that at some point in his life, a good point in an otherwise horrid one, someone nicknamed him PPP. It mattered to him at the time and made him happy. I think his childhood was far from joyous, so it's a way of making him remember a time from his past without the horror that the rest of it brought."

It made sense, and he nodded thoughtfully. In the low light from the outside wall lamps, at the distance she was from him, even in a bath robe, Rick thought she was stunningly beautiful. *Fuck, how can she look so damn sexy holding folders and wearing terry-toweling?* "Good night, Pat, have a lovely dinner."

She raised her glass in a toast and smiled back.

Rick turned away, reluctantly, and walked across the gravel driveway to his car without looking back. Driving to his home, he couldn't help but think again of Patricia, and examine his feelings for her, which at best, he realized were confusing, at worst, dangerous. He realized, with a dawning horror, that not only was he attracted to her, but deep down, in a place he didn't want to visit, he wanted to act on it.

She intrigued, and possibly even beguiled him, and he had no idea why, or how he could even feel that way. He had made a stupid mistake with Angie, spent months separated from Amy and Juliet because of it, and miraculously had been given a second chance. Life had been fantastic as a family ever since. He loved Jules, and adored his daughter, yet there was no doubt he was attracted to Pat, *why?* And, even more troubling; he worried that possibly, she was attracted to him.

Was it possible to have a professional relationship with a woman, where both had desires but it just stopped at being flirtatious? He thought it was, but could those feelings get in the way if one or the other wanted more? He shook his head, angry at himself; he did not need this sort of complication in his life. He was not going to risk losing Juliet again, no way. And, he shouldn't need to remind himself; there was a woman's life at risk too, she had to come first, and she deserved Ricks total focus.

By the time he pulled into his driveway, he felt better about the whole situation, especially when he saw the time. Amy would not be in bed yet, and he would be able to read her a story.

****

A little after midnight, Thomas Holmes, stood in

the doorway of his wife's study watching her reading files. He had a bad feeling about this police investigation thing she had been drawn into.

He knew criminal psychology was her passion, and he had suffered through endless litanies of her postulating that someone like her should be attached to police departments to assist in tracking down serial killers and violent offenders. He found it tedious but had long since learned to keep his opinions to himself. Patricia was not backward in coming forward, when he dared to voice any opinion that differed with hers, about her career.

He was angry with her. Not only had she seemed distant with him all night at dinner, but she had virtually ignored their friends, which was damned rude. Grayson, and Michael were not just friends, but work colleagues, and he was trying to get their support for the senior surgical residency at the hospital. He had explained to Pat just how important the night was, and she seemed to go out of her way to sabotage it for him.

"Pat, when are you bloody well coming to bed? Do you know what the time is?"

She glanced up at him, seemingly annoyed at the interruption, then the antique silver German timepiece on her desk. "It's ten past twelve, Tom. I will come to bed when I'm ready. I'm not feeling tired now. I'm not stopping you though. I will be up directly." She turned back to the open file.

Her dismissal of him only made him angrier. "Now, look, Pat. What's all this nonsense about? You've been like a moody cow all night, now this; staying up half the night."

She laid her hands flat on the desk and took a slow

deep breath. "Nonsense? Did you call what I do nonsense? A woman's life is at risk, and I have been asked to help. For once, the police have realized they need help in understanding a murderer's mind. Don't you dare call what I do nonsense."

"Now you listen here." He stood up straight and pointed a thin finger at her from across the room. "I've put up with them consulting with you, and if you want to work with them fine, so long as it doesn't impact on our life, or put you in danger. But you ignoring our friends over dinner and treating them like they are an imposition in your hectic schedule, is damn well interfering in our lifestyle. I won't put up with it."

She stood up, palms still flat on the desk. "*You* won't put up with it? Is that what you said? Since when do you determine my life for me? You better get out right now before I start throwing things. Don't you ever tell me what I can or cannot do. Tonight, was fucking boring, Tom. I can't stand your friends, but I put up with them for you. Usually I don't show how tedious the whole thing is when I see them, and their boring wives. I should have feigned a headache and stayed home, if I have any regret it's that. Now leave me alone, and let me get to work." She picked up the clock and held it as if she was ready to throw it at him.

Tom turned and left her to it, slamming the door behind him. She thought she could tell what he was thinking by the look on his face? *Two can play at that game, bloody bitch.*

Chapter 12: My Memoir Entry
Graduation Day

I admit it. I consider Angel, as she will always be to me, though for what reason I will never know, the point where I finally graduated from the university of life, and death. But, I must also acknowledge, in many ways it was amateurish.

Understandable, I suppose. I rushed things, and she only lasted four days. I came home from work in a state of great excitement with plans for that night's entertainment, only to find her hanging from the cuffs in the wall, lifeless. I had even brought her a hamburger, and the ungrateful bitch had given up the ghost. Well, it didn't go to waste, I ate it while considering my next move.

I had bought an even bigger chest freezer and put it in the shed when I had re-opened the business. I had checked out sizing because, unlike my father, I was not intending to put just the one body in there, but several.

I had invested in some heavy-duty plastic drums, with lids and they would fit on top of each other two high inside the freezer. The drums were for the entrails and organs. The house had a septic tank for sewerage, so the blood would be flushed down the toilet, and I had been investing for a while in plastic drop sheets for wrapping the joints of meat up in, once I had butchered the corpse.

I am not explaining all this to sicken readers with weak stomachs, and I apologize if that happens. The reason for pointing all this out is to highlight my planning skills. I had been working on this phase of my life for a long time; I had not hurried. Yes, finding Angel was fortuitous, but I had been ready for her for some considerable time.

I decided to strip the meat from the choicest cuts, transport it to work and put it through the mincer. The idea had only become more appealing with time, rather than less, but the meat had to be fresh, of course I wanted people to somehow share in my work, yet not become ill.

Is it a contradiction in terms to be having my 'fun' with women, killing them, but not wanting to make others sick from eating spoilt meat? Maybe it is dear reader. I will leave such judgements to you.

As I am not a strong man. I had devised a pulley system to winch Angel upside down from her position on the floor when I undid the cuffs. Once suspended I could let the blood drain out, get rid of the messy bits into one of the tubs, and begin my human butchery lesson. I had, naturally, already done some studying of anatomy at the Midland Library and used their photocopier to record some of the diagrams of the more complex joints I would need to cut through.

I didn't finish until after midnight, and boy, was I tired? The last hour had been spent cleaning up, as every good butcher does at the end of his shift. The wooden block, knives, and floor underneath Angel all had to be scrubbed with boiling hot water and bleach. And, I needed a long hot shower before I allowed myself to go to bed.

It was nearly one in the morning when I crawled under the covers, tired yes, but with a feeling unparalleled to any I had experienced before. I was already looking forward to the next time. I intended learning from my mistakes. it was going to last much longer in the future. I promised that to myself as sleep opened its golden wings and engulfed me.

****

It took a few months before the next opportunity presented itself. I had spent some time out and about at night, looking for a playmate, but it hadn't happened. I had become discerning, meaning that I didn't want to kill just anyone, I had to *want* to do it, and the victim had to be appealing. It wasn't as if I was compelled to do it, so by waiting it only increased the sense of anticipation. Some women I came across, I couldn't see the attraction in them. One that I did see and like, was holding hands with a boyfriend or husband, so again she was lucky to have been out with him, rather than alone.

I should at this point add that I had finished cutting up Angel's body within a day, relayed the meat to the sausage mincer at work and neatly packed the bits that were left covered in plastic, inside the freezer.

To the best of my knowledge, the sausages went down a treat, at least I never heard a complaint coming back from customers who had bought the 'Old English Pork Sausages.' Occasionally I would notice people through the windows out into the customer service area, pick up a cling wrapped pack, and it would be all I could do not to break out in hysterical fits of laughter.

I remember once, my manager, Ian asked what I found so funny when I noticed an elderly couple shuffling away from the meat fridges, a pack of my 'specials' in their hands. I shrugged it off by saying that the couple reminded me of a comedy sketch TV show I had seen over the weekend. He didn't ask me further, just shook his head and went back to ignoring me. I learned a lesson not to laugh out loud again. I had to remind myself, that there was a *reason* for mincing the human meat other than my amusement. It assisted in getting rid of the bulk of the body. If I was to continue down this path, disposal was a very important problem, and I had resolved it.

Driving home that night, I did give in to gales of laughter causing tears to stream from my eyes and down my cheeks as I imagined the old age pensioners that night eating their dinner. He would say something like *"Here, Betty, these sausages are lovely, are they different ones?"* And she would reply *"No Bob, just the usual Old English Pork."* So, the old man, who clearly loved his wife, would end by adding: *"must be the way you cook them, Betty."*

Honestly, I had to pull my van over to the side of the road as I nearly wet myself laughing so hard.

It was Halloween, when I took my next victim. I treated myself to a night at the movies in Midland. They were playing a triple feature of horror films including *Scream 2, I Know What You Did Last Summer*, and my favorite *The Night Flier*. I had gorged myself on salted popcorn and Cola and was in a fantastic mood as I drove home well after midnight.

Imagine my surprise, when I saw stumbling along the side of the road, what looked very much like an actress from one of the films. She was quite young, she appeared from behind, walking in the glare from my headlights, and she was wearing either a very long T-shirt or a very short white dress. But what made it interesting was that the back seemed to have tears in it and blood dripping through those holes as if she had been stabbed a dozen or more times. Well, to say I was stunned would be an understatement.

I pulled over onto the gravel shoulder of the road, jumped out of the van and ran back to her. From the front, I could see she had short spiky blonde hair and she was struggling to walk in a straight line. She must only have been eighteen or so. The front of her outfit also seemed to have stab wounds and blood too, and I remember thinking: *how can she be still walking with all those wounds?*

"Are you all right?" I asked as we met in the red-light reflection of my tail lights.

"I'm lovely," she replied as if she didn't have a care in the world. "Were you at the party?"

Okay, call me stupid but, it was only then that it dawned on me she had been at a Halloween party, and the outfit she wore was fancy dress. I knew she was staggering along the shoulder of the road because she was under the influence of alcohol, or drugs, or both. I knew I had to have her. How ironic, to dress up like a murder victim, and then get murdered?

"Oh yeah, I was there, with Jim, I'm Paul remember?"

I was brilliant. She looked at me crookedly and nodded vaguely and I thought she didn't remember me, but realized she was drunk and didn't want to offend me. "I'm going this way; do you want a lift?" I nodded in the direction we had both been traveling in.

"That would be great, yeah thanks."

And that was how easy it was. We walked to the van and when we got to the passenger side I pretended to drop the keys, as I bent to pick them up I pulled my jeans leg up and slipped the knife out of its sheath. I held it to her throat and made her get in through the sliding door. Perhaps it was the fact that she was drunk, but she even did as she was told and cuffed herself up.

Would you believe, dear reader, when we got out of the van, which she did without prompting, she said: "Are we going to have sex?"

That was such a delightful question to ask me, I almost spared her.

Her name was Lola, and she lasted much longer than Angel. For the first week, I barely hurt her at all, but then, much to my surprise, I began to tire of the sex and light pain games and wanted more. I wanted to see and feel her fear, and that was when I began to enjoy myself. I managed to stretch her time out to almost three weeks, but by then, she was more of an annoyance with her constant whining. At least this time I had the pleasure of ending her life myself when she whined one time too many.

I cleaned up Lola's mess efficiently, and effortlessly. I had some music playing in the background, jazz, from memory, and whistled as I worked. I stopped every now and again, eyes closed as the music got to me, then when the solo finished, went back to work

Once again, I took my lunch box filled with pieces of meat to work and sausage sales went on as per normal. But, dear reader, truth be told I was tiring of that, the humor didn't have the same effect. I barely even smiled any more when I saw customers with my home brand Old English Pork, it just all seemed so...boring. I don't know why, the sex had been fun, killing Lola even more so, but for some reason, I wanted more. Something was missing, but what?

Over the next few weeks and months I gave my world some serious consideration and came to a few conclusions. What was the point in living if there was no risk? How could I continue to enjoy myself, but up the ante so there was more excitement in it? Another thing that was eating away inside like a cancerous growth was that I wanted a bit of recognition. Now, I'm not saying I was dumb and wanted to get caught, I'm not mad after all. But, I wanted people to fear me in general. I wanted to be Perth's boogie-man, and that, right there, was when I thought I would put my considerable talents to some forward planning and gain the fame that I believe I so richly deserved.

In Lola and Angel, I had committed the perfect crimes. No one even knew they were dead, they were just...missing, and where was the fun in that? I could have carried on forever, finding playmates, making sausages for Dalton's and storing body parts with the victims just listed as missing, but, dear reader I wanted more. I wanted notoriety, fame even. What was the point of having a superior intellect if I didn't show the world I possessed it?

I decided my next killing would be more public, and so began a period of intense thinking how I could bring that dream to reality. Firstly, I needed a location. Was it fate, but that weekend I saw an article in the Sunday Supplement on the history of Lake Monger. It is a man-made lake just on the outskirts of Perth. What attracted me to this place as a premier site for my next killing, was the name of the place. Have you ever heard of a more dreadful sounding place?

Once I had the location gurgling in my mind, I needed a victim, and in a blinding flash of inspiration I knew I wouldn't do it just once, but twice. The papers would have a terrific title ready-made: The Lake Monger Murders. Dear reader, can you imagine my excitement? The Lake Monger Murderer; now there was a name to conjure fear.

Chapter 13
An Assortment of Excerpts from Newspaper Articles

West Australian Newspaper. Friday February 13th 1998:

Jogger's Body Found Murdered at Lake Monger

Lake Monger has this morning been closed to the public as police and forensic investigators comb for clues in the horrific killing of a female jogger overnight at the popular lakeside jogging spot in Leederville.

Marlene Hornborough found the victim's body suspended upside down from a tree while walking her dog, which she did every morning before work. "It was like a scene from a horror film." A visibly distressed Mrs. Hornborough said to this reporter. "There was blood everywhere; the poor girl had been hacked to death." She went on to say before her husband led her away.

Police are remaining tight lipped at this point, but sources say they are baffled. They believe the victim was a regular late night jogger, but they are not releasing her name until family have been notified. It appears she was attacked in a wooded area at the Northern end of the lake where the path left the lakeside and curved in between some trees. It is believed the killer laid in wait, hidden from view, until the victim ran by.

West Australian Newspaper. Saturday February 14th 1998

Body Identified in Lake Monger Murder

Police this morning named the victim in the horrific Lake Monger Murder as 19 years old Hayley Martin. Hayley worked as a physical trainer in the Heart and Muscle Gymnasium in Leederville and was a regular late night jogger around picturesque Lake Monger.

Police say Hayley was jogging alone around eleven pm on Monday when she was attacked. Internal sources had said that while Hayley's acquaintances would be investigated, her killing showed all the hallmarks of a random attack. Why she was suspended upside down in a tree no one knows, though some people are theorizing it is some form of satanic ritual.

Occult specialist, and lecturer in anthropology Theodore Van Neilson said that bleeding of a sacrifice would normally be done in an upside down state to collect the blood, which would then normally be used in rituals. A police spokesman scoffed at the suggestion of a ritualistic killing stating that the blood had not been collected, and Miss Martin had been killed before her throat had been cut. When asked why he thought her body had been suspended, he said: "Because the killer is a bloody madman, that's why."

Friends of Hayley's are in shock, though one said

she had repeatedly warned her not to jog alone late at night. She said, Hayley had loved life, and loved to exercise in the open, with the city lights and water as a backdrop.

Family are in deep mourning and have asked for privacy at this tragic time.

Police spokesperson Nicola Landon, said joggers should always be vigilant, and not do it alone, especially late at night. She went on to say police patrols would be stepped up in the area, and that an arrest would come quite soon.

Sunday Times. Thursday 19th February 1998

Police re-enactment and Lake Monger Memorial for Hayley Martin

Family and friends are joining in prayer to celebrate the life of Hayley Martin today on the banks of Lake Monger following the televised re-enactment last night of the events leading up to her murder.

Hayley's mother and father will attend the memorial and spoke briefly at the press conference, appealing for witnesses to come forward. "Hayley was a beautiful innocent soul, who had everything to live for," Sally Martin said.

Detective Sergeant Daniel Travers admitted they were no closer to an arrest after the brutal murder almost a week ago, and asked that anyone who saw Hayley jogging, to come forward. They were very keen to speak to anyone who was in the park between eight and midnight. Inspector Travers said that they have been very pleased with the response so far by the public, but he said that someone would have seen the killer, and often it could be a small detail that leads to an arrest.

Turn to page sixteen for pictures of Hayley, and of the actress who dressed in the sports clothing for the re-enactment.

West Australian Newspaper. Friday 27th February 1998

Police No Closer to an Arrest in Lake Monger Murder

Detective Sergeant Daniel Travers, in charge of the Hayley Martin murder investigation, admitted today that police were so far not able to make an arrest in the brutal killing, despite a televised re-enactment.

"We have interviewed hundreds of witnesses, but we still have no clear idea who the murderer is," he said outside Police Headquarters today. "It would appear to be an opportunistic, random attack, and this type of killer can be extremely difficult to catch without significant input from the public." He went on to say: "Someone out there saw something. They may not know they saw the killer, but if there is anyone who was in the park on that night that has not made a statement we are pleading for them to come forward now. Also, if anyone has had a bad experience in the past while out alone at night, please call the hotline number and report it."

West Australian Newspaper. Thursday May 16th 1998

Lake Monger Murderer Strikes Again

A second woman has been found stabbed to death and suspended upside down from a tree only two hundred meters from the location where Hayley Martin's body was discovered, three months ago.

While Police refuse to divulge the identity of the latest victim it is believed the young woman was last seen in the Northbridge night club and restaurant precinct and taken to Lake Monger where she was murdered.

Forensic medical examiners have confirmed blood analysis shows extremely high concentrations of alcohol which would have made her more easily abducted. Previous victim Haley Martin was jogging around the lake when she was attacked.

Both victims had been stabbed repeatedly, until death. Then a pulley and winch arrangement used to suspend the bodies upside down from a limb of the tree.

Police are refusing to speculate whether this is the same murderer or a 'copycat' killing until all evidence has been examined. They have promised a press conference later today.

West Australian Newspaper. Monday May 20th 1998

Where Have all the Joggers Gone?

The once bustling pathways around picturesque Lake Monger remained deserted over the weekend. Where once hundreds if not thousands of locals would *walk, run, or skate around the Lake when weather permitted, only ducks, swans and this reporter dared tread despite twenty-nine degrees Celsius sunshine.*

Occasional police patrols broke the stillness, but the feeling I had was that the man dubbed The Lake Monger Murderer was nowhere to be seen. Perhaps he has moved to the banks of the Swan River, or the foreshore at Cottesloe; he would be hard pressed to find a new victim here.

I spoke to Tracy Onscott and her friend Frederica Hapstadt, who used to jog the lake every evening for over five years: "We won't be going to the Lake anymore, it's too dangerous." Feelings seemingly echoed by lots of other people.

Since police admitted they were investigating their belief that the two killings were committed by the same person, Lake Monger has been left like a ghost town.

****

And so, I was famous.

Oh, the joy of discussing the murderer with co-workers, and agreeing that the perpetrator was a monster. I found myself becoming such an expert on the subject that I wrote several letters to the editor of the newspaper, criticizing the police for not keeping our parklands safe. Then I pulled what I consider to be my masterstroke. I suggested to the editor, that might it not be one and the same killer who had murdered Carly Biddle all those months prior?

I had no family or friends, but my fans through the letters to the editor wanted to know me. I'm quite sure of that.

I had to decide what I was going to do next. It had to be something even more audacious. Something so

bizarre, everyone would sit up and take notice. I spent a
lot of time thinking what my next move would be.

Chapter 14
A Troubled Soul Laid Bare

The squad room was a hive of activity when Rick arrived in the morning. Extra uniformed officers had been brought in to man the phones, which had been located along five trestle tables joined together to form one very long desk along the back wall. Detective Sergeant Micky Macklin was overseeing that operation. Much like a triage nurse, his job was to prioritize the detectives time. A TV plea for help, always brought hundreds of calls, and sorting the timewasting ones from the occasional vein of gold, was an important job.

The Detective Chief Inspector allocated jobs, based on Mickey's recommendations, as the case had now grown well above the authority of a Detective Sergeant, even though it was well accepted that Rick was the senior lead.

Before he could sit at his desk, he heard his name being called though the open door of the DCI's office. He walked in and was taken aback by the amount of paperwork scattered all over the desk. Rick noted his boss looked haggard; as if he had aged ten years.

"Grab a seat, Rick. Tell me straight, what's the deal with this Patricia Holmes?"

"What do you mean, Boss?" Rick first thought was that she had complained about him, and he was going to be reprimanded.

"She phoned me first thing this morning, she wants to work with us. She did not have your mobile phone number so got me through the switchboard. Apparently, she has been up most of the night reading the files you took over and wants you to go to her house to go over them with her. She is taking some leave of absence to help us, because she says you have her hooked. Specifically, she mentioned working with you. Anything I need to know here, Rick?"

Rick smiled, "I'm delighted to have someone of her caliber working with us, she will be an asset."

He nodded, clearly deep in thought. "Rick, we are fortunate that we have the support of Commissioner Monkton, otherwise I'd never get permission to have a psych attached to a major murder investigation. None of the other states have a psychologist on their payroll."

"Pat doesn't want to be on the payroll, and she certainly doesn't need the money. If this case didn't interest her, she wouldn't want to do it. I say we snap her up I think she will be invaluable."

"If we do this, there has to be some rules. We must control her in terms of information, and not have her control us to further her career. Once we have the killer, she can write as many papers and books as she likes. If we are going to give her carte blanche with case files and the like I need to know she is on our side. She can observe and advise with interviewing suspects and witnesses but not actively take part in them. I'm not having some smart lawyer using her involvement to get a case dismissed. I also think for her protection, she needs to have an officer with her full time, and clearly you have the rapport with her. How do you feel about coming off all other duties and working with her until we catch the guy, or she leaves to go back to her day job? I'm thinking we bring her on board for seven days."

Rick took a moment to think about things. On the plus side this was a new initiative and one he felt was interesting rather than the run of the mill police work. If they were successful in unmasking the killer, and saving June Daniel's life, it could make his career, and herald a new era in criminal investigation in West Australian Law Enforcement. He also enjoyed Pat's company, and found her an interesting, intelligent, and very perceptive person. Even if they failed he knew he could learn a lot from working closely with her. Then, of course, was the undeniable fact that if they failed, he could be ridiculed, so possibly the move could be a career ender.

"Boss, I'm not one hundred percent clear on what you mean. Are you saying that for the duration, Tyler is no longer my partner, but Patricia Holmes is? That I work with her and if she comes up with a theory I follow her leads, with her in tow?"

"Yes, but you report to me in advance of any leads she may come up with so that as a team we can support you."

"So, she puts up or shuts up and we give her one week to do so?"

"Pretty much, yes. Any longer than that, if she isn't successful, it isn't fair to her teaching job, and patients she works with at Graylands. She has taken some leave, but sooner or later she must go back to her work. But, Rick, I know you've had some marital problems in the past, which is why we are having this chat. I've been told Patricia Holmes is a very attractive woman. If you think this could be a potential problem with your wife, say so and I will get her to work with someone else. This isn't an order, Rick; it's asking if you want to volunteer."

"I'm up for it. But I ought to run it by Juliet, rather than have her find out from someone else. Things have been great since I moved back in, and I don't think this will affect anything, but, I should let her know. Give me fifteen minutes and I will give her a call."

"Happy wife, happy life, Rick, I'm all for that. Yeah, go talk to her, let me know what decision you come to."

****

"Hey Babe, it's me," he said when Juliet answered the phone on the fourth ring.

"Oh, hi. This is a surprise, what's wrong?"

"Nothing is wrong, but something came up. I've been asked to volunteer for special duty, and I thought I would get your opinion."

"Sorry, who is this? It can't be my husband; he never asks my opinion about his job." She laughed.

He smiled, knowing she was kidding, but there was also a lot of truth in what she said. "That was your old husband, this one wouldn't accept this job if you were against it. And, to be fair, you might be."

"Oh, I see. You're not going undercover and I won't see you for two years, are you?"

"No, love, nothing like that. The DCI has asked me if I would work with Pat full time on a week's trial basis. She has taken leave of absence from the University and her patients to help us out with the case. Colin wants her babysat, but also for me to take the lead on any theories she comes up with regarding the bunch of old case files I gave her to look at."

"Why would I be against that, Rick?"

He drummed his fingers on the desk; *here it comes.* "When you took me back, Jules, I promised you I would not only never lie to you again, but that I would share things with you that I hadn't before about my job. You should know that Pat is a very attractive woman, she would be my partner for a week at least, and not Tyler, and we would be spending a lot of time together."

"Wow, Rick. You've blown me away here. But from what you've told me she sounds fascinating. I trust you; I believe you will keep it professional."

"You're amazing, Jules. You know that, right?"

"Just don't *you* forget that."

"See you tonight, love."

"Hey, Rick? Before you go."

"Yeah, still here."

"I appreciate you asked me, I love you."

"Love you too, Babe."

****

Detective's David Rollick and Charmaine Hilton knocked on the faded and paint peeled front door. They were following up on a lead from a neighbor, called through to the hotline, that the man inside was not only a 'weirdo' but had been seen carrying a large brown suitcase and putting it into his car. The timing was consistent with the day the case had been dumped at Midland.

Adding fuel to the fire was that the neighbor had also reported there seemed to be a never-ending stream of young women knocking on the door and leaving shortly afterward.

"Who is it?" Came the muffled yell from inside.

"It's the police. We would like to ask you some questions, please," Dave shouted back.

"Okay, I just got out of the shower, hang on."

"A shower?" Charmain asked quietly. "Sounds suss to me, at this time of day."

It was that sixth sense that saved her life, and a blatant disregard for procedure that ended Dave's. "Let's give him a chance; maybe he works nights."

Inside the home, Brad Michigan calmly took the pistol from the shelf under the coffee table. He wasn't going to fall for the old: "I'm from the police" knocking on the front door trick. He had built up quite a considerable business manufacturing, and selling meth-amphetamine, but he had made plenty of enemies along the way.

He'd amassed over three million dollars, which was sitting in a Canary Islands bank account, and if it was to all come to an end, so be it. But he wasn't going to go quietly.

He pulled the slide back on the side of the muzzle, and stood in the passage, ten feet from the voices he did not believe were police. "What's this all about?" he yelled.

Dave stepped in front of the door, while Charmaine moved to the side. Instinctively she slipped her hand under her black jacket and grasped the handle of her gun. Dave was a big man and had effectively shouldered her out of the way. "It's just some routine…"

He didn't get to finish the sentence, as a sudden, ear-shattering, noise deafened her. A hail of bullets ripped through the wooden door, picking Dave up and throwing him backward. His chest disintegrated in mid-air, and he died before he hit the ground.

Charmain was frozen, in deep shock; her partner was dead. She didn't need to feel his pulse to know that. In a daze, she heard the click-clack of the lock being undone, then the handle turned. She was about to be shot as well, and she was petrified.

The door was yanked open as she stepped back further. Her training came to the fore and she pulled her gun from its holster. She had the drop on him. Brad Michigan's eyes were only on the dead body on the footpath. He heard the word freeze from his right and turned as Charmaine's finger tightened on the trigger. She fired repeatedly, in shock, in an unconscious reaction.

From a second-floor window across the street, an elderly man watched, and smiled. He was fed up with the drugged-out troublemakers who came and went from the obvious meth lab. He had reported it time and time again to the police, but they had done nothing about it? Report that a serial killer lived there though and it got action straight away.

He smiled, faintly, and pulled the blind back down.

****

She was ready when he rang the doorbell and opened the door for him within seconds. Her short hair glistened, and she wore a crisp white shirt and black pants, with high heel shoes. She looked professional, but chic and sexy. Her clothes fitted her perfectly, and as she turned ahead of him after telling him to come in, he noticed the outline of hidden bra straps through the silk top.

Rick felt a little under dressed in his dark blue

jacket which covered a pale blue shirt and black tie. He followed her down the hall, and couldn't help himself, he glanced down at her rear but could not tell what type of underwear she wore, but once again noticed she had a perfect bottom. Admonishing himself, he jerked his eyes away. *Stop that right now.*

He followed her into her study where he saw her desk which had been cluttered last visit, but now was neat and tidy. At one end was the pile of files he had given her, but three of them were lined up side by side in the middle.

"The coffee pot is on, Rick, would you like one?"

"Not right now, Pat, thanks all the same. I'm very keen to know what you've gleaned from the files."

"Before we get into that, Daryl called; he said you are to be my partner for a week, on a trial basis. How do you feel about that?"

"The DCI ran the idea past me, and I volunteered. I think you will be a great asset to the squad, Pat, your insights, and reading of this guy's mind, will be invaluable."

She stared at him and shook her head imperceptibly. "Yes, but how do you *feel*?"

He held her stare, and wondered to himself exactly what kind of answer she wanted to hear from him? "I feel very good about this, Pat. I didn't come here under sufferance, or because I was ordered to. I'm looking forward to spending time and working with you."

She sat down, behind the desk, and he sat down too. She moistened her lips with the tip of her tongue, and then smiled. "So you don't feel like you've been press-ganged into this, and your mates will be laughing at you behind your back?

"No, I don't. Possibly some of them may take the mickey out of me, but I'm a big boy, and can handle a bit of ribbing. Especially if we can come up with a result."

She smiled, and nodded, as if happy with his answer. "Just so long as I'm not causing any problems for you." She pointed at the files. "So, what I was looking for with the files, was an escalation. Someone who started out small and worked his way up to the big league. After all, it's not like overnight he started killing. Of the cases, you've brought me, I can't find that escalation, which is perplexing."

"Pat it's hard to find a file if you don't know what you're looking for. I searched within the parameters you gave me. I couldn't find any attempted violent rapes that fit, no real animal cruelty that leapt off the page, no assaults against women that matched your criteria. The closest unsolved investigations I could find I brought to you."

She nodded and peaked her fingers under her chin. "I'm not being critical, Rick, not at all, I just thought there would be some signposts along the way. You see the mind, when it fractures, is usually caused by a build-up of things. We are the sum of our life experiences after all, so unless this man grew up in another state or another country, it's strange that there isn't any build up here. This leads me to think of a few possibilities. Now I stress this is only educated guessing, for want of a better expression. But here's what I am thinking."

"Don't hold back, I'm all ears."

She smiled and licked her lips again. "All right, let's look at what I think we have here: As a child, he had a horrific life, but he doesn't see it that way, to him his upbringing was normal. To some extent that has carried forward into his adulthood; he thinks he is normal and everyone else has the problems. His mother left, essentially abandoning him. This left PPP with a dad who was at best troubled and at worst a monster. The way PPP is taking his victims screams out to me that that was what triggered it. This much so far I'm sure about, he fits into the pattern of that type of upbringing, but then I think it got worse. Either he was taken into care, or he was fostered out, or of course both. He could have been a ward of the state where he was bullied because he was so small and then was lucky enough to be picked up by foster parents, or a family member took him. Sadly, I think he was abused in that relationship too, and I'm going to stick my head right into the noose here, Rick, this is pure speculation based on one of the case files you brought me. I think he was abused homosexually."

"How can you possibly know that, Pat?"

"It's not what I know, it's what I think, and let me remind you, I could be wrong about some of this; that's the problem with theorizing. But, reading three of the files you brought me has given me more insights than I had before. Let me come back to that when I talk to you about one of these files. Because I believe he was locked away in a home, and then taken in by a someone who completely and utterly controlled his life. So, his escalation if you like, was steeped in fantasies. He imagined doing things, hurting animals and people in all sorts of bloody and disgusting ways, but he didn't get a chance to act out those vivid dreams until he became an adult. By then he had lived eighteen or more years as if he were the central character in a horror movie. One phrase he used in the first note, '*are we having fun yet?*' keeps coming back to me. There is a reason he said that, and it bothers me because to him mutilating and killing is somehow fun, but then he must ask if we are having fun *yet*, as if there is far worse to come."

"I've always thought from the start; he was enjoying himself and that he would kill more people."

"Well, you are perceptive, Rick, and I believe you're right. But, I'm positive he killed several times before the body in the suitcase. I'm sure this one was one of the very early ones, if not his first. To me, it feels like it's the initial killing."

She pushed the folder over toward him and eagerly he picked it up and opened it. "This can't be right, Pat, the victim is male. I almost didn't give you this one because of that reason. Gordon Bridges was a closet gay, and he picked the wrong one and was knifed to death in his car at a park."

"Yes, the circumstances of the murder are all quite right, but he was stabbed forty times, which is about the same number of wounds as Bridget Schaeffer. If this was a homophobic killing, why was there never a second one? The weapon seems to be similar, in fact, I think it was the same knife. Gordon Bridges suffered a frenzied attack, from inside the car, so the victim knew his attacker, else why did he let him inside? If this wasn't, as I believe, a random attack, then what does that tell us about the killer? Intricate planning. He lured Gordon Bridges to the park to meet him there. He let him in the car, and then our man brutally killed him. And, he did it in such a way that the police would think it was a gay hate crime. Can you not see the type of planning it took to get him, a married man, to the park at night time, kill him and throw the cops off the scent?

"So, let's hypothesize, remember, Rick, this is all about hypothesizing. They knew each other, possibly introduced by the person who took him in as a youth, or perhaps his homosexual abuser guardian. He was perhaps shared, much like a book from a library, except it was for sex. Somehow, PPP went from one to the other because he had to, until the time came when he decided, no more. Think of this too, Gordon Bridges was married, with children and he chose to go out at night and have sex, leaving his children at home. Doesn't that remind you of our man who was left at home by his mother in the company of an abusive father."

Rick sat, and stared, dumfounded by the leap of perception that could find a link between two diametrically opposed cases. "So we look at all his acquaintances, let's go to the station and read the interview statements." He urged.

"And look for whom? Who can you cross reference with, other than the witnesses you have from the current cases?"

"Okay, point taken, what else do you have? You have a certain look to you, like you're holding the best until last."

She pushed another folder over toward him. "This one, actually two to be precise, is where he really came of age, the launching pad if you will into the body in the suitcase."

"The Lake Monger Murders? But the M.O. is nothing like what followed."

"You don't think it was the same type of homicidal madman showing how clever he is? You don't see the similarity in dumping a body is a suitcase so it is found, and hanging a woman upside down in a tree in a park used by thousands of people so it is found? *Look at me, aren't I so smart and you cops are so dumb? Are we having fun yet?* It just feels so right to me, Rick. I told you I thought he evolved, he learned, he got better, and he sought the limelight. He wanted to be famous, and in a way, with the Lake Monger Murders, he found the infamy he wanted.

"I'm sorry, I don't see it. Yes, I can see there are similarities, but there are also aspects that are nothing alike."

"Check the knife that was used, I bet you a thousand dollars, it's the same type of blade."

"Even if you're right, there's not a lot of help in that case, it went nowhere. He stopped after the second killing so they had no witnesses, no DNA, absolutely nothing."

"Yes, he stopped. Why would he just stop? Because he got bored, he had to up the high, and how much higher was the body in the suitcase? I will have another bet with you, that he was one of the people interviewed, he would have been a jogger, or dog walker in the park, he wouldn't have been able to resist that. That's how his mind works, he needs to feed his ego. In my opinion, this man is as narcissistic a person as I have ever come across. Now, there is something else, call this good luck rather than deductive reasoning. My husband, bless him, has a less than endearing quality, which annoys the heck out of me at times."

"Really? What's that?"

"He insists on reading out loud to me over breakfast the letters to the editor when something irks or interests him. And, what's more, he gets all hot under the collar with some of the people who write in. Seriously he does my head in when he reads to me some of the crap that some people feel strongly enough about to write to the editor of the bloody newspaper. You get these holier than thou opinionated readers with nothing better to do with their life than write in for other opinionated idiots, like my husband, to read and want to debate about. It is a hive of self-righteous clap-trap, and sometimes, what happens is that one letter will trigger responses from other like-minded souls, and before you know it there are full blown conversations between these people."

Rick laughed, he too couldn't understand the mentality of people who write to the papers to vent an opinion. "I'm with you, Pat, but what's that got to do with the case in point?"

"I remember one such outpouring after the second murder at the Lake. I mean fair enough, *everyone* was talking about the sheer brutality of the killings at the time, it was horrific. But my husband read to me a series of letters over a period of two or three weeks or so, and as I recall, one guy was vocal, extremely vocal. Even at the time I thought it was strange that he would be so indignant, but then he got even more bizarre in my opinion. What he started doing, after ranting and raving about how useless the police were in keeping our parklands safe, was to suggest another previous murder was committed by the same man. Interestingly you brought me the file to it as an unsolved case."

"Which one?"

She held up a hand to quieten him, and he realized she would get to it in her own time.

"Now, my question is this: Why would he bring it up in the newspaper, being such a public forum? He was not, apparently, a relation of the victim, if he was you could understand his outrage. The answer, again in my opinion, was that he wanted recognition for the crime and in so doing, could further show how pathetic the police were in not catching the murderer from a previous case, as well as the current ones. So, Rick, I think our writer of letters, is our killer, and that he killed this young woman after following her one night on her way home from her job."

She slid the last folder toward Rick, who, sat open mouthed; stunned at her understanding of the human mind. He slowly opened it and began to read the case notes about Carly Biddle's stabbing.

"Pat, she suffered a single stab wound to the chest? The investigators thought it was a sex crime, it's nothing like our guy's known M.O."

"They are not the same cops who thought Gordon Bridges murder was sex related were they? Rick, this wasn't a sex crime; it was more like a crime of passion." Once more she held up her hand to stop him interrupting. "I know what you're about to say. You wonder how can I make that kind of leap. Well, looking at the case as a whole, and, following my reasoning with the other files, it fits. That's all I can say. I believe it was done by someone who coveted her; who worshiped her from afar. In his warped twisted way, he wanted her, and she refused him when he made his feelings known. Then he struck out, a single stab wound, which killed her instantly."

"But her dress was opened."

"Not when she was killed it wasn't; she was stabbed through her dress so it was closed. It was opened afterward so he could see the body he had idolized and wanted for so long."

"But the cops interviewed anyone and everyone who knew her, and everyone checked out."

"Of course they did, that's what I've been telling you all along. Naturally the killer wasn't wearing a sign that said *I did it*. Rick this is the case I was looking for, he is here, somewhere in the witness statements, hiding in plain sight."

Rick shook his head, he just couldn't get it, there was no way it could be this simple. "Pat, how can you be so sure?"

"Okay, let's say it's not our man. Who else would kill her and why? If it was done for sex, why not abduct her, take her somewhere and rape her. A single stab wound, to me says a crime of passion, he struck out in anger. There were no signs of a struggle, no screams heard, she had no skin under her finger nails, so she didn't fight back, why? Because she didn't have time. He struck out, and she died. Then her dress was opened so her body could be viewed, but there were no signs that he touched her indecently after death, so if it was sex related, why not?"

"Pat, I'm not saying you're wrong, I'm just having trouble getting my head around this. There is no evidence here, just your belief, and I must say your arguments are very persuasive. It's the first time I've ever looked for clues to prove the theory, it's usually the other way around."

"For me, the clincher is the letters to the editor.

They were well over a year after Carly Biddle's death, closer to two years! Okay, if it was your daughter, sister, neighbor even, then I could understand burning a candle for her. But this murder and the deaths of the two women at Lake Monger bear no similarities to each other at all. Therefore, the only theory that makes any sense at all to me is that the killer wanted people to know that he had struck before, and, that he had gotten away with it. There was a flurry of letters following his one, most even suggested that other unsolved deaths could be attributed to the same murderer. Can you not imagine how that fueled his ego? He's got people talking about him, and while the general conversation was how awful this killer is, to him he hears adulation."

"So, you think if we trawl through the hundreds of interview statements for the four murders, you think we will spot our man, that his name will appear in each case as a witness?"

"I do, unless he used a fake name, but, I don't think he would have. He would have enjoyed knowing you were interviewing him and not realizing who he was. Plus, he believes he is smarter than you, so to him; he would have had nothing to fear."

"I know it's a long time ago, but do you recall what name he used when he wrote to the editor?"

"No idea. I didn't read them, just listened to excerpts that were read out to me."

He took his Nokia phone from his pocket and dialed a number. "Boss, it's me, Rick. Can you send Tyler, or one of the others guys to the West Australian? You remember The Lake Monger Murders?"

****

What a fucking dump. Clive Peppercorn thought, as

he rapped on the wooden door, painted a horrible shade of green, for the second time that day. This time he could hear a noise from inside so he knew the man he had come to interview was at home.

He took his I.D. from his inside pocket and raised his eyebrows at the colossal waste of time his day had been. As he looked up, he noticed the reams of spider webs across the alcove ceiling which made him jump. If there was one thing that gave him the absolute-fucking-willies, it was spiders. That was yet another thing to piss him off, and all he wanted was to go home and have several beers, with scotch chasers.

Right, I am not fucking going any closer to the fucking door. He took two good sized paces back, which took him down the large stone steps. A particularly nasty looking black bugger was in the process of weaving its way down a silken thread. *Probably to see what the fucking knocking on the door was all about. Good job I saw the fucking thing; if that fell on my head I'd shoot the fucker.*

He had been re-interviewing witnesses who had admitted to being at the Midland dump. This was his last call then he could go home. *The whole case is fucked up. Fuck me, how many times am I supposed to ask the same bloody questions, to the same fucking people?*

"Yes, who is it?" Came a nervous sounding voice from inside.

"It's the police, Mr. Rankin, it just a routine follow up to a statement you made a while back."

"Oh, is that so? Umm look, just hang on, I must wash my hands, I was peeling vegetables. Won't be a minute."

Yeah, that'd be fucking right. You take your fucking time; I've got all fucking night to wait around under spider fucking city.

Several minutes passed, which seemed like half an hour to the increasingly irritated detective. Eventually, he heard draw bolts being pulled, and locks being turned. *Oh, for fuck's sake, is this Fort-fucking Knox?*

Eventually, with a squeal of unoiled hinges, the door opened to show a slim-looking man, wearing a thick polo-necked woolen jumper and black track pants that looked like they hadn't been washed in months. "Sorry about that, this door doesn't get opened much since I shut the shop down; you caught me when I was busy."

Right, that's all I fucking need, a fucking faggot. "No worries Mr. Rankin. I did call earlier, but no doubt you were at work."

"Yes, that's right, I've not long got home, and was preparing my tea, would you like to come in and join me? What's all this about? It's exciting to have a policeman call on me in the evening."

Oh, yes sunshine, you'd love my truncheon shoved up your arse, wouldn't you? "No thank you, sir, little lady at home with a cold beer and bowl of spaghetti with extra chili waiting for me."

"Sounds delightful," he replied as he leaned against the doorframe, still wiping his hands on a tea towel. "How can I help you, detective?"

That fucking spider is only inches away from his head, but I'm not going to say a fucking word. Fuck me it would be funny if it dropped on him.

He held up his I.D. "Detective Clive Peppercorn, Mr. Rankin. I'm just following up on the report you were good enough to make about being at the dump on the day the body in the suitcase was found."

"That's an interesting name; Peppercorn. Do you think your distant family were farmers?"

"Fifth generation Australian, so probably convicts more than farmers." *This guy gives me the fucking creeps, like he is undressing me with his eyes.* "Sir, in your statement you said you were at the dump in the late morning, is that correct, or could it have been later?"

With a flick of the wrist, he swung the tea towel onto his shoulder, then folded his arms. The spider inched ever closer to his hair, and Clive could barely conceal a grin.

"Oh, now let me think, it's *such* a long time ago, isn't it? I remember I got up late, had my breakfast, and got stuck into the gardening. It was long overdue. I have this lemon tree that was just so overgrown. Anyway, I pruned the heck out of it, mowed the lawn, well I call it a lawn, but it's more weeds, if you know what I mean. Then I took it all to the dump at Midland. Now, maybe it might have been twelve or so, but it wouldn't have been much later than that."

"Sir, we now believe the person who left the suitcase is of slight build and drives a white colored van. Did you see anyone who could possibly resemble that description?"

"Slight build, what, you mean short and skinny? No, I didn't see anyone like that. I did see a big burly guy who was hairy, and when I say hairy, gawd, he was like a bear. He had his wife with him, but I don't think she was as hairy." He laughed at his own humor, which made Clive's skin crawl.

The spider was only two inches away now. *Fuck, I need to keep him talking and see if it lands on him.* "Did you notice anyone else at all, or notice a white van?"

"Can I be honest?"

"Please, being a policeman, I appreciate honest answers."

"Well, I'm one of those people who just doesn't look at vehicles, I wouldn't know a Ford Commodore, from a Holden Falcon."

"It's umm, the other way around, sir."

"What do you mean?"

"Ford Falcon, Holden Commodore." *Fuck it.* The spider started back up its strand, away from the cupcake's head.

"See what I mean? No, I didn't see a white van, sorry. And I didn't see anyone I would describe as slight in stature. Are you sure you wouldn't like to come in for a while?"

Clive Peppercorn shook his head and stepped farther away. "Thanks, but no thanks. That's all I need to ask. Good night, sir."

He walked back to his car, shaking his head, and resisting the urge to vomit. He didn't realize that in stepping back, and down the step, to avoid the spider, Paul Rankin was standing higher than him during the interview. That made him look taller. Had they been on the same level, he would have realized if anyone could be described as diminutive, it was Paul Rankin. Then, if Clive had asked what type of vehicle he drove, he may have discovered it was a white van.

Chapter 15: My Memoir Entry
Incandescent Rage

I am not usually susceptible to rage, dear reader. Apart from when I killed Carly I don't recall ever feeling the kind of anger I felt when I saw the news conference.

I mean seriously, how dare he feel sorry for me? He wants to sit down over a beer and have a chat to see if he can help me? And then jail me? How dare he condescend to me like that. He had his chance to help me, and did he? No, he did not. He abandoned me to a fate worse than death. It was his fault I became what I am, he could have helped, as he promised me he would if ever I needed it, and boy, I needed it then, and where was he? Nowhere to be seen, that's where.

Well, now they've done it. The instructions I had given them were clear enough, they were to acknowledge I existed, not try to belittle me. I would tell them in no uncertain terms whose fault this was. The kid gloves were coming off.

But, that was to be just the start. I knew it was time to begin stage two and turn the heat up on Rick himself. I had been plotting this affair for months, and I had plans and counter plans, and counter-counter plans for all sorts of eventualities. He had no idea I knew where he lived, his dumb wife's name and habits, and, where his daughter went to school.

****

I know I have skipped over some months, but there wasn't too much of great note to tell. I wanted to do some serious planning on my next victim and out of the blue realized that the key to fame was not in the abduction and play time with the victim, but in the way that the body was found. The two women at Lake Monger were very good cases in point, people stopped going to the park, like some people stop going to the ocean to swim after a shark attack.

Suspending the bodies in a tree in a frequently used park had been lapped up by the media and my adoring public. I must add here that in hanging them upside down I used a pulley and winch system. After all they were far too heavy for me to lift. The ropes I had bought, using cash, from a very large hardware type supermarket in a different suburb. The winches I found in a salvage yard. Knowing the police would try to back track them, I stole them, and covered it by buying a chain saw. At the time, I knew I would find a use for that later when I pruned the lemon tree.

Everyone had been talking about the murders, so it made sense that my next unfortunate would need to be even more public. I needed something to not only shock but hold everyone's interest. I needed inspiration.

Completely out of the blue, one day I had been wandering around the Midland Park shopping center during my lunch break. I saw a woman coming out of a shop called The Bag Shop. It was an establishment selling all sorts of women's handbags, briefcases and, you guessed it: suitcases. The woman concerned held no appeal to me, she looked to be Vietnamese, and I have previously mentioned I have no time at all for that race of people after what they did to my father. Anyway, she was quite short, and the suitcase she was wheeling out of the shop looked huge in comparison. It was bright red, with castors on the bottom, and I remember thinking: *Hmmm, I could cut her up and fit her inside that suitcase!*

Anyway, I kept walking having a bit of a laugh to myself how much fun it would be to literally do that to her. And then it struck me, *what if I* did *do that to her?* I stopped suddenly as the enormity of that thought hit me. An old aged pensioner riding one of those motorized buggies with the long orange flag reaching up to the sky for visibility's sake, ran into the back of me.

Bloody hell! I thought, and the idea went right out of my head as the back of both of my legs hurt. The old bloke was decent about it, very apologetic and all that, though he did blame me for stopping suddenly, which, to be fair, I had. We had a bit of a laugh about it all while I rubbed furiously to get the circulation going again.

Later that night, I was watching a new horror movie I had rented from the Video Crash shop in Mundaring called *Psycho Cab Driver*. It was one of those Spaghetti horror films, made in Italy with dubbed English voices, and featured lots and lots of blood and gore. I have always enjoyed those sorts. The cabbie was helping a woman with a suitcase, and he was intending to murder her. Suddenly the memory of the woman with the suitcase returned to me.

And so, the plan was hatched. I found and abducted Melanie from the shopping center car park, which was child's play using the crutches I had bought from the chemist shop. I feigned a fall near my van as she was walking across the carpark, no doubt leaving her children at home, as they all do. Of course, the stupid bitch came over to help, and I held the knife to her throat and she came quietly.

Oh, dear reader, did we have some fun? She tried so hard to please me, she was priceless, my favorite by far. But all good things come to an end, and naturally enough I did tire of the constant: "Please let me go, please let me go," when clearly that was never going to happen.

Leaving the body at the rubbish dump, I thought, was another genius idea of mine. I had the suitcase inside the rear of the van and I had pruned the lemon tree in the back yard using my chain saw, for some branches to obscure it. I was lucky when I arrived as there was no one else at the tip face, so the case was the first thing I jettisoned, then I quickly dumped the branches and was on my way out before someone driving a car with trailer full of their own pruning's, came along. I turned my head away as he passed.

I figured that a brand new looking suitcase would be too much of a temptation for someone, and they would have to look inside. I know if I were at the dump and saw one, I would wonder what it contained.

I lapped up the publicity over the following few weeks. The papers and TV news were full of me, again, though this time it felt different. The Lake Monger Murders was more outrage and indignation, but the Body in the Suitcase was more, dare I say, grudging respect. And then they had the re-enactment for when she disappeared from the shopping center and naturally I wanted to watch it because I wanted to phone in and be a witness, and that's when I saw my old friend, Richard.

Dear reader, I cannot adequately describe how I felt when I saw him. He had come a long way from his constable days. He was a Detective Sergeant in charge of the case, pleading for help from the public to catch me. But, where was he when I needed help? In a flash, I saw my life as it could have been. If he had come to help me, I never would have been in the situations I had suffered through, as I had.

I wanted him to be the one to come to me, and yes arrest me, put me on trial so I could tell the world my story, find the fame I deserved. And, in that fame, I could also make sure he was ridiculed. Everyone would know those people would not have been murdered if he had only kept his promise and came to check up on me.

I had had another, some might say, bizarre fantasy, many years ago. What if Richard had himself adopted me out of that hideous place? He could have been my surrogate father, and I know I would have liked that. I could have been safe from Stubsy, my uncle, and Gordon bloody Bridges. Richard would have taken me shooting, I would have liked that too. I've never fired a gun and would like to know what it feels like. But all those opportunities were taken away from me, by the one man who could have saved me.

For the next few weeks, I planned my revenge. I was in no rush. He had a high profile for a while, and I had given him that fame. How ironic was that? That made it easy for me to track him down and follow him. I found out where he lived, I watched him first at his dump of an apartment, and then miraculously he moved back in with his wife and daughter, what had gone on there I could only guess at the time, but I made it my purpose to find out.

Wearing my best disguise, I got close to her, his wife, and listened to her conversations. The bastard had been unfaithful! How could he have done that? At one time, he was my idol, but he had an affair and his wife had dumped him; my opinion of her went up into the stratosphere. But she took him back? Then, I lost respect.

From my observations of mother and daughter, I knew the kid was a peach, no question, and I hated them both for that. How come she got to live a life with a loving mother and father when I had to suffer, day after day?

I was in no hurry, by taking things very slowly it made the pressure build up for Rick when he didn't make an arrest. The press was all over him, he was made to look useless, and all the time I crowed at my success.

Slowly the plan came together in my mind. The next victim I would make about him, tell them that I was going to carve her into small bits and send each piece to Rick, so that the longer he took to stop me, the more parts she would lose. Then, I decided I would give them a witness, and then she would die horribly. Who would get the blame for that? Rick would. Oh, dear reader I had such fun while coming up with my perfect plan.

I once saw an English horror movie; I cannot remember who was in it or what it was called. But one of the actors when asked how his plan was coming along replied that things were going 'swimmingly.' Well that was how things went for me: swimmingly.

The abduction, the note to the cops, and then I watched from, not so far away, as they interviewed my witness. Oh, it was fun. I realized that once Rick knew I had been watching him interview the witness I gave him on a platter, he would have to take the blame for not stopping me. That would be especially true when it all came to an end and it came out in the press he had once known me, yet he hadn't recognized me when I followed him, how wonderful would that be?

But, then the fun stopped. Rick changed the rules of engagement, didn't he? He insulted my intelligence.

I had started watching the televised news conference about me, elated to see that Rick had been demoted. There was now a Detective Chief Inspector in charge. Oh, did I laugh at that? You bet I did. He had been muzzled, that much was obvious, and he looked morose and dejected the whole way through and I reveled in his misery. I thought the story of the mystery witness was rubbish, a childish hoax to try to trap me. They would need to get up far earlier in the morning to trick me.

But then, he went and spoilt it all. Telling my adoring public that I was sick, how dare he? What's worse; I don't even drink beer!

I had to be careful, after all I was smart enough to know that feelings ran high in the police department over my case. I had to be sure I would live through it all to be able to tell my story, and not get shot dead in some midnight raid when they eventually came to arrest me. I knew they had to find me eventually, that was inevitable; all the TV shows had the killer caught, after all I'd given them enough clues, so it wasn't the capture that bothered me, quite the reverse. I wanted to be caught because only then could I be famous and in that fame, drag Rick down in the mud.

I knew there would be a book deal, and probably a movie, not that they would let me act in it, I'd be in jail, but they would acknowledge me for all the crimes I committed. I wouldn't be the small insignificant victim I had been all my life, I'd be up there in lights, and I couldn't wait. Even in jail I would be a hero among the inmates, no one would dare abuse me there, not with my fame they wouldn't.

So, I wanted to get caught eventually. But I wanted it to be me handing myself in, not my front door kicked in, shots fired and me sprawled across my bed riddled with bullet holes, while some corrupt cop stuck a pistol in my hand to make it look like I had wanted to fight. I'd watched lots of movies and knew that often happened in life. Giving myself up was one thing, I was happy to do that, but how to do it in such a way that even that would make me look like a hero, and good old Rick look like an incompetent coward?

And then, dear reader, it all came together; the perfect plan. I could make it all happen to my set of rules. It was a good plan, it would work. He would suffer, as my father had once threatened me with: *A fate worse than death.*

Chapter 16
The Needle in the Haystack

Loretta Starling was a local freelance journalist with dreams. She thought she was good enough to be an international correspondent, or a Sixty Minutes anchor. She had practiced, in front of her dressing table mirror over a hundred times how she would phrase her line: "I'm Loretta Starling, Sixty Minutes, Goodnight."

All she needed, she knew, was just one big break that would get her name up in lights, and she strived more than any other Perth reporter to find it. Unfortunately, for the four years she had been doing her job, that break had eluded her. She had been to a scene too late or missed the exclusive through all sorts of bad luck and bad timing, but she knew she was better than all the rest. One day, she was sure, her time would come, so she kept practicing her Sixty Minutes sign off, and dreamt of traveling to exotic and dangerous places where she could look down the camera lens and say her line to her adoring millions of viewers.

True, she sold stories on a regular basis; enough to make a living, but generally they were powder puff pieces. She went to courtrooms in case anything interesting developed, sat at the airport on the off chance a Hollywood actor arrived incognito, and dreamt of stumbling across the one big break that would rocket her into journalistic heaven.

She had spoken to the big-time reporters when she could, to beg for information as to how she could find her opportunity, but all they gave her was a load of well-meaning clap-trap about hard work and persistence. She knew that. What she wanted was the magic bullet that would take her there faster. After all, at twenty-eight years old, she wasn't getting any younger, and she knew, that for female reporters, her looks were as important as her brains. Therefore, she had a shelf life, and every day she didn't find her panacea was one day less she would have at the top, once she eventually made it there.

Everyone was talking about the big murder investigation, the Body in the Suitcase, and that was now being linked to the poor woman, June Daniels, who had been abducted. A race against time, and every reporter and his brother were working it. There were never less than eight of them hanging around the front door of Police Headquarters, and for that reason, Loretta had been rather sneaky. She had followed a car through the boom gate protected car park behind the building so she could discreetly watch the rear entrance.

She had been sitting in her car since quite early that morning and had run out of snacks, and she was bored. She knew this was what it took to be a reporter, watching and waiting, but she knew she had to give up soon and follow one of the cars out; she needed to find somewhere to pee.

She had just told herself *ten more minutes, then I'm out of here,* when she saw a car arrive at the boom gate entrance. She picked up her camera, just in case, and watched the dark blue car circle around as the driver looked for a vacant space. As the car slowly made its way down her aisle, she hunkered down but just caught a glimpse of a woman sitting in the passenger seat, and she instantly remembered her.

Loretta had been covering a murder trial about eighteen months prior, and she watched Patricia Holmes giving evidence as to the mental state of the accused. It was gritty and harrowing stuff, not at all for the faint-hearted, and Loretta had found it fascinating. So much so that she had sought out and asked for an interview with Mrs. Holmes and had been granted it.

Though she wouldn't talk about the specific case she had given evidence about, she did espouse on how she believed that criminal psychologists should be used in major police investigations on a regular basis. They could help give insights into personality traits and assist in identifying serious criminals much earlier than was currently being experienced. She believed that 'Profiling,' which had become big in America with the FBI, would one day catch on in Australia.

Once Loretta saw Detective Richard McCoy get out of the driver's side of the car, after he had parked, it all fell into place, and Loretta aimed her camera. Her telephoto lens tracked them across the car park as she took picture after picture of them. She looked through the viewfinder, clicking away, with her mind racing. She realized how glamorous the woman looked, and how Rick looked the opposite. Sure, he was dressed well enough, but his unkempt hair, stubbly beard, and jacket creased from sitting in the car reminded her of Beauty and the Beast. The headline flashed across her mind: COPS BRING IN FAMOUS PSYCHOLOGIST TO TRACK DOWN SERIAL KILLER.

It was just at that moment Mrs. Holmes stumbled

as her stiletto heel rolled over something and instinctively she reached out a hand and grabbed Rick's arm to stop herself from falling. But, what Loretta saw, as she snapped away, was the look that passed between them as he put his arm around her lower back to help. They stared at each other, momentarily, and Loretta took a series of pictures which to her clearly indicated, that if they weren't having sex already, they soon would be.

She flung her car door open and dropped the camera on her seat while climbing out in one fluid motion. By the time she reached them, her hand-held recorder was on, and the would-be lovers had recovered. They had reached to the rear door where Rick was about to enter his code into the keypad.

"Mrs. Holmes, remember me, Loretta Starling? Can I ask if you've been brought in to work on the abduction case with Sergeant McCoy?"

"What the hell are you doing here?" the angry cop asked while Patricia looked flustered, like a kid caught shop stealing. "This is a restricted parking area."

"Is using Mrs. Holmes skills to profile the killer top secret then?"

"What on earth do you mean by that?" Rick looked around, obviously hoping to spot a uniformed cop who could evict her out of the car park. Naturally, there wasn't one and she humorously lamented on the cliché: there's never a cop around when you need one.

"Well you're sneaking her in the back entrance. I would have thought that someone of Mrs. Holmes reputation would be worth using the front door."

"Miss Starling, this is not the back entrance, and Mrs. Holmes is not being snuck in. You're being melodramatic, and foolish. We have no comment to make."

"So, you are part of the investigation team then Mrs. Holmes?" And the look on both faces was all the confirmation she needed: she had her story.

"Loretta, I do remember you, you interviewed me some time back, and you did a very good and thoughtful piece on me for the Sunday Supplement. Please don't print my involvement here, you could do irreparable damage," Patricia replied.

"Damage to who? I'd have thought you being brought in was your dream job. It's in the public's interest to know that the police are so desperate for a lead they would bring in a psychologist." Loretta loved the way she sounded, *if only this were being videotaped, I'd be a super star.*

"Please listen, Loretta. The police are working on several lines of inquiry, but the person they are looking for is extremely dangerous and unpredictable. If you print my involvement, it could make him very angry, and he might react. I'm just here as a volunteer advisor, that's all. I'm not being paid, and it's not my job. My husband and I are friends with the assistant commissioner and he thought I might be able to offer some advice. You're making a mountain out of a molehill, and it could do real harm if you print."

"Miss Starling," Rick interrupted, "you know I cannot comment on operational matters, but it's vital Mrs. Holmes assistance remains out of the public's domain, for now. How about if I give you my word that when the time is right, I will give you the story, so long as you don't go public right now?"

Loretta nodded, *sure you will, you must think I'm*

236

dumb if I'd fall for that one. She tried to look thoughtful, as if she were seriously contemplating not divulging what clearly was the biggest potential story of her career; one that could finally launch her toward her dream. "So, just for clarity's sake, you are asking me to bury your involvement Mrs. Holmes because you think this nutcase, might do something even more manic because he would think that you think he is insane?"

"Loretta," Patricia pleaded, "we are dealing with an extremely troubled personality. It's impossible to predict how he will react to your story. I urge you, please don't risk anyone else's health and safety until after he's caught. Then, if you want you can have an exclusive with me, and I will tell you anything you want to know about him."

"But what if you don't catch him anytime soon? And another reporter finds out about you?"

"We are more concerned with the victim he is holding hostage. Your story could tip him over the edge, and he kills her. Is one story worth that? Give us a few days to follow the leads we have, that's all we ask."

"So, in your professional opinion this man is *that* dangerous."

"He *is* that dangerous."

****

"Pat this is Detective Chief Inspector Colin Harris, Boss, this is Patricia Holmes."

He stood up and reached his arm out to her across his cluttered desk. "Mrs. Holmes, I want to thank you for helping us out like this. Please have a seat. I've organized an office for you both to use and have had the three complete case files with witness statements delivered so they are waiting for you. I'd love to hear your thoughts as to why you think this is our man. Tyler is across at the West Australian Newspapers office checking out those letters to the editor."

"Before we get into that, Boss, I've got to tell you a reporter recognized Pat in the car park and buttonholed us. I think we may have convinced her not to go public, but I'm not so sure. The shit may well hit the fan if she goes to print."

"Fuck! Sorry Pat I hope the odd cuss word doesn't offend you."

She smiled, "I've heard the word before. The situation can't be helped now. I'm all for buckling down and getting to work and try to find him quickly."

"True, what's done is done. I suppose it had to come out sooner or later. If you would though, just so I can get my head around all of this, please give me a quick run through of your thinking. Rick here has been singing your praises, since he met you, but why do these three case files stand out?"

She sat and crossed one leg over the other and gave him a summary of her thoughts. Rick and Colin sat silently, digesting what Patricia outlined. Rick had heard it all before, but this was the first time that the Inspector had met her, and he watched his bosses face to try to get an insight of his thoughts.

Colin Harris cleared his throat. "Pat, that all sounds feasible, I agree, you make a very plausible, but highly circumstantial case.

"Well, that's what I do. Let's be honest, you wouldn't need me if he had been anything less than he is; you would have caught him. I could be wrong about one, or more, of those three cases being attributable to him, that's true. There is only one way to find out. If

I'm right he knew the first two victims, and by cross-referencing the witnesses I hope to find him. I also think he couldn't resist the urge to have been a witness at Lake Monger. To be fair I'm less sure of that, but it fits with what I consider to be his profile. Then, the engineered leak would have thrown him off his kilter, he may fear you are closing in sooner than he would have liked, this could go one of several ways."

"And if this reporter does publicize that you've been brought in as an advisor? What will that make him do?"

"Hmm, that's not so easy to answer. But in my opinion, he is a true narcissist. He craves recognition, and he demanded you acknowledge him in a press conference because he needed to feel like you all agree he is the best there has ever been. Rick said a couple of things which on top of this man's sense of malice he holds against him, will have angered him. But, if he hears you all believe he isn't superior at all, that he is mad, then I worry what he will do, what retribution he will take. Today was unfortunate and I just hope this Loretta Starling agrees to keep the story to herself, at least for a few days."

"Let's hope so. I will try to talk to her myself, who does she work for? Maybe I can bring some pressure to bear."

Pat shook her head slowly, "When she interviewed me, she was freelance. If she doesn't agree to hold off for her own reasons, she will sell to the highest bidder."

"I see. Look, every other lead we have is petering into nothing, everywhere we look it's one dead end after another. So, right now I'm hoping you are right and you can give us something to work with. I'm afraid that in terms of witness statements not much would have been computerized unless something unusual was noted, and I'm guessing from what you've said he probably didn't stand out from the crowd. I've sent word out to the original lead detectives to be prepared to be interviewed by you both. I've asked that they have their notebooks ready, just in case they noted something which at the time wasn't deemed important enough to put into the record. If you require anything else, you only have to ask."

Rick stood up and opened the office door for Pat. She nodded toward the DCI who returned the gesture, then picked up the type written sheets she had prepared as a profile and began to read.

****

Three hours later they had jointly worked their way through the reports, scene of crime pictures, and witness statements covering the murder of Gordon Bridges. They had read the interviews of his wife and family members, work colleagues, friends, and those who were suspected of being homosexual lovers from an address book found hidden in the back of his desk at his place of work. They had studied the forensic report of the car, and noted the unidentified gloved fingerprints taken from it. There were numerous statements taken from known sexual offenders.

"Rick," Pat began, "is it me, or does it seem to you like the investigation from the very beginning centered around looking for a gay hate killer?"

He stared back at her, experiencing mixed feelings about the investigation. On the one hand, they were his colleagues, and he was naturally biased to protecting them from undue criticism. But, deep down, he had to agree with her assessment.

Her hair was mussed up on her left-hand side where she had a habit of resting her hand while she read. She had also undone the top button of her shirt and every now and again, as she moved, he caught the faintest glimpse of her beige colored bra strap; a sight which he found remarkably exciting.

"Pat, I know what you are saying, but I have to say, from what I'm reading here, I probably would have come to the same conclusion. None of the fingerprints taken match our man."

She sat back in her not too comfortable chair, tilted her head to one side, and as if by magic, the right-hand side of her shirt ballooned out. He could clearly see the bra strap reaching down toward the cup. If she just leaned forward a bit, and the blouse stayed sticking out he would be able to see the top of that cup. Like a schoolboy, he yearned to see more.

Fuck, I must stop thinking this stuff,

"I know what you're thinking, Rick." She stared pointedly, and Rick squirmed.

"You want to be loyal to them because they are fellow officers. But, one thing I think I know about you is that you would not have jumped to that conclusion. You would have exhausted *all* avenues before you made a judgement call. I realize the prints don't match, but that just proves he didn't want them taken. He would have worn gloves. There is one group of people who have not been interviewed, and I'm quite sure you would have attempted that."

Rick bowed his head, feeling a sense of relief that he had not been caught out as a pervert. "What group is that, Pat?"

She didn't reply. Slowly the realization dawned on him. "Jesus, you're right. He was a Public Trustee; what about the families and inheritors of the estates he managed?"

"Tunnel vision. It looked like a hate crime, so that's the type of killer they looked for. Now, that would have been fine if he had been murdered by that sort of person, but I don't believe he was."

"Fuck, we're going to need a court order after all this time to get those records, that's always assuming we can get a judge to agree to giving us one. Damn, they should have at least looked at them; you're right, Pat."

"Here's what I think. Let's consider the timing of this. If I'm right our murderer was a young man back, then. What if my earlier thoughts were correct; that he had been in care or adopted, and while he was underage, his affairs had been managed by Gordon Bridges?"

****

"Mauri, long time no see," Rick began as they shook hands, "this is Patricia Holmes, a consultant who is helping us out with the June Daniels abduction case. We'd like to talk to you about the Gordon Bridges unsolved murder you worked on."

They had driven south to the Rockingham Police Station where the detective now worked.

"Yeah, I know, your DI was on the phone this morning warning me about it. Why is it so important now after all this time?" He sat back down behind his desk. He had the look of a cop approaching retirement, his once white shirt was grubby, and stretched taught across his expanding belly. If he had started the day

242

wearing a tie, it had long since been discarded, and he looked long overdue for a haircut.

"We feel there is a strong possibility our guy was your killer, and we are chasing up background information."

"Bollocks."

"Why do you say that, Mauri?"

"Like everyone I've been following the suitcase murder and have heard on the grapevine about the developments with the abducted woman and the threat to send you parts of her body. No way it's the same guy."

"Again, why do you say that?"

"The park was a known haunt for car sex between couples, and the public toilets was a 'beat' that had a reputation as a place for men to meet to give each other blow jobs. There was a glory hole in the cubicle door for Christ's sake. Bridges obviously propositioned the wrong guy who went nutso and killed him. It was a dead end from the start. We door knocked the area, even set up an undercover cop over a few nights to hang out at the toilet so we could interview the queers who met there, to see if any of them had come across anyone acting weird, but like I said, the case went nowhere."

"Sergeant, do you mind if I ask you something?" Pat asked

"Sure, shoot."

"Did you ever consider it was anything other than a gay sex meeting that went wrong? Was Bridges a regular visitor to the park?"

"We couldn't prove he was a regular there, but we do know he had sex with other men, he was a fag. We looked at his acquaintances, family, and wife; she knew he was bisexual and put up with it for the kid's sake. Darlin,' if something walks, sounds, and looks like a duck; it generally is."

"And, did you ever consider it was one of the clients he had."

"Nah, why would it be? Besides even if it was, there was no way to get those records from the Trustee's office without a Court Order, and there was no evidence to support asking for one. It would have been a waste of time."

"Okay, Mauri, thanks for your time, I appreciate it." Rick stood and offered his hand to shake.

"Are you guys saying I fucked up here? That I should have looked deeper?"

"Sergeant," Pat answered. "Right now, we have no evidence, that's what we are looking for. But we think there is a very real possibility it's one and the same killer. That as a young man he was a client of Gordon Bridges, and for whatever reason, he lured him to the park with the intention of killing him. But I suppose at the time, you did the best you could, there is no suggestion you did anything wrong."

He looked crestfallen, and Rick grudgingly changed his opinion of the man "Mauri, it's a theory at this point, we have our reasons for thinking that's what happened, but I agree with Pat, there is no suggestion of any wrong doing on your part. It would have been nice if you'd looked at his client list, but I can understand why you didn't."

They stayed mostly silent in the car heading back down the freeway to the city, each lost in their own thoughts. The traffic was quite heavy, and it was after six when Rick pulled into her driveway.

She turned in her seat so she partly faced him, in doing so she lifted one leg under the other which caused her skirt to ride up her thighs, and the shirt ballooned out again. This time, she was leaned slightly forward and the bone colored bra cup came into view. *Fuck, she is one hot woman.*

"I'm beginning to respect what you guys do, day after day, Rick. I started out today with high hopes, that we would make inroads into this case, but we are no further advanced than when we started. It's disappointing, isn't it?"

"Police work is sometimes about the mundane. Asking questions repeatedly, and sometimes you're right, for all the work, nothing breaks. I spent weeks on the suitcase murder, full time, and realistically got nowhere. I wish cases were solved quickly, believe me, but you must be in this for the long haul, and know that in the end you made a difference. Tomorrow things could break, and what looks impossible tonight, might become clear in the morning. This is what we do."

"Tom is out at a Rotary Club dinner, do you feel like a glass of wine, or a beer before you go home?" She smiled and tilted her head to one side.

To Rick, the invitation was clear, sitting as she was, with the look of hope, and what looked like need, in her eye. Half of him was pleasantly surprised, and the other half was screaming at him to say no.

He slowly shook his head. "Pat, I'd like nothing more than to continue this inside, and have a drink with you. But if I leave right now, I should be able to get home in time to read my little girl a bedtime story, and that, when I can make it, is the highlight of my day.

Another time, maybe?"

"Rain check sounds good. She turned back to open the door, still leaning slightly forward, and the gap in her shirt exposed the entire bra covered breast to his gaze. He almost wavered.

Driving away he was torn. He wanted to turn around and go back.

Richard Bryan McCoy, you are a fuckwit. Remember back, just a few months ago, living alone, in that dreadful apartment, pining for Juliet and Amy? Now grow up, keep your dick in your pants. Go home and hug your daughter.

He realized he was driving ten kilometers over the speed limit. Tomorrow was another day, he realized, as he eased off the accelerator.

Chapter 17
The Day the Sky Fell In

Rick and Patricia arrived at the squad room just after eight in the morning, right after the mail had been delivered. That was when the nightmare began.

"*Rick, Patricia, get in here now!*" Colin Harris's voice boomed across the incident room. They glanced at each other and hurried over.

"What's up Boss?"

Sitting on the middle of his desk was a parcel wrapped in brown paper. It measured around twenty centimeters long, ten wide and seven or so high. In black permanent ink was Rick's name and the address of the police department.

"Fuck no, don't tell me." Rick gasped and sat down.

I was about to open it, but as you're here, and it's addressed to you..." The DI tossed him a pair of latex gloves. "Not that there is a lot of point, everyone in the postal service has touched the outside, still, forensics may get something from inside. They are on their way, I just got off the phone with them."

Pat stood by the door, hand over her mouth, horrified. Slowly Rick pulled on the gloves. He gently picked up the box and turned it upside down to get to the edges that had been sealed with clear sealing tape. He peeled it back with his thumbnail wary that there could be fingerprints on the sticky side. As he pulled the brown wrapping paper away, a single sheet fell out, and the three of them leaned over to read it.

Dear Rick
I thought you might need a hand to catch me.
You want to chat with me over a beer, do you? You had your chance, and you don't get a second. We will meet one day, but it won't be over a beer. Will you be ready for me?
Are we having fun yet?

PPP

Inside the paper was a purple plastic lunch box, with a pink lid. The type a child might take to school. Rick looked up at Colin, who nodded back. Gently but firmly he grasped the tab on the corner and peeled it open.

"Oh my God!" Pat gasped and turned away, her hand firmly clamped over her mouth. There nestled inside the box lay a human hand, the left one, which had the wedding ring finger missing.

****

Thirty minutes later the squad was assembled for the inevitable meeting. Four people stood at the front of the room, before the white board: Assistant Commissioner Monkton, Patricia Holmes, Rick, and Detective Inspector Colin Harris. In central position was displayed a large photocopy of the note they had read earlier. There was the usual hubbub of noise between officers until the loud, angry voice of the DI quietened them.

"Right, shut up everyone, there is no time for chit chat. We have received another piece of our unfortunate victim; her left hand to be precise. If she is still alive we must acknowledge she has very little time left now and I want everyone to give her a hundred percent effort to try to save her life before it's too late. Are we clear on this?"

Every police officer signaled their agreement.

"I was here most of last night, going over your reports and witness statements, and quite frankly, so far you lot have brought me nothing we can use. We are no closer to nailing this bastard through normal police procedures than we were a week ago. From this moment on I want you all to act think and feel as if June Daniels was your wife, mother, or sister, we need to get serious and find her, are we clear on that?"

"Mrs. Patricia Holmes is with us; she is helping us understand what kind of person we are dealing with. She has made considerable inroads, so far and has come up with some good theories, and I want her to tell you all what kind of man we are dealing with."

"Sir, as from this morning's paper, the whole world knows we have brought in a psychologist. I picked this up on the way in." Detective Joel Crittenden held up that morning's West Australian. The headline screamed: *POLICE BRING IN TOP PSYCHOLOGIST TO HUNT DOWN 'EXTREMELY DANGEROUS' KILLER.*

Rick and Pat both groaned at the same time, they had not had a chance to see the newspaper, and it was the kind of headline they had been dreading.

"Right, well we knew this would happen eventually, but with June Daniels losing her hand, the medical examiner worries that the blood loss and shock she must have suffered means that she could die sooner rather than later, if she is not dead already. Pat, would you please give the squad the kind of summary you gave me yesterday."

As if rehearsed, the three men took a step away, leaving Pat standing alone, like a deer caught in the headlights, and she nervously began her summary.

"Thank you, Detective Chief Inspector. Let me start by saying that what I do does not in any way undermine the job you perform. I have the utmost respect for dedicated police officers who do this work. Anything I can do to help is just that; help. Please think of it this way: you might look at a crime scene and search for clues and evidence. I look at the same scene and ask why that way, what was he, or she, thinking. What was their frame of mind, and what led a person to the point where they took that action? By reading hundreds of case files, and studying the mental states of serial killers over the years, places like the Profiling Department of the FBI have made great strides into understanding that word: why. And if we extrapolate that further, if we can understand the why, then sometimes that can help lead us to who. I hope I've explained that well enough.

"I was asked to look at the suitcase murder, and the June Daniels abduction, and I have drawn several conclusions from them. Our man then went on to murder Bridget Schaeffer in such a way that it gave more insights into his mindset. I've also looked at past case files to look for what I call his footprints in the sand, that he left before he became what he is today. I believe we have found three such cases, though let me stress I believe there were more, but the bodies were never found, because PPP didn't want them found."

She went on to explain her theories in detail, then paused. "If you corner him he will do one of three things, kill you, himself, or surrender. I think PPP wants to give himself up to become famous. But, he is not quite ready yet. He has some master plan that he has worked on for a long time, and I worry what that plan will be."

"Yesterday, Rick and I combed through the full case file and witness statements for the murder investigation of a Public Trustee from a few years ago, by the name of Gordon Bridges. I believe this was our killer's first victim. Unfortunately, the investigating officer, who I think is a good man, and I mean no reflection on his abilities, jumped to a wrong conclusion."

Some of the officers appeared to fidget nervously. "I'm not here to criticize anyone, he saw the case from a certain perspective, one which a lot of policemen might also have made. Unfortunately, he did not consider Bridges' work clients were suspects, and I feel it was there that our man could have been found. I hope a court order is granted so we can see who his clients were."

"We hope to get that today; we have the Public Prosecutor's Office working on it for us," Colin interjected.

She nodded her appreciation then carried on. "Today Rick and I are looking at what I believe was PPP's second murder, and then, the third and fourth. Some of you know about those, they occurred at Lake Monger."

There was a very sudden outburst by a detective she didn't know. "So you are saying PPP was the Lake Monger Murderer?"

"Yes, I believe he was. That was the beginning of his phase where he wanted fame, he wanted that recognition, adulation even, he so desperately craves. It was there, where he honed his skills and it became a precursor to the Body in the Suitcase." She nodded her head to add emphasis, then explained why she thought what she did, and explained about the letters to the editor, linking the earlier killing.

"For me there are two very scary things in the latest note. Firstly, it's a repetition of an early question: *are we having fun yet?* And secondly, it's the attempt at humor in offering Rick a hand to catch him. More than anything else, these two things show me that we are dealing with a true sociopath. Genuine sociopaths are rare. They do not experience guilt or remorse, no feelings at all. You can't plead with him, he doesn't understand mercy, you can't threaten him, he doesn't feel fear, or worry about consequences. You can't hurt him, either; he has been hurt all his life."

"All right, thanks Patricia," Colin Harris said. "Now, Tyler, tell us what happened with the West over these letters."

"I've got print outs for them all, and they do make for interesting reading, sir. At first, I thought they were just the ravings of some self-righteous do-gooder, but then they got quite weird. And if I didn't know Mrs. Holmes explanation I would have wondered why suddenly he started talking about other possible victims killed by the same murderer, including Carly Biddle. The clincher is how he signed the letters, I'm sorry to say it was PPP. Naturally they didn't keep envelopes, there is no way to trace where they came from, especially after all this time. They didn't even have the originals."

"Is there anything he says which gives away who he is, what he does, where he lives?"

"Nothing that I could see, sir, nothing obvious anyway. Perhaps Mrs. Holmes can spot something."

"Please guys, call me Pat. I'm not into all this Mrs. Holmes stuff. Yes, I'd like to read them; it proves he murdered Carly Biddle, and by association, it also proves he was the Lake Monger Murderer, as I suspected. If we could only get the client list of Gordon Bridges to cross reference, I'm sure we will spot him."

"We will find out about the Court order today, I will push harder. Where are we at with re-visiting, the previous witnesses?"

"Nowhere sir, we're about halfway through, but so far nothing," Clive Peppercorn offered.

"What's the latest from forensics? And that photo, did we get it enhanced?"

"Nothing new from both, boss," Sergeant Brighton answered.

"As I said earlier, you guys are bringing me nothing. I want a full team to go to Midland Post office, question everyone, he must have mailed the parcel yesterday, someone would have seen him. Being Midland Shopping precinct there could be CCTV. He may be disguised but we know he is of slight build. Tyler, I want you at forensics, push them for quick results on the parcel, the hand, the lunch box, give me something. I am going to see June Daniels husband, and deliver the news. Pat, and Rick find PPP for us. Let's go."

It was well past lunch time when Rick and Pat had finished reading the last piece of paper in the box containing the evidence for Carly Biddle's murder. He was stiff and sore from sitting for too long, and while he didn't want to admit it, bored. "Fancy a sandwich or something from the canteen for lunch?" Rick asked.

Pat nodded, looking distant and deep in thought.

The café on the top floor wasn't overly busy and they got a table by the windows, Pat selected a salmon salad plate and Rick took a beef casserole with vegetables. They agreed to phone Detective Barlow, who had run the investigation, straight after lunch, who, Rick had discovered, had transferred to run the CID Department at the Kalgoorlie Station. Being five hundred kilometers away it was too far to drive for an interview.

"What's your first thoughts, Rick?" Pat asked as she took a bite of her salmon with lettuce strands forked up against it.

"A good solid investigation. I can't see too much they did wrong. It looked like it might have been the ex-boyfriend for a while there, until that played out."

"I agree. I can't see that they did anything wrong or missed any connection. The fact that she was killed on her way home from work, suggests the killer fixated on her there. Unfortunately, it's a big shopping center, so there's not just the supermarket she worked at, it could be someone who works at one of the other shops and he saw her from afar. Come to that he may not work there at all; he could have just seen her while he was at the bank, or post office, and she was on her lunch break. He could have stalked her from that point on. It kind of has that feel, that he watched her, stalked her, and that night she rejected him."

"We could go there and re-interview all that we can, but, of course there is no guarantee PPP still works there after all this time, if he ever did."

"I think he may, Rick. He would tend to be a creature of habit. He would like order and the stability of repetitiveness in his life, it would give him comfort. But with over three hundred witness statements, not one of which matches up with Gordon Bridges case, that would take a lot of time."

"But surely we could narrow that list down. For example, we could ignore all the women, and married men. You said that PPP would be single and incapable of a normal relationship."

"True. Although that said, there is a slim possibility he could be married. Peter Sutcliff, the Yorkshire Ripper was, and his wife never suspected a thing. I don't think that's the situation here, but it's possible. But, even so, that still leaves a lot of potentials. And remember, this man will be difficult to detect by talking to him. And, in doing so, we will alert him that we are closing in. No, without Bridges client list to compare against, I think we should go through the Lake Monger case files and see if we can spot him there. I think he would have made sure he was interviewed at some point. If we get a double up of names, then we can move quickly without warning. Rick, you have realized I'm sure, that the parcel was sent from the Midland Post Office, which is the same shopping center Carly Biddle worked?"

He nodded. "I wondered when you would mention

that." He smiled. "I also realize that because we police tend to believe there is no such thing as coincidence, it does also offer proof that your theory is correct. I'm sure we will also find a shop there that sells the type of lunch box that the hand came in. Yes, he knows this shopping center very well. I bet there are two or three places that sell suitcases too. Is it also a coincidence the dump he used is Midland? I think not."

"Even though we don't have anything concrete, I feel we are closing in, albeit slowly."

Well, when we get back we will phone Jack Barlow, and see if anyone stuck out in his mind, but not enough for him to put in the statements. Meanwhile I will have the DCI put someone onto looking there for lunch boxes and suitcases, not that I think that will throw up a suspect, but it couldn't hurt; you never know."

When they got back to the station, Rick placed the call but was informed that Detective Inspector Sam Barlow was out of the station but should be back around two thirty. Rick left his extension number and asked for the call to be returned, and that it regarded an old case of his that had been re-opened. While they waited, they opened one box each of the Lake Monger Murders evidence and started reading.

"Rick." Pat glanced up after a while. "I didn't make the connection before, but these two bodies were hung upside down and had their throats cut after death. Didn't you tell me the Medical Examiner thought that the body in the suitcase had been hung upside down before death?"

"Yes, he thought that by the ligature marks and blood lividity. Oh, I see what you mean; yes, it's a signature, isn't it? Why didn't I realize that before?"

"It's easily missed if you didn't work on the case." She smiled at him, and he smiled back. It was true, this had never been his case, and other than water cooler chat, he had no information prior about the investigation.

"Why hang them upside down, do you think?"

"I really don't know. It can't be for the sex angle; it must be something else. I suppose it makes less mess, from a practical point of view. You realize, of course, he used a pulley and winch to hoist them up in the tree. More proof of his small stature."

"Hmmm, I suppose, but then again a cut artery sprays blood a long way. No, I don't think it's that. I could understand in the case of cutting Melanie's body up, it would make it easier, but in the Lake killings, they weren't dismembered. The supply of rope and winch, as usual, turned into a blind alley. Common rope bought from Bunnings and the winches were old and rusty. Could have been in the killers shed for years."

In that moment, he almost had it. On the peripheral of his consciences he thought of an abattoir, with carcasses swinging upside down on a conveyor chain across the ceiling. But before he could make the leap, the phone rang. "McCoy."

"Detective Inspector Barlow, returning your call, Sergeant."

He sat up straight, instinctively, as if he were sitting in front of a superior officer, rather than speaking on the phone. "Thank you for ringing back sir, I appreciate it very much. It's regarding the Carly Biddle case. It's been re-opened because of a connection with a recent murder and abduction, and we think there is a very good chance that it's the same perp. I'm going to put you on hands free mode, Sir, if you don't mind so my partner, Patricia Holmes can listen in." He pressed the speaker button.

"Yes, I'm aware of the background; your DCI called and said you would be in touch. I remember the case, and I did glance through my notebook from that time, but I didn't spot anything that will be helpful. The fact is that it was one of the most frustrating jobs I've ever worked on. We walked in, thinking it would be a simple one to solve, but it just went nowhere."

"What made you think it would be an easy crime to solve, sir, what was your first instinct?" he asked, leaning forward in his seat.

"She was single, lived with her sister; both parents were overseas traveling at that time. She was mousey and not prone to going out at night partying. She hadn't had a steady boyfriend for a while, and the last one she did have was in a happy relationship with her replacement. At first, we thought it was him, because he had no alibi that would take scrutiny, but there was no motive. Our next thought was that it was something to do with her job, that she had been bullied, or had had an argument with someone there. He, or she, followed her home until she got to where she was killed; it was a quiet street, mainly high fences at that spot, and she was murdered under a huge willow tree. So, we interviewed everyone at work, and like most work places everyone thought it might be someone else, but really, when we interviewed each of them we couldn't find a suspect. In fact, the more of her colleagues we spoke to, the more unlikely it seemed that it was someone from there."

"Why was that sir?"

"Just that everyone checked out. There was the usual bunch of assorted people who work in the same place. Some were likeable, others were horrible, but true to say most of them liked the victim. There was no hint from anyone that there was an issue between her and any of her colleagues. She was good at her job, and doing payroll, she was everyone's friend on pay day."

"I see, please go on, sir." Rick glanced at Pat, who looked to be listening with rapt attention."

"We talked to everyone else at the shopping center, asked if they had noticed someone hanging around, or who had been watching her, but no one had. It was a dead end every which way we turned."

"Did you get an indication from any of the witnesses that something, anything, wasn't, quite right? Just a feeling? We know our guy would have enjoyed being interviewed. We also know he is of slight build."

"Look, Sergeant, all of the young blokes that worked in the shopping center had chips on their shoulders, like the world owed them a living, you know the type. The middle-aged ones seemed normal, and again, no one stood out that I can recall. It was also a long time ago. We thought we might find a suspect by telling them that we had found a DNA sample on the body when we took theirs, But, no one refused to give a sample, or even batted an eyelid. If one of them was the killer, they would be the best liar I've ever come across."

"You took DNA samples from all of them? The results are not in the file."

"No, well they wouldn't be. We didn't get them tested, it was just a bluff to see if anyone got antsy. It would have been expensive to test that many samples, and we didn't have the budget. If we could have narrowed it down to one or two prime suspects, fine, but then again, you must understand there was no sample that had been left on the body, so we had nothing to compare it to. It was a bluff to see if someone cracked."

"Yes, I see sir. Would the samples still be with the forensics department, or, would they have been disposed of at the time?"

"Do you have something to match it to now?"

"Yes, we have lots of traces."

"Well, you'd have to check. So far as I know they were never destroyed, but then again, after all this time, they may well have been by now."

"So, sir, going back to the investigation, your best guess at the time was a random sexually based attack?"

"Not personally, no. I always felt it was more personal than that. But when the case went cold, and we had no suspect, the powers that be overruled me, and I can't blame them for that. I always had the feeling that the fact she had been stabbed, and then her dress opened after death, was suggestive of a more personal attacker, but, there was nothing to prove that that was the case. The DI was of the belief that sooner or later he would strike again, but he never did, not so far as I knew."

"Sir, I'd like to thank you for your time, it's been very helpful, especially if we can locate those DNA samples."

"Good luck with that. Tell me, what makes you think it's the same man killed Carly Biddle, and your woman in the suitcase? I'm intrigued how you linked them."

"It was Assistant Commissioner Monkton's idea that because of the bizarre nature of the two murders and an abduction we are investigating, we bring in a very well credentialed psychologist to consult: Mrs. Patricia Holmes. She and I have been trawling old case files."

"I see. Monkton has always been a bit of a radical. Mrs. Holmes, thank you for not jumping in with questions, unannounced, I would be happy to answer any you may have of me now. It always bothered me that I hadn't done enough for Carly, I'd like to help in any way I can."

Pat blanched and glanced toward Rick. She cleared her throat and leaned toward the phone so the microphone would pick up her voice. "Thank you, Inspector, I must say it's wonderful to be included in such an important investigation, I just hope we can find June Daniels alive. Sir, if you don't mind me asking, I'd like to know what your instincts told you about any of the witnesses you talked to. Our man would have been young, probably around early twenties I would guess. He is small and thin, possibly almost effeminate. He would have acted incredibly smart, almost condescendingly to you as well as being very quick thinking. Of course, he would have expected to be questioned, and would have been prepared for it. Knowing that, could you cast your mind back to everyone you spoke to and tell us if anyone at all stands out in your mind?"

"Hmm. Bloody hell, you don't want much, do you? Do you know how many people we questioned who could fit that description?"

"I was just hoping that because of his feeling and

acting superior to you, that in itself may have made you take note at the time and remember him now. But, it was quite a long time ago, and you've interviewed a lot of other suspects since, I do understand that."

"Look, let me sleep on this, I will wrack my brain, you have my word on that, and I will phone you tomorrow if I come up with anything.

She called her number out to him and they said their goodbyes. Once the phone was hung up, Rick turned to her.

"Can you make a start on the boxes, while I go and see the DCI and see if we can find those DNA samples, it could identify PPP if we can." He held up his hand to silence her. "I know what you're going to say, even if we do find them it will take days to get a match, but I'm hoping they can at least give us a blood type from them; we know PPP's."

She shook her head, "Rick, I'm sorry to rain on your parade, but detecting a blood type from a saliva test is theoretically possible, but by no means definitive. It would take more testing not less, and the result you end up with would not be foolproof. I daresay it would also be expensive. The only way to tell a blood type is from testing blood itself, or semen. I do believe you should find the samples and test them, it will certainly help convict PPP when we catch him, though I doubt you will have the answers in time to save June Daniels."

He nodded. DNA tests were expensive, and slow. Determining a blood type from saliva would not be easy, he was clutching at straws, he knew that, but he just knew they were getting close. "You're right, Pat. I will go and report it to the DCI, let him get the ball rolling and see if they still exist. I will be back in a minute."

Ten minutes later he returned and sat back down in front of the open box. Pat looked up, and he shrugged. "He's sending Tyler over there to see if they can be tracked down."

At that moment, his phone rang and he fumbled in his jacket pocket to pull it out. Once in his hand he pulled the aerial out with his teeth and barked his usual answer into it: "McCoy."

"Rick, it's me. I'm at Amy's school, did you finish work early and pick her up? Oh, God, please say you did." Juliet's voice sounded frantic; nearing hysteria.

"No, Jules, I'm at work. What's happened?" he replied instinctively standing up from his chair.

"Amy, she's been picked up by someone else, she gone, Rick, she's gone, she been taken."

Chapter 18: My Memoir Entry
Ducks All in A Row

Granted, dear reader, the day didn't start well; the stupid woman died on me!

I suppose the shock of losing her hand was too much for her, and yes, I guess I should take the blame for that. But, once I had the thought about lending them a hand to catch me, well, it was irresistible, surely you can see that? I cauterized it well enough so she didn't lose too much blood, I mean; it was bloody inconsiderate of her.

She could have lived; I was willing to let her. If the cops had caught me and she was still alive; albeit missing a couple of bits and pieces, I would have let her go back to her family.

I thought I had been careful enough I had wanted to send them her leg next, and I couldn't very well do that after I found her hanging by her one good wrist, lifeless in the cool room. The police may well be stupid, but the medical examiners they use are not. They would be able to tell that the leg had been removed after death.

After I ranted and railed against the damned woman for a bit, I calmed down and realized it was probably for the best. To be frank I was tiring of the whole thing. What had seemed like a brilliant plan had become boring. I mean I didn't even have sex with her because I wanted to keep her alive as long as possible, and I thought forcing her to have sex might demoralize her further. Then there was the feeding and cleaning up the waste. It wasn't as much fun as I thought it would be.

So, realistically, her dying, once I had become accustomed to the idea, wasn't all that bad. She had served her purpose; they had sat up and taken notice, and finally acknowledged that I was a superstar. So, it was only fit and proper that I moved on to phase two.

While I was disposing of her corpse, cut into nice neat pieces, into the back freezer, I decided I would just move everything else forward, and I smiled at the thought. Detective Sergeant Richard McCoy; he was the real enemy. And, when I had completed that task, it would be time to hand myself in and find the fame I so richly deserved. I knew in my heart that this scrapbook you are reading, would go on and become a best seller, it had to. So, I had to make sure I was alive to publicize it through a high-profile trial.

While I set about my tasks I turned the radio on and picked up the news bulletin, which was live from Police Headquarters. I raced back through to the house and switched on the TV. Half of me was delighted when I realized the police on screen were talking about me, but what the hell? They had brought in a psychologist? Did they think I was deranged? How dare they discount my superior intellect, strategy, and planning ability as the work of a madman? I listened in stunned silence, the damned woman was working with Rick, and they told the reporter I had 'an extremely troubled, narcissistic personality?'

That made me mad, incredibly so. I paced up and down and wanted to punch a hole through something. I would have too, if I didn't value my hand so much, and had something thin enough to be able to do it to. I was always going to make Rick pay, now he would pay an even higher price. I shook my head to myself, knowing I would have the last laugh, and Rick wouldn't know what hit him.

I had always yearned for the day when everyone knew my name, like they did all the famous serial killers. I would no longer be the man who everyone walks past and doesn't notice, the man who has been bullied since childhood; *I would be famous!*

Once I had cleaned up the mess and disinfected every surface with steaming hot soapy water, I went down to the local shopping center and bought some toys. After all, I was going to have a child as a houseguest and I wanted to give her some things to amuse herself. I am many things, but I am not, heartless.

I dressed in one of my favorite disguises. I'd been to her school several times, and watched her mother pick her up. Like a lot of others, including my own before she left me, Juliet is self-centered and lazy. She waits for little Amy outside the front gates of the driveway. There she stands talking away, with mothers like her, like a gaggle of geese. But Amy's classroom is around the rear of the main administration building. I wouldn't be seen by her from the street when I made my move.

Now, before I can tell you of my plan, it's time to let you, dear reader, into one of my biggest secrets. But, to tell you it, I must first take you back in time

When this phase started with my uncle, I hated it, like everything he did. But, it's funny how things work out. These days I love that one thing that he made me do all those years ago.

I will not go into the details of the sex acts between my uncle and myself, suffice to say they were as hideous as they were relentless. He showed no quarter, gave no mercy and I had no choice in the matter. What made it worse was he always, but always asked me if we were having fun yet. That was his saying, and he used it every time he raped me. Was I having fun? Of course, I wasn't.

Long hair was fashionable then, and when mine was sufficient, he liked to brush it for me. Next came the dress ups. He brought home this very frilly mini dress, a teenagers training bra, and girls under pants. These were the kind of things you would expect a twelve or thirteen-year-old girl to wear. Naturally I refused, and he punched me in the face and when I raised my hands to staunch the flow of blood from my nose, he kneed me in the stomach, and I dropped to the floor.

"How fucking dare you say no to me," he screamed at me as I lay writhing. "I saved you from the orphanage, and you will fucking do anything and everything I tell you to do or I will take you straight back there. Once I finish telling them all you are nothing but a raving queer boy, your life will be hell in that place."

I had little doubt in the front part of my brain that he wouldn't send me back there, he had way too much fun with me. But then again, if he did and he told those lies about me, just how bad would my life get then? I was not a queer, but at Parkerville, there were several strong boys who were gay and violent. To be used and abused frequently by people like that and be too small to fight back would be more than I could bear. There is a saying in Australia, 'Hobson's choice.' It means you have no choice at all, and, I had, no choice either. The devil I knew could be a lot better than the devils I didn't.

So, I put the bra, panties, and dress on, after I washed the blood off my face, and then faced the inevitable.

The only good thing I can say about that night was that the sex didn't take long. But of course, as you can imagine, it didn't stop there. There were more clothes, and the underwear got sluttier, school uniforms, French maids, and then came the make-up. I was expected to not only wear young girl's clothes, but to be made up so I became a young girl, and if I do say so myself, I realized one day, I looked pretty. At first that thought was abhorrent to me, looking like a girl, but, over time, I adjusted, and after a while, I thought I looked, well, can I say hot?

I remember one night after I was ready for the usual, I stared at myself in the mirror, and I suddenly 'got it.' To all intents and purposes, I was a girl. No one would be able to tell that I wasn't. I had always been small and slight, but with long hair, make-up and wearing girl's clothes I almost fancied sex with myself. I was beautiful, and I did not look like a boy any more. All I needed were breasts, but that didn't seem to bother my uncle, he liked me to act pre-pubescent.

From that day forward, while I still did not like the sex, I began to enjoy dressing and looking like a girl, and later, like a woman. It was somewhere to retreat to, where I could feel better about myself. Once I got into it, I did appear to have breasts because of the padded bras I wore. Now, I don't want you to think dressing up for me was about sex, it wasn't. If men choose to do that for those reasons, that's their thing and I mean no disrespect. For me it was more like, well my life had been hell, and this was a chance to be someone else who hadn't had an awful life. It was a pretend world, and a harmless one.

After my uncle died, I came up with a name for when I went out like a woman: Charlotte Bingham, I took the first and last name from characters in movies I saw. It was so refreshing that people noticed me, where they never had before. Men looked at me, not that that had an appeal, but when I was just me, women never looked. It was liberating to feel noticed, and liked.

So here is my big secret: the reason they never got a decent witness statement about me? Most of the time I was dressed as a woman.

I watched the cops interviewing people and it was always: 'did you see a man...' Honestly, I nearly wet myself. I even let them interview me at Lake Monger, and the stupid policemen wrote my name down as Charlotte Bingham. He asked for identification and I made an excuse, that when I jogged in the park I didn't take ID with me, and I watched his eyes closely. He didn't have a clue.

Even my voice: I could make it sound very feminine. In fact, I don't believe anyone talking to me, would think I wasn't who I was pretending to be, even if they knew me. I proved it once by dressing up in 'my best' and going shopping in the supermarket where I worked. It was dangerous, I know, but I spoke with Hazel on the checkout about the weather, and what she was doing that night, and she had no idea it was me.

****

And so, I went to Amy McCoy's primary school, looking prim and proper, as if I belonged there. I walked right in through the side gate, from the staff car park, and waited just outside the administration building for little Amy to come out. Once I saw her I called her name and waved to her. She looked perplexed, but because I looked like I belonged there she came straight over.

I squatted down so I was eye to eye with her. "Amy, mummy sent me to pick you up, she isn't feeling too well, I work with your daddy. My van is out the back here, let me take you to her."

I stood up and held out my hand, and like a little lamb she took it. We sang songs all the way back, and I promised her chocolate milkshakes and biscuits when we got there. I swear, it almost broke my heart when I locked her in the cool room, because she was so sweet.

****

I knew he would cause a kerfuffle. He was a policeman after all, and his daughter had been kidnapped, of course he would flood the school with cops. But really, what could anyone say? Amy was taken away by someone who looked like a school teacher. That's always assuming anyone saw me at all, which I doubted. It was finishing time and kids were running everywhere, I honestly didn't see anyone give me a second glance. I was just one more woman picking up a child.

It would have been a shame if anyone did see me, because the cat would be out of the bag. But, I was planning my endgame, and I had just one or two more

270

jobs to do before I handed myself in.

I left Amy to play in the cool room with her new toys, of course by then she was crying and wanted her mummy, which was tiresome. I knew right then I wasn't cut out for parenthood. I tried to tell her mummy was coming for her later, but the little smarty-pants then questioned why I'd told her she was sick.

In the end, I pushed her in the cool room and shut the door so I didn't have to put up with the whining any longer. I had to go and buy a mobile phone; I had never had need of one before.

Still dressed as Charlotte, I drove to the city and got there in time to find a phone shop in the main mall. I flirted outrageously with the young man as I got him to show me everything about the phones that came with a pre-paid SIM card. I told him I was buying them for presents, so didn't want to do any paperwork for ownership. He explained that with these types of phones, none was necessary. When the SIM card ran out of credit, it could be re-charged at any participating shop, so it was anonymous. Wonderful technology, isn't it?

I bought three, and had so much fun licking my lips, and touching the man's arm, I even offered him my 'fictitious' phone number, which he wrote down, no doubt thinking he could screw me anytime he wanted. Oh, aren't men just so dumb? I toyed with the idea of luring him to his death, but with Amy in the cool room, and getting so close to my confrontation with Rick, I decided against it. He is a very lucky man. He even put some charge into the batteries for me, so that they could be used straight away.

You may be wondering: why three phones? Well I

had befriended a guy about my age in the Midland phone shop when I had sat next to him in a lunch bar. I had done it quite intentionally to get information about mobile phone technology, and the traceability of them. I was aware that at the end of nineteen ninety-nine the analogue phone network had finished, and we had joined the digital revolution. I thought that meant that mobile phone use could be tracked; and I was right. Over a lunch of toasted ham and cheese sandwiches, my new friend told me all about it. Phone carriers could trace a phone while it was on air, so if I hadn't done my homework they could have found me when I used the phone. Therefore, my intention was to make a call to Rick, then dispose of the handset immediately, then use a second for the next call.

I knew I wouldn't be calling more than three times, probably only twice, but it always pays to be careful. I've got where I am today by forward thinking, after all.

I went to a little bar called Solo's, to kill some time. I wanted Rick to suffer, so I was in no hurry to phone him and give him his ultimatum. I sipped a glass of white wine, in my most feminine way, and thought about how he would react

I watched the bulletin on the TV, mounted high on a wall bracket. I even comically put a shocked hand over my mouth as I watched the breaking news story about the little girl abducted from her school. Everyone in the bar shut up and listened; I suppose there's nothing like a little lost child story to get people's attention. Even Rick, bless him, begged for her safe return. I swear it warmed the cockles of my heart to see him so upset.

It was while I was eating some crumbed Whiting

fillets an overweight, office worker, whose tie was crooked, and shirt untucked offered to buy me a drink. Well, my blood ran cold. The wedding ring on his finger clearly showed he was married, yet here he was trying to pick me up and have sex with me. I smiled my best smile, as I pictured sticking my knife, which was hidden in my handbag, into his throat and twisting the blade. *Well,* I thought, *it could pass the time, so long as I don't get his blood on my nice clothes.*

Over the next hour, I let him think he was Don Juan, and charm me out of my underwear. He kissed me, but I stopped his hand traveling too far up my leg under the table: "No, not here."

"How about we go out the back, let me show you a good time, you've got great tits."

Seriously, this guy is making my skin crawl. "What makes you think I'm the kind of girl who would go down a dark alley with someone I've just met?" I whispered in his ear, trying to sound a little husky.

"Well, I think you're the kind of girl who would love a good fucking, and out the back is pretty dark, no one will see us." His hand squeezed my thigh and started heading north again, so I grabbed his wrist and pushed it down, more firmly.

"But you're married, what about your wife?"

"What she doesn't know won't hurt her." He took my hand and put it on his crotch, which I must admit was impressive, and throbbing. "There's plenty of meat for both of you. Come on, you know you want to, why else did you come into a bar by yourself?"

"I only came in for a meal, and to kill some time."

"Come out the back with me, and we can pass some time together. Come on, live a little, I bet I can make you cum like a freight train."

Oh, my God. Cum like a freight train? I will be doing not only his wife, but the entire female population of Perth a huge favor by killing this idiot. I looked at the dainty watch on my wrist. *Yep, it's just about the right time now.*

"All right, you talked me into it, let's go." I finished my drink, picked up my handbag and stood up.

The fat pig downed his beer, and I watched as he waved to his mates, gloating, no doubt about the easy lay he had picked up.

You should have gone home to your wife; honestly, you should have.

I followed him out the door, then around to the right. At the corner, he turned and waited for me, probably to make sure I didn't change my mind. I smiled, trying to look like I was gagging for it. When he turned back I slipped the knife out of my bag and turned the handle upside down so the blade didn't catch what light there was.

I took my jacket off and put it on a windowsill; I wasn't going to risk getting blood on that, it was my best one. I kissed him a few times, just for fun. He was breathing like a pig; grunting and groaning. Once again, I stopped his hand going to my crotch. "It's the wrong time of the month for me; let me go down on you," I whispered.

Even though it was dark, I could see his eyes glaze over as he must have thought all his Christmases had come at once. It could have been the darkness, or he was distracted, because he didn't see that I had turned the knife around. Mind you, he was frantically undoing his belt and zipper at the time. Once he exposed himself, I pirouetted like a ballet dancer, and as quick as a cobra strike, I cut his throat.

That's when the fat man got his filthy blood on my arm, which only made me angrier. I followed him down as he fell, stabbing, non-stop. He died quietly, spluttering and wheezing, rather than screaming. I suppose it's quite hard to scream with your throat gaping wide open. I decided his wife would be better off without him, and it took all my willpower not to kick him in the face; the disgusting, unfaithful, pervert that he was.

Quite calmly, I turned on my heel, and walked away, feeling as calm as ice, stiletto heels echoing the noise against the alley walls.

****

It was just after eight-thirty, and I was standing outside the Myer's Department store, leaning on a convenient rubbish bin to drop the phone in afterward, I made the call I had been looking forward to. I smiled as the number chimed its ring tone, and I heard three or four sirens in the distance. *They found the body, excellent.*

I put on my deepest voice when I heard the man himself answer his phone: "McCoy."

"Hi, Rick, it's PPP. I've got your daughter, Amy, isn't it?"

Chapter 19
The Ultimatum

Within six minutes of Juliet's phone call police cars converged on the school. What few parents were left there were asked to wait to answer questions, though a frantic Juliet had already run from person to person asking if they had seen her daughter, so they were aware a child was missing.

The teachers completed a search of the grounds and buildings, confirming that Amy was nowhere to be found. The headmistress, Ms. Stanza, generated a list of all children's parents with addresses and phone numbers, and was checking off names of parents who were still hanging around, so that those who had left earlier could be phoned or visited by the police for witness statements.

Rick's car skidded to a halt and he was out of the car running to Juliet before it came to a stop. She burst into fresh tears when she saw him. They clung to each other, her sobbing into his shoulder.

"Where has she gone, Rick? Who would do this to us?" Juliet wailed.

"We'll find her, Jules, we will, I promise."

He was torn. He wanted to go and conduct his own investigation and start questioning people, bang heads together if he had to, but he knew he was in no fit state to objectively hold interviews. Amy was the light of his life, and if he caught up with whoever took his little girl, their lives would not be worth living.

His thoughts of revenge were interrupted, "Mrs. McCoy, my name is Patricia Holmes, please call me Pat, I'm so sorry for what you are going through, if I can help in any way, I'd like to do that."

She didn't answer, her face stayed buried in Rick's shoulder and he ran his hand up and down her back. He had not spoken a word to Pat, all the way there in the car, though she had tried to talk to him. Each time she had he had held his hand up to silence her, so he could concentrate on driving as fast as he could make the car go, with its siren blasting a warning to other road users.

"Babe, in your handbag, do you have a recent photo of Amy?" he asked, gently. She shook her head that she didn't.

"Okay, I'm going to send you home with Pat, here, and two officers to get one. One officer and Pat will stay with you, just in case Amy comes home, or there is a phone call from a parent that has taken her for a play date. The other cop will bring the picture back here so we can circulate it and see if anyone saw her. If we have two, please send them both, one we will get copied for the patrol cops to have to search the area, the other we will get on TV. Jules, I promise I will do whatever it takes to bring her back home, trust me." Juliet nodded her acceptance.

He turned to Pat, would you mind staying with Jules for a bit, I'd really appreciate it."

"Of course I will, I'd be happy too, but can I have a very quick word with you before we go?"

He nodded, then beckoned uniformed officers over and explained what he wanted them to do. One gently guided Juliet to the patrol car, another would take Juliet's car. Rick turned to Pat, "what is it Pat?"

She took a deep breath, then gripped his lower arms in her hands. "Rick, I can't even begin to imagine what you're feeling right now, but please listen to me. You know who has done this, don't you?"

He stared back, blankly, then shook his head. "You can't think this is PPP?"

"Rick, in life, there is no such thing as these sort of coincidences, you know that, don't you? He would have been planning this move for a long time. Don't lose sight of that, and don't play into his hands by panicking and doing exactly what he wants you to do. He will see this panning out a certain way, don't allow it."

"Pat, you're wrong, there's no way he would know where Amy went to school, there has to be another explanation."

She stared back, solemnly. "It's him Rick. That news conference has tipped him over the edge, and my involvement has made him retaliate. He wants to punish you even more than he did before. Planning is his hallmark; this is how he rolls. He would have been watching you, long before his first note to you, once he saw you on TV. Please believe me, stay vigilant, I know this is tough, but you need to stay focused, out think him."

She turned away and hurried to the patrol car.

Rick watched her go, slowly shaking his head from side to side. *Could it be? Surely not, she's wrong; she has to be.*

****

The next two hours passed with Rick in a daze. He was conscious of the investigation, and took part, but he felt, and acted as if he were on automatic pilot. His brain churned over, repeatedly asking himself the question: *could it be PPP?*

The thought was too horrific to contemplate. Every time his mind wandered to the possibility he dragged it straight back, he simply could not bear the thought of his angel in the company of such an evil man.

TV crews showed up and held interviews with Colin Harris and Assistant Commissioner Monkton. When Rick was asked for a comment all he could say was: "Please, whoever has got my little girl, Amy, give her back, I'm begging you."

Numerous officers had been dispatched to the parents' homes that had left the school earlier, having picked up their children before the alarm had been raised. The school color photocopier had been utilized to make duplicate pictures of Amy, but each radio report in did not bring any useful information. It seemed the children in Amy's class had been intent on getting to their parents for reasons varying from arranging play dates, or having something to eat as quickly as possible, to have noticed where Amy had disappeared to.

They acknowledged she had been in class, as per normal, and all had left at the same time, clutching their bags and books. But what had occurred after was a mystery. The first glimmer of hope came from a radio call from Constable Patrick McSweeney. Rick was talking to the DCI, when the radio squawked to life with an announcement of the police car's call sign.

"Go ahead Oscar Romeo one seven," Colin Harris answered.

"Sir, I'm at the home of Mrs. Ravensthorpe, her

daughter Colette is in Amy's class, and she thinks she saw Amy talking to a woman near the administration building as they were on their way to the front gate. She thinks she heard the woman call out to Amy."

"Did she think it was another parent or teacher?"

"Sir, I asked if she had ever seen the woman before, and she said she wasn't sure. She was in a hurry to get to a birthday party, which was why they were not home when we called earlier."

"Tell them I am on my way," Rick said.

Colin Harris grabbed his arm. "No, you're not, Rick. I will send Tyler, you cannot possibly be involved, and you know that."

"It's my little girl, please, I have to be. I'm going mad, here."

"Rick, go home be with your wife, she needs you with her, there is nothing you can do here. I will get Tyler there with a sketch artist. Let us handle things, and I will call you the moment anything develops, I promise. We've got something like sixty officers searching for her, we will find her. Go home, your wife, needs your support."

Rick hung his head. Without another word, he turned on his heel and walked away, as Colin spoke back into the microphone. "Stay there, keep them company, I'm sending a detective and a sketch artist."

Back in the car, Rick gripped the steering wheel and rested his head on his hands. He wanted to scream with frustration. He had never felt so helpless, or so inadequate. Eventually he shook himself from his malaise and started the engine, and within minutes pulled into his driveway. A lone patrol car was parked on the street.

He was almost at the front door when it was flung open and Juliet ran out with a female officer, and Patricia close behind. "Any news Rick, have they found her?"

He reached for her, when he knew she could tell by his face there was no new information. He hugged her to him as she broke down with fresh tears. "Babe, do you know Colette Ravensthorpe or her parents?"

She leaned away from him, searching his face, "Vaguely, why?"

She says she thinks she saw Amy talking to a woman near the admin building. Maybe it was another mother who took her to play with her daughter. She could have parked in the staff car park, and that's why you didn't see her leave."

"But that doesn't sound right, Rick. There are signs all over the gate no entry to parents, it's for staff only."

"Sweetheart, I don't know any more than that. I've been ordered off the case; I can't be involved; they think I will be too emotional to be able to make the right judgement calls, and they are probably right. Maybe it wasn't a woman, maybe she was mistaken, but they are sending Tyler and an artist over now to get what they can. I've come home to be with you and wait for developments."

Her shoulders dropped, and she turned away. "Pat, thanks for staying, I'm sorry to burden you with this, I will get you taken home. I will phone you as soon as there is any news." He turned to the officer who had stood quietly waiting. "Please run Mrs. Holmes home."

Pat watched Juliet enter the house before turning back to him. "Rick, I'm so sorry this has happened. I feel responsible. If I hadn't got involved and that damned reporter opening her mouth, maybe this wouldn't have happened. I know in my heart this is something to do with PPP, but who this woman is, baffles me."

"I can't see how this can be anything to do with him. It sounds like a woman took Amy for a play date. PPP has nothing to do with Amy's disappearance."

She shook her head, biting her lip, clearly wanting to say more. "What, Pat, what are you not saying?"

She sighed, loudly. "I don't know anything, and it's so damned frustrating, but I can tell you what I think. Firstly, I can't remember the last time a woman abducted a child this age from a school ground, can you? I'm not saying it's impossible, but if it was a woman, you would think she would be emotionally unstable, but this does not look like the work of an unstable female, does it? It suggests planning, and guts, if not sheer audacity, not luck. Amy was spirited away with almost no one having seen anything out of place. Who else do we know comes up with this sort of strategy? Secondly, if I am right, it can only mean one thing: June Daniels is dead, and he has moved his schedule forward, because she is of no more use to him. I believe the news story about me being brought in, and your insult at the press conference has tipped him over the brink into out and out revenge. Possibly this woman is innocent, maybe it's a teacher, or a parent who stopped to ask her something, or maybe it wasn't Amy this other child saw. But everything about this abduction reeks of PPP's work. I'm sorry Rick, it's your daughter, and I'm very worried for her, but we must think clearly and not ignore the obvious."

"You know you can be quite heartless, can't you?"

She reacted as if he had slapped her. "Oh, Rick, is that what you think: I'm saying these things because I have no heart? Nothing could be further from the truth. I'm saying them because I *do* care."

"So, what exactly do you suggest I do?"

"There isn't anything that can be done until he gets in touch, but, he will contact you. This is only the first step; I'm sure of that. You need to be ready for him. This is just one rung on the ladder he has created for you to climb.

"Well, he can do anything he likes to me, I just want Amy safe." He turned away. "Constable, can you run Mrs. Holmes home."

****

The first phone call came from Tyler just around seven o'clock. "Boss, it's me. I've questioned the girl, and I'm sorry to say it's a dead end. It may or may not have been Amy, and it may or may not have been a woman she was talking to. When I pressed her, she wasn't sure, it was more something she saw peripherally, and an impression that it was a woman."

"I see, thanks for letting me know," he replied, his heart sinking as Patricia Holmes' words echoed in his head.

"Boss, I'm not giving up, neither is anyone else, hang in there. Is there anything else I can do for you and Juliet?"

"Just find our little girl, Tyler, please just do that."

"I'm sorry, Jules," Rick said to his wife who was standing by his side, "It looks like a dead end with Collette Ravensthorpe."

She looked more depressed than anyone he had ever seen before as she turned to go back to the couch where she had been sitting, staring silently into space. "We will get her back, Jules, I promise you, don't give up hope."

The second call came after eight. It was Colin Harris. "Rick, I'm sorry to report we have nothing for you. All parents have now been interviewed, and other than the report of Amy talking to someone who was possibly a woman, we have nothing. We've searched the school grounds and buildings, door knocked the houses closest to the school and we are coming up empty. We have also searched the local parks, same result. I've got patrol cars sweeping the streets in the area and they will be doing that all night. I'm so sorry we don't have any better news for you. Hopefully by the morning there will be calls through to the Crime-stoppers phone appeal, someone, somewhere must have seen something."

Rick now felt as depressed as Juliet looked. "Thank you, sir, I appreciate all you've done."

"How's Juliet holding up?"

"We're just holding onto hope that she is safe."

"I'm going to send a female officer from victim support, she will be there in the morning and will stay with you both. Then, if you need to leave Juliet won't be on her own. Is that okay, Rick?"

"Yeah, that's, umm, a good idea sir, thanks."

For the first time in his career, he hung up the phone on a superior officer.

The next phone call arrived fifteen minutes later. "McCoy."

"Sergeant McCoy, it's Loretta Starling, you gave me your card with your mobile number the other day when we spoke. I just wondered if you had any comment that I could circulate for you to help find your daughter?"

His blood turned to ice in his veins and a rage took over him. He walked out of the lounge room so Juliet didn't hear his response.

"How much did you get paid for that story? Was it enough for you? Was it worth antagonizing the killer so he kidnapped my daughter?"

"Do, you know that it was the same man, Sergeant?"

He bit his lip, suddenly realizing she was just trying to make him say something she could put in print. The more sensational the better. "You're a piece of work, aren't you? Do you even care that your actions may well have caused the kidnapping of a child? How would you feel if it was your daughter? But then, I'm guessing that you are such a cold-hearted bitch, no man would want to have children with you." He hung up the phone.

He thought she would call back, to argue, but the phone didn't ring again until later. By then, he was ready to climb the walls, as Juliet sat morosely staring into space.

"McCoy."

"Hi, Rick, it's PPP. I've got your daughter, Amy, isn't it?"

He was speechless, for a moment, a mass of conflicting emotions ran through him, with rage, and fear being uppermost. Suddenly, he found his voice, "You? You took my daughter? I will kill you. Listen to me; if my girl is not returned safe and sound I swear to you I will hunt you down and kill you if it's the last thing I do."

"Rick, Rick, Rick, you disappoint me. But then you've disappointed me before, haven't you? I can hang up if you like, and you can try to hunt me down to kill me; I don't care either way. But, you haven't had a lot of success so, far have you? Let's be honest here, you would never get to me in time to save her. Is that what you want? Your girl is fine, playing with some toys, *for now*. How long she stays safe is in your hands, not mine. She's quite a peach, isn't she? A credit to you both. Now, I have not touched her, *yet*, but as I said, whether she stays safe is up to you, and of course your wife, Juliet, isn't it?"

Juliet stood by his side, her hand on his shoulder, trying to listen in to the call. "Please, let her come home. You can have me, do whatever you like to me; just let Amy come home." His tone sounded frantic, begging, even to him.

"Oh, that's very good Rick, personalize her, use her name, you've obviously been to hostage negotiation school. You see? You can do so much better when you try. Now, how badly do you both want to see your daughter alive again? Oh, I know, silly question, let me re-phrase that. How far are you *both* prepared to go to see her alive again?"

"I will do anything you want."

"Now, Rick, clearly you weren't listening, so I'm going to try one more time, and if you ignore me again, like you did once before, I will hang up, and Amy dies. I said, how far are you *both* prepared to go to see her safe? Now hold the phone so that Juliet can hear me as well, I want to talk to *both* of you."

"Please, please, please let our daughter go, she hasn't done any harm, she is just a child," Juliet pleaded when Rick tilted the phone so she could join in to the conversation.

"Juliet, can you hear me now, I can hear you okay, but it's important I speak to you both. Listen carefully now; you have a choice to make."

"Yes, we can both hear you, tell us what you want." She gripped the phone around Rick's fingers.

"Okay. See? Now that's good, now you get the picture. First up, I'm sorry but I cannot in all clear conscience keep calling you Juliet, that's what Rick calls you and that leaves a bad taste in my mouth. So, I'm going to call you Julie, is that all right? Of course, it is. Next, I did a drive by of your house, and didn't see any cop cars out the front other than your blue one in the driveway, Rick. So, we must agree to keep it that way, this is between the three of us, agreed? If I get even the merest whiff of another cop being involved I will break off contact, and Amy dies, are we clear on that?"

"Yes, there won't be anyone else involved, you have my word," Rick said for both.

"Yes, well, your word doesn't count for much, so this time on the merry-go-round I will be watching you. You won't know where, or when, but I will be there, somewhere. If you let me down again, I will know, and Amy dies a horrible death."

"I don't know you, tell me when we met before, and what I did to deserve this."

"All in good time, Rick, but honestly, I'm not an idiot, so please don't treat me like one. Didn't you have an affair and Julie kicked you out? You have history of deceit. Don't bother arguing or trying to justify things that cannot be justified. I've had my eye on you for a long time. The fact is: your word isn't worth much in my opinion."

"He made a mistake, yes, but he regretted it and has been the perfect husband ever since. Everyone is entitled to a mistake," Juliet shouted, the edge of hysteria in her brittle voice.

"Julie, love, you're sure you don't mind if I call you Julie, do you? I'm doing this in part for you. Don't you suspect he is up to his old tricks again with that rather dishy psychologist? Didn't you see the rather cozy picture of them in the paper, the way his arm was around her?"

Rick turned red. "I swear to you Jules, on everything I hold dear, I haven't done anything with Pat. And, that picture was taken as we were walking across the car park and she stumbled and would have fallen if I hadn't grabbed her."

The mocking sound of laughter came echoing down the phone.

She stared at him, slowly nodding. "Really? Nothing happened? But you've at least thought about it, haven't you?"

Rick felt snookered, with PPP on one hand taunting him, and Juliet on the other looking for someone to blame. "How can I even answer that? Have I thought about sex with other people I've met or seen? Probably, and I bet you've seen guys you have fancied too, that's natural, if you ask me. But it doesn't mean you act on those thoughts. I promised I would never stray again, and I haven't, and won't. You and Amy are everything to me."

"Oh Bravo, Rick, very slippery, a bit like an eel. As fascinating as this is, let's move on, I'm sure you two have a lot to talk about after this call is over. But one piece of advice, Julie: I've been watching Rick, and don't believe a word of what he says about Mrs. Holmes, they're at it like rabbits. Now, moving on, it's all well and good you saying, Amy is just a child, but I was a child once, and I hadn't done anyone any harm either, but it didn't stop people hurting me. In the case of your husband, he could have helped me, but he chose not to."

"Tell me your name, I don't remember ever refusing to help anyone, especially a child. I think you have me mixed up with someone else."

"You see, Rick, right there is your problem. You didn't care then, you just pretended to, and you cared so little since you don't even remember me. Well I remember fine, and there is no mistaken identity. Anyway, now is not the time to talk about that. But, it's a nice lead in to what I want from you both to free your daughter You see Rick, because of you I suffered, and now it's your turn to feel pain, so here's the deal, are you both listening?"

"Yes," they both replied in unison.

"Good, you have a choice. I will free Amy, but I have to have Julie in her place."

Chapter 20
Face to Face with the Devil Incarnate

Patricia Holmes, felt a mixture of anger, and frustration, in equal proportions. By the time she had been delivered back home, the person she was most angry at, was Rick. *Why can't he see I'm right, and how can he call me heartless?*

Tom, was in the kitchen, preparing a meal. She briefly filled him in and told him she would fix herself something to eat later, she was determined to work. "The answer is in the files, I know it is, and I'm going to find it. I made copies of the Carly Biddle witness statements and brought them home."

He nodded, morosely, almost ignoring her. They hadn't spoken since the argument a few nights before. Pat went to the rack and took out a bottle of wine and a glass from the shelf above and disappeared back into her study.

Sitting behind her desk, sipping from the glass she had filled, she went back over everything she thought she knew about the man they were hunting. *Small man, thin, intelligent, egotistical, arrogant.* She sat up straight, and put her glass down, she had had a thought. Pat rummaged through the papers until she found what she was looking for: the phone number for Detective Inspector Barlow. She dialed the number and pleased when she heard his voice answer hello.

"Hello sir, it's Patricia Holmes, I'm terribly sorry to call you so late in the evening, but there has been a serious development here in Perth, and I thought I would take a chance and try to get hold of you."

"Ah, Mrs. Holmes, no I don't mind you phoning me at all, what's happened there?"

She ran him through the events surrounding Amy's disappearance.

"You really think it's the same man?"

"Yes sir, though I'm having a tough job getting Rick to listen to me. But, he is so upset over his daughter; I can't blame him for not being able to see the wood for the trees. Have you had a chance to think about the witnesses and if so, did anyone jump out at you as being overly confident, if not cocky?"

"As it happens I did have a think, and someone has come to mind. I didn't like the little pipsqueak one little bit at the time, but there was no evidence against him. His story checked out, but, back then I wanted it to be him, if that makes sense. He just didn't feel right, and after you saying he would act condescending, well, this guy did in spades. He didn't have an alibi, but there was nothing whatsoever to suggest he had done it."

She felt a tremor run though her body, and she leaned forward at her desk. "Go on, sir, please."

"He was small as you said, but I wouldn't say effeminate; he didn't give the vibe that he was gay. He was just, well, weedy, for want of a better description. One of the earlier interviewees had said that this guy had the hots for Carly, but was such a coward, he would never find the nerve to talk to her."

"Go on please, sir, this is fitting in very well with my profile."

"I remember fronting him with the accusation that he had harmed her, and he just stared at me. Usually, when you accuse a suspect, they can't help themselves but talk and talk and talk to convince you they were innocent, but this prick? Well, he just stared back at me, insolently. Then when I called him a smart arse, he said he felt sorry for her parents and that every staff member fancied Carly and if we focused on him we would miss the real killer. I didn't think of it at the time, but the thing was that every other staff member didn't fancy her. By all accounts she was very plain looking and was stand offish to all the men, some even thought she was a lesbian. Our guy, she just ignored like he was a dog turd. Is that what you were looking for?"

"Oh yes, sir, that's perfect. What was his name?"

"Rankin, Paul Rankin."

****

After she hung up the phone she sat back in her chair, and despite knowing Rick's anguish, realized she was enjoying the thrill of the chase. She wrote the name *Paul Rankin* on a sheet of handy paper, and ran several circles around it, almost going through the paper with her enthusiasm. But, she had to admit it was only Detective Barlow's intuition; there was nothing else to suggest that Paul Rankin was the killer. His name did not come up in any of the witness statements for the Lake Monger Murders or the suspected gay killing of Gordon Bridges. Of course, she had known it wouldn't come up in that case, unless they got the list of his Public Trustee clients. Was Paul Rankin's name there? She would bet her house that it was, but for now there was no corroboration.

Was it a coincidence that Paul started with a P, and

the killer wanted to be known as PPP? There was certainly no other P's in his name, but she felt that that was right, it was more likely to have come from a nickname, than his real one. He was far too intelligent to use his own initials, but it must have meant something to him. Everything had a reason or a purpose. *What else was there?* She wondered, as she took another sip from her glass of wine.

She spluttered and dribbled as she experienced a blinding epiphany. The woman seen talking to Amy. *A woman!*

Wait, wait, wait; hold the damned phone, let's think this through. She rummaged on her desk and found a pencil, then flipped the nearest sheet of paper over and began to write, but such was her excitement she snapped the lead off. "Fuck!" she exclaimed, then yanked open her drawer to find a writing implement that she wouldn't break.

1. Small build and height

2. Known to have used disguises to avoid suspicion.

3. Sexually abused as a child, probably by a male family member, step-father or in foster care.

4. Gordon Bridges was killed at a park frequented by gays and was himself bi-sexual—theory: he had sexually abused the young PPP from a position of authority—most likely a client as Public Trustee.

5. Abducts women, not men, often from shopping centers—theory: his mother abandoned him causing him to hate women in general. He has sex with the women he abducts to prove to himself his masculinity.

6. If he has gay tendencies, could this have been exacerbated by being either forced, or could he have willingly, dressed as a woman/girl in his formative years?

She threw the biro down. *Amy was abducted by PPP dressed up as a woman.*

It made sense; it all fitted together, but where was the proof? She shook her head; it was the police's job to find the proof; hers was to come up with a profile of the killer. She picked up the phone and almost dialed Rick's number, but paused. He was going through hell, and in effect had been removed from the case. She checked her notes, jotted his name and number on the same sheet of paper, and dialed.

"Hello?"

"Inspector, it's Patricia Holmes, sorry to trouble you at night, can I talk to you please?"

"Yeah, hang on let me walk outside, there is a bit of background noise here. Funnily enough I almost thought of calling you to see if you wanted to come and check out a murder scene. At first, by the carnage, I thought it was PPP that had struck again; multiple stab and slash wounds. But, it would appear this killer is a woman."

"What? Please tell me everything, it's vital. I now believe PPP dresses up as a woman. In fact, the reason for my call was to tell you I believe strongly it is PPP who has taken Amy McCoy, and he did it while wearing woman's clothes, and make up, to avoid suspicion."

"Jesus Christ. Let me send a car to pick you up and bring you here, I'd like you to see his handiwork first hand if you're up to it. It's in the city, a bar called Solos on Hay Street, the East end."

"It will be quicker if I drive, I'm on my way."

She hung up the phone and gathered up the case files in her arms. Such was her haste; she didn't think to tell her husband she was leaving.

****

She could see the ocean of flashing blue and red lights in the distance, and the traffic was congested because of it. Eventually she got to within a hundred meters and swung the car to the left and parked illegally. *Fuck it; if I get a parking fine I do.*

She got out, locked her car, and walked quickly toward the festive looking lights.

There was a crowd of people milling around the cordoned-off area and she fought her way through to the front. "Officer," she called out to the uniformed man. "I'm Patricia Holmes, here to see Detective Chief Inspector Harris."

"Yes Ma'am, step through." He lifted the blue and white tape which had been strung between the building and signpost and she ducked under it.

All the interior bar lights had been turned on, but it was still dim. There were several patrons and staff who were sitting, waiting, or being interviewed in the far corner, with two detectives. They were using two tables, books open taking notes as they questioned them in turn. She saw the DCI behind the bar alongside Tyler, who was beckoning for her to approach.

"Thanks for coming so quickly Mrs. Holmes," the DCI began. "The body is out the back, untouched except for the ME. I've ordered it to be left so you can see firsthand this mad man's work, if you choose to. First though, tell me your story, because I've got some CCTV, and while the picture quality is crap, we think it is a woman who stabbed this man to death. She and the

295

victim spent close to an hour talking, before they went out to the back alley."

"Hi, sir, Tyler."

Tyler nodded, but he didn't speak. He looked serious to the point of moroseness, which Pat attributed to his partner losing his daughter.

"I got Tyler to come here because he interviewed Collette Ravensthorpe. On questioning her though, we cannot really confirm that she saw Amy with a woman."

"Yes, about that. Look, in my opinion, when a child tells you what they saw, and an authority figure questions it, it is normal for that kid to back pedal."

"I was very non-threatening. I hope you are not suggesting I made her change her story?" Tyler jumped in, defensively.

"No, no, Tyler, not at all. I'm sure you would have been very gentle. But you are still a policeman, and a child fears and respects you. She would have been frightened she would mislead you and would be more likely to recant than make something up. Especially as you were the second officer to interview her in such a short space of time. Her stress levels would be sky high. It would have been better if a child psychologist questioned her, but that's not a criticism everyone was trying to do the right thing by Rick. So, I suggest, we go back to her original statement, which is likely to be the truth. That was that she thought she heard a woman call Amy over, and that she saw her squatting down, partially obscured, talking to her. Now, if she couldn't see the person, how would she think it was a woman? By the clothes she wore."

"Okay, that makes sense, but we still don't have a

concrete description we can use."

"No, but do you have a description of the clothes she wore? When most men dress up like a woman, they tend to go over the top, try to be more feminine. Frills, colors, overly sexual underwear, that kind of thing. You say you have CCTV of this murderer, Amy was kidnapped this afternoon, this killer struck tonight. Ask Collette if this woman on CCTV is wearing the same clothes."

Tyler snapped his fingers. Firstly, he raised his eyes, and looked happier, yet at the same time he shook his head admonishingly. "You're right, Jesus Christ, why didn't I think of it? The description of what the woman was wearing does pretty much fit the CCTV. I'm sorry I missed that, sir, I'm a bloody idiot."

"But—" the DCI said turning his attention from Tyler back to Pat. "—Surely he wouldn't have dressed up, took Amy, drop her off somewhere, and then come into town and go to a bar for dinner and a few glasses of wine? That doesn't make any kind of sense."

She shook her head, feeling exasperated with them. "Sir, you've *got* to stop thinking conventionally with this man. Everything he does is planned, he had a reason for coming to town, just like he has a reason for everything he does. I would suggest a likely scenario is that he had two things to do, and they were some time apart, he came to the bar to kill time between performing those two things. If that's the case, this murder was coincidental, or done for fun." Suddenly, she snapped her fingers, as Tyler had done. "Correct me if I'm wrong. The man that was murdered, I bet he is married? Wait, let me go one better, he was killed in the same manner as Gordon Bridges, and Bridget

Schaeffer, and he is wearing a wedding ring?"

"Yes, he was married. All three killings were mirror images of each other, overkill you might call it. But Bridget Schaeffer wasn't married."

"No, she wasn't, but that was a set-up. She was killed to discredit Rick. PPP wouldn't have realized he had killed her in the same way as he killed Gordon Bridges; he just wanted it to appear different to the victims you already knew about to muddy the waters. Our man, hates people who are unfaithful, I think that's because as a child his mother left him with his sadistic father when she went to the shops and never came back. That is why the man in this bar was killed in the same way as Gordon Bridges, they were both being unfaithful to their wives; PPP killed them because of the infidelity."

"Ok, I can go along with that theory, but why dress up like a woman?"

"You mean other than make you, and especially Rick, look stupid when you are searching for a man, when all the while he looks like a woman? Well, there is no doubt in my mind, PPP has been abused sexually from a young age. Now if you go along with me that far, then let's think about the kind of man that would do that to a young, possibly effeminate looking boy. I think he made him dress up like a girl, and over time, that became habit, almost normal behavior if you like. The icing on the cake for him is, as I've said, while you are questioning people trying to find a man, he gets to laugh his head off because you can't find any witnesses to describe him."

"Okay, I get it, but how does it help us find him?"

She paused and bit her lower lip. "Sir, did you get

the Court order for Gordon Bridges' clients?"

"Yes, we can pick them up tomorrow morning. Other events overtook it, with Amy being snatched. The Trustee's office will hand the files over at nine thirty."

"Yes." She wrung her hands together, sensing victory was close. "Tomorrow morning, we can compare the list of names with the witness list in the Carly Biddle case and we will know the killer, I am convinced of that. Detective Inspector Barlow gave me the name of someone he felt at the time wasn't quite right, but his story checked out and he had nothing else to go on. If that same name appears in the trustee files, tomorrow you will be able to arrest him. Can you can get a hold of them tonight? If not, I think it will be in time to save Amy, he won't rush that, though it is unfortunately too late for June Daniels."

"Why do you say that?"

"Sir, if she was still alive, he would not have taken Amy yet. He moved to the next stage of his plan against Rick, because she died, or he killed her so he could escalate things after Rick insulted him. That stupid reporter put my involvement in the paper, which made him even angrier, and he brought his plan forward to take Amy."

Tyler looked troubled. "Umm, I'm not sure I should tell you this Pat, because, well, it's private. But, you mentioned PPP's hatred of unfaithfulness. Rick had an affair with a woman, who told Juliet when Rick tried to break it off. During the suitcase investigation, they were separated. They did make up, she forgave him, and he turned his life around ever since. These days he won't even go to the pub with the boys."

"Oh, my God. Now it all fits into place. Rick and

PPP met years ago, and something, occurred, for which PPP never forgave him. He became a serial killer, and his crowning glory was 'The Body in the Suitcase.' Then who should he see on TV conducting re-enactments? Rick. So, he follows him, probably out of interest at first, though some form of revenge would have been on his mind, most likely to murder him. He would have been dressed up as a woman, so avoided being recognized, and that was when he realized what Rick had done. The person he hates more than anyone else in the world had done the very thing he detests with a passion. So, his hatred for Rick intensified even more. Now he didn't just want to kill Rick, he wanted to make him suffer as an adulterer. In a way, I feel so much better now."

"Why? He has Amy."

"He won't kill her, not yet anyway. He wants to make Rick suffer so he will string this out. Amy is a child, and while PPP is a sociopathic narcissist, and will kill anyone without any qualms, he will identify with her being a child and blameless, as he was blameless when he was young. She is safe for now, I'm quite sure of that. I do think we should tell Rick, it will put his mind to rest."

"With respect, Pat, I don't think we should," Tyler said. "I've worked with him for years, and the old saying 'still waters run deep' is very true of Rick. If we told him, I know what he is like; he will go and break into the Trustees office to get at those files tonight and get himself in all sorts of trouble."

Colin Harris nodded his agreement. "If you're sure she will be safe overnight, let's leave off telling him. I'm going to try to get someone to release the files to us tonight. I'm doubtful that will be successful, being a government department. No one will be there this time of night; but it's worth a try. Yes, he and Juliet are suffering, but they are together. First thing in the morning, or earlier if I can get them, you and I will go to the Public Trustee and get those files. Then we will find out who he is, get a search and arrest warrant, and send in the Tactical Response Group to save Amy. Now, did you want to see the body?"

"No, that's one nightmare I can do without, thanks."

****

Her mind raced, as she drove out of the city toward her home. She ran through a mental checklist to make sure she hadn't got anything wrong. She worried that they had not told Rick her suspicions but counterbalanced it with the logical arguments put forward by Tyler. She thought that PPP would want Rick to suffer and would be in no hurry for any confrontation. Still, it bothered her, she liked Rick, in more ways than one, and knew he was going through hell, but, she reasoned, would he be any better off if she told him her thoughts? He had already accused her of being heartless. She agonized that she got something wrong, but eventually felt satisfied that she hadn't.

Her mind turned to the one aspect that bothered her. Why had PPP gone to the city, and then spent two hours in a bar? If he had two tasks to fulfil, and had to wait, in between as she had hypothesized, why the city, and what could those two jobs have been?

The city is big, with lots of busy shops on a Friday night. PPP could find anonymity there, that's a given. Whatever he went to buy, he wanted to gain time, and use the crowds so that he wouldn't easily be tracked down. So, Okay, he came in to buy something, but what could that thing be? More women's clothes? Surely not? It must be more important than that.

Question two: whatever he bought, he then decided to kill time in a pub, why? Why not go home? Answer: he wanted to use it in the city. Whatever it was, if it was something he wanted to use, rather than wear. Perhaps he worried that in using whatever it is, it could lead to his discovery if he went to his house. That discounts clothes, surely?

At that moment, her mobile phone rang in her bag on the passenger seat, which startled her. She fumbled inside, took out her pink Motorola and flipped it open one handed. She was expecting it to be Rick. "Hello?" she answered, nervously.

"Pat, it's me, where the bloody hell are you? I brought you in a coffee to find you had disappeared, without a single word. I've been worried sick."

Bugger, I forgot to tell Tom. "Oh, Tom I am so sorry. I dashed out without a thought, please forgive me. I've been at a crime scene with the police. PPP has killed again. I am on my way home now and I will tell you all about it when I get there. I'm about ten or fifteen minutes away."

"A crime scene? Jesus Pat, isn't this getting all bit too close to the bone? It's not dangerous is it, you working like this with the cops?"

She sighed, ignoring the pun he had made unintentionally: A surgeon saying it was close to the bone? "Tom, I'm doing something I always wanted to do, you know that. No, I don't think it's dangerous, and I did say sorry for getting so distracted that I ran out without telling you I was going. I will be home soon, let's talk then, I'm driving, ok? Sorry I made you worry."

They both disconnected at the same time, and she tossed the phone onto the seat. *Now, what was I thinking?* Only then did it hit her what PPP had gone to the city to buy: a pre-paid, disposable mobile phone. With that realization came an understanding why he would wait in the pub: to telephone Rick. He wanted to do it from the city so that if Rick's calls were being traced, he could dispose of the phone and be just another woman in the late-night shopping crowds.

She pulled over, again parking illegally, snatched up her phone and flipped it open. With a sinking heart, she noticed it only had one bar of battery power. *Damn, I knew I should have replaced the bloody thing.* Of recent times, it had been playing up, the battery life had become shorter, and shorter. She loved the pink flip style of phone, but the battery life was dreadful.

She dialed Rick's number, expecting to hear the traditional 'McCoy' barked at her, but she didn't. "Hello?" she heard him say quietly, and she knew by his tone that PPP had phoned.

"Rick, it's Pat, my phone is going to die soon so I don't have long. He has called you, hasn't he? Whatever you do you must not do what he says. He has killed again tonight, I think his name is Paul Rankin, tomorrow morning, early, we will know for sure. You must not do anything before then. Do you hear me?"

"This is not a good time, Pat. I'll talk to you in the morning, goodnight." He hung up on her.

Damn the man, he's not thinking straight. Fuck, is it any wonder with Amy in the hands of a madman?

She got six digits of Colin Harris's phone number in when her phone screen went black and died. "Arggh," she cried, and threw the useless thing on the floor on the passenger side of the car.

In the next instant, she realized that if she had called the Chief Inspector, and he acted on her information, it could have caused a problem for Amy. Colin would have been forced to move, and PPP could have seen them arrive. If he had contacted Rick, as she now believed he had, his radar would be on high alert. Then, feeling cornered, he would have killed Amy, out of spite, and then probably himself. There had been numerous cases where sociopaths had done that when confronted.

She knew full well that his type of narcissistic personality craved the limelight; even if it was to die as a martyr. He would either kill himself, or hand himself in, there was no way to know which side that coin would land on. A lot would depend on whether he thought he had a choice. She had no doubt that his first option would be to surrender, if given the chance, so he could become famous. The narcissist in him would love that. But that would only work if he was permitted to make that decision. But, if he thought he had no alternative, he would kill himself and anyone else he could take with him.

She had to do something, but what?

Think damn you, think. Paul Rankin, do I have his witness statement? She grabbed the pile of copied files she had taken home for her homework and flicked on the overhead light. She riffled though page after page within the manila folder marked Carly Biddle.

She found it, very brief, but there it was with the

other interviews of staff in the meat department. *Oh, my God, he's a butcher, why didn't I think of that before? That's why the bodies are hung upside down, like meat carcasses in a fridge. That's also why the bodies were dissected so well, he is a bloody butcher, not a medical student or surgeon. It's him, it's him.*

She could find a phone box and call Colin, but she had a feeling if she did, she would be condemning Amy to death when the police raided his house. Life had no value to Rankin, his own, or anyone else's, why would he bother surrendering in a raid carried out by armed police? Fame; that was the most obvious thing that would appeal to him. If she could get to him first, if she could assure him she would drag Rick's name through the mud, and at the same time make him famous, maybe *she* could save Amy.

Who is better qualified to convince a madman than me? This was what I lived and trained for: to be face to face with a serial killer and talk him down.

She ran her finger down the page until she found his address. Mundaring. That was another clincher: it was so close to Midland. Next, she reached for the glove box and took out her map book and looked up Phillips Road. Satisfied she could find it, she started the car, and pulled back out into the traffic. She was going to meet a serial killer, for the first time, outside of a mental asylum or courtroom.

Chapter 21
Hope and Good Intentions

"You can't be serious, swap my wife for my daughter? I'm not making that choice," Rick shouted.

"I understand, Rick. It's is a tough decision. Okay, I will let you know where you can find Amy's body, after I finish with it."

"*Wait,*" Juliet screamed, "*She's my daughter too. Don't I get a say in this? I'll do it, tell me what to do.*"

"Jules, you can't, you can't sacrifice yourself like that, and besides, he may not let Amy go anyway."

"Oh Rick, stop judging other people by your own low standards. Unlike you, when I give my word I keep it. I have said I will free Amy, and I will once I have Julie. Now, are we going to have some fun, or not?"

"Rick," she pleaded, "I'm going to do this, you can't stop me. You wanted to give yourself to him to save Amy, why can't I do the same? She is our daughter, and if one of us has to die to save her, who says it should be you and not me?"

"Are you listening to your wife, Rick, are you hearing how wonderful this woman is? Why would you have screwed that other thing, when you had a woman like this at home?"

Rick hung his head in anger, shame, and frustration. Tears spilled from his eyes as he realized Juliet would not be swayed.

"So, are we in agreement?"

"Yes, tell me what to do," Juliet replied quietly.

"Wait, what are you going to do with her? We deserve to know."

"Tsk, tsk, tsk. No Rick, you don't deserve to know anything. So far as I am concerned you gave up all rights to Julie when you had sex with that other woman behind Julie's back. And if that wasn't bad enough, now you're at it with Mrs. Holmes. What she does with me, is between us, not you. But you should know, I may, or may not kill her. I may just want to talk to her and tell her all about what a rat you were all those years ago. Or, I may have sex with her. And, finally, I might kill her, but it is my choice, not yours. Do you understand, and do you agree Julie?"

"Yes," she answered, trancelike.

Rick was incapable of speech; He had never felt so helpless in his life.

"Good. Now, Julie, you will take Rick's mobile phone, and Rick, you will stay home. I will call now and again on your landline, to make sure you stay there, do you understand me?"

"Yes, I get it." His mind raced, trying to find a way out of the dire situation he was letting Juliet walk into.

"Good, because, if you are not there when I call, or if I call and the phone is engaged, well, firstly how can I tell you where to pick up little Amy from? And, secondly, I will know you have lied to me again. If you make me think that, both Amy and Juliet die. Let me hear you say you understand my instructions, Rick."

"I understand." He choked.

"Good boy. Julie go and get in your car, and drive toward the city, slowly, and take Rick's phone with you. At some point, I will be behind you, making sure no one is following you. I know your car, and the route you will take. When I'm convinced you have not lied to me, I will flash my headlights, and phone you. Then and only then will I tell you where to go to meet me. Then you will throw the phone out of the window. I will be watching to make sure you do. When we meet, I will take you to Amy in my car, and then, we will take her to somewhere safe. I will call you at that point, Rick, and tell you where she is. Only then can you leave the house and go and pick her up. Do we all understand?"

"Yes."

"Yes."

"Good. What are you waiting for? Let's go and get your daughter, Julie."

The phone went dead. Juliet turned to Rick, "I forgave you, and you fucked her? You made me think our lives were perfect and you screwed her?"

"I didn't, and I never would have, I swear it to you."

"Can you hear yourself, Rick? Why should I believe you when you admit you thought about doing it with her?"

Before he could answer, the phone rang again, and he expected it to be PPP, "hello?"

"Rick, it's Pat, my phone is going to die soon so I don't have long. He has called you, hasn't he? Whatever you do you must not do what he says. He has killed again tonight, I think his name is Paul Rankin, tomorrow morning, we will know for sure. You must not do anything before then. Do you hear me?"

"This is not a good time, Pat. I'll talk to you in the

morning, goodnight."

He hung up and looked at his wife, who was sneering. "She calls you, at a time like this. I trusted you, how stupid am I?"

"Jules, I swear you have this all wrong, he has played with your mind, tricked you. Pat was calling to try to help save Amy. I promise you, she and I have never done anything like that, and never would have."

He reached out and put his hand on her arm, but she shrugged it off. "Don't touch me."

She snatched the phone from his hand and walked out. He wanted to run after her, wanted to convince her, but he knew he had thought of being unfaithful, and he was ashamed. He heard her car start and pull out of the driveway. He was left alone

****

Phillips Road was long and dark, very dark. There were very few street lights for most of it until she ventured around a curve and saw a lone lamp on a crooked pole, opposite an old shop front building. She slowed down, and by the dim light could just make out the faded and peeling painted sign that said Rankin's Meats. It was strange to see a single shop, among houses while on the opposite side there were no homes at all, just park or bushland; it was hard to tell which in the dark.

She stopped the car thirty meters past the building, so she was in shadow, and turned off her ignition. The building looked as if it was empty, there wasn't a light anywhere, and the front windows had been painted over to stop passers-by looking in. She could see in the gloom the shadow of the house attached behind, but there were no welcoming lights there either.

No one is home. There's nothing for it, but wait.

Her plan, such as it was, was to knock on the door when he got home and try to talk to him. Five minutes later, she changed her mind, *let's have a look around the back, maybe there is a way in, Amy could be inside, and I can free her.*

She got out and closed her door quietly behind her, then making even less noise, opened the boot of the car. In the side compartment was her breakdown torch, which she picked up, then she had a second idea, and took the wheel spanner from the tool kit. Suitably armed, she locked the car and crossed the road, keeping to the shadows as much as possible, as she approached the shop.

Up close, the building looked even more derelict. It clearly hadn't had a coat of paint in years. She tried to find any part of the window where the coating had worn away so she could see inside. Right up against the corner, there was a spot and she squatted down low, and shone her torch through the gap.

It was as she expected an old closed butcher shop to look like, with a long refrigerated counter, wooden chopping block, and old signs of meat cuts on the wall. It looked like a set from a horror film, and a shiver ran down her spine.

Next, she went around the side of the building to the wooden front door, which appeared as if it hadn't been opened in years. The alcove was strewn with cobwebs hanging down from the corners, and once again she felt she was visiting a haunted house. *There must be a rear entrance,* she decided, and took off to investigate, glad to get away from the cobwebs.

As quietly as she could she walked from shadow to

shadow to the corner and then around it after peeking to make sure the coast was clear first. It was as quiet as a grave and that thought didn't please her at all. There was a gravel alley behind the house, which was overgrown with weeds, and trees which overhung the corrugated iron fences. It was very, very dark.

Pat was glad she had the torch as she stepped as quietly as she could, but the gravel scrunched under her shoes. When she drew level with the rear of the shop, she found a double gate, the same height as the fence, and covered in sheets of iron so she couldn't see through. There was a hand hole through which she thought she could reach to open the latch, located on the inside.

Taking a deep breath to calm her nerves, she put her hand through; hoping upon hope there wasn't a big dog on the other side that would bite her. Her fingers closed over the draw bolt and she see-sawed it to and fro, until it opened. The mechanism and hinges had been well oiled, which took her by surprise, so the gate opened quietly, and she stepped through, then latched it closed behind her.

She turned the torch off, just in case *he* was home, and stood still to let her eyes adjust to the dark. She was standing on a paved area, obviously used to park a car, though the flag stones were uneven with neglect. It then turned into a path, that lead to the back veranda of the house. There was a straggly old tree to her right, and weeds nearly a meter-high struggling to grow in the crowded flower beds either side of the path. To her left was a large old shed.

Being careful where she placed her feet she tiptoed to the shed, not daring to turn the torch back on. There were no windows, just a door, secured by a gleaming big padlock which looked almost new. She tapped on the door. There was no answer from inside.

She contemplated using the wheel spanner to break the clasp which held the padlock but thought she would check out the house first. *If I force an entry, and Paul Rankin is not the killer, I'm in a lot of trouble,* she warned herself. *I'm here to reason with him, not break into his home.*

Her heels made their inevitable noise on the path as she started off toward the main building, and she cursed her choice of footwear. *Right, like I should have gone home and changed first.*

The sheer magnitude of what she was doing came home to her. She was being stupid, no, more than stupid, *far more*. She turned to leave, she needed support and help, and was going to call the DCI from the first call box she could find.

Then she heard a vehicle approaching, and her heart missed a beat. She prayed it wasn't PPP, but a neighbor returning home. Like a petrified deer, she couldn't move, and slowly the sound got closer. It was only when she saw the glow of the headlights turn into the alleyway; she came to her senses and looked around for somewhere to hide.

****

Juliet cringed every time he touched her during the drive, but she tried to hide it, for Amy's sake.

She had done as she had been told, her mind racing with fear, and anger at Rick's betrayal. Finally, a car behind her flashed its headlights, and Rick's phone rang.

"I'm here," she said hoarsely.

"Toss the phone out the window, so I can see, and then find a place to pull over. We'll take my vehicle to get Amy."

She wound down the window and held her arm out with the phone in her hand. She wanted to be sure he saw she was doing as she had been told. She dropped it, then put her indicator on and pulled out of the light night time traffic, and parked. She saw in the rear vision mirror the glare from the headlights of the vehicle pull up behind. She took a deep breath and got out of her car and hurriedly walked to the white van.

Once she got in she had to stifle a scream; a woman was sitting in the driver's seat. She saw her smile, and then heard the unmistakable voice of PPP. "You weren't expecting this, were you, Julie? Come on, hop in, belt on, we've got a long drive ahead of us. What shall we chat about? Oh, I know, we can talk about what a bastard your husband is, that will be fun, won't it?"

That was when he put his hand on her thigh for the first time and tugged her skirt up. She blinked back tears, and took a deep breath, desperate not to vomit.

****

The skin across Rick's hand was cut and bleeding, yet he couldn't feel a thing. Within minutes of Juliet leaving he had come to his senses and realized he should have taken charge and done something, anything to stop her. Or he could have called PPP's bluff and gone with her. How could he just stand there and let his wife go to meet with a murderer? He had lashed out and punched the lounge room door, splintering the thin timber which covered it, and knocked a hole all the way through.

Think fuck you, think, he told himself. He knew he had to do something. He could not stand by and do nothing. He forced himself to calm down, while blood dripped from his exposed knuckles onto the carpet. He began pacing up and down, his brain rattling ideas around, and one by one he discounted them. *I can't call this in, if I do, and they search for her car and PPP sees them, he said he will kill Amy and Jules too, so that's out.*

I can't leave until he phones me…

He stopped dead in his tracks. *Wait, wait, wait, how does he know the home number, it's unlisted? There is no way he could know that, or is there?* He shook his head in exasperation, realizing that he had Juliet; all he had to do was ask her what the phone number was. He started pacing again and then stopped. *Fuck, why didn't I think of it before? I can divert the phone to Juliet's mobile.*

On the kitchen bench was Juliet's Nokia. He realized all he needed to do was to lift the landline handset and enter *21, her number and # and hang up. The home number would then divert to her mobile if it rang, and PPP would have no idea he was on the move.

Hot on the heels of that feeling of hope, he crushed it. *So, okay, I can leave the house and PPP won't know, but where do I go?*

Again, he started pacing up and down, he needed help, he was desperate, but he couldn't call the DCI; that was too dangerous. *What about Pat?*

He snatched up Juliet's phone and punched in her mobile number, and again his heart fell through the floor as he listened to the recorded message: *The number you are trying to reach is switched off or not in*

314

a suitable reception area.

He barely restrained himself from throwing the phone against the wall in a blinding rage. He resumed pacing again. He thought back to the last call he had received, what was it Pat had said? He searched his memory. He'd barely listened when he realized it was her, after the call from PPP. The look of near hatred on Juliet's face had made him want to hang up. *What did she say?*

He stopped and screwed up his eyes in concentration, forcing his subconscious to recall the conversation. Slowly, agonizingly slowly it came back. *She said he'd killed again. She knew he had phoned us, how the fuck did she know that? She then said that they were going to have proof who he was in the morning, what proof? What would she have in the morning that she couldn't have today? Fuck: The Trustee records, of course. She had said someone's name, what was it?*

It started with a P, of course it started with a P, PPP? Hello? Peter? No, it wasn't Peter, it was Paul YES, Paul. Paul what?

He opened his eyes, suddenly feeling calm, yet his blood turned ice cold. The hairs rose on the back of his neck and arms, as he recalled going to the house in Mundaring. *The kid, Paul, ten or eleven years old. The boy who seemed so calm, the one who ate his breakfast after finding the bodies of his father and mother. Paul Rankin. Fuck I'm so dumb! His father murdered his mother, and then kept her body in the freezer. Then, when he couldn't take the guilt any longer, he killed himself and made an orphan out of his son Paul.*

How could I have forgotten that? HOW?

But what did I do to let him down? God I'm an

idiot. Pat said he had had an abusive father, and Paul told me his dad was cruel, but he loved him. He thought his mother had left home, but instead she had been murdered. I should have remembered this. It's all my fault.

He hung his head in shame as it all came flooding back. Paul had been taken to Harkerville orphanage, and he had checked up on him, once by phoning Cynthia Barnsley. She had said he was doing fine and had made a new friend, a boy named Jeremy. *I should have done more, shouldn't I? I should have gone to see him.*

Part of him railed against that: as a police officer, he was not in the habit of checking up on victims. They had victim support for that role. If cops checked up on the welfare of every person in need they came across, they wouldn't have time to catch offenders. But, Paul had wanted to hold his gun, and he had promised him that if he stayed out of trouble, when he was old enough Rick would take him to a gun club and teach him to shoot.

Is that it? Is that what all of this is about? A broken promise to take him shooting when he grew up?

Rick sighed. He went into the bedroom, pulling his keys out of his pocket as he walked. Under the bed was the locked gun cabinet where he put his revolver, under lock and key, every night when he got home. That was one of Juliet's rules, so Amy could never get to it and have an accident.

He removed the Smith and Wesson .38 revolver, still in its holster from the case, stood and clipped it inside the rear of his trousers and walked back into the lounge room. He diverted the phone, slipped his jacket on to hide the gun, grabbed Juliet's mobile from the bench top, and sprinted to the front door. He was going to save Amy and Juliet, or die trying.

****

Colin Harris turned the TV down and picked up his mobile phone when it rang. He had been watching his wife's favorite show with her: *Sea Change*. They both preferred comedy shows, and almost never watched crime dramas; too real-life for Colin. She pressed the mute button on the remote to quieten the TV, she looked annoyed at the interruption. He had only just arrived home and had sat down when his mobile chirped its happy tune.

"Colin Harris."

"Hello, look I'm sorry to call you so late, it's Tom Holmes, Patricia's husband, is she still with you?"

Colin sat up straight in the chair, the man sounded worried and angry, the tension was palpable. "No, Tom, I've only just got home, she left me ages ago."

"Well she's not bloody well here, and quite frankly, I'm annoyed at the intrusion this damned volunteer work has had on our lives."

"Have you tried to phone her?"

"Of course I've bloody well phoned her; I spoke to her ages ago and she said she was on her way home. She said she would be here within fifteen minutes, but she never made it. Her phone is dead or switched off, either way the bloody thing won't answer. She told me the other day it was playing up."

"Give me your number Tom, I have a feeling she might have gone to visit Rick, that's Sergeant Rick McCoy, his daughter has been kidnapped. I will call him and see if she is there for you."

"Sorry about this, love," he said to his wife who looked like she was getting more upset by the minute, as he dialed Rick's mobile phone number. He was dismayed when it rang out.

Why wouldn't he answer? His daughter is missing, he should be waiting, phone in hand for news. He crossed the room to the hallway where his briefcase sat on the table. Behind him the volume increased on the TV. He rifled through it and found his address book. After checking the number, he dialed Rick's home. "Hello?" Rick's voice shot out from the phone.

"Rick, it's Colin Harris, I have a very worried Tom Holmes calling me looking for his wife who is long overdue at home, is she with you?"

"*No*, she is not with me."

"Calm down, Rick, I'm not suggesting anything untoward, but Pat appears to be missing. Are you in the car, it sounds like you're driving?"

"No, I'm not, must be a bad line, I have to go, sorry."

The line went dead, and Colin stood with phone in hand, more confused than at any time before. *What the hell is going on?*

Damn them, Pat disappears, Rick hangs up on me, something is going on. What? He stood tapping his phone against his forehead and realized there was only one possible explanation for their behavior. *Pat has figured out who PPP is, she's told Rick, and they are on their way to save Amy. I must stop him; Rick will kill him.*

His wife stared at him as he dialed another number, then back to the TV. "Tom," he said as it answered. "I'm concerned for Pat too, she is not with Rick, and he is acting strangely. I'm worried she may have figured out who the killer is, told Rick, and they are going to confront him. Is there any of her notes there that might give us a clue to who or where she has gone?"

"Jesus Christ, I knew something like this would happen. Why did you drag her into this? Hang on let me go to her study."

Minutes dragged by as he paced up and down, ignoring the requests from his wife as to what was going on. He had a very bad feeling, and over the years, he had learned to trust those feelings.

"Colin, I'm back in her office and the files I saw her working on are all gone. All there is, is a sheet of paper, it looks like some sort of typed witness statement: on one side, and her handwriting is on the other. That's where I got your phone number from. It's a list of things about PPP dressing up like a woman, and a name circled several times: Paul Rankin. Who is Paul Rankin?"

"I've no idea, Tom, but I will find out, I will get back to you as soon as I have news."

He hung up. "Sorry love, I have to go back to work." He raced out the door. She stared at his departing back, and shook her head, then turned the volume back up. She was a cop's wife, after all, and had seen this behavior many times over the years.

On the way to his car he dialed Tyler's number. He was climbing in when it answered. "Tyler, it's me, sorry I know its late, meet me at work, we have a problem."

****

Pat could almost hear her own heartbeat as she cowered behind the wheeled rubbish bin on the rear veranda. She concentrated on keeping her breath from panting, knowing she would be heard if she panicked any more. *What was I thinking coming here?* She berated herself as the gate opened, then a white van drove in. She dared not stick her head up again to watch, but heard the car door open again, and then the steel gates close.

A white van; the vehicle driven by the man suspected of leaving the suitcase at the dump. Any lingering doubts disappeared in a vapor cloud; *It's him, and he's going to find me here in his garden – what was I thinking?*

Then she heard a male voice. "Come on Julie, bring the hamburger and fries for Amy, she must be starving by now."

Julie? That can't be Juliet, surely? What's she doing here?

"You promised you would let her go."

Oh, the bloody fools, why couldn't you wait until tomorrow? Now he's got two hostages, three, once he finds me.

"And so, I shall, love. Let's go and see her, and have a good long chin wag, shall we?"

She heard the other door open, and then close. Pat's mind raced. *If I stand up now it will be on my terms, but if I stay hidden and Rankin discovered me, it will be on his. Then I will lose all credibility.*

Without thinking any further, she quietly put the wheel spanner on the ground and stood up. Trying to look casual as she leaned on the bin she said in a voice that sounded calmer than she felt: "Hello PPP, or should I call you Paul, or Mr. Rankin?"

Rankin whirled around, startled. "Who the bloody

hell...what are you doing here?"

She watched as he opened the handbag he was carrying and in the dim light saw him pluck something from it. The moonlight glinted off the blade and she saw it was a knife. The fear factor she was already feeling climbed several notches. Juliet cowered back against the van. Suddenly, Pat saw this could get very ugly, very quickly.

"Paul, its Patricia Holmes, I've been helping and advising the police. I'm a great admirer of your work. I came to ask your permission for an interview, I'd like to write a book about you, I think we could both be very famous. I love your outfit too, by the way, you look incredible."

****

Colin and Tyler arrived at headquarters within moments of each other. Both parked not in the car parking bays but at the rear entrance, effectively blocking the driveway for anyone else who might want to do some late-night work in the squad room.

"We need to find an address for a witness named Paul Rankin, Tyler, and quickly."

Tyler knew better than to ask why.

As he led the way through the passages to the Major Crime squad room Colin explained what had happened. "We cannot send in the TRG in case we spook him, but either way we could be in trouble. If we don't do something, I'm worried what will happen, either we will have some dead hostages on our hands, or a dead suspect."

"I get you, sir, I've known Rick a long time; if this Rankin has his daughter, I wouldn't want to be in his shoes. And, if Amy has been hurt, he has no hope at all."

They raced through the building, flicking light switches on as they went, until they arrived at the office Rick and Pat had used. There on the floor surrounding the large desk were the evidence boxes that somewhere contained the address that would lead them to the killer.

"Fuck, this could take all night," Tyler exclaimed, dismayed at the number of witness statements in the boxes.

"No, it won't, the name is from the Carly Biddle murder inquiry. Pat was looking for confirmation from Gordon Bridges' clients." He grabbed the box, reached in, and pulled several manila folders out which contained different aspects of the investigation. Handing Tyler a handful of witness statements they both sat down and started flicking through sheets of paper looking for the name.

"Got it!" Tyler yelled, a few minutes later. "Fucking hell, why didn't we think of it before, he's a fucking butcher, not a medical student. No wonder the dissections were so neat. It's Mundaring, sir, I just hope we get there in time."

Chapter 22
The Gathering

They were in an untidy, dusty, sitting room, with horrendously outdated furniture. The two women sat beside each other, on a chocolate brown fake leather couch while the killer held court standing at the doorway so neither could get past him.

"What are you doing here, Pat? He told me he would let Amy go, I didn't need you here." Juliet nodded her head in Rankin's direction.

Pat noticed she was barely holding onto her temper, she seemed on the verge of hysteria. "Don't worry, Juliet, I'm here to help, everything will be all right." She held her hands out to calm her.

"As lovely as this get together is, I told you, and Rick what would happen if you told anyone, all bets are off. You both need to shut up now and let me think." PPP alternated between waving the knife from one woman to the other. He looked to Pat like he could snap at any moment. She had to take charge, and quickly, but Juliet had her own ideas.

"You promised me you would free Amy, now you won't even let me see her?" Juliet screamed.

"Oh Julie, stop your whining. Why do you women always, *always,* whine? I gave you my word, and I will keep it, but don't test my patience. Your husband's lover turning up has taken precedence, and we need to have a little chat. I would have thought you would have wanted to hear about Rick's adulterous shenanigans with the shrink."

"Now, you just wait one minute, Paul," Pat said. "I came here of my own free will to meet you and talk to you. I could have just told the cops where you were, but I didn't. I have not, and never would, have any sort of 'adulterous shenanigans' as you call it with Rick. So, don't tar me with that brush, thank you. Yes, the man showed his feelings, and made no secret that he wanted sex with me. I'm sorry to tell you that, Juliet, but I am very, can I repeat *very,* happily married to my husband of twenty-six years. For goodness sake, my husband is a surgeon, not a bloody cop. I mean, please."

The silence hung in the air, and Pat imagined what Juliet must be thinking by the look on her face: *The bastard, the bloody bastard. If I ever get out of this mess I will murder him. The lying cheating bastard, how could I have believed in him?*

Pat watched her take a long, slow deep breath. "I'm not whining; I just want to see my daughter."

"Right, that's it. You, shrink, stay here, and you Julie, come with me and I will put you in the cool room with Amy. You can give her the food, and once I finish here I will come and get you. You are a huge disappointment to me, Julie, and an unnecessary distraction. I need to talk to the good doctor here about far more important things than your daughter."

She stood and followed him down the long passageway. He didn't put any lights on and he unlocked the adjoining door between the house and the shop, then led her to the cool room, behind the counter, with the sharpening steel hanging through the handle.

He swung the heavy door open, and the light spilled out from inside. Juliet heard her daughter cry out.

"Oh, baby, mummy's here." She ran past him and into the prison and picked up Amy, hugging her, crying tears of joy. "You're safe now, baby."

But the door swung shut behind her with a muffled clunk sound. She was reunited with her daughter, but, they were locked in, and Juliet realized they were far from safe.

****

Pat's mind raced, she knew she had one chance to survive, and to do so she would need to call on all her training, cunning, and guile. She knew she had to convince PPP that she was on his side, and that would be no mean feat. One slip, one thing said wrong, and she knew he would kill her, and not lose one moment's sleep over it.

She sat, with one leg crossed over the other, her fingers laced over her knees, so that she would appear to be polite and respectful. Her body language would be as important as the words she used. She heard his footsteps coming back down the passage, and took a very deep, calming, breath.

Paul Rankin, with knife in his right hand, sat across the arm of an old-fashioned chair, near the door, and looked back at her. "I'm not an idiot, you know, so don't treat me like one," he began.

Here goes; it's show time. "May I call you Paul?"

"It's my name, why wouldn't you?"

This has not started well. Concentrate; win him over.

"Paul, I did not come here to treat you like an idiot,

I came here with a proposition. I admire you; you've done what a lot of us would like to do but lack the courage. I would like to live the rest of my life vicariously through you, write your story, make you famous, that is of course, if that's what you want."

He shook his head. "May I call you Pat, or is that what Rick calls you, in which case I will call you Patricia."

"My friends and family all call me Pat, but Rick does call me that too."

"Well, Patricia, there is an old saying, 'Don't bull shit a bull-shitter.' I don't believe you, and even if I did, why would you think I need the likes of you?"

"Paul, irrespective of what happens tonight, what you think of me, or whether you kill Juliet, Amy, and me, tomorrow morning, they are coming to arrest you, and they will be armed. Do you know why they are coming for you?"

"Because I've given them enough clues?" He waved the knife in the air.

"Rubbish." She shook her head emphatically. "You haven't given them any clues, you've taunted them, and hid clues. Brilliantly, I must say, but, at no time did you make it easy for them. But then again, why should you? They're slow, so bloody slow, and you are fast on your feet. If they hadn't brought me in, you could have kept ahead of them for years. I'm sorry for that, but realistically, it's time this all came to an end. You should enjoy the fame that your deeds deserve."

"So let me get this straight, you are saying they will capture or kill me tomorrow because of you? And, you came here to tell me that? You don't think I will kill you for causing that. Are you mad? I'm told a lot of psychologists do in fact go mad."

"Really? Now who is bullshitting a bull-shitter?"

He grinned, and Pat realized it was his way of smiling, but being so socially incompetent a grin was the best he could manage. "You're not scared of me, are you?"

She uncrossed her legs and leaned forward. "Let me clarify that. Am I scared you will kill me? Yes, I don't want to die, who does? Do I think it's likely you will kill me? No, I think not, because I hope I can make you see that your reign has come to an end, but how it ends is up to you. You can be shot dead, like Bonny and Clyde, or live on, and bask in the glory of all you've achieved, like Charles Manson. Do you know how many followers and fans he has? My God he has women by the hundreds who want to marry him and have his babies. Every time he comes up for parole the whole world sits up and takes notice. You, Paul are an Australian Folk Hero, like Ned Kelly. What I would like to do is tell your story, from your perspective. Everyone is interested in serial killers, and we've never had one quite as clever as you."

"Why has it come to an end, enlighten me."

"Because of me. You are a great killer, probably the cleverest serial murderer in Australian history. I'm sorry, but I discovered who you are by looking at your footsteps in the sand, as I call it."

Before she could blink, he was upon her. He flew across the room, straddled her lap, lifted her head by grasping her hair, and held the knife to her throat. She felt her skin being nicked and a trickle of blood run down her neck. She wanted to scream, to fight, and struggle, but deep down, she realized this was bravado, like a small child who doesn't get his own way. She forced herself to smile at him, and the seconds dragged by.

"Patricia, I asked you to enlighten me, not brag. No doubt you are a very clever woman, But, don't try to make me feel like I am stupid, I warn you for the last time. Now tell me why has my reign come to an end, as you so eloquently said?"

She knew, because he had not murdered her, he was posturing. Yes, he was dangerous, yes, he had no conscience, and would lose no sleep if he killed her, but he was also intelligent, and egotistical. This was her chance to stand up to him and win him over. She put on her coldest voice, the one she used with her husband when he *annoyed* her.

"Paul. If you are going to kill me, kill me. If you want to talk, then take that *fucking knife away from my throat!* I am not some young woman you've abducted and terrorized. I came here to meet you. Now, stop fucking about, I am more than happy to tell you why they are coming for you tomorrow, but I will not respond to threats, or a knife pressed to my throat."

The seconds dragged again, but he did not slash her neck, and the pressure on the razor-sharp tip eased. "Well, you're quite the potty-mouth, aren't you? I don't like woman who swear."

"And I don't like a knife being held to my throat. Let's make a deal, you stop threatening me, and I will stop swearing."

It was bizarre, on so many levels. A man was kneeling across her lap who had murdered God alone knew how many people, yet he was dressed as a woman. And, she had to admit, quite an attractive one.

He had the '*look at me*' mentality of a child, yet would kill her without blinking an eyelid; an eyelid that was covered in make-up.

"Do you really think we can be friends?"

"I'd like to be, but friendship is a two-way street, it takes two people to become friends. Do *you* think we can be friends?"

"I have a scrap book, you know," he said as he lowered the knife to his lap.

"You do? That will be very useful, Paul. How far back does it go?"

"To when I was five. Please tell me, how did you discover me."

"I will, but please get off my lap. I am married, and my husband would not appreciate another man sitting across me, and I don't like it either. Friends yes, but please don't take advantage of that."

Slowly, he climbed off, head bowed low. "I apologize, Patricia, in my life I have not had many friends."

"Good job I came along then." She smiled her very best smile, and watched him dismount and sit alongside her, but still held the knife, pointing at her. He shrugged, waiting for her to begin.

"Paul, I'm not being egotistical, please understand that. But I am very perceptive. I have also made it my life's work to study people like yourself. I got my Master's degree in criminal psychology and a doctorate in psychology *and* psychiatry. When I finished at university I won a six-month internship with the FBI's Criminal Behavioral Unit. I have always wanted to work with the police as an advisor, or profiler because of people like you, Paul. Serial killers fascinate me. I'm saying all of this because at first the attraction was assisting in your capture, but the further I dug, the more I wanted to write your story. I thought, that the best way to do that was approach you before the cops come rushing in. When they come, their adrenalin will be high, accidents happen in situations like that, suspects are shot. I can tell you that once your name is confirmed tomorrow morning as being one of Gordon Bridges Trustee clients, they will send the Tactical Response Group to raid this house. In doing so, they may well shoot first because they believe you are armed, and because you have hostages. The DNA samples the police took during the Carly Biddle murder, have also been found. They are being tested as we speak. You were tested when you were questioned over Carly's murder, and you've left samples galore more recently. Because I dug up your old cases, you have been discovered."

"Who told them I was armed?"

"I did. Well, let's face it you do have a knife, who was to say you don't have guns as well?"

"But, how did you find out about Mr. Bridges?"

"Paul, this is what I do. I was asked to advise when you sent your first note. I looked at the Body in the Suitcase murder, and quite frankly I saw your brilliance. But I knew you didn't just start there. I asked to look at unsolved murder cases where the victim was killed with a knife. Lo and behold I saw your signature, the one you displayed with Bridget Schaeffer, and it was the same with Gordon Bridges. I knew it was a personal murder, not random. His client files were never requested at the time, but, they will have them early in the morning. Next, I looked at Carly Biddle's murder. I saw someone who cared for her, and again it was a very personal killing. So, I knew your name would pop up in both cases. I asked the senior investigating police officer who had stood out in his mind as being a very good actor that showed arrogance and intelligence. Detective Barlow remembered you Paul, he didn't like you but he couldn't prove anything. Then there were the Lake Monger murders, I felt sure you would have been a witness, that you would want the fun of being questioned about your own crimes, yet I was wrong then."

"No, you were right, but I was dressed like this, the stupid cop couldn't even pick he was talking to a man. I enjoyed myself."

She smiled and nodded her head. "That makes good sense, Paul, lots of joggers are, after all, women. The letters to the editor though, Paul, that was a mistake. I understand that you wanted some recognition, I totally get that, but you made two mistakes. Firstly, you pointed the finger at yourself for Carly's killing, and secondly you signed them PPP. What does that stand for, by the way?"

"Are you saying I am not smart?"

"No, not really, I'm not saying that at all. If the police hadn't brought me in, they wouldn't have a clue. You were right, they are a pretty dumb lot. But I've spent years studying people like you, I knew where to look, the early signs, the mistakes made in learning your craft before you got as brilliant as you are now."

The silence was deafening, as she could clearly see he was thinking about things, but his face gave no indication of which way he would go. She lowered the tone of her voice, to nearly a whisper. "It's over Paul.

I'm sorry, but it is. The only question left is how you want it to end, as a hero, alive, letting me tell your story, or a dead martyr to a lost cause who will be forgotten in weeks."

"You asked me where PPP came from. One of my earliest memories is visiting a friend who lived up the street. He was older than me and he had a broken leg. He was getting everyone to sign the cast, but I was too young to write, so I drew a pirate. He nicknamed me Pirate Prince Paul. Of course, he moved away, eventually. Everyone I ever liked either ignored me, or moved away."

"I won't move away, Paul." She reached out and gripped his arm.

"I was going to give myself up anyway, but Rick must pay. He knew I went into care, and he pretended to like me. He just abandoned me there, at Harkerville, and it was awful, Patricia. I wouldn't send a dog there. I was eleven years old, my father had just killed himself after murdering my mother years before. Rick was one of the cops who answered my call, and I thought he cared, but, he didn't. I could have turned out differently, I could have been someone and not ignored by everyone I met. It's his fault I turned out like this."

"He has suffered, Paul. He is a nervous wreck now. I could see in Juliet's face she doesn't love him anymore, not after I admitted he made passes at me. Let her live, and Amy, then she will leave him; he will be alone. I will write your story, and tell the world it was his fault. I will do that for you." She gently squeezed his arm, trying to make him believe her sincerity.

"No, you don't get it. He took away my life, now I'm going to take away what's his, see how he likes it. I deserve that."

She was losing him, she could tell. He was staring down at the knife, twirling it in his hand. How to get him back on side?

"Paul if you kill them, I believe Rick will kill you. He is a cop after all. He will think he could have won Juliet back, but for you. He will get to you in the cell, fake a hanging, or pay someone to knife you in the shower. He is a nasty piece of work; you were right all along about him. It doesn't surprise me he was a rat back then after the way he treated Juliet. But if he kills you, you won't see the fame I will create for you. If you let them live, he will lose his family anyway.

He sighed a long drawn out sigh and shook his head. "I suppose you're right. Will you visit me in jail?"

"Every chance I get. Especially if you let me tell your story. I will be your editor, working with you on your book."

Suddenly, there was the deafening noise of a smashing window from the front of the building and the sounds of approaching footsteps over broken glass.

"You too? You lied to me?"

As if in slow motion, she watched him turn toward her, his face showing his rage. His right-hand travel in its arc through the air, and the knife blade disappeared into her stomach.

"No, please no, I didn't…"

But the knife was yanked out and stabbed into her again.

****

Rick raced through the shop without a glance at the cool room, not realizing that was the prison. His footsteps scrunched over broken shards caused by the rubbish bin he had thrown through the glass entrance. He kicked open the door leading into the house with gun drawn, hell bent on getting to his wife and daughter before Rankin could do anything to them.

He turned the corner into to the living room and saw a scene from a horror film. A woman stood over Patricia Holmes, hand raised with a knife in it about to stab again. There was blood everywhere. Rick, acting on instinct, fired his gun twice, as he had been trained, without realizing he had pulled the trigger.

The soft nosed bullets took Paul Rankin high on the right-hand side of his torso, which spun him around so he fell back onto the couch, alongside the bloody mess that was Pat. He tried to inflict more stab wounds on her, but Rick saw he couldn't lift his arm; the bullets must have smashed his shoulder. Still holding the gun ready to fire again if needed, he crossed the room and snatched the knife from Rankin's grasp.

"This-was-all-your-fault, Rick," he mumbled. He slowly slid down the couch to lie prostrate over the arm. Unconscious or dead, Rick didn't care.

He dropped his gun and bent over Pat. Carefully he slipped one arm around her neck, the other he reached under her thighs and in one motion lifted her. He turned and dropped to his knees and gently laid her on the floor. Next, he removed his jacket, balled it up, and held it over the wounds in her stomach, trying to staunch the flow of blood.

One handed he took Juliet's phone out and dialed the emergency number. "This is Detective Sergeant Richard McCoy; a woman has been stabbed and is bleeding profusely at 1606 Phillips Road in Mundaring.

I need an ambulance with para-medics *now*."

He dropped the phone to use both hands. "Oh, Pat. What have you done? What are you even doing here?" Her eyes fluttered open. "The ambulance is on its way, you're going to be fine, Pat. Stay with me, don't you bloody die on me."

"Cool room, shop, Amy, Juliet. Alive."

He looked up, torn between staying and slowing the blood loss, and getting to them.

"Go. Tell Juliet, I was lying to Rankin when I said you made a pass. Was trying to get his confidence..." Her eyes closed and her head lolled to the side.

"Pat. *Pat*." He touched the side of her neck; there was a very faint pulse. She was going, fading fast.

"No damn it *no*." He began CPR but realized as he pushed down on her chest, he was not stopping the blood loss, and he could see it oozing out from under his jacket.

He moved so he sat across her, straddling her stomach, using his weight to push the jacket over her wounds, then concentrated as he counted the compressions. Minutes passed; he had no idea how many. Suddenly, he was startled by hearing Colin Harris's voice echo down the passageway.

"This is the police, we are armed and coming in, lay on the floor and do not move."

"*In here*," he screamed. His sweat dripped from his forehead, and he heard their footsteps across the smashed shards of glass in the shop.

"Jesus Christ what's happened here?"

"Help me with her, she's dying."

It was then he heard the welcome sound of the ambulance siren, as it split the night.

Afterword (Part 1)

It was a very pale and drawn Patricia Holmes who lay in her hospital bed holding her husband's hand, listening to yet another litany from him as to why he never wanted her to work with the police again. She was far too weary to try to explain to him, for the twentieth time, that while she had been wounded, the experience of being on the front line of the hunt for a serial killer, she would not have swapped for anything. Ironically, she realized, she had never felt so alive, right up to the time she had nearly died.

She feigned tiredness and asked if he would leave her for a while to get some sleep. It was so much easier than arguing with him. He said he would come back that night, and quietly left her alone with her thoughts.

She had been very lucky to survive; she knew that. She had been told it was Rick's CPR, and stemming of her blood loss, that had saved her life. Overall, she would describe herself as being confused about her feelings for Rick. She believed had he not burst in when he had, she would not have been attacked, and would have got Paul Rankin to hand himself in. She sincerely believed that he wanted that. He thought she had lied to him when Rick broke in, and hence the attack.

But, she had to consider Rick's state of mind, after losing his daughter and wife to a man who had intended to murder them.

It was...complicated. She kept trying to explain that to her husband. There was no simple explanation; it was all if's. If Rick, hadn't smashed his way in, if she had a few more minutes to get the knife from him before Rick broke in. So many variables. Not that he wanted to listen, he just wanted to tell her not to do it again, that she *owed* it to him, and their children. One day, she thought, she would tell him she didn't owe him anything. That her life was hers to decide how she would live it. But, that day hadn't come just yet. She had no doubt that it would though, especially if he told her one too many more times, that she owed it to him to stop.

What she didn't try to explain, and never would, was her feelings of attraction for Rick. That was the most confusing thing of all. They were from different walks of life; they were both married, and they should not ever be any more than friends or work colleagues...yet deep down, she wanted more. She wanted to live again, she wanted to feel wanted, valued, and loved.

Tom and she had slipped into a life of...boring normality. Like wearing comfy slippers, she would describe it as. Hardly exciting anymore, and it hadn't been that for years. They lived together, shared a bed and holidays in equal proportion, yet what they hadn't shared in a very long time was sex. She had lain awake in bed while Tom snored, on two or three occasions and wondered what it would be like with Rick. She found herself touching her most intimate place, and fantasized about him taking her, using her body to satisfy his lust, and by proxy; hers. She would never, ever admit that to anyone.

She winced in pain and wondered how long before she would be permitted to have some more pain killers. As if by magic, a nurse who had earlier introduced herself as Irene, entered with a small tray that held the syringe, and Pat felt elated. She licked her lips knowing she would soon get some relief from the incessant burning from her stomach. The pain was growing, exponentially.

"Patricia, you have a couple of visitors, do you feel like talking to them? It's Juliet McCoy and Amy," the nurse said quietly.

She nodded, her eyes never leaving the nurse as she slipped the cap off the needle and inserted it into her drip line. "If you start to get drowsy and want rescuing from them, call for me and I will come straight in. I don't want you over exerting yourself."

Almost immediately the drug took affect and she felt serene. She blinked rapidly, grateful. "Thank you, Irene, I needed that. Mmm, okay, you can send them in."

Juliet and Amy held hands as they entered, and both looked troubled. *Amy is going to need a lot of help to get over this.* She thought. "Hello Amy, we haven't met before, but I'm so glad to see you." She smiled her best smile.

Juliet looked down at her daughter and nodded for her to speak. "Thank you for coming to save me. Mummy says the nasty man might have hurt me if you hadn't come."

"You're very welcome, Sweetheart. I'm glad I was there to help. He is a very bad man, but he's gone now, you don't ever have to worry about him again."

"Baby, you go and wait with Daddy outside now,

Mummy wants to talk to Pat alone," Juliet said.

Amy nodded and turned around and walked back to the door. "Bye, bye," she said and gave a little wave.

"Bye, Amy. I hope I see you again soon."

Pat turned her head on her pillow. "Please come and sit, Juliet. I know why you're here."

She shook her head. "I want to thank you for coming to Amy's rescue, I guess you didn't know he had me with him as well. Did you do it to save her, or get yourself made famous?"

"I know you don't know me, and I suppose no matter what I say, if you chose to, you could think I was lying. I promise you I went there because I wanted him to surrender and I thought I could make it happen and save Amy. I thought I had a chance of talking him into handing himself in, that if I put on an act and make him feel like I wanted to make him famous it would appeal to his narcissistic side. I knew his personality type would kill himself and anyone he could take with him or surrender if he thought he could become famous. All he wanted was recognition, for once in his miserable life, and for people to like him. Everything I said was to garner support and make him believe in me."

"Rick told me he tried to call you back, but your phone was turned off."

"It wasn't turned off; the battery had died."

She nodded, still looking deeply upset. "I'm trying, I'm trying really hard, but I don't trust him anymore."

Pat reached out and took her hand in hers. "Juliet, he never, and I do mean never, made a pass at me. I only said that he did because I knew Rankin hated anyone who was an adulterer. I needed him to think I wasn't like that, so he would trust me. I also knew he hated Rick, so I deliberately made him sound bad. I'm sorry about that, but I had to do it. It wasn't true. Juliet, Rick loves you. You know, there was one time, I asked him in one night for a coffee when he took me home. My husband was at a Rotary dinner, and Rick could easily have thought it was an invitation for something more. It wasn't, it was just for a drink. But, do you know what he said?"

She looked back at Pat, two tears welling in her eyes. "What?"

"He said that if he left then he could get home in time to read Amy a story and be with you. He is a good man, and he loves you, don't let the ravings of a lunatic turn you against him. He raced to that building, smashed in through a glass door to rescue you both with no thought for his own safety."

"But he admitted he had thoughts about you, isn't that just as bad? After what we went through, for him to think about it says to me he isn't satisfied."

He thought about seducing me? Wow.

She slowly shook her head, determined to bury deep her innermost feelings. "You know what? If he were married to me, I'd be more worried if he didn't think about sex with other women. It's how middle-aged men are wired; they can't help it. Trust me, I'm a psychologist. They are at heart hunter gatherers, but the difference between Rick and a lot of other men is that he learned from his mistake; you are the only woman he wants to be with."

"Am I being stupid?"

"No. You're not. Rankin tried to manipulate you, and he is very good at that. You showed incredible bravery in agreeing to sacrifice your life for Amy's. I think you are an awesome woman, and so does Rick. Go and be happy, grant yourself that right, you both deserve it."

"What about you?"

She smiled, "well if Tom has his way my days of working with the police are over."

"You don't sound so sure though?"

"Well, it's not my choice, is it? Me getting stabbed has probably stopped any invitation to come back again, liability issues and all that. But I think Tom knows me well enough to know, that if I was asked to help again, and the case interested me? I'd say yes. I think I have a talent for this, and I totally get why people like Rick do what they do. Time will tell Juliet, we will see."

Afterword (Part 2)

So, now I have two people to get even with. One day I will get my revenge, they have not heard the last of me.

They took great delight in telling me that lying bitch lived, damn her. She's like a cat with nine lives, I should have slit her throat. Next time she won't be so lucky.

I need to come up with a plan, lull her into a false sense of security, then, when she least expects it...

Maybe I will let her write my book, get her to trust me, I could say sorry. Then, one day... She won't see it coming. Yes, I can do that, I can apologize to her, tell her I was wrong, and beg her forgiveness. She can't compete with me on a mental level; I'm much smarter.

But Rick, he is the real culprit. Thanks to him, I've got a deformed shoulder, that will never heal. But, I will get even. The trick will be to make everyone think I'm harmless. If I'm smart, they will think: *Paul Rankin? Oh, he wouldn't hurt a fly.*

I will be on my best behavior; I can fool them; I have lots of time. I'll be back. Next time, they will suffer. Oh, God, how they will suffer. I will give them both a fate worse than death.

The End

Patricia Holmes and Rick McCoy will return, in: Glimpse, The Beautiful Deaths. The second instalment of the Deadly Glimpses Trilogy.

Stephen B King
Perth, Western Australia.

A word about the author…

I was born in the UK, what seems like an epoch ago, and moved to Australia at age sixteen. I was a long haired rock guitarist and poet/songwriter, before real life got in the way, and I gave it all up for love.

I've always felt I had tales to tell and won short story competitions and published poetry in my wilder, younger days. More recently, I've written and published five novels. While they have all been police procedural thrillers, mainly focusing on serial killers, they all have a love theme running through them.

I believe love, and family are everything. Anything else you gain in life is a bonus.

I live in Perth, in Western Australia and am fiercely patriotic, and parochial. My wife is amazing in that she not only puts up with living with a writer but encourages it. I've been blessed with five children, and I adore them all.

http://stephen-b-king.com